EMBRACE THE SUCK

AN OPS PROTECTOR ROMANCE

GIULIA LAGOMARSINO

Cover Design courtesy of T.E. Black Designs

www.teblackdesigns.com

Photography by Reggie Deanching @ RplusM Photography

https://www.rplusmphoto.com

Cover Model: BT Urruela

https://www.facebook.com/B.Taylor.Urruela

❀ Created with Vellum

For Horatio

CAST OF CHARACTERS

Cash Owens- Owner of Owens Protective Services, sniper, and overall badass.

Eva James- deadly mistress of throwing knives and Cash's...person

Team 1:

Jerrod Lockhart- Complete hardass, rule follower, and generally the guy considered to always have a stick up his ass.

Edward "Edu" Markinson- Hater of hospitals, slow drivers, and references to anything in the '80s.

Brock "Rock" Patton- Wannabe model, obsessed with his looks and constantly combing his hair...A ferocious fighter for a man so obsessed with his looks. Also, as a side note—he can't act for shit and hates the word 'loins'.

Scottie Dog Thacker- Tactical vomit expert, hater of flying planes, and always up for a good time. If you're with him, have a barf bag in hand. Has never had even a sip of alcohol in his life.

Quinn Lake- Awesome geologist who is terrible at telling people no. She's a runner—running from situations so she doesn't have to grow a spine and deal with confrontation. Awesome at Battleship and Twister.

Team 2:

Marcus "IRIS" Slater- His name stands for *I Require Intense Supervision*. EOD expert that has taken up a new love...blowing up shit.

Jane Layne- IRIS's sidekick in real life and in her mystery novels. Also known as Shayla Jacque. Absolutely despises technology, and goes so far as to use a typewriter to avoid it.

Mick "Slider" Jeffries- Not Slider from *Top Gun*. Sorry, ladies, I know he was gorgeous, but it's not the same hottie.

Tate "Thumper" Parsons- No, not named for the adorable furry rabbit. Thumper got his nickname after losing a foot to an IED. Now using a robotic foot, he is probably the fastest person on the team.

Bree Wilton- Financial guru, killer of the boardroom, and newly appointed partner in her firm. Wilts under the sun. Hates hiking, dirt, bunnies, and generally all things that don't come with a luxury sticker.

Team 3: Now known as The Ditty Boppers

Eli Brant- Fierce team leader, but will put you in your place with a good practical joke when necessary.

Red Warren- Funny, meat-eating, California-hating, rifle owner. Proud to take out the bad guys in any way possible.

Zoe Thacker- Screenwriting badass that hates guns, refuses to eat meat, but loves a good gunfight.

Bradford Kavanaugh- Son of a senator, terrified of mummies, scarabs, and basically anything from ancient Egypt. Loves practical jokes, except when they're about him.

IT Department:

Rae Dennon- Sarcastic, witty, badass woman. Terrified of nothing, will take down any man with little effort, and has an intense feud with Dash.

Dash- Awesome with computers and a skilled fighter. Constantly being compared to Rae, the sexier version of him. Still trying to convince Fox he's just as awesome.

Black Ops Team: Also known as The Three Js

Jack Cox- Team leader who loves aviator sunglasses as much as a good gun fight. Willing to take one for the team as long as the mission is long and hard…just like his johnson.

Johnny Wood- Dangerous cowboy, loyal to Rafe—a man that would kill his own mother if it finished the job. Respects a man willing to get the job done.

Jason Long- Number 3 of the baddies. Dangerous and dark, always full of threatening wisdom. Stay out of his way.

The Other Guys:

New Guy- Also known as FNG- Doesn't have a death wish, but firmly believes he can never be killed. Willing to take horrible risks to prove he's unstoppable. Medic and smart as a whip, but also one of the most ridiculous men you've ever met.

Jones- Spotter for Cash during their military days, with a bad attitude since losing the use of his leg. Like you really need one of those.

Rafe- Evildoer posing as the good guy. Or is it the other way around? Dangerous antihero with not a single redeeming quality who stays hidden in the shadows. Unknown relationship to Cash.

Liberty- Pretty ballerina with hidden talents. Obsessed with Rafe and willing to sacrifice anything to be with him. Or is she???

Fox- Works in training, has an undeniable fascination with throwing knives, and loves singing show tunes…sometimes a little too much!

Anna- Gorgeous Hollywood star that has captured Fox's twisted heart. Her looks aren't nearly as deadly as her right hook.

The Young Squad:

Asher White: This suit-wearing enigma has a thing for dangerous jobs, fast women, and…trains. Yes, you heard that right! Don't come between a man and his love of locomotives.

Chase Carter: Tattooed badass with a bullring in his nose. His wacky personality is nearly as irritating as his love of playing Monopoly.

Patrick Cook: This is no ordinary gigolo. Hang onto your hats ladies! You're not just getting a striptease with this stud!

EMBRACE THE SUCK

Origin:

Popularized in 2003 by Marines in Iraq
"The suck" also known as "friction"
This friction—that which appears easy in war is difficult in reality.
Troops, in their resilience, in effect, mitigate the chasm of difference
between training or planning and the often harsh realities they face on
the ground. And they do it with aplomb, because they must.

—Retired U.S. Army Reserve Col. Austin Bay

OPS Meaning:
We cannot control everything that happens to us. But we can control
how we react to it.

1

CASH

WITH MY ARMS crossed over my chest and the most vicious look on my face, I should have had these ladies squirming in their seats. Betty was on her box in plain view. That alone should have let these ladies know just how much trouble they were in.

"Leaving OPS without telling a single person," I ticked off on one finger, taking a step away from my desk as I began to pace.

"Breaking into a client's home," I added to the list.

"Befriending said client." I spun on my heel and glared at the four ladies still sitting in their seats as if they weren't in a world of hurt. "Do you have any idea how serious this is? Eva, I expected more of you."

She snorted slightly. "Since when have I ever listened to you?"

The answer was easy, and she knew it. The fact was, Eva never listened to me. Since the day I met her, she fought back against doing things my way, and it was clear now that wasn't about to change. Still, as the boss's fiancé, I had hoped she would play by the rules just a little bit.

"And Zoe, you just had a baby."

Her head moved slowly in a cocked position, as if she was examining me like a bug. How was it possible these women could make me feel like I'd done something wrong when they were the ones that left OPS without telling anyone, broke into a client's house, then hid out there without any of us knowing! And frankly, that was the biggest issue. How did we have four women hiding out without a single one of us catching on? We cleared the house every time we left. The cameras and sensors showed absolutely nothing. It was baffling to say the least.

But that was beside the point at the moment. I got a little off track with my thoughts, and didn't pick up on the fact that all four women were now plotting my demise. Based on their looks alone, I was already dead and they were trying to decide where to dump my body. I swallowed hard and tried my best to hold my ground. I was the owner of this company, and I would not falter.

Zoe very slowly got to her feet and sashayed closer to me. "I'm sorry, I must have heard you wrong because I could have sworn you said I just had a baby."

Yep, there was a threat in there somewhere. It was undeniable. Very slowly, I looked behind me at the line of men who belonged to these women. They held their ground just like me, but obviously, they knew better than me. Red gave a minute shake of his head, telling me to back off. But I was the boss around here, and I wouldn't be dictated to by people that didn't even work at this company.

"That's right. You have a baby," I said firmly. "You should have been at home, not off gallivanting across the countryside."

"Gallivanting," she grinned. "I had no idea that's what I was doing."

"I'm not the bad guy here," I said, finding my balls buried deep inside my body. "We were on an operation. I don't care if you're bored or in need of adventure, none of you have the right to leave this property without expressed permission, and you definitely can't show up at a client's house. You got lucky that Jane enjoyed your little adventure. That wouldn't be the case in every situation."

"I wasn't aware that having a baby excluded me from having any fun," Zoe quipped.

"Fun? No, but interfering in a job? Absolutely."

"We never interfered at any time," she shot back. "Maybe you should take a lesson from us in stealth."

"Yeah, for a security company, you somehow managed to miss five women wandering around the house the entire time you were there," Eva said mockingly.

This was going nowhere fast. If I had any hope of regaining control, I was going to have to put my foot down hard. "This is not a debate!" I shouted. "Yes, you were fine this time, but any other job, you could have found yourselves dead. We do not work under these circumstances. Your husbands have jobs to do, and they can't be distracted by their wives suddenly going missing! Not to mention, that you could have been in danger and we wouldn't have known it—"

"Because you didn't know we were there," Eva interrupted. "I think that says more about you than us."

I was fuming, partly because she was right. We somehow missed all of them and I couldn't figure out how it was done. But I was also pissed as hell because I didn't like to reprimand them when they clearly got the drop on us. We should be working with them to find out what they did to infiltrate our system.

"This will not happen again. Am I making myself clear?"

Anna raised her hand ever so slowly. I bit my tongue, because frankly, I didn't want Fox getting pissed at me for mistreating his woman. "Yes, Anna?"

"Say it's necessary for us to tag along."

"If it was necessary, we would already know about it."

"Yes, but what if you were…say, kidnapped. Would you want us to sneak in and get you out?"

"And why would a group of highly intelligent, extremely well trained men get kidnapped?"

"For every one of you out there, there's someone faster and smarter than you," Quinn noted.

She had a point, but that didn't mean I wanted them sneaking in to rescue us.

"Boss," Fox stepped forward, keeping his voice low. "She has a point. Just one small distraction, and we could find ourselves in a predicament."

3

"Since when would you ever admit to being distracted to the point that you'd allow yourself to get kidnapped?" I hissed.

"Say one of us is vomiting," Scottie stepped forward. "You know, on a plane after a very intense flight."

"Yeah, and maybe Kavanaugh freaked out because there were mummies on board and we had to detain him," Red added.

"It could happen to the best of us, boss," Scottie nodded.

I stared at them all incredulously. "You're professionals!"

"Yes, but we're only human," Red pointed out.

"You're human," Scottie muttered. "Fox is a special breed."

"Thanks," Fox grinned. "There's no one quite like me."

"And why isn't IRIS here?" Red asked. "It was his woman that allowed these shenanigans to go on. Why isn't she getting the speech on what not to do?"

"She was the client," I bit out.

"All the more reason for her to understand what she did was wrong," Fox said. "But seriously, you have to admit, our women were awesome. If it weren't for them getting drunk and making all that noise, we might never have known they were there."

"And what's your point?" I bit out.

Fox frowned at me. "Um…I thought it was pretty self-explanatory. We should use them."

"Are you insane?" I snapped. "An actress, a geologist, a screen-writer, and—"

"Careful, boss," Scottie cut in. "This is Eva we're talking about. She's almost as crazy as Fox now."

I slammed my eyes shut and took a deep breath. I would not lose my shit right now. "The point is, despite the fact that they somehow outsmarted us this time, they have no place in our operations. They got lucky, but they may not next time. I'm not willing to risk my woman's life for five seconds of pleasure."

"Five seconds?" Fox grunted. "Boss, you need to step up your game if all you're getting is five seconds."

"I'm not talking about sex," I snapped. "I'm talking about them getting five seconds of pleasure."

"That's even worse. She's your woman. You should be giving seventy percent of the pleasure."

"Really?" Scottie asked. "You think seventy percent is the number to go with."

"Were you thinking higher or lower?"

"Equal shares," Scottie shrugged. "I don't mind putting in the hard work, but why should I only get thirty percent?"

"Because you're the man," Red interrupted. "You have to keep her happy if you don't want her wandering off to someone else."

"And the same could be said for us. A displeased man won't stick around for thirty percent."

"Unless it's a very good thirty percent," Fox said. A dirty grin crossed his face in a way that made me shiver in disgust. "Thirty percent in my bed goes a long way."

"Enough!" I cut them off. "Christ, I don't even remember what we were talking about anymore."

"Sex," Fox said, pulling a stick of beef jerky from his pocket. He tore it open and ripped a piece off in his mouth.

"What are you doing?" I asked incredulously.

"Eating. I thought that was pretty clear."

I wasn't about to get into this further. If he wanted to switch from Funyuns to beef jerky, that was his business. "We were talking about the fact that our girlfriends and wives decided to tag along on a mission, regardless of the risks they were taking on. We can't allow this to happen again. All it takes is one time and we'll be paying for the rest of our lives. Are we all in agreement on that?"

They nodded reluctantly, and just as I was about to turn around, Fox grabbed me by the arm. "Maybe we should have a contingency. Like...if we do get kidnapped, they're allowed to help, but only if the risk is minimal."

"Yeah, or...one of them could learn to fly a plane. That way if said pilot gets...oh, I don't know...nauseous, there's a backup person."

"That's not a bad idea," Red agreed. "Flights are starting to make me nauseous, and it has nothing to do with the flight. It's the smell."

"Fine," I bit out. "We can have a contingency plan, but we'll create it and hide it somewhere that they'll only find in case of an emergency. Deal?"

"That sounds fair," Scottie nodded.

"We can not at any time allow them to think we condone this behavior. It'll only come back to bite us in the ass."

They all nodded as I turned back around and faced the women that recently caused me way too many headaches. "Alright—"

"Who wants to learn to be a pilot?" Fox cut me off. All the ladies raised their hands, completely ruining my entire plan. I glared at Fox, which was pointless. He wasn't intimidated by me in any way. "Training begins tomorrow! Dismissed!"

The ladies got up, chattering amongst themselves excitedly. Everyone filtered out of the room, leaving me standing there staring at empty chairs. When had I gone from the boss to just another guy in the room?

"It was bound to happen," Red sighed. "None of those women were going to become housewives."

"I would have settled for them listening to directions."

Red snorted out a laugh. "Yeah, that was never going to happen either." He clapped me on the shoulder and walked away. "It was a good speech, though."

2

BREE

THE TOWN CAR pulled up outside Hobbs and Morris Enterprises, just an hour before everyone else would arrive. As my door opened, I placed one stiletto heel outside, careful not to flash anyone the goods underneath my tight pencil skirt. I was professional at all times and refused to allow my standards to slip at any time.

Pushing my glasses up on my nose, I stepped out of the car and took my briefcase from the driver. "Thank you, Gerard."

"You're welcome, Ms. Wilton. Mr. Hobbs will be in soon, and he'd like you to meet him in his office."

"Thank you."

I marched to the front door, walking swiftly through as the doorman held the door for me. "Jeremy," I nodded, earning me a smile in return. My heels clacked on the marble floors as I made my way to the elevator. My assistant Derek was standing in his usual spot, just outside the elevator doors with my tea in hand. As I approached, he took my briefcase from me and handed over my tea. This was our routine every day, seven days a week. He always anticipated what I needed, and in return, he had one of the most coveted positions in the company.

"You have a meeting set up with Mr. Hobbs for seven forty-five.

I've already pulled the figures for this week and have all the usual information you request, along with the figures for the new branch that opened last week in Paris. You also have a conference call with Dwight at nine o'clock, and I rearranged your lunch with Marcus for an hour later to fit in the staff meeting you requested."

I nodded along as he continued on with my schedule for the day. There was hardly any downtime, and my lunches were always working lunches, despite my bosses insisting that I take an actual lunch break. I worked twelve hour days five days a week, and ten hour days the remaining days. And then there were the business dinners that I needed to attend, and there was always some opening or charity function for the good of the company. I basically went home only to sleep. But it was all in an effort to achieve the one thing I'd been working toward since the day I wrote my first high school paper on American finance. I would have my name on the building soon, and nothing would stop me from achieving my goals.

The elevator doors opened swiftly, as if they knew I had a schedule to keep and didn't have time for delays. Derek opened my door for me and walked over to my desk, laying out all the files I would need for this morning. He rattled off the remaining information I would need to get my day started and then quickly exited. The great thing about Derek was that he knew I wasn't one for idle chit-chat. I had a job to perform, as did he. It was why we worked so well together.

I checked my emails, insisting on doing it myself to avoid any unmitigated disasters. By the time I finished, I had just five minutes to make my way up to the top floor to speak with Mr. Hobbs. Leaving my tea behind, I popped a mint into my mouth and headed back to the elevators. I made quick work of my mint, making sure there was nothing in my mouth by the time I stepped out onto the fortieth floor.

"Good morning, Sandra," I nodded to the receptionist.

"Good morning, Ms. Wilton. He's ready for you."

"Thank you." I walked past her down the hall to the last office. It had a beautiful view of the city, one I hoped to get by the end of this year. Everything was running perfectly for me. The job was already in the bag. Pushing his door open, I walked inside and took a seat across from him, crossing my ankles as I sat up straight. "Good morning, Preston."

"Bree, you look lovely this morning."

"Thank you."

"Walter was very impressed with you last night."

A small smile tipped my lips. "I always research potential clients before any event."

He nodded, smiling as he leaned back in his chair. "I know. He wasn't the only one impressed with you last night. There were several companies that took notice of you. Some tried to talk me into ripping up our contract so you could go work with them."

"I have no desire to leave the company."

"I was hoping you'd say that."

This was it. My moment had finally arrived. At the age of thirty-five, I was going to get my name on the wall. Women would look up to me, knowing they too could have it all with a little hard work.

He leaned forward on his desk, linking his hands together as his brows furrowed. "It's come to my attention that you haven't taken any of your time off."

"Because I don't need it."

"You work seven days a week," he pointed out.

"And I am the most efficient person you have on your staff."

"Yes, but…Bree, you'll burn out if you don't take some time off."

"Like I said, there's no need for time off. I do my best work when I'm up against a deadline."

He sighed and leaned back in his seat. "I've been speaking with HR. They need you to take your time off for the past five years."

"Five years?" I asked incredulously. "Preston, we're in the middle of several large deals. I can't take time off."

"Your assistant…Daniel?"

"Derek."

He nodded. "He's got everything under control. George will step in while you're on sabbatical—"

"Sabbatical?" I asked incredulously. "Preston, I cannot take a sabbatical right now. It's impossible."

"It's necessary. The company needs this for tax purposes.

Accounting has been on my ass for the last six months about the time you refuse to take off. Do you have any idea how much time you've built up?"

I had an idea, and if he suggested I take it all, I would walk out right now. Well, that wasn't true, but I'd be very unhappy.

"Bree, you've built up enough time to take off six months."

"Preston—"

"Now, I've agreed to you taking off three months this year and three months next year."

"But George can't possibly take over my position."

"He'll have to since that's his new position," he said with a grin.

My breath caught in my chest as I stared at Preston, hoping to God he was finally going to put me out of my misery and make the announcement of a lifetime.

"When you come back from your sabbatical, you'll be moving to the top floor. Your name is already on the door."

A wide grin split my lips for the first time in ten years. I did it. I made all my dreams come true. "Thank you, Preston."

"You've earned it. But your sabbatical starts next week. You'll have this week to get George up to date on your current files. After that, I don't want to see you in this office for three months."

"That's a really long time. And shouldn't I dive in right away and get started—"

"Bree, you take the sabbatical, or you don't get the job. That's my only stipulation. And do yourself a favor, go do something you would never dream of doing. Live for once."

"I live all the time."

"By a schedule. Go lay on a beach somewhere. Go see the Grand Canyon, or take a trip to Paris."

"I already have a trip to Paris scheduled next year."

"For work," he clarified. "I meant for you to do something that doesn't involve work in any way."

"No offense, Preston, but that doesn't sound relaxing at all."

"You've been in the business world too long if you can't find relaxation when you're not working."

"Maybe that's true for some, but when you enjoy your work, it's not really work, is it?"

"Don't go around telling everyone else that," he grinned. "Half the people in this company only see this as a job."

"That's because they have no drive."

"Three months," he clarified. "And if you come back even a day sooner, you'll be turned away."

I stood with a smile and held out my hand. "It'll be hard, but I can do it. And I won't let you down."

"I know you won't. That's why you got the job. Enjoy your last week of work."

"I will," I grinned as I turned and headed for the door. One week of work and then three months of hell. I could handle this. I hadn't been bored since I was seven, but I'd find a way to deal with it. I had to. I was about to get my name on the building.

"Wait, you're actually taking a vacation?" my sister Grace said when I called her that night.

"It's not my idea. I would have started work on my new job immediately."

"So, they're forcing you to take a vacation. Paid?"

"Of course."

"Wow...and you're upset about this?"

"Why would I stop working when everything is going my way? This is what I've worked for my whole life."

"Yes, but that's the point. Work isn't supposed to take over your life. When was the last time you went out on a date?"

"I go out on dates all the time."

"No, those are social events that you drag some poor schmuck along to. He's there to make you look good, and that's the extent of it. I doubt you even remember their names."

"Of course I do. I always go with James."

"Yes, James. The man that's in love with you, but you won't give him the time of day."

"Because he's not right for me. He thinks he knows me, but he doesn't."

"Honey, I hate to point this out, but nobody knows you. Your head is constantly buried in work."

"Because I've been working toward my goals since I was in elementary school."

She sighed over the phone as I poured myself a glass of wine. It was my little way to wind down at the end of the night. I had the same routine of drinking a glass and then going through my nightly facial routine before falling into bed for precisely six hours.

"Bree, do you even know where you're going?"

"On sabbatical? I thought I might spend my time researching the company and my new position. I want to be ready when I go back."

"You've been researching that position for the last ten years. There's nothing more you can learn in the next three months, let alone three minutes. Why don't you go on an actual vacation?"

"And what would I do? Lay on a beach all day and be bored out of my mind?"

"I would love to do that. I haven't had a vacation in years."

"You could come with me," I said excitedly. I didn't particularly want to spend my sabbatical with my sister, but spending it alone sounded even worse.

"I can't afford to take the time off right now. Charlie needs braces and Ella is in the middle of ballet."

"Their father can take care of that."

"Braces and ballet are expensive. That's why I can't take the time off."

"Oh, well, what if I covered the costs?"

I knew before she answered what she thought about me loaning her money. She was a proud woman that always did everything for herself. And I admired that, but I needed her right now, and I had more money than I knew what to do with.

"Bree, that's very nice of you, but it just wouldn't fit into my life right now. It's the middle of the school year. I can't just leave everything behind to go on vacation."

"Other teachers do it all the time," I pointed out, though I secretly hated that they did that.

"And I'm not one of those teachers. I may not have the same drive as you, but I do have the same work ethic. I will not take random time off work to go on vacation."

"Fine, but you're missing out on a lot."

"You don't even know where you're going," she pointed out.

"Maybe I could go visit Aunt Tilly," I said as the thought popped into my head. I always liked seeing her when we were little."

"Aunt Tilly died three years ago."

"What? Why didn't anyone tell me?"

"We did tell you."

"No, Aunt Tilly was my favorite. I would have remembered something as important as her dying."

She sighed heavily, making me feel even more guilty about the whole thing. "You were in the middle of a big deal at work. Don't ask me what. None of us actually know what you do. Anyway, you had to meet some deadline and missed the funeral and the wake. But you did send a beautiful bouquet of flowers."

Most likely Derek's doing. I would never have missed her funeral. I bit my lip and tried to remember hearing anything about my favorite aunt dying, but nothing came to mind. However, I did remember a huge merger a few years back. It helped me get the office I was currently residing in.

"Okay, Aunt Tilly may be out, but I could still go down to Alabama and visit Grandpa. He always has the best jokes. Remember when he told us he unscrewed his head at night so he could admire himself?"

"Yeah, Grandpa died five years ago."

I opened my mouth, ready to yell at her for not telling me, but figured it was probably my fault. Most likely she did tell me and I ignored it for my job. God, I was the most irresponsible family member.

I sat down at my desk, placing my wine next to my keyboard. "Why didn't anyone tell me I was being so self-centered?"

"We have, pretty much every time we see you. And by my calculations, that was two years ago when you dropped by for Christmas Eve

GIULIA LAGOMARSINO

and left the same night because someone called with something important and you just couldn't miss it."

"It *was* important," I stressed.

"You left in the middle of Dad saying grace."

"It wasn't something I could avoid. If I didn't leave right then—"

"Yeah, yeah. Some deal would have fallen through."

Wow, my sister had a terrible opinion of me. I had no idea. "Well,
maybe I'll come see you."

"Please don't. I have no time to clean and with all of us busy with
work and school, you'll be bored out of your mind."

"Are you really telling me not to come?" I asked, somewhat hurt by
that.

"Listen," she sighed. "You know I love you, but you only think
about you. This is about my family, and I've wasted way too many
years subjecting them to long-ass winded complaints about how you're
never around. I won't make them pretend to be interested in you now."

For just a moment, I felt a twinge of hurt that my own sister didn't
want to see me. Or apparently, subject her family to me. But in fairness,
I didn't know the age of her kids or even what her husband did for a
living. I really was the worst sister ever.

"I'm sorry," I whispered, feeling absolutely horrible.

"For what?"

"For being the worst sister on the face of the planet. For not paying
attention to anything that goes on in your life."

"Honey, I've known this was the way you'd turn out since you
were ten and had more interest in learning about the stock market than
playing Nintendo with me. It's the way you are, and I've come to
accept that."

"But what does that say about me?"

"That you're ambitious?"

"So ambitious that I have no idea what's going on in your life?"

"Relax, once you start this new job, you'll forget about me and go
back to your life again. It's the way it always goes. We did this seven
years ago."

"We did?" I asked, not remembering that at all.

"Yep, pretty much the same conversation. A few minor details changed. Aunt Tilly and Grandpa weren't dead, but Waddles had just died, and the house on Elm sold."

"No!" I said in astonishment.

"And when you start this new job, the same thing will happen, so enjoy it while you can."

"I'm like…the worst person in the world."

"No, just extremely driven. We've always known it. It's why we stopped trying."

They stopped trying because I was too wrapped up in my own life to remember to have any sort of relationship with them. That made me like the weird second cousin that hardly anyone spoke to. I really sucked at this relationship stuff.

"Look, do yourself a favor and take these three months to find something out about yourself."

"But I already know everything about myself."

"You know everything about your work self. Why not go somewhere that's completely the opposite of you? Go hiking or see something you have no interest in seeing. Just for fun."

"That doesn't sound fun," I pointed out.

"Maybe not, but it'll give you something to talk about when you get back to that tower you call work."

"We don't talk about personal stuff," I pointed out.

"Okay, you can call and tell me about it. If you remember my number.

"I have no desire to get dirty or sweat."

"Maybe it'll be good for you."

"Maybe it would be the worst trip of my life," I pointed out. "Maybe I should just go to the beach."

"Well, whatever you decide, just make sure it's something that can keep you entertained. I can't see you lying on a beach staring at the waves all day, even though that's what I would do."

I grimaced at the thought. She was right. I needed something that would keep me moving. "I'll do some research and let you know what I decide."

"Of course you will. God forbid you ever do anything without researching first."

"Now you sound like Mom."

"I take that as a compliment. Let me know what you decide."

"I will." I hung up and opened my computer. If I was going to be on vacation for three months, I would have to make sure my time was packed with things to do so I didn't get bored. By the end of the week, I would have the next three months mapped out with exciting things to do.

I chugged my wine and opened my browser. "Okay, what do people do for fun?"

3

THUMPER

I BREATHED in the morning air of the desert and watched the beautiful sunrise from the bed of my pickup truck. Sipping my gas station coffee, I let the cold air wash over me. It had been years since I'd come out here—long before I lost my foot overseas.

I glanced down at my new robotic foot and grinned. I hadn't come out here with the old one. I guess part of me was scared to test how it would hold up while hiking. But this new foot came with a shoe that fit perfectly over it, specialized to allow my foot to do everything it could before. It was really a work of art. At first, I was testing the prototype for a friend that was an engineer. Since then, he sent me upgrades whenever he was trialing a new design. This was his latest, and it worked perfectly. Now I just had to be brave enough to actually get out there and test it out on the terrain.

Despite wanting to shut down on this trip, I brought my phone anyway so I could send Tank video footage of how the foot held up. I took another sip of my coffee and mapped out my day. I wanted to start at the beginning of the trail through Arches National Park and work my way through, really spending time at each rock formation.

Hopping down from the bed of my truck, I got back in the driver's seat and set off to see the beauty in front of me. I always assumed that when I came out here, it would be with someone special, but that blew up in my face the minute I lost my foot. While it didn't bother me in the slightest, that's usually where I lost women. I thought it was awesome. A robot for a foot was freaking cool, but women tended to see things differently.

I stopped first at the Balanced Rock, imagining how I would scale it —if that were legal. Visitors could climb over nearly all rock formations, but I was pretty sure trying to climb up the Balanced Rock would be frowned upon.

"I'm telling you, I could scale it."

"You can't, because you would get arrested!"

I closed my eyes, wondering if they saw me yet. I could hide behind the rock and maybe slip away unnoticed. I moved quickly, running over the uneven ground to the rock. It was large enough around that they wouldn't see me right away.

"He's got to be here. That was his truck." I recognized Dash's voice immediately. Why the hell he was out here was beyond me.

"Unless someone drove his truck out here and he's somewhere else completely," New Guy added.

"Right, someone stole his truck to come hiking at Arches."

"You never know. It could happen."

I slinked along the base of Balanced Rock, trying to stay out of sight. They followed me out here. I could kill them. I wanted this trip to be peaceful, something I wouldn't get if the two of them were with me. I was just lucky no one else joined them.

"I would have come out here with him had I known he was coming here," New Guy huffed.

"That's sort of the point. He didn't want us tagging along."

"This has to do with his foot," New Guy surmised. "He's been so upset since IRIS used his foot as a torch."

"It's not about his foot."

"He's projecting his frustrations in a negative way. It's our job to pull him out of his funk."

"Do you hear yourself? His teammates said he was fine. They told you he was fine. Cash told you he was fine. Hell, Fox said he was fine. Do you have a hearing problem?"

"If you don't believe me," New Guy snapped, "then why are you out here with me?"

"Because you would die out here on your own. And because Cash ordered me to follow you."

"Bullshit, I can handle a few rocks."

I heard his yelp and peeked around the corner just as he slipped and started sliding down a large rock. Dash grabbed his hand, keeping him from tumbling down to the base and possibly catching his foot and breaking it.

"Yeah, you can handle a few rocks."

"I could. One slip and everyone thinks you can't handle shit."

"The problem is," Dash started, "that you think you can't be killed. If you came out here on your own, you'd die for sure and no one would know it."

"Would not," he grumbled. "I'm very resourceful."

I was stuck in my current position. The trail back to the truck was wide open. If I made a run for it, they'd spot me for sure and then I wouldn't be alone the rest of the trip. I looked around for inspiration and found a hefty rock at my feet. Picking it up, I tossed it a few times in my hand before lobbing it toward a second large rock formation.

"What was that?" New Guy asked.

"What was what?"

"Didn't you hear that sound? It was like a rock falling. Do you think he's over there?"

I peeked around the edge just as New Guy started sprinting across the rocks in search of me. I chuckled to myself as I watched him frantically looking for me. When Dash gave chase, I abandoned my position and hot footed it back to my truck. With any luck, I'd be long gone before they even realized it. I glanced over my shoulder several times, thankful I was in the clear. I cranked the engine and roared out of there, skipping the next leg of my journey. I had to throw them off my scent, which meant going to the end of the trail through Arches. I could see The Windows another time.

Glancing in my rearview mirror a few times, it was pretty damn clear I lost them. Now I just needed a place to hide out for the rest of the day so I didn't have them dogging me the whole time. I really wanted to see the Delicate Arch, but wasn't ready to take the trail directly to it. So, I parked and hiked it up to the overview. It wasn't as good a view, but for today, it would be fine.

I was hiking for about ten minutes when I came across a woman arguing with herself. Saddled down with a pack that looked more like something a person would carry if they were climbing Mount Everest, she didn't look like she knew what she was doing.

"Ugh! You can do this, Bree. This buckle goes to this one," she muttered to herself as she tried to adjust the straps.

I should have kept walking. After all, I didn't know this woman, and this journey was about me, relaxing before I went back to the daily grind. Besides, the point was to get away from women. The last thing I needed was to stop and talk to one, especially one that didn't seem to know what the fuck she was doing. But as I hiked past her and saw her struggling to figure out something as simple as a backpack, I couldn't do it.

Sighing, I turned around and walked back down the steep trail to her. "Do you need some help?"

She huffed out an unamused laugh. "Why? Does it look like I don't know what I'm doing?"

"Kind of."

"Well, you'd be right. I have no idea what I'm doing. I don't know what this strap does. I don't know why there are so many hooks. I don't even know what this compartment is for!" she shouted, pulling at the compartment at the top of her pack.

"Where did you get this?"

"At some hiking store," she grumbled, wiping the sweat from her brow. It was barely sixty degrees outside and she was sweating.

"And did you tell the salesperson where you were going?"

"Yes."

"And they sold you this pack?"

"I asked for the best, so this is what they gave me. Why, is it not right?"

She finally looked up at me and my breath caught in my chest. Fuck, she was gorgeous. This was bad. I needed an immediate extraction. Suddenly, Dash and New Guy were a lifeline I needed. I couldn't be around this woman when I was supposed to be enjoying this little adventure on my own.

"Um…" I shook my head and tried to get the image of her pouty lips out of my head. When that didn't work, I tried to imagine her face as less symmetrical than it really was. I even tried to imagine she had a long crooked nose instead of the cute, slightly upturned nose that sat perfectly between two plump cheeks. Hell, just thinking about her facial features had me growing a vagina.

"It's fine. I mean, if you're hiking in the Alps. This pack is better suited for scaling Everest. If I were you, I'd go back right now and demand a refund."

"Right now?" she asked incredulously.

I nodded, my neck refusing to stop my head from bobbing up and down. "Right now. Right this minute. You should tell them they're a bunch of scam artists and demand a refund."

"But I just got here!" she said incredulously.

"Right, well, sometimes you have to do what's morally right."

It didn't make sense. Hell, I sounded like a crazy person, but I needed her gone. Right now, all I could see was her beautiful face. But soon she would stand up and I would see so much more. Her thighs, her ass, her feet. It was all downhill once you saw a woman's feet. Were they petite and cute? Did she have perfect toes or were they long and unsightly? Yes, it was ironic that I had a thing for feet when I was currently missing one. And my foot was nothing special to look at. Hell, I had hairy toes and flat feet. But men weren't supposed to have cute feet. We were supposed to look like cavemen. But women…show me a gorgeous foot and I was lost.

Not that I had a foot fetish. God no. I just thought feet were sexy. Some men were leg men or breast men. I was a foot man. I shook my head, trying to get the idea of her feet out of my head. This trip was going south fast. "Anyway, I would take it back immediately and get a refund. Your pack is too heavy. You'll never survive out here in the heat."

With that, I turned on my heel and headed up the steep incline to the overlook. My skin tingled and not from the sweat I was now emanating. No, I was sweating because a gorgeous woman was behind me. I had successfully avoided women for most of my life, only taking them home for a night when I needed to let off some steam. I saw how Eva turned Cash into a lunatic that shot everything to hell to save her life. And every man after her that dropped everything they were doing for a woman. And what did it get them? A big pain in the ass.

"Ah!"

The scream behind me had me spinning around and rushing down the trail to aid the woman that was now lying on her back with her foot wedged between two rocks. I tore my pack from my back and tossed it aside as I took in the potential injuries. The woman was crying with mascara running down her face as she tried to hold it together.

"Okay, don't move."

"Why would I move?" she snapped. "My foot is stuck!"

"I know, and I know it hurts, but I'll help you."

She sniffed and pulled out a hanky, wiping at her nose, which made me frown. Most people just used the back of their hand. "It doesn't hurt. I just really suck at doing this."

"Doing what?" I asked against my better judgment.

"This!" she said, raising her hands in the air as if to say all of it. "I'm not an adventurous person. I work in an office. I make deals happen. I'm a fucking professional!"

I flinched back at her sudden anger over falling on her ass. Suddenly, I wasn't so sure this woman was actually injured. It was more likely her frustration was at a boiling point and I was witnessing a meltdown. Yet another reason to run away, but I couldn't leave until I was sure she was okay.

"I'm going to check your foot now, okay?"

"Whatever," she snapped, laying back on the ground, making sure to put her pack under her head. Some might have misconstrued the move as her making a headrest for herself. But I saw it for what it really was. Getting a good look at her now, it was clear that she was a very prim and proper woman. Her hair was slicked back perfectly in a ponytail without a hair out of place. And she wore lipstick. Actual fucking lipstick while hiking. Who did that? Even her clothes were more like fashion hiking gear—you know, the kind people wore for photo shoots to look pretty, but you wouldn't actually wear them hiking.

Shaking myself out of my obsession of staring at her, I gently pulled her foot out from between the rocks and tested her foot. "Does this hurt?" I wiggled it from side to side, not feeling anything broken.

"No, it's fine."

"Really?"

"Yes, it's fine. Only my pride is wounded."

"You're...so, you're not injured?"

"No, I just realized that I'm not cut out for hiking!"

I looked around, wondering if anyone came with her, but didn't see a soul in sight. "Is this your first time?"

"Yes," she sighed, closing her eyes.

"And you came out to Arches. Alone."

"Yes, okay?"

My brows furrowed as I stared down at the woman before me. "Why?"

"Does it really matter why? Why did you come here?"

"Well, I'm physically fit for this. And I've been hiking before. This isn't out of the norm for me."

"Yes, but why did you come?"

"Because it's peaceful. Aside from when teammates follow you out here," I grumbled under my breath.

"Well...maybe that's what I wanted. Peace."

"And you thought you would do that alone. Where are you even from?"

"New York, okay?"

I snorted, trying my damndest not to laugh at her, but seriously... this was getting more hilarious by the minute.

"How about we sit you up?"

I held her elbow as I helped her into a seated position, which was a terrible move because now my face was just inches from hers. Her breasts were so close to me that when she took a breath and exhaled, they brushed against me. Fuck, I did not need this right now.

"So, you're good. You're fine. Everything's fine," I stumbled over my words. "Uh...so, have fun and maybe get some better shoes."

"That's it?" she scoffed. "You're just going to leave me here?"

"Well, you did say you wanted to be alone."

"Yes, before. Now, I got my foot wedged, I'm carrying the wrong pack, and I have no fucking idea how to actually hike!"

"It's not too hard. You climb the trail," I said, motioning to the dirt path ahead of me.

"Yes, but that's for people with stamina. I work out, but that doesn't include hiking in the heat."

I frowned at her. "It's sixty degrees."

"Yes, and I always have air conditioning in the summer."

"It's fall," I clarified.

"Everything is temperature controlled for me. Even my bed is temperature controlled. And now I'm out in the desert and I'm wearing black. Black! I should have known better. Doesn't it suck up the sun or something?"

"The sun is barely out. I doubt that's what's making you sweat."

"It's probably that they're fleece-lined," she grumbled.

That gave me pause. "Wait, you're wearing fleece-lined leggings?"

"The salesperson told me the temperature can swing drastically. I didn't want to get caught in the cold and freeze to death."

"But...you're hiking during the day."

"Yes, and now I'm sweating. Thank you so much for pointing that out."

Sighing, I got to my feet and held out my hand. "Maybe you should just go home."

"I can't," she said, her voice coming out as a squeak. "I can't go back to my job."

"Oh," I winced. "You were fired?"

"No, they made me take a vacation. For three months! Can you believe that? Who takes a three month vacation?" She slammed her hands down in the dirt, sending up a plume of dust. "I didn't want to go on vacation. I was perfectly content with my busy days and paperwork that constantly needed to be filled out. I was in my element. I was making deals and lots of money. How dare they stop me!"

I was confused, to say the least, and while I had this sudden urge to flee because this woman seemed like she was missing a few bolts, I couldn't help but want to ask what this was all about.

"So, your job forced you to take a vacation and your solution was to come someplace you wouldn't like and do something you knew you would hate?"

She shot me an evil look and then picked up a handful of dirt and tossed it at me. But the slight breeze blew it back in her face, causing her to choke on the dirt. I cupped my hand over my mouth so she wouldn't see me smile as she threw her hands on the ground and screamed some more.

"I hate this place!" she cried, covering her face with her hands. "I hate the dirt and I hate the heat. I don't even like wearing leggings! I miss my heels!"

I nodded along as she threw her temper tantrum. As funny as it was, I felt slightly bad for her. The woman was clearly having some sort of psychotic break, and laughing at her would only make things worse. "Listen, why don't I get you out of here. Are you staying in a hotel?"

"A yurt," she mumbled under her breath.

"You're..." I nearly started laughing, but reminded myself that she was already losing her shit. "Well, that should be interesting."

"They didn't have any hotel rooms available," she muttered. "But I got a really nice one with a shower and toilet inside, so how bad could it be?"

She had no idea, but I wasn't about to drop that bomb on her until she saw it for herself. There was no point in subjecting myself to more of her anger until absolutely necessary.

I held out my hand and waited for her to take her. Slowly, she got to her feet and tested her weight on the foot that got stuck between the rocks.

"Okay?"

"Yeah."

"Here, let me take your pack."

"Are you sure? It's kind of heavy."

I snorted at that. "Lady, do I look like I can't handle the weight of your pack?"

Her eyes roamed over my body, narrowing in on the shirt stretched across my biceps. Then she removed the pack with a wince and hefted it over to me. I grabbed it and nearly dropped the damn thing. I was fucking strong, but this pack had to weigh twice as much as her. What the hell had she put in this thing?

I slung it over one shoulder and motioned for her to walk ahead of me. Mostly because I didn't want her to see me struggle to carry the damn thing. And as a bonus, I got to stare at her ass the whole way down the trail.

"Where are you staying?" she asked.

"My truck."

"You're sleeping in your truck?" she asked over her shoulder. "How can you be comfortable like that?"

"I slept on the ground when I was in the military. Sleeping in my truck is like a luxury hotel."

She wrinkled her nose at that. "A luxury hotel includes a king-sized bed, a spa, and room service. But I suppose it is better than sleeping on the ground."

"So, your work forced you to take a vacation," I muttered. Big surprise. "Where exactly do you work?"

"I work in finance. I just became a partner, which I've worked my entire life for. Weekends aren't a thing for me, and there's no such thing as a nine-to-five day."

"You're awfully devoted."

She glanced over her shoulder with a smile. "I love it. I get lost in the numbers and budgeting…it's thrilling."

I raised my eyebrows at the enthusiasm in her voice. "I'll have to take your word for it. So, when you say finance…"

"Oh, we work with huge corporations down to personal finance. I started out in personal finance, but soon, I was working with some of the largest corporations."

"Wow, that's impressive. How old are you?"

"Thirty-three."

That was damn impressive. She must have worked her ass off from the moment she entered college. Not that I hadn't done the same, just down a different path.

"You're very driven."

"I've known it's what I wanted to do since I was little. I was always obsessed with numbers," she said wistfully. "I'm something of a math nerd."

"You were?"

"Still am," she smiled over her shoulder, nearly falling on her ass in the process. I rushed forward and grabbed her arm so she didn't tumble down the path and break a few bones.

"Watch where you're going."

She jerked her arm out of my grasp. "I'm perfectly capable of walking down a hill."

I widened my eyes as she turned away and started walking again. This woman wasn't cut out for walking on anything but a busy sidewalk.

"So, what exactly do you do?" she asked as she started walking sideways down the hill.

"Protection services."

"Like a bodyguard?"

I smirked at that. "Yeah, we deal with that stuff."

"And did you go to a special school for that?"

"I was in the military."

She scoffed at that. "Boys and their toys."

"Uh...not toys, weapons we use to defend our country."

"That's what I meant."

"It's not what you said," I muttered under my breath.

"I've never met someone in the military before. Then again, I've been so focused on my own career that I've been so blind to everyone else around me, so my sister told me."

"I wish I could be blind to everyone else right now. I came out here to get away from them."

"Do you not love your job?"

"Yeah, I do. I just don't want to be around them all the time. They're...an eclectic group of people."

"I wish I was always at work."

She continued to stumble her way down the path, carefully avoiding rocks and slowing down when she started kicking up dust.

And her outfit...she looked like she was modeling for a hiking magazine.

"Can I ask why you came here instead of...a spa?"

"A spa would have been nicer," she panted. The path took a steep decline and she grabbed onto a boulder, leaning against it as she tried to breathe. "It's so hot out here. I could be in a sauna right now."

"A sauna is hot too."

"I know that, but it's good for your skin, your lungs..." She waved her hand in front of her face. "I feel faint." She glanced up at the rising sun. "Is it just me, or is that sun really bright?"

Her flushed red face would be sexy if she were under me in bed, but out here in the sun, it only showed her intolerance for any kind of exertion. "It's barely up yet. How do you expect to survive hiking out here?"

She pulled a water bottle from her pack and chugged it. "I'm always up for a challenge. Granted, this one is not exactly what I'm used to, but I'm no quitter."

She stood, shoving her water bottle into her pack at the same time. But she was off balance and fell sideways, screeching as she fell and started to roll down the hill.

I pursed my lips and nodded as she tumbled in a very ungraceful manner until finally coming to a stop when the ground leveled out. "That seems about right."

I finished the walk down, holding in my laughter as she sat up and started throwing a temper tantrum about the sun, the dirt, and everything else around her. I sighed and grabbed her by the arm, hauling her up.

Her tear-stained face was streaked with dirt, which kind of made her adorable, not that I would ever tell her that. No, this was a woman any sane man would steer clear of. She wasn't worth the hassle, even if she was sexy as hell.

"I hate this place," she cried, shoving her face into my shoulder.

I cringed at the sudden contact and shoved her gently away by the shoulders. "Yeah, we should keep going."

I walked around her and headed to the parking area without looking back. My back was killing me from the weight of her pack.

And now that I had hiked all the way down the trail, I didn't exactly want to make my way back up again. I shoved the pack in the back of her car and stepped back as she slammed the door.

"Thank you…"

"Thumper," I answered, earning me a weird look. "And you are?"

"Bree."

I nodded. "Bree, a word of advice, go find yourself a spa and relax for your vacation. You weren't made out for hiking."

At her shocked expression, I turned and headed back to my truck. I'd start fresh tomorrow and hope I didn't run into Dash and New Guy along the way.

4

BREE

"Go to a spa," I muttered to myself as I got in my car and slammed the door. "Go to a spa," I repeated. "Like I can't handle a little hiking? So the first day was bad. That doesn't mean I can't handle this. I can handle anything! I'm Bree Wilton. I was made to tackle the highest hills and the deepest waters."

Although, I couldn't swim and I had never climbed a hill if I didn't have to, but that was beside the point. Nobody told me what I could and couldn't do. I would prove to Thumper that I could hike in Arches National Park if it was the last thing I did.

I watched his truck drive off in a cloud of dust. Okay, it would be hard to prove it to him when he was leaving, but knowing that I knew I had proved it to him would be enough—After I got a shower and a better pair of shoes. He wasn't wrong about those people selling me the gear. It was way too heavy, and looking back on my shopping experience, it was clear they saw dollar signs the moment I walked through the door in my heels and suit.

I followed my GPS back to my lodgings. I wasn't entirely sure what a yurt was, but it couldn't be that bad. I had a shower and a bathroom, so I was fairly confident that it would be fine. But when I pulled into the…location I followed on the map, I was certain I was in the wrong place.

I parked in what I assumed was the parking lot and headed to the main tent. This couldn't be right. I pushed my sunglasses up on my forehead and squinted into the morning sun. Disbelief sank in my gut as I looked around what appeared to be a campground. Tents were spread out on the property, and though I saw it on the internet, some part of me didn't actually believe this was where I would be staying.

Still, there was a bathroom and a shower. I would be fine. I straightened my shoulders and headed through the tent where a woman awaited behind a reception desk. Her bright smile was way too cheerful for the hot tent she was sitting in. A slight breeze emanated from the ceiling fan above, and I got the sneaking suspicion there was no air conditioning out here. I would roast.

"Can I help you?"

"Yes, I have a reservation. Bree Wilton."

She smiled up at me, circling my name on a paper. "Mhmm. Yes, we have you down to arrive today and you're staying with us for two weeks. You're going to love it here." Her bright smile was just a tad too cheerful for me. "You'll wake up to the most gorgeous views and hear the most soothing sounds at night." She finished gathering my paperwork and handed it over. "You're in the third yurt on the right. You even have a deck," she said, as if that was a luxury only select guests were offered.

I took the paperwork with a forced smile. "Thank you." I looked through the paperwork and frowned. "Um…there's no key."

"Mhmm," she nodded.

"I need a key," I said again, wondering if she hadn't understood the question.

"Oh, there are no keys. However, there is a padlock. To unlock it, just enter the last four of your social. Have a nice stay!" she said with way too much cheer in her voice.

I nodded, but I wasn't at all confident that this stay would be happy. In fact, I was pretty sure I wouldn't even make it one night. I turned and headed outside, sliding my sunglasses back on my face. I could do this. I wasn't a wimp. I drove down to my yurt and parked outside. I popped the trunk and grabbed my largest suitcase first. Hauling it out of the trunk was a struggle, but after much wiggling, I finally got it free and rolled it over the dirt to the deck.

"Okay, this isn't that bad. There's a seat for me to sit on the deck and do...deck things." I grunted as I pulled the luggage up and rolled it across the zipper. "I can't believe all that's standing between me and a potential murderer is a zipper."

Bending down, I entered the last four of my social, then slowly unzipped the tent. Tears sprang to my eyes when I saw the inside, and it wasn't out of joy. Sure, there were wood floors and a bed, but all the luxury of a hotel was missing. Blinking back my tears, I stepped inside and checked out my accommodations for the next two weeks. Surely, I had the wrong tent. I had requested the luxury tent. I walked around the space, but saw no hidden rooms revealing a bathroom. No shower either. There was a sink, but I couldn't figure out how to turn on the water. It was basically a basin, but no spout for the water.

"This can't be right. They didn't give me the right yurt."

Turning on my heel, I grabbed my suitcase and wheeled it back across the deck, over the dirt, and struggled to stuff it back in the trunk. There was no way I was in the right place. I had a shower and a bathroom—basic luxuries that any normal person would expect to find in a hotel!

After driving back down the dirt road to the main office, I stomped inside, ready to sort out this mess. Her bright smile pissed me off, but I held my temper. I would not lose it and act like the crazy lady from New York.

"Hi, I was just in here a few minutes ago."

"Yes, I remember. Bree Wilton. Yurt 3."

"Yes, but I think there's been a mistake. See, I signed up for a yurt with a bathroom and a shower."

"Oh, yours has one."

"No, it doesn't."

"Yes, it does," she said way too cheerily.

I bit my lip for a moment, trying my best not to yell. "See, I know what a shower and a bathroom look like. There's not one in my yurt."

"Of course not," she laughed. "None of the bathrooms or showers are in the yurt. There's a community bathroom just down the road from you, along with a shower."

"A…community…you mean I have to share it with others?"

"That is what a community bathroom means," she whispered, like she was letting me in on the secret.

"No, I paid for my own. I should be in a different yurt."

"I'm sorry, we don't have any available."

"But I paid for it."

"Ma'am—"

"When a person puts a deposit down on something like this, it's expected to be held until said person arrives."

"I understand—"

"I don't think you do, because if you did, I would have a fucking bathroom and shower in my yurt!"

Her eyes went wide as I raised my voice and swore at the poor woman. It wasn't her fault that I couldn't handle nature, but it was her fault that she gave me the wrong accommodations.

"I'm sorry. I shouldn't have yelled."

"Ma'am, none of our yurts have a private bathroom or shower. It clearly says on the website that there are showers and bathrooms on the property."

"No, it said they came with every yurt."

"And they do. They're just not in the yurt."

I stared at her for a minute, trying to figure this out. "Who the hell would come out here and stay someplace they don't have a private bathroom? That's insane!"

"Um…we actually get a lot of business," she said uncertainly.

I took a deep breath. I would not lose my shit right now. Everything was fine. There had to be something else available. I refused to give up. "Listen, I'm sure there's something else nearby. Maybe another hotel you work with?"

"Of course."

"Perfect."

"But they're most likely sold out."

My heart deflated, but I wouldn't give up until I'd called every single one and ruled out any possibility of a hotel. Turning in a huff, I stormed out of the main office and drove back to my yurt. I didn't bother with my luggage this time. I was only staying until I found another hotel. Reception was spotty at best. I called the first hotel, the one with the most luxurious rooms and expensive room service.

"Yes, I'm looking for a room."

"What...please?"

"What?"

"Date..."

"I'm sorry, the reception is terrible. Did you ask what date?"

"Yes."

"For tonight."

"I'm...booked...October."

"You're booked until October?"

"...yes...try...you."

The line went dead. I took a deep breath and looked up the next hotel. It took forever for the page to load, but ten minutes later, I finally had a hotel number. "It's going to be okay. You'll find a hotel and take a nice long nap in the air conditioning."

I dialed the next number, and the next, but every hotel was booked. Hours passed as I struggled with poor internet and terrible cell reception. Every hotel said the same thing, they had no openings until October. The final hotel on my list was actually a motel—something I had never considered as an option until this very moment. But how bad could it be? At least I would have air conditioning and a bathroom. That was a world up from where I was currently.

Twenty minutes later, I had a room booked for ten nights and I was on my way out of the camp of tents and unclean people who shared bathrooms. Never again would I enter this campground. And the best part was, I was still roughing it, doing something unexpected.

However, that excitement was soon deflated when I saw the motel I'd be staying at. The sign was hanging sideways from the rusted post and half the lights were burnt out on the sign. I hadn't had high expectations for the motel, but I'd hoped it at least was a step up from the yurt. Still, I hadn't seen the inside yet.

I was smarter this time, taking only my purse inside with me after grabbing the key with the squishy keychain attached. It was like something out of a bad eighties film. Unlocking the door, I prayed the inside was really a palace. The eighties bedspread made my heart sink and the box TV with no remote made it even worse.

I pulled out my phone and immediately dialed my sister for some perspective. "Wow, twice in a week. You must really be bored."

"Grace, this whole trip is a disaster. I booked a yurt, but apparently it has a community bathroom and shower."

"Uh-huh."

"So, I got myself a motel, but it's like…a super creepy motel with a box TV and a bedspread out of the eighties."

"Wow, talk about your bad luck."

"And now I don't know what to do. There's nothing in the area and it's too late to drive around and find someplace else to stay."

"So, are you going for the rat-infested motel or yurt with no bathroom?"

"I don't know! What would you do?"

"Pull back the bedspread."

"Why? Do you think it's better underneath?"

"Not really," she muttered.

Creeping closer to the bed, I pinched the corner of the bedspread between two fingers and swiftly yanked it back. Something squirmed across the bed, making me yelp. I jumped back, nearly dropping the phone as I huddled in the corner breathing harshly.

"Oh God, something ran across the bed."

"What are you doing now?"

"Why does that matter?" I snapped.

"Just wondering. If it were me, I'd go ask for another room, but I'm guessing that's not in the cards for you."

I dropped my head in my hands. "This is such a disaster. Go do something you wouldn't normally do! That's what you said. Now I'm out here in the middle of the desert with cockroaches and no bathroom and probably no cable either!"

"Were you really planning on watching cable while you're at a national park?"

"Yes, because that's what people like me do! I wanted luxury, but I listened to you instead."

"Wow, way to place all the blame on my shoulders."

"You're the one that told me to do this! Be like Dad! That's what you said," I argued.

"Yeah, but I talk to you once a year if I'm lucky. I haven't seen you in three years."

"Hey, I always send presents to your kids on their birthdays." It was like she thought I totally forgot about her.

"Yes, last year you sent Ella a new ballet bag."

"It was adorable."

"Yes, for a six-year-old."

I frowned, trying to do the math in my head. "Wait, I thought Ella was the younger one."

"The younger one?" she snorted. "Wow, really classy sis. Ella's sixteen."

"She is?" I gasped.

"Yes, you saw her first recital twelve years ago, not that you'd remember that."

"I'm sorry," I said sincerely.

"Look, you've always been ambitious. I learned a long time ago not to be disappointed."

"By me, you mean."

"Well, yeah."

Shocked, I slumped down against the wall, trying to figure out where the time went. There was so much I missed over the years, and apparently, my family didn't even concern themselves with the fact that I was so absent from their lives. They just assumed this was the way it would always be. And once I took this new job, it would be even more likely that I would miss holidays, birthdays, or any other family functions. Hell, my father could die and I wouldn't notice.

"I'm a horrible person," I groaned.

"You're not a horrible person. Maybe a horrible sister, daughter, granddaughter, pet owner, and neighbor, but you're not a horrible person."

"Thanks. That makes me feel so much better."

"Listen, stop feeling sorry for yourself. Get up off your ass and go back to the yurt. At least that was clean. So what if you have to share a shower or a bathroom? Is it really the end of the world?"

"Possibly. I would be much happier in New York."

"I have no doubt about that, but if you don't do this now, you'll always be wondering what might have happened on that trip, if only you had seen it through. You'll have the next fifty years to work your-self to death."

"I suppose that's true," I muttered.

"And who knows, you might actually like it out there."

That made me laugh, and God knows I needed a laugh as I sat in this crusty, dusty motel filled with creepy crawly bugs. "I did meet a hot guy."

"Yeah?"

"His name was Thumper."

"Like the rabbit?"

"I have no idea."

"Was he hot like a model or hot like he was sweating profusely?"

"Definitely not a model. He was...rugged."

There was a pause on the other end of the line. "Rugged? Since when is rugged your style?"

"Since never, but he did carry my pack for me."

"That's...nice?"

"He had tattoos."

"And that's a bad thing, I'm guessing."

"It's...well, it doesn't fit into my world."

"I can guarantee that most of the men that fit into your world will not be found hiking at a national park."

"That's not true."

"Uh-huh. Did you tell anyone where you were going?"

"Yes."

"And how many of them asked where that was?"

I stayed silent, not wanting to prove her point.

"Listen, go back to the yurt. Stay the night and see how things go. You might find you actually like it there."

"I might end up dead. Do you know it only has a zipper to keep people out?"

"Yes, I do often hear about people breaking into yurts and murdering people in their sleep."

"You do?"

"Okay, well, this has been fun, but I have actual things to do that don't involve solving your problems of yurt versus motel."

She hung up without another word. I hauled my ass off the floor and left the motel behind, pulling up to the yurt just a half hour later. After hauling my luggage inside and getting it somewhat organized, I plopped down on the bed and stared up at the canvas ceiling.

"What the hell am I doing here?"

5

THUMPER

I STARED up at the stars from the bed of my pickup truck. This was just what I needed—solitude. It had been way too long since I got away from it all and just enjoyed the peace and quiet. Though, to be quite honest, I was getting away because OPS was becoming overrun with women. Not that I didn't like them all, but staying in a house with all those men, and then the women on top of it...it was all too much.

A man couldn't think around all those female voices. And they were all so damn curious. I could still remember what it was like when Eva first joined us at the safe house. She was like a scared kitten, too afraid of everything to make a move. I liked that about her. Call me sexist, but she kept her mouth shut and let us do our jobs. For the most part. But then Fox got to her. It was always Fox. If there was one key element that made all these women crazy, it was Fox.

Knife-throwing, excitement, weird food—that guy had a way of drawing the ladies in, and I'm not talking sexually. Well, besides Anna. What she saw in him, I would never understand, and I didn't want to. What did a guy have to do to find a normal girl that wasn't turned on by danger, didn't fancy throwing knives, and was actually scared when danger approached?

I sighed as I fluffed the pillow behind my head. With the chill settling into the night, I zipped up my coat and let my eyes slide closed. However, the peace of the night was soon interrupted.

"Do you see him?" Dash said.

"It's dark as fuck out here. How the hell would I see him?"

"Don't you have super vision or something?"

"I can't die. That doesn't heighten all my senses and make it impossible for other things to happen, like bad hearing."

"Do you think he went wandering around in the desert?"

"At night?" New Guy asked. "Why the fuck would he do that?"

"I don't know. Why would he come out here all alone? If you ask me, it's a sad day when a man goes out to the desert alone and doesn't invite his friends."

I pulled the pillow from under my head and smashed it over my face. I couldn't believe they followed me out here, or that they found me after I ditched them. A man could only take so much, and these two were pushing my boundaries more than any other human being could.

"Did you check the truck?"

"I thought you checked the truck," New Guy answered.

"I was taking a piss. That's why I said *I'll be over here taking a piss. You check the truck.*"

"Maybe I would have heard you if you weren't muttering all the time. You know, it's important to speak clearly."

"I do speak clearly. Name one time I didn't speak clearly."

"Apparently, when you told me to check the truck!"

"That's your opinion."

"No, if any other living creature were standing here, he would say the same thing. He would say you muttered."

"Any creature? So, if a skunk passed, you'd want to ask him?"

"No, are you fucking crazy? Then I'd smell like you."

"Oh, you're really funny," Dash snapped.

I bit the pillow, doing my best not to pull out my gun and shoot them both. I could do it. I'd just toss them over a cliff and say they were standing too close to the edge as they took a picture. It happened all the time.

"Clearly, he doesn't want to see us or he wouldn't have ditched us."

"Why do you have to say it like that?" New Guy asked.

"Say what, like what?"

"*Clearly*. There's nothing clear about anything. You only say clearly when it's obvious."

"It was obvious. That's why I said clearly," Dash snapped.

"No, we missed him at the Balanced Rock. We have no idea if he meant to ditch us or if it was just bad luck. So clearly, clearly doesn't apply."

I shot up in the bed of my truck and tossed my pillow at them. "Would you shut the fuck up? Some of us are trying to enjoy some peace and quiet around here!"

Dash turned to New Guy with a huff. "Clearly, he's been hiding from us the whole time."

"Ah-ha! See? You said it too. You meant it that way."

I jumped out of my truck and grabbed New Guy by the collar, shoving him up against the truck. "Would you just fucking stop? I came out here to get away from all of you, and you fucking followed me out here!"

"Well, that's because we wanted to make sure you were okay. Which clearly you're not."

"I swear to God," I snapped, my cheek shaking with anger. "I will fucking pull out my gun and shoot you right now if you don't stop saying *clearly*."

He snapped his lips shut, but I could see the laughter in his eyes. He was dying to open his mouth and say it just to piss me off. Meanwhile, Dash jumped into the bed of my truck and started moving stuff around.

"There's not nearly enough space here. Someone's going to have to sleep in the truck."

"Nobody's sleeping in my truck," I grumbled, shaking New Guy off. "Go find someone else to bug for the night."

"It's already dark," Dash argued. "Where exactly do you expect us to go?"

"Anywhere but by me."

"You would do that to your own teammate? That's not cool."

I hopped back into the bed of the truck and rearranged my bedding. "I would do it in a fucking heartbeat. This is my truck, my vacation, and I didn't ask you to tag along."

"But...we'll freeze out here," New Guy said pathetically.

"Not my problem. Where's your truck?"

"We uh...sort of can't find it," Dash confessed.

"You can't find your truck?" I asked incredulously. "Where exactly did you leave it?"

"Well, see...we were looking for you at the Balanced Rock, and then we wandered off. Long story short, we ended up here."

"So, you didn't lose it. You just don't want to walk back and find it."

"No, we're pretty sure it got towed," New Guy nodded. "Yeah, we watched from a distance as it got hitched up and taken away."

"Why didn't you go claim it?" I asked irritatedly.

Dash laughed at that, but I wasn't sure why it was funny. "Dude, we couldn't be those guys that ran after a tow truck, insisting the vehicle belonged to us. We'd end up on YouTube."

These guys were driving me nuts. But there was no getting rid of them tonight. "Alright, you can stay for one night, but then I'm driving you into town and you're leaving me alone."

"Scout's honor," Dash said, holding up five fingers.

"Yeah, what he said," New Guy nodded.

I turned and got back to work on my bed.

"Except..."

"Except what?" I sighed, knowing I wasn't getting to sleep anytime soon.

"Well, Cash kind of told us to make sure you didn't do anything stupid."

"Me? What could I possibly do that's stupid?"

"Well, you did come out here all by yourself," Dash answered.

"Yes, to be by myself. That's hardly stupid."

"But you just got that new foot. Maybe it's a sign."

I pinched the bridge of my nose, already thoroughly irritated with the direction of this conversation. "What could getting a new foot be a sign of?"

"Depression."

"Anxiety," New Guy countered.

"A need for a new life."

"Or to end the one you have."

"Wait, you think I came out here after getting a new foot to off myself because a new foot would remind me of the life I had before I lost my foot by blowing it up?"

"Hey, people react in strange ways," Dash quickly explained. "That foot represents—"

"A foot. That's all it fucking represents. I had a foot. Now I have a robotic foot. I run faster than all of you, and if I lose this one, I just get a new one. That's all it fucking represents."

"See, I'm sensing some hostility here," Dash said to New Guy.

"Exactly what Cash was talking about," he agreed. "Maybe we need to get him a healing stone."

"Or a pilates class."

"Ooh, they have those wristbands with the calming beads on them. Maybe that would work."

"Or I could pull out my gun and kill you. That would definitely relieve some tension," I snapped. "Now, leave me the fuck alone so I can get some sleep!"

I plopped down on my makeshift bed and curled up on my side. Tomorrow, I was finding a hotel or someplace I could lock these fuckers out. It was bad enough that they interrupted my vacation, but now they were destroying my peaceful night under the stars.

"Psst," one of them hissed in my ear. I practically jumped out of my skin, swinging back hard to get the bastard away from me. "Hey, calm down. You're so tense."

I spun around and faced Dash with a death glare. "How about I sneak up on you and whisper in your ear?"

"I didn't really think I was sneaking. You're ex-military. I shouldn't be able to sneak up on you."

"I was trying to fucking sleep!"

"That doesn't matter," New Guy said, appearing at the tailgate. "Once a Marine, always a Marine."

"I wasn't a fucking Marine," I snapped.

"Really? What were you?"

"Navy," I snapped.

New Guy frowned hard. "*You* were Navy? Well, that explains a lot."

"Like what?"

"Well, why you blew off your foot. Any experienced boots on the ground guy would know not to blow off his foot."

"Would you just fucking shut up and let me sleep?" I yelled.

"Yeesh. Someone's testy. Hey, scoot over."

"What?"

Dash patted me on the back. "I'm trying to lay down here. Scoot over, man."

"You fucking scoot over. "This is my bed."

"Yeah, but I'm your friend."

"You're an annoyance."

"If he gets to sleep in the bed, so do I," New Guy said, climbing into the bed of the truck.

"There's not enough fucking room!"

"Yes, there is. We'll just squeeze in." He squirmed between Dash and me, shoving me into the wheel well and crushing my nuts. I groaned, trying not to curse seven ways to Sunday over the current situation I found myself in. I just had to get through tonight.

"Hey, is it alright if I drape my arm across your stomach?" New Guy whispered in my ear like a creep. "It's just, my arm is kind of squished and I like to snuggle with a pillow at night."

I slowly turned my head to face him. If he couldn't read the fuck off look I was shooting him, he would feel it in a minute. Luckily for him, he raised his arm and scooted away from me.

"I'll just tuck my hand into my jeans so there's no touching. No touching you, I mean. Not that I'll be touching myself. That would be weird with the three of us in the bed of the truck. I just meant my hand would be firmly away from you. Not touching you in any way."

I didn't bother responding. I just rolled over and closed my eyes, praying for morning to come swiftly. That or death. Hell, I didn't have a death wish when I came out here, but a few hours with these guys and I was ready to be committed to the psych ward for evaluation.

"Were you really in the Navy?"

The early morning sun should have been refreshing. Instead, I was cranky as hell because my back was all out of whack. At least my bedmates were gone. I rolled over and stretched, groaning when my back cracked in the most unpleasant way.

Sitting up, I shook my head when I saw New Guy and Dash cooking something over a fire. "What the fuck are you doing?"

"Squirrel?" New Guy asked, holding up the stick with the impaled rodent.

My stomach turned at the sight of the bloody animal. I could eat in the wild if I had to, but why would I? I could go to a restaurant with coffee made from something other than the dirt they scraped off the ground.

"I'm heading out."

I jumped out of the back of my truck and headed to the driver's side as they scrambled to put out the flames, kicking dirt over the woodpile.

"Wait!" Dash shouted. "We'll come with you!"

"No, thanks. I'm good."

"But…we don't have a truck!"

I hefted the door open and grinned at them. "Call Cash. I'm sure he'll get you sorted out."

I slammed the door before either of them could say anything else. I saw New Guy running toward my truck as Dash unzipped and started spraying the fire with piss. I put my foot down and shot out of there just as New Guy leapt into the back of my truck. Cranking the wheel, I swerved from side to side as he screamed in the back, rolling from one side to the other and trying to hold on for dear life. I slammed on the brakes, making him slide forward, then hit the gas and laughed as he fell out of the back.

As I drove off, I watched in the rearview mirror as he rolled in the dust, then got up and shook his fist at me. Grabbing my phone, I called the pain in the ass responsible for this.

"Please tell me they're still alive," Cash said.

"You should have thought about that before you sent them out to stalk me."

"You took off without any warning."

"I explained everything to IRIS before I left."

"Yeah, and it was a shitty excuse. Why are you really running?"

"I'm not running," I snapped. "I wanted a fucking break with some peace and quiet. There are women everywhere and they make horrible decisions. Is it too much to ask that I get away for a guy's weekend without women storming in and fucking things up?"

"It can't be a guy's weekend if you're the only guy."

"Says who?"

"Everyone!"

"Yeah?" I laughed. "Point me in the direction of these so-called rules. I'd love to read this book that tells me who is allowed on a guy's weekend, and what constitutes using the phrase."

"Alright, fine! There's no fucking rulebook, but you could have at least kept them alive."

"They are alive," I said, putting him out of his misery. "They lost their truck, so I left them at the campground after New Guy tried groping me in my sleep."

"Did he know it was you?"

"Yes."

"Did you cut off his hand?"

"No, he shoved his hand down his pants so he would keep his hands to himself."

I heard his heavy sigh over the phone and could imagine him rubbing Betty in his pocket, wishing he could take Sally 2 out for a little fun. "You know, there are some things a boss doesn't need to know."

"You and me both. You can deal with them from now on, and leave me the fuck alone."

"When are you getting back?"

"When I feel like it."

I hung up, feeling slightly better about the situation. But there was no way I was sleeping in my truck again, not after last night's disaster.

46

Before I even hit Moab, I saw some campgrounds with yurts. That would be interesting to say the least. I'd never stayed in a yurt, but it couldn't be too much different than places I'd stayed in the military. Hell, if it had a bed, I was good to go.

I parked outside the main office and headed inside, giving the woman behind the counter my most winning smile. After all, it might be my only shot at getting someplace to stay.

"It's getting hot out already," I grinned.

"You're not from around here, are you?" She had a crooked smile, but was still beautiful. If she gave me a yurt, I just might see if she wanted to join me for the night.

"No, I'm not. I came out here to get away from it all."

"And where is *it all*?"

"Kansas," I answered honestly.

She looked at me for a moment, then started laughing. "Yeah, we get lots of people from *Kansas* trying to get away from the hustle and bustle."

I didn't quite know what to say to that. I actually told the truth, but she didn't believe me. "And do you happen to have any yurts available to someone looking to get away?"

"We did just have one become available, but it's very pricey."

"Is it a million dollars a night?"

She laughed at that, throwing back her head. "No, you're funny. It's three hundred a night."

"I'll take it."

I handed over my card and shot her a wink as she continued registering me. I didn't know how long I planned on staying, but she had it available for ten nights, so I took it.

"You're the last yurt on the right," she smiled flirtatiously. "If you need anything, you know where to find me."

"I just might take you up on that."

I headed out to my truck and grabbed my bag, hauling it over my shoulder. After the night I had last night, I was going to sleep the day away without any distractions. It would be hot in the yurt, but I could handle that. Strolling down the path, I entered the code on the lock and unzipped the tent, then walked into paradise.

A king-sized bed awaited me, complete with a living room and a small sink. At the back of the tent was a wall that separated the toilet and the shower from the rest of the room. And there was even a clear opening to allow me to stargaze at night. Tossing my bag down, I flopped on the bed and closed my eyes.

"Peace at last."

I dozed off as the sun rose in the sky and covered me like a warm blanket. I could lay here all day and forget anyone else existed.

"Ah!"

A shrill scream jolted me awake, making me jump from the bed and pull my gun. I slipped easily into work mode, moving across the tent quietly as the screaming continued just outside. Peeking around the canvas, I cleared the area to my left before stepping through the opening and swept my surroundings for the threat.

A woman in a robe and hair towel ran across the dirt path, screaming as she ran toward a yurt. I moved swiftly in the direction of the communal showers, busting in the door as I prepared to fire on the enemy. There were three shower stalls, all of them with closed curtains. Approaching the first, I tore back the curtain, prepared to fire, but it was empty. The second was the same, and when I approached the third, I was about to rip back the curtain when a snake slithered out from the stall.

Relaxing slightly, I opened the curtain to find it empty. Sighing, I holstered my weapon and grabbed the reptile. "All of this over a fucking snake?"

I walked outside and tossed it a good distance from the showers. Then I marched over to the yurt the woman entered, ready to rip her a new asshole.

"Hey!" I shouted, standing just outside. "What the fuck was that?"

"Excuse me?" she snapped.

"You were screaming like an insane person. I thought someone was trying to murder you!"

I heard her footsteps march across the floor, and saw her outline through the canvas. When she tore open the zipper, I understood exactly why she was fucking screaming.

"You."

She sighed, crossing her arms over her chest. "What are you doing here?"

"I'm sleeping here."

"This is just my luck," she muttered.

"Hey, as I recall, I helped you out yesterday."

"And I said thank you."

"Woman, you can't run around screaming because there's a snake in the shower. I could have killed someone."

She huffed out a laugh. "That's just ridiculous. Why would you have killed someone?"

I pointed to the gun at my hip and shot her an *are you fucking stupid* look.

"Why are you carrying that? Don't you know those things are dangerous?"

"No," I said in mock surprise. "Is it really?"

"Do you know how many people die at the hands of a gun every year?"

"No, but I know how many people die at the hands of the idiot holding the gun."

"Are you mocking me?" she asked, her face pinched in anger.

"No, simply pointing out that a gun doesn't have hands and can't discharge itself."

The look on her face could melt steel, but it didn't affect me in any way. Well...mostly. I would never admit that it stirred something inside me down south. That was insane. This woman was the complete opposite of me, and a pain in the ass.

"Was there anything else you wanted?"

"Not a damn thing. But the next time you scream, there had better be an actual emergency."

"Or what?"

"Or you might just find out what I do to people that cry wolf."

I turned and stomped down the stairs, cursing myself for rushing off to save a woman who didn't need saving, but a gag that would shut her up.

6

BREE

I QUICKLY ZIPPED up the tent as the irritating man marched off. If I was smart, I would have asked him to check my yurt before going to make sure no other critters were inside. But my pride wouldn't allow me to rush after him now. I hauled my suitcase up on the bed and flung it open, pulling out some decent clothes to wear. It occurred to me as I was rifling through the clothes that a snake might be lurking inside, but I pushed through the fear, refusing to let it take over.

I didn't care how much money I spent on this yurt, I was getting the hell out of here before any other creatures decided to make their way into my tent or my laundry. Seriously, who shared showers? It was disgusting. I rushed around the room, tossing all my items in my luggage, ready to hit the road before lunch. If I was lucky, I would get out of this Godforsaken state and into civilization before nightfall. I highly doubted there were any of my favorite hotels out this way. Maybe I'd find a Hilton Hotel, or at the very least a Holiday Inn. As long as it wasn't a motel, I'd take it.

I grabbed my purse and was about to head out when my phone rang. I was going to ignore it, but it was my boss calling. Maybe he was asking me to come home early.

"Hello, Preston. How are you?"

"I'm great. I was just calling to check in with you, see how things are going?"

"Oh, you know…" I looked around the yurt in disgust. "Just wonderful."

"That's great. I want lots of pictures. You know, many around the office didn't think you'd make it out there."

"Really?" I asked, pissed that there was someone out there that doubted my abilities, even in a situation like this. "Oh, I just love this stuff. It's been so long since I've gotten away."

He laughed raucously, which only further enraged me. "I knew it! There's a bet going around the office for how long you'd make it. My money was always on you," he said conspiratorially. "I told them all, you can do anything you put your mind to. Don't let me down. I have a lot of money riding on you."

The last thing I wanted was my boss losing money on me, especially when I was getting such a big promotion. "Well, you can tell them I'm having the time of my life."

"I knew it would be good for you."

"But I can always come back early. The job comes first, and I wouldn't want to leave you shorthanded."

"Not at all. You're due the time off, so take it."

"Really, I don't mind," I urged.

"I told you, HR insisted. I'm really just calling to say that I've put all the paperwork through. When you get the chance, look over the email I've sent and have Becky in HR file it. After that, you're good to go."

"I'll look at it right away," I promised.

"It's really no rush. I'm sure you're enjoying the sights way too much to stop and look at paperwork. Anyway, I've got to get back to the grindstone. Have fun!"

He hung up before I could argue the finer points of why I should be back there, but it was no use. As he said, HR demanded it. I grabbed my bag, ready to leave when I remembered what he said about nobody thinking I could do this. When I stopped to think about it, it really pissed me off. I had always been able to do anything I put my mind to. So, I stayed out here for ten days. I could do that. I could rough it with the best of them. Maybe I wouldn't step foot in a shower for ten days, but damn it, I would not give in and run home.

If I was going to make it out here, I was going to need help. My pack was too heavy and I really wasn't an outdoor girl. I should have just gone to the beach. It would have been so much more relaxing. Still, I needed the evidence to show all those pricks at the office. My eyes drifted to the yurt opening. There was only one way to handle this, and it was going to be painful for me in the short term.

Steeling my spine, I marched to the opening and waltzed my ass straight through. I didn't care what I had to pay this man, I would get him to help me if I had to offer him my first born. One step outside and I was already sweating more than I had in my entire life. I wiped the sweat from my brow and raised my fist to knock. Except, it was canvas, so there was no place to knock.

Clearing my throat, I shouted, "Excuse me, Mr…" Crap, what was his name? "Thumper."

A loud snore ripped through the silence. Great, he was sleeping. "Mr. Thumper!" I shouted.

Still, I was only met with silence. I was about to turn around and walk away when I saw his zipper wasn't closed all the way. I could just walk right in there and wake him up. It was his own fault, after all. He should know better than to leave it open. I slowly unzipped it and stepped inside, creeping along like a thief in the night.

I winced as the floorboard creaked slightly. I held out my hand just over his shoulder and was about to give him a small shake when he spun around suddenly, shoving his gun in my face. I held completely still, my heart pounding wildly in my chest as I held my breath. My nostrils flared in fear as my eyes stayed locked on the gun just inches from my nose.

For a brief second, I looked at the man who had just been sleeping. His eyes narrowed in on me before he quickly pulled the gun out of my face and rolled completely to face me. "What the fuck are you doing in my tent?"

Still shaken by the near-death experience, it took me a moment to gather my wits. "I…I came to ask for your help."

"And you thought you'd let yourself into my yurt?" he asked, sitting up. He started patting the messy bedding, looking for something as he continued to basically ignore me.

"Um…there was no place to knock."

He grunted in response, which only irritated me further. "Mr. Thumper—"

"Mr. Ha! That's a funny one."

"What's a funny one?"

"You calling me Mr." He tore his blanket from the bed, then snatched some kind of metal thing from the other side of the bed.

"As I was saying, I need some help. See, I'm supposed to be on sabbatical, and my coworkers think I can't make it out here."

"Because you can't," he said as he lifted his pant leg.

I stared in shock as he started massaging the skin where his leg abruptly ended and a stub remained. "You don't have a foot!"

He finally looked up at me, his eyebrow quirked like I was stupid. And I guess I was, because he clearly knew he didn't have a foot.

"You're quick. I can see why they gave you the job."

"But…you…yesterday…"

"Again, you speak so eloquently. Are you like this at work too?"

My cheeks burned in humiliation. Obviously, I knew there were handicapped people out there who dealt with missing limbs, but I'd never seen it firsthand. It was a shock, to say the least. I watched in utter fascination as he rubbed some kind of lotion on the stub, working it into the skin of the thinner portion of the leg.

"Um…how…what happened?" I asked, taking a seat in the chair across from the bed.

"Shrapnel. Got too close to a bomb and nearly blew myself up," he grinned. "Luckily, I only lost the foot."

"And this is…" I gestured to the robotic-looking foot he was slipping onto his leg. He pulled it on just like a sock, then pressed the foot to the ground.

"This is a robotic foot. It allows me to walk, run, even feel sensations."

"How is that possible?"

"It has sensors in the bottom." He lifted his foot, showing me little circles on the bottom. "Touch it."

I shook my head quickly. That seemed wrong somehow. "No, I couldn't."

"You couldn't?" he laughed. "It's not going to bite you."

"No, I know, but it seems insensitive."

"Insensitive would have been when you pointed out I was missing a foot."

"I'm so sorry—" I said quickly, but he cut me off.

"Relax. I don't offend that easily. You didn't hurt my delicate sensibilities. Now touch it."

"No," I shook my head.

"Touch it!" he demanded.

"No, you can't make me!"

"Lady, just hold out your hand and touch it!"

The canvas behind me ripped open and I spun around with a squeal. Two men stood there, staring at us in amusement.

"When I heard *Lady, touch it,* I really hoped I was walking in on something slightly more interesting than this."

I stood quickly, ready to bolt. With my humiliation at a fever pitch, I wanted nothing more than to go hide in my yurt for the foreseeable future.

"How the fuck did you find me?" Thumper snapped.

"Easy. I followed the trail of women drooling over you." The man stepped forward and held out his hand. "The name's Dash."

"Dash, as in…"

"I run really fast," he said with a glint in his eyes.

I held out my hand and shook his, glancing back at Thumper.

"He's not really the one you want to meet. I'm FNG," the other man stepped forward. "I can't die, so if you're looking for someone to hang out with, I'm the better option."

"You…I have so many questions. Are you robotic also?"

Thumper snorted behind me. "He survives on stupidity."

"Not true. You've seen it with your own eyes," FNG said pointedly.

I was so confused by what was going on here. "I'm sorry, what exactly does FNG stand for?"

"Fucking New Guy," Thumper grunted.

"Except, I'm no longer the New Guy. We have three new recruits, yet somehow, I haven't had the pleasure of getting a new name."

"They have to name you?" I asked.

"I'd be happy if they just used my real name."

"Which is?"

"Oh, it's—"

"Do you guys have a point of being here, ruining my vacation?" Thumper asked.

"You're not the only one entitled to a vacation," Dash pointed out. "Maybe we just wanted to see the great state of Utah."

"You followed me here. You saw I'm alive. Now you can leave."

"Why would you not be alive?" I asked.

"Can't a man take a vacation with everyone following him around?" he asked as he stood. "I came here to get away from everyone, and you followed me! That's the opposite of getting away."

My brows furrowed as I looked past him to where a wall separated the room from something else. I marched past him to the other side of the yurt. "Do you have a shower?"

"I just want some fucking peace!" he continued.

I gasped as I saw the shower head hanging from the ceiling. "You do! How did you get this? They told me none of the yurts had showers!"

"I go where I'm told," Dash shot back.

I stormed around to the other side of the wall and gasped a second time. "And you have your own toilet! How is this possible?"

"You can go home. I don't need someone to follow me around. Especially someone with a death wish."

"I don't have a death wish."

"What makes you so special that you get a shower and toilet?" I yelled, staring in longing at the facilities.

"Maybe it's my charm!" he shouted.

"I'll have you know that I've wished a few times in my life that I could die."

"You did not," Thumper shot back.

"Okay, no, but if I wanted to, it's just not possible. There are worse things than death, you know."

"Yeah, like not having a shower or toilet," I argued. "Seriously, why did you get it?" I asked as I walked back out to him.

"Would you forget about the toilet? You don't want to be here anyway!" Thumper shouted.

"But now I have to be, so the least you could do is switch yurts with me!"

"No, and I'll tell you why. It's privileged assholes like you that think they should get their way. And why? Because you're a woman? I could pull that card too, but I don't. You know why I got this yurt?"

"I would love to know." I crossed my arms over my chest and glared at him.

"Because it was available. They had an opening and I came along at the right time. I didn't cry or complain or use my charm. I just said I needed a fucking yurt. That's all it came down to."

I stared at him with my mouth gaping open, not sure what to say. This man was so infuriating. He didn't realize how easy he had it with his handsome face and cute dimples. I didn't have dimples, and even if I did, no one would look at me the way I was sure half the female population looked at him. "Well...I'm not an asshole."

"That's not what I was—" He let out an animalistic growl at the ceiling before turning back to me. "Would you just leave and let me get back to my vacation? I've spent more time with you than I have on my own, which defeats the purpose of getting away."

"I'm not leaving until you agree to be my guide. I can't go home without pictures proving that I can make it out here."

"No, because you can't make it out here, and I'm not destroying my sanity to make you look good."

"I'll take you," Dash offered.

"Ooh, me too. I love a good hike."

I smirked at Thumper and turned on my heel. "It's nice to know there are still true gentlemen in the world. I'll just grab my things."

"Don't fall off the cliff taking a selfie!" he shouted after me.

"Don't fall off the cliff taking a selfie," I muttered to myself in a mocking way. Like I would actually be stupid enough to do something like that. Actually, come to think of it, I might do something like that unknowingly, but he didn't know that. I pulled on my long-sleeved t-shirt and grabbed my pack, slinging it over my shoulders. It felt even heavier than yesterday, and when I took a step, I almost fell backward.

"Whoa, what are you wearing?"

I slowly turned so I didn't topple over, and looked questioningly at the men standing just inside my yurt. "I'm wearing hiking gear." I glanced down at my outfit, wondering what exactly was wrong with it.

"In all black," Dash questioned. "Are you trying to kill yourself faster?"

"Black is slimming," I argued.

"It also attracts heat. You'll roast in that. And why are you wearing long sleeves?"

"The man at the store said to wear long sleeves in the heat to keep me cooler."

New Guy snorted and sauntered over to my bed where my suitcase was sprawled out. "You want loose clothing. That shirt will make you sweat even more, which will make you need to drink more water faster. And there aren't exactly a lot of places to stop for a refill."

"Oh, I have that covered. I packed extra water bottles."

Dash rubbed a hand over his face, then motioned for me to hand over my pack. I slid my thumb under the strap and struggled to get it off, but it was too heavy. "Um...I might need some help."

"You're not carrying this thing," he said as he slipped it off my shoulders. "If you trip, you're going down hard."

"But I don't have another pack."

"Then we'll get you another backpack in town. I'm sure they have them for unsuspecting tourists."

I bristled at the description, but couldn't deny it was true. "What's wrong with it?"

"First, this thing is made for a hike on Mt. Everest."

That was the same thing Thumper said the other day, but I wouldn't ever tell him someone else agreed with him. Dash opened the main compartment and started pulling stuff out.

57

"Second, how many water bottles are you carrying with you?"

"The guy said I would need to be prepared. He said I could get stranded out there and die without enough water."

"Have you actually studied Arches at all?"

"Well…I looked at a map?"

"You drive through it," he continued. "Keep extra water in the back of your vehicle. You only need one water bottle in your pack, and you should really have a stainless steel water bottle to keep it cold. These plastic bottles won't help when you're hot."

"Oh, I have one of those," I grinned, happy I got something right. I pulled out the bottle and showed it to him.

"Here," New Guy said, shoving clothes into my hands. "Change into this. It'll be cooler than what you're wearing."

After changing and grabbing my water bottle, the guys headed out with me to the parking lot. Apparently, I didn't need my pack since today we were just exploring off the main road. They didn't say it, but I had the feeling they didn't dare go off trail with me, which was fine.

"Hop in," Dash said as we approached a truck.

"Um…that's a truck."

New Guy sighed heavily. "I suppose it would be bad to drive in a truck?"

"Well, my car is a convertible. We can drive with the top down."

"Trust me, it's going to be hot enough. You're going to want the break from the sun."

Disappointment hit harder than expected. I shouldn't be so upset over not getting to ride in my convertible, but it was so cute and pretty compared to this monstrosity. People would mistake me for someone that liked hiking. But, they were being nice enough to be my guide, so I'd go with them.

After driving past the Balanced Rock, we stopped at The Windows. It didn't look too far from where we parked on the side of the road.

"You ready?" Dash grinned. "This is amazing."

I disagreed, but didn't want to ruin this for him. "Sure."

"Don't sound so enthusiastic. This is nature at its finest!"

"It's hot and dirty."

"Wow, you really aren't an outdoors girl, are you?" New Guy huffed. "Let's go."

They took off ahead of me, walking way too fast for my little legs to keep up. I wasn't small, but compared to these guys, I might as well be a midget. Their long strides ate up the path in much less time than mine. I struggled for breath as I rushed behind them, having to stop several times to press a hand to the stitch in my side. Holy crap, this wasn't for the faint of heart.

"Hey!" Dash shouted. "You okay?"

I waved at him, unable to speak at the moment. He walked back to me and bent over, staring at me funny.

"What's wrong?"

"Just...out of breath."

"But it's pretty much flat."

"So?"

"So, how are you out of breath?"

"Because I'm not used to this," I snapped.

His eyebrows shot up in surprise. "Walking? Do people normally carry you around?"

"I walk on concrete. I walk in heels. I don't walk on dirt in tennis shoes."

"Yeah, you should really have on hiking shoes."

"Is that really helpful to point out right now?"

"And this technically isn't dirt. It's sandstone."

"Thank you very much for the history lesson."

"It's not history. It's geography."

"Are you going to correct everything I say?" I asked, glaring at him.

"That depends. Are you going to keep saying the wrong thing?"

"Can we just move this along so I can get my pictures?"

Staring at me for a moment, he turned and crouched down. "Come on, I'll give you a lift."

"What?"

"Just get on. I'll get you to the main attraction."

"I will not be carried like some toddler that can't walk on her own."

"Well, you kind of can't," he grinned.

With all the determination I could muster, I pushed myself into an upright position and soldiered on. I might not be athletic at all, but I could do this, even if it killed me. Well, I still had to work, so I might need to be carried back. But I would make it at least as far as The Windows.

By the time we got there, I was sweating hard and panting like I'd just run a marathon. It was pathetic, but after drinking all my water, I felt slightly better.

"Okay, let's do this," I sighed, pulling out my compact. I checked my makeup in the mirror, grimacing when I saw it was all gone from having sweat so much. I wiped my face and took out my hair to brush it through.

"What are you doing?"

I looked up into the shocked faces of Dash and New Guy. "What do you mean?"

"You're...brushing your hair. Why?"

"When I take selfies of this, I want to look flawless, like this was a breeze for me."

"But...you're brushing your hair."

"Right."

"But your hair was fine."

"Maybe to you, but my coworkers have never seen me look anything but professional. I will not allow them to have something to laugh at."

"They'll be laughing at you when they see you looking like a doll while you're hiking," New Guy muttered.

"Thank you very much for your commentary, but it's not needed." I snapped my compact shut and continued brushing my hair. After another ten minutes, I was perfectly styled...or as perfectly styled as I was going to be in the heat in the middle of the desert.

"Alright, let's get some pictures and call it a day."

"What?" New Guy snorted a laugh. "That's it? We came all the way out here to snap a few pictures and leave?"

"What did you think we were going to do?"

"Um..." He looked to Dash for help. "I assumed we were going to hike. Isn't that what you bought all that gear for?"

"Look, I understand that you enjoy this sort of thing, but clearly,

I'm not cut out for sweating, hiking, or any kind of outdoor activity. I just need some proof that I was here."

"But you're going to show them you stopped in one spot. That's not really going to convince anyone that you spent any quality time here."

"Look, just smile for the camera and pretend you're having a good time. That's all I ask of you."

Dash rolled his eyes and walked over to me, draping his arm around my shoulder as I preened for the camera.

"Everyone say *Arches!*"

They didn't say it, but I got my photo. We moved around a few more times to get different views, but after ten minutes, I was ready to get home.

"And that's a wrap. We can get back to that tent thing we'll pretend is a hotel. I'll take a nap in the heat and pretend there's air conditioning, and then tomorrow we'll do this all over again."

I turned just in time to see New Guy grimace. "I can hardly wait."

7

THUMPER

IF I HAD BEEN SMART, I would have left while they were gone. I could have done my own hiking and avoided seeing them this afternoon. I knew she wouldn't last long. She might have grit in the financial world, but out here in the desert, she was a wilting flower.

The rumbling of Dash's truck had me rolling over and groaning. They were going to come here and try to share my yurt. Well, there was no fucking room. I wasn't sharing with them. I pressed the pillow over my head and pretended to be asleep.

"What a fucking waste of a day," I heard Dash mutter.

I chuckled to myself, but kept playing opossum. Through the pillow, I could hear Dash and New Guy trying to get inside my yurt. Still, I snored on.

"It's got to be his birth year."

"What's his birth year?" New Guy asked.

"Like I know that?"

"You snoop on everyone. Don't tell me you haven't looked in his file."

Dash finally conceded. "Alright, I have, but it's not like I memorized his birthday. What would I possibly need that for?"

"For breaking into his yurt!" New Guy shouted.

"Well, I didn't exactly think about that two years ago when I was reading his file!"

"We'll just have to wake him up," New Guy sighed.

"He's not sleeping. He's ignoring us."

"How can you tell?"

"Because when Thumper snores, it's a long, loud snore. This is too melodic."

"His snore is melodic?" New Guy asked, not believing him.

I extended my snore, adding in a slight snort in the middle for effect.

"See? He's trying to snore. Anyone can hear that."

There was silence for a moment as I continued with my charade.

"I don't hear a fucking thing. Since when are you the snoring whisperer?"

"That's not a thing," Dash countered.

"Okay, the snoring master."

"That would imply that I snore and I'm the best at it. I don't snore."

"Then what would you call it?"

"Why do I have to be called anything?" Dash argued. "Do you realize we're standing outside a yurt, arguing about what to call my snoring knowledge while he's in there pretending to be asleep, snoring on purpose all so he doesn't have to let us inside?"

"He would never do that to us," New Guy snapped.

"You bet your ass he would. He's fucking laughing at us under that pillow."

"Hey, what are you guys arguing about?"

I groaned when I heard Bree's voice. This was never going to end. All I wanted was some fucking solitude, and the peanut gallery was making that damn impossible.

"Nothing."

"It's not nothing," Dash argued. "Thumper locked us out."

"Why would he do that?" Bree asked.

"Yeah," New Guy added. "Explain why he would do that? We're lovable. We're his teammates."

"And he came out here to be alone. And it's Thumper!"

"Thumper's a great guy," FNG snapped. "He would do anything for anyone."

"Christ, you don't have to put on a show. He's awake and he knows you're faking it. Don't make this worse," Dash said.

"Wait, so he's really awake in there?"

I snored louder just so Bree might believe me and walk away.

"Do you hear that melodic snoring?"

"Yes."

"She does not," FNG snapped. "There is no difference between his regular snoring and what he's doing now."

"No, I definitely hear it," Bree said. "It's got a sort of...melody to it."

"Thank you!" Dash shouted.

They continued to bicker, and I really thought I could hold out, but it was getting to me, and no amount of smothering myself with a pillow would make this situation better. I tossed it off my head and stomped toward the opening.

"Enough!" I shouted. "Fucking arguing about the melody of my snoring? Are you fucking kidding me? Take a hint. I don't want you here. If I did, I would have invited you along, or not ditched you last night. At the very least, I wouldn't have put myself through the last ten minutes of listening to you argue about the sound of my snoring! Now do me a favor and piss off!"

I turned and stomped away, heading to the bathroom to take a shit. I would sit there all fucking night if it meant ignoring those fuckers. I walked into the bathroom area and tried to slam the door, but there was no goddamn door. Where the fuck was a door when you needed it?

I sat down on the toilet fully clothed and dropped my head in my hands. This was the worst vacation ever. I should have pulled a Fox and left without telling anyone where I was going. Not that it would matter. The tracker in my arm would tell anyone where I was. Only Fox was crazy enough to rip it out of his skin no matter how many times Cash made him get another.

"What are we supposed to do? We can't just sit out here all night," FNG snapped.

"You're damn right I will. He's being a pain in the ass, and I'm not leaving until he lets us in. I didn't haul my ass all the way out here to lay out in the fucking desert all night and get eaten by wolves or bison!"

"Alright, alright! Fuck, can we at least get some food before I park my ass out here for the foreseeable future?" FNG asked.

"Fine, but no onion rings."

"What? You can't tell me what to get."

"Hey, I get enough onion smells when I'm around Fox. I don't need it with you too."

"Fuck you very much. I'll have you know I never smell like onions."

The bickering died down the further they got from the tent. Assuming I was finally home free, I walked back out into the main area of the yurt and parked my ass in a chair, wishing I had a beer. Or a bottle of vodka. Hell, I'd take a White Claw if it meant I could get the tiniest buzz in the world. But sadly, I had no liquor, no food, and no peace.

I was in my chair, snoring and minding my own business when I was woken up by a screeching sound so loud that I jumped out of my chair, ripped the tent open, and rushed out into the night. It was like I was back in Afghanistan, wide awake and searching for the threat so I wasn't immediately killed. Except, we were in Utah, and that screaming sound was coming from the yurt beside me.

I pulled my gun from my waistband and ran toward Bree's yurt. Her squeals were frantic, making me rethink leaving her alone out here. I knew better than to rush in, guns blazing, but if her hysterical cries for help were any indication of how bad things were, she might be dead before I got to her. No one should have to be so terrified that they screamed like that.

"Bree!" I shouted, pushing the canvas aside as I rushed into the small space.

I expected to see a lone gunman or maybe a snake again. But what I didn't expect to see was Bree standing on her bed, jumping on her tiptoes as she tried to outrun a fucking bunny.

"Oh God! Get it Thumper! Get it!"

Staring at the cute thing nosing around her bed, I sighed and holstered my weapon. I scrubbed my hand up and down my face, hoping I was really seeing things that weren't there. This was fucking ridiculous.

"Thumper!" She stopped jumping just long enough to shoot daggers at me. "Why are you just standing there? Get it!"

"It's a rabbit."

"And your name's Thumper," she pointed out.

"Right, but it has nothing to do with rabbits. At least...I don't think it does," I said after I thought about it a moment. "Then again, it kind of makes sense."

"This is not the time for you to have an existential crisis!"

"Who, me?" I pointed at myself, then tossed my head back and started laughing. "Lady, if anyone's having an existential crisis, it's you."

"Mock me all you want," she snapped, heaving angrily as she pushed her hair out of her face and tried to balance on the bed. I watched as her eyes kept flicking to the poor thing on the floor, just sitting there watching her with fascination. I was surprised it hadn't run away with all her screaming, but apparently, it knew it was more deadly than her. "Just get that rodent out of here!"

"That's not a rodent. If you want, I can go outside and bring you a rodent."

She screeched angrily as her long brown hair flopped around her. It had a slight wave to it, probably from the heat, and no matter how many times she pushed it out of her face, it wouldn't stay back. I shook my head, refusing to notice these little things about her that didn't matter.

The fact was, if I wanted to get out of this woman's presence, I was going to have to remove the bunny from her yurt. Then I could go back to my peace and quiet, and pretend she wasn't next to me at all.

"Alright, alright!" I shouted. "Stop yelling. I'll get the damn bunny out of here."

"Thank you!" She reached behind her, snatching the pillow off the bed and shielding herself as if the bunny would attack at any moment.

I slowly approached the animal. All I had to do was grab it and throw it outside. But as I approached, the rabbit suddenly went rigid, his ears standing straight up as he watched me out of the corner of his eye.

"It's okay, little bunny. I know the mean old lady looks crazy, but I promise she won't cut you up for dinner."

"Old?" Bree said, offended by my comment. "Who are you calling old?"

"If the shoe fits," I muttered.

"I'll have you know that I wear very stylish shoes. Shoes that young people wear. Shoes that even hookers want!"

I slowly looked up at her still perched on the bed. "Lady, I don't give a fuck about your shoes. I'm having a conversation with a rabbit. Do you really think it matters if I tell him you're old or young, or what the fuck kind of shoes you wear?"

She shrugged slightly as she thought about it. "Maybe not to you, but I think he should know I have nice shoes. I wouldn't want his bunny friends to think this isn't a cool place to hang out."

"Right, because you want more bunnies lingering around."

"Okay, you're right about the additional bunnies, but you still don't have to call me old. Would you just get him out of here?"

I shook my head as I got down on my knees. "A minute ago you were worried the bunny wouldn't like your shoes. Now you want him out of here." I scooted a little closer, holding out my hand to the bunny. "Come on, buddy. I'm not going to hurt you."

I crept slowly toward the beast, but when I was just inches away from grabbing it, the damn thing sprung at me like a leopard, scaring the crap out of me.

"Oh my God!" Bree screamed. "It's like those killer rabbits from the *Monty Python* movies!"

"It's possessed!" I yelled, scrambling backward and falling on my ass as the damn thing jumped over me and started running around the room.

"Don't just lay there! Get him!" Bree yelled at me.

Glaring at her, I got up and started chasing the damn thing around the room. I lost sight of it when it ducked under the couch and didn't come back out. Drawing my gun, I laid flat and began to belly crawl across the wooden floor.

"Don't shoot it!" she shrieked when she saw my gun.

"Shut up," I gritted out, keeping my eyes on the target. "I'm just going to scare it."

Nope, I was shooting this fucker after all the trouble he put me through. I'd be eating rabbit stew while she cried over how much the damn rabbit would have loved her shoes if only she'd had a chance to talk to him. Maybe all his bunny friends would come to his funeral and I'd make a surprise attack. We'd have rabbit stew for the rest of the trip.

As I got closer, the bunny's white cottontail came into view. "Gotcha," I muttered, waiting for it to come just a little closer. With my finger on the trigger, I started to apply pressure.

"No!" Bree jumped off the bed, scaring the rabbit away from me and out the front of the tent. "Run, bunny! Run!" she shouted, holding the sides of her pants as she screamed at him.

I slammed my fist down on the ground and got to my feet, stomping over to her. "What the fuck did you do that for? That was my dinner!"

She spun around and shoved her finger in my face. "You said you weren't going to kill it, but I knew you were lying!"

"Then why the hell did you call me over here? If you wanted to make friends and gossip about shoes, you shouldn't have called me!"

I bent over and rested my hands on my knees as sweat dripped from my head. That was way too much fucking work for vacation. Finally, I stood up and speared Bree with my most deadly look. "Well, I hope you're happy now. I have no dinner now."

"Happy?" she sneered. "Don't say it to me like that. Why would I be happy that you had to tear my yurt apart because you wanted to eat a rabbit for dinner?"

"I didn't have to do anything," I snapped. "If you hadn't left the canvas open, you wouldn't have animals in your tent!"

She opened her mouth to argue, but then snapped it shut. Satisfied that she wasn't going to say anything further, I turned and stormed out of the yurt and headed back to my own.

"Damn woman," I muttered. "I came out here for a vacation and got stuck next to a woman who doesn't know how to use a zipper."

I started slamming things around the room, pissed off that my trip was going so badly. I walked back to the bathroom and unzipped, sitting down on the toilet. It was the only place to get some peace and quiet. Minutes passed where I breathed in and out, calming myself down. I was finally breathing normally again when another scream ripped through the night.

I clenched my teeth and refused to move. "She's fine. It's just another fucking rabbit."

"Thumper!" she screamed, her shrill voice wracking my nerves.

"I'm on the shitter!" I called back, refusing to be snowed again.

"Help! Oh my God!"

"Just talk about your damn shoes. The poor rabbit will be so bored, he'll kill himself in five seconds!" I shouted.

The sound of her screaming and running around the yurt made me wince at how much destruction she was causing. I could picture her tearing the fucking place apart as she tried to escape the furry bunny. Chuckling to myself, I shook my head and finally found the humor in this whole fucking trip.

"Thumper, I really need some help!"

"I'm not falling for that again!" I began to whistle a cheery tune to drown out the sounds of her crying wolf yet again. I shouldn't have fallen for it the first time, and I definitely wasn't this time.

"Holy shit!" Dash shouted. "What the fuck is that?"

There was some kind of bleating sound that had me momentarily wondering if there was actually a problem, but then I laughed and reminded myself this was Bree.

"Oh shit. Oh shit! Thumper, get your ass out here!" FNG shouted. "Get me out of here!"

"It's stuck in the yurt! Holy do we get it out?"

That had me standing up quickly and pulling my pants up as I ran out of my yurt, still zipping up as I came to a sudden halt at the sight before me. "Holy fuck!"

"Get it out of here!" Bree shouted from inside.

The problem was, whatever the hell this animal was, its horns were stuck in the canvas, and the more it wiggled, the more riled up the animal got.

"Where's FNG?" I asked, trying to figure out how to get inside.

"He's in the tent with Bree."

That gave me pause. I turned and grabbed him by the collar. "Why the fuck is he in the tent with Bree?"

"Because she screamed and the stupid fucker ran in there!"

"So he wasn't in there before?"

"What the fuck are you talking about?"

"Was he in there with her before this asshole stuck his horns through the canvas?" I shouted.

"No!" He ripped my hands from his shirt and pointed at the tent. "We have bigger issues than whether or not FNG was trying to *FNG* your girl. Get it?" he grinned.

"She's not my girl. She's *a* girl. A girl that likes bunnies and prevented me from eating rabbit stew!"

"Guys?" FNG called out. "Not to put any pressure on you, but this big ass thing is still trying to eat us. And now he's trying on Bree's underwear!"

"Like, actually trying it on?" Dash asked.

"He's got it on his head. I don't think he understands where it's supposed to go. And purple really isn't his color."

"Wait, she wears purple panties?" Dash asked. "Are they lacy?"

"Yes, and silky too."

"That's really not good underwear for the desert."

"Not very moisture-wicking," I added.

"That's why I go commando," Dash nodded.

"Don't your balls stick to your leg?"

"Hey!" Bree shouted. "Yes, they are silky. Yes, they are purple. Would you like me to get him a color more suited to his skin tone, or would you like to help me get out of this fucking tent?"

"No, leave the purple on. That way we can identify him as the perpetrator!" Dash shouted.

"Are you planning on having the police do a lineup?" FNG asked.

All this talk of her purple panties was making it rather uncomfortable down south. Not that I cared what color her panties were or if they were silky. Although, I did like to run my hands across the smooth silk on a woman's buttocks.

I shifted uncomfortably, adjusting myself in my pants just as Dash looked over and down at the placement of my hand.

"Are you thinking what I'm thinking?" he asked.

"Are you thinking about fucking a sheep or the color of her panties?"

He stared at me incredulously. "Her panties. Who the fuck would get a hard on thinking about sheep?"

"You know, you hesitated. It makes me think you actually were thinking about the sheep."

"That's something you would only think about in a romance novel."

"What kind of fucked up romance novels do you read? And what kind of author would think it's funny to talk about fucking sheep?" I asked.

"Guys? Are you still there?" FNG called out. "Any time you want to help us out, we're willing to run out of here and get to safety."

"Okay, okay!" I shouted, holding up my hands as I stared at the ass end of the beast. "Um…Bree, I'm going to come around back and get you out."

"Hey, don't forget about me!" FNG shouted.

I took off as Dash shouted, "But what am I supposed to do when it gets out of there?"

I didn't bother answering as I rounded the yurt and pulled out my pocket knife. Tearing into the canvas, I slid the knife down until it was long enough for Bree to get out. Before I could even finish, she started tearing it horizontally, then jumped into my arms, nearly impaling herself on the knife as she clung to me in desperation.

"Go! Go! Go!" she shouted in my ear, clinging to me like a spider monkey.

"I'm going. Stop yelling in my ear!"

I heard FNG running behind me after climbing through the canvas after Bree.

I rushed around the tent with her crawling up my front, making it nearly impossible to get anywhere quickly. Just seconds later, the entire yurt collapsed in a pile of canvas.

"It's a fucking Bighorn Sheep!" Dash shouted, his eyes wide.

"Is that supposed to mean something?" I asked, trying to set Bree down. She wrapped her arms around my neck even tighter and refused to let go.

"It's a ram!" Dash continued to freak out. "A fucking ram!"

The tent shifted and the beast appeared, looking deadlier than any animal I'd ever seen before. It took a step forward, effectively cutting me off from Dash.

"It's gonna kill us!" Bree screamed in my ear, swinging herself around to my back and choking the hell out of me.

"Uh...okay, don't panic," Dash said as he scrolled through his phone. "It says...do not make eye contact."

"It's staring right the fuck at me!" I shouted.

"Calm down! Turn sideways and walk slowly down the slope."

"There's no fucking slope, Dash. I'm on flat ground," I reminded him.

"Right, uh...if you are on higher ground or if you face the ram, it may see this as a challenge. Holy shit, don't look at him and get to lower ground!"

"There is no lower ground," I yelled back. "Give me something useful!" I shouted as the ram slowly faced me.

"Oh...Oh!" Dash continued. "It says they're herbivores, so he won't eat you!"

"That won't matter if he charges me!"

I turned, ready to run for my life when another man approached, standing tall with his arms in the air. "Hold on there. Just do as I say and everything will be fine."

"Okay," I nodded, my heart pounding out of control as the sheep now turned to face the new threat. It pawed at the ground and lowered its head, reminding me of a bull about to charge the matador.

"Don't worry. Just follow my instructions. Stand tall."

"I am standing tall!"

"Now, yell *mint sauce*."

"Don't you mean mint jelly?" FNG asked.

"Yeah, my mom always served mint jelly with lamb," I agreed.

"This isn't a fucking lamb, and he's not the one about to be eaten," the man yelled.

"You know, he's right," FNG looked at me. "That ram is probably thinking we'd taste better with mint sauce, which begs the question of why we'd yell it."

"Would you just fucking yell it?" the man snapped.

I rolled my eyes and yelled at the sheep, "Mint sauce!"

"Louder! You need to scare him!"

"Mint Sauce!" I yelled at the top of my lungs.

"All four of you!"

"Mint Sauce!" echoed around the desert as we all yelled at the sheep.

He turned and galloped off into the night. Sagging in relief, I dropped my arms from under Bree's legs and let her drop to the ground.

"Thank you so much," I said to the man. "How did you know what to do?"

"I come out here all the time. It's good to know what to do when approached by a wild animal."

I nodded, thankful I hadn't pissed myself. "So, why did it work to yell mint sauce?"

The man threw his head back and laughed. "It didn't. I just wanted to see how many times I could get you to do it."

He turned and walked away, still laughing at us. I fell to my knees, still breathing hard from the sheer terror of almost being mauled by a sheep. I'd come across a lot of scary shit during the war, but never something as unknown as a gigantic sheep ready to kill you.

"That was a close one," Dash laughed. "Had my heart thumping for a minute."

"Me too," FNG said, coming out from where he was hiding.

"You pussy. You hid behind me the whole time," I snapped.

"I wasn't hiding. If you got killed, someone had to be next in line to protect Bree."

"Yeah? If the sheep had already charged, how would you protect Bree?"

He looked stumped for a moment, then he stuttered… "Well, I would have stood in front of her, giving her a chance to get away."

"You're the one always saying you can't die, but you hid from a sheep."

"Hey, I might not be able to die, but that doesn't mean I want those horns piercing my skin. There are worse things than death."

I glanced behind me at Bree sprawled out on the ground. Her arms were spread wide as she stared up at the sky.

"Hey, you okay?"

"I want to go home. I'm not cut out for the desert. I hate sand. I hate sweating. I hate rams. I hate not having my own shower. I hate—"

"Yeah, we get it," I interrupted. "You hate a lot of shit."

8

BREE

"WHAT THE HELL did you do to my yurt?" an older man came running over yelling. He stared at the collapsed yurt that was torn to shreds, then swung his gaze over to me still lying on the ground.

"You!" he stabbed a finger in my direction. "I knew you'd be trouble the moment you called for the reservation."

"Me? How did you know simply by talking to me?"

"Because you didn't know what you were talking about. It's always you city slickers that cause trouble. Now I have no yurt for the next booking!" Then he turned to Thumper. "And you!"

"Hey, I had nothing to do with this."

"You're standing right next to the yurt," the man snapped.

"Right, but I..." Thumper winced as he looked at the yurt. "I was only trying to help. See, there was this Bighorn Sheep, and its horns were stuck in the canvas—"

"Whoa, there was a sheep stuck in the canvas?" His gaze swung back to mine. He stormed over to me just as I started crawling backward. Thankfully, Thumper stood in front of me, but that didn't stop the man from shouting around him. "Did you bring food to your yurt?"

"I…" My eyes swung to Thumper and then back to the man. "I was hungry!"

"There are strict rules about eating in the yurts, and now you know why!"

"I do?" I asked, getting to my feet.

"You aren't supposed to bring food to your yurt because it attracts wildlife! This is on you! You're cleaning up this mess…all of you!" he shouted.

"Hold on a minute," Thumper cut in, much to my relief. "She's the one that rented the tent. This is on her."

He stepped aside as he jerked his thumb in my direction. I narrowed my eyes at him for turning on me.

"You jerk!"

"Hey, you had the bunny and now the sheep. This is on you, lady."

My mouth gaped as I stared at him incredulously. I'd known some real assholes in my time, but the way he turned on me was downright ruthless.

"I don't care who is responsible. You're all at the scene of the crime, and none of you are leaving until you've cleaned up this mess!"

"Technically, it's just them," Dash cut in. "We're not even guests here."

"Yeah," New Guy strolled over to him. "We just stopped by. This is on them."

"I want this cleaned up by morning or I'll call the police," the man yelled, then turned and stomped away.

I spun around and faced Thumper head on. "This is all your fault!"

"My fault," he barked out a laugh. "You heard what the man said. You weren't supposed to bring food in your yurt. This is on your head."

"If you had come when I yelled for help, none of this would have happened!"

"You cried wolf with that damn bunny," he argued. "A fucking bunny! And you left your tent open. What the fuck are you even doing out here?"

"I told you—"

"Yeah, yeah. Trying to prove some point to a bunch of coworkers so they don't think you can't hack it. Well, guess what? You can't, and now the rest of us have to pay for it."

"Uh, not me," Dash cut in. "As I told that guy, I don't even have a yurt. Naturally, I would be happy to help out, but *someone* didn't have room at the inn for two friends who were just trying to do their jobs. So…yeah. This is all on you."

Thumper stormed over to him and grabbed Dash by the shirt. "You will stay and fucking help or I'll make sure Cash knows about Jamaica."

His face paled slightly. "You…you don't know anything."

"I know about the job you supposedly took. Do you think he would like to know about the woman you met?"

He swallowed hard, his eyes flicking to New Guy. "Fine. I'm in."

"What was the job?" I asked curiously. "And who was the woman?"

"Yeah, who was the woman?" New Guy asked.

"Where do we start?" Dash asked, walking away from us.

"What was the job?" I asked again. Why wouldn't he just answer the question?

"It doesn't matter," Dash muttered.

"It clearly does if you're letting Thumper blackmail you with it," New Guy cut in. "And this woman…would I like her?"

"Would you think about something other than your dick?" Dash snapped.

"Yeah, like what was this mystery job," I reiterated.

Thumper clapped his hands together, cutting off the line of questioning. "Alright, now that we're all on board, let's get to work and get this shit done." They all turned and started walking away as if that was the end of it all.

"I demand to know what this job was!" I stomped my foot. "I'm not lifting a finger to help until I get some answers!"

They all stopped and turned to face me. "Let's get one thing straight," Thumper finally said. "You aren't part of our work. We don't know you, we don't share secrets, and after this is all cleaned up, we'll go our separate ways and never speak again. Are we clear?"

I really hated the man. I mean, yeah, he was sexy and growly…all of which shouldn't affect me in any way, yet somehow did. I hated men like him, ones that thought because they had a dick, they could throw their weight around. But he carried it off perfectly, probably because he looked like he wasn't just talking out of his ass.

Still, the man clearly didn't like me, and there was no love lost on my end either. "Crystal," I said, standing in challenge against him. He could talk down to me all he wanted. That didn't mean he won, just that I wasn't going to play his game.

"Then let's get to work."

I was filthy, exhausted, and worst of all, my things were ripped to shreds in that yurt. Everything I owned in this godforsaken desert was on me. My legs gave out as I walked into Thumper's yurt and sank into a chair. By the grace of God, he offered to let me stay the night. I pretended not to be completely shocked by the offer.

"I'm taking a shower," Thumper grumbled as he walked past me.

"Me too," Dash said, following him.

Thumper spun around and held his hand up, stopping Dash. "It's a single shower. You can wait your turn."

FNG slumped down on the couch, sighing heavily as he closed his eyes. "I need some food. I'm fucking hungry."

"So go get some."

"You're not staying here!" Thumper shouted as he tossed his clothes over the shower wall.

"Sure, you tell us to stay to help clean up, but then we're not allowed to get some shuteye," Dash snorted. "That sounds very reasonable."

"My bones hurt," I complained. "How is that possible?"

"You just need to spread out and relax," Dash said, coming up behind me and rubbing my shoulders. I moaned as he dug into my muscles and relieved the pain from carrying all that shit around. "Do you really wear purple panties?"

"Gross," I said, smacking his hand away.

"What? It's a serious question."

"You're a pervert."

He took a seat beside FNG, who was now sitting at full attention. "I'm just curious why you went with purple. Most women go for seductive colors like black."

"I happen to like purple."

"Because you're no fun in the sack?" he asked.

"Excuse me, but what would you know about what I like in bed?"

"Oh, hey," he said, holding up his hands. "I didn't mean to sound offensive. It's just, women that wear purple in bed tend not to be... exciting in the bedroom. It's a study," he pointed out, as if that made a difference.

"Really? So, you ran this study?"

He snorted, "Man would I love to run a study like that." When I didn't return his smile, he cleared his throat and continued. "No, it was in a magazine. It was all about the colors you wear in bed and what that means."

"And what colors do you wear in bed?" I asked curiously.

His sly grin said all I needed to know about him. "Much like I am right now, I wear nothing."

My nose wrinkled at that, but my eyes had a mind of their own and drifted to his crotch. "So...right now..."

"Free as a bird," he clucked. "It's the only way to go."

"The only way to ensure you can get in and out as quickly as possible," New Guy pointed out. "What color are you wearing right now?" he asked me.

"That's none of your business!"

What was with these guys? Didn't they have anything better to talk about than sex? And why did they feel it was okay to ask me about my sex life? I was a complete stranger!

"I just figured that we've been through a lot together..." New Guy started.

"And that gives you the right to know intimate details about my life?"

He shrugged, leaning back in his seat just as Thumper came out of the shower with only a towel wrapped around him. I got up and immediately stormed past him to take my own shower. I would do practically anything to escape these perverts.

I quickly undressed, tossing my clothes over the top of the wall just as Thumper had. But when I tried to turn on the shower, I couldn't figure out how to do it. The shower head hung from the ceiling, but there were no knobs on the wall. A small chain dangled above me, and I reached up to pull it.

Cold water washed over my body making me squeal and jump out of the way. "Oh, God! That's cold!"

I heard them laughing at me in the other room, obviously in on the joke that I wasn't aware of. The water died off a minute later, leaving me even colder than when I first stepped in, which was hilarious since it was so hot outside. Grabbing the bar of soap, I quickly ran it over my body and sudsed up my hands. Looking up tentatively at the chain again, I pulled it and stuck my head under, scrubbing my soaping fingers into my scalp.

I danced from toe to toe as I washed under the cold water. Every minute or so, I had to pull the chain again. I would cut off my own hair right now if it meant it didn't take so damn long in the shower. My nipples were so hard they could cut glass, and while I wouldn't normally care right now, there were perverts sitting out there that wouldn't hesitate to point it out.

The water shut off and I wrung my hair out, then reached for the towel. Except, it wasn't there, because I forgot to bring one. "Shit," I muttered, sticking my head around the wall. "Um…I need a towel."

"Don't have one," Thumper said, still sitting in his.

Pursing my lips, I let out a huff of annoyance. "You have one on you right now."

He glanced down, then up at me. "So, I do. Would you like it?"

"If you would be so kind," I said with all the politeness I could muster.

He stood and slowly walked over to me, then his fingers slipped around the knot and pulled it loose. I swallowed hard as the towel slid from around his waist. My eyes grew wide as he caught it in front of him and held it there, just barely hiding what was behind it. Then he tossed the towel right at my head. I jerked it away to get a peek at his package, but he was already turned around.

I heard Dash's chuckle as he shook his head. "I told you, purple underwear."

Embarrassed, I ducked behind the wall and quickly wrapped the towel around my body. I leaned back and closed my eyes. I couldn't go out there until I was firmly in control of my mortification.

"What's that about purple underwear?"

"She's a prude. Didn't you see the way she was looking at you? It was like she'd never seen a dick before."

I scowled, wanting to go out there and tell him just how many dicks I'd seen, but that would probably only egg him on.

"And purple underwear means what exactly?" Thumper asked.

"Purple means she's a prude. Don't get into bed with her. You won't be satisfied."

My jaw dropped at his insinuation. Not that I would ever get into bed with any of them, but I didn't like to be classified or shoved in a box without first being able to demonstrate a thing or two.

"And what color exactly would mean she's a great lover?"

"Well, obviously red means she's a tiger in bed. Pink is immature. Yellow, she'll submit to you."

"What about black?" New Guy asked. "Black has to be racy as hell."

"Perverted."

I didn't need to see the look on Dash's face to know he was grinning.

"But the color you really want is orange."

"Orange?" Thumper asked. "Why?"

"Orange means you're passionate, playful, even violent in bed. Just imagine she's a sex kitten."

I'd heard enough of them talking about me like I wasn't just behind a wall. I stormed out, hands at my hips as they all turned to face me. "I'll have you know that I wear every color of lingerie."

Dash pointed at my underwear laying on the ground. "White. Means you're puritanical. Not great for bed." He slapped his thighs and stood. "Anyway, I'm off to take my shower."

He strolled past me, but at the last second snatched the towel from around my chest, leaving me stark naked in front of New Guy and Thumper. I screeched as I turned, covering myself.

"Need the towel," he grinned, then strolled away.

"Holy shit," New Guy muttered.

Thumper quickly stormed over with his shirt, shoving it over my head and yanking it down my body. Then he maneuvered my arms until they were through the arm holes as they should be. His eyes lingered on my hard nipples for just a moment too long. Then he stomped over to his bag and pulled out a pair of boxers, tossing them at me.

"Here, unless you want to bare down there all night with these guys."

I did not want that, so I pulled them on with as much grace as I could muster while trying to keep myself concealed. I stabbed my finger at New Guy as he continued to stare at me.

"Get it out of your head."

"What?" he asked, still staring at my chest.

"There will be no threesomes or…other dirty things happening."

"Orgies?" he asked, his face quirking up.

I narrowed my eyes at his playful tone. "Don't get any ideas."

I turned for the bed, but Thumper shook his head. "Don't even think about it. This is still my yurt and my bed."

"But…it's a king-size bed. There's plenty of room for me."

"And me," New Guy stood up.

"Shut up!" we both shouted.

"You've ruined everything about my vacation so far," he said, stalking toward me. "There's no fucking way you're ruining my night."

"I'll stay on my side!"

"You'll stay in that chair," he pointed to the one I'd been sitting in before.

"But—"

"Of course, you could always spend the night outside with the Bighorn Sheep."

I wanted to yell and rail at him, but I knew he'd make good on his word and kick me out. Even sleeping in a chair was better than being outside.

"Fine." I turned and stomped over to my chair, slumping down in it. It was one of those deep ones that were nearly impossible to get out of, and I knew I'd have a crick in my neck by the morning.

I shifted to get comfortable, and watched as he sat down on the edge of the bed and peeled the sock off his leg, taking the robotic foot with it. As much as I knew I should turn away, I was fascinated with watching him care for his leg. I knew that probably sounded ridiculous to anyone else, but this was a world I knew nothing about. A man like him, so strong and capable, showed absolutely no signs of missing a foot being a hindrance. That spoke louder than words about his character, even if I did think he was an ass.

"Your turn," Dash said to New Guy as he strutted out of the shower.

New Guy got up and caught the towel right as Dash stripped it off and tossed it at him. I closed my eyes tightly, pretending to already be asleep so they didn't know I had just seen Dash in the nude.

But I knew I was caught when I felt Dash's warm breath caress my skin. "Nude is so much better than purple."

9

THUMPER

I JOLTED myself awake with my own snoring. That meant it was pretty loud. I always woke myself up when the snoring reached higher decibels. Rolling over in bed, I sat up and stretched my arms over my head. I had to piss, but I was too lazy to put my foot on, so I got up and hopped to the bathroom.

I could do with another five hours of sleep, but I'd be lucky to get two. I finished up and started hopping back to the bed just as Bree stumbled over to the bed and plopped down on her face, spread out like an eagle. I thought about joining her and just shoving her to one side, but her body was too tempting. If only her mouth wasn't attached to the rest of her.

I started hopping to the chair, cursing myself for not putting on my foot when I had the chance. I flopped down with a sigh and leaned back to close my eyes. I heard the familiar crack just before a bullet tore through the flesh of my bicep, missing my bone by less than an inch.

"Get down!" I shouted as I rolled out of the chair. Dash was already on his feet, ducking down as he made his way to the entrance of the yurt. New Guy ran to Bree, diving over her and pulling her to the ground on the other side of the bed.

"Who the fuck is shooting at us?" New Guy shouted.

I army crawled across the floor, snatching my bionic foot from one side of the bed and making my way to the other side. "Dash! Status check!"

"What's going on?" Bree screeched, her eyes wide as she stared at me with pure terror.

I leaned against the bed and pulled on the sock, attaching my foot and locking it into place.

"I can't see a fucking thing!" Dash responded.

"FNG, go out the back and secure the perimeter."

"Do what?" Bree shouted.

"Bree, stay down until I tell you to come out."

"What's going on? Is that blood? How did that happen? Oh my God! This is not a vacation!" The panic in her voice was already pissing me off. I could tell she was going to be one of those women that asked a lot of questions instead of doing what I said.

"Listen!" I snatched her by the arms and shook her until she stopped rambling. "Just stay down until I tell you to move!"

"But you're bleeding and you only have one foot, and I was sleeping two minutes ago, and now I'm in a war zone, and—"

"Lady! Shut the fuck up!"

At my harsh tone, she snapped her lips together and stared at me like I'd slapped her. I only wish I had. At least I would get some enjoyment out of this. Certain that she would keep her mouth shut, I gave a tight node and shoved her back to the ground.

I grabbed my Sig off the table and huddled at the end of the bed before shouting to Dash. "Cover me!"

I raced across the yurt, weapon trained on the entrance as I moved into position across from Dash. I saw New Guy slip out the back just as Bree popped her head up.

"What's going on?"

"Get your head down!" I shouted. "Do you want to get it blown off?" I turned back to scan our surroundings, but it was impossible to see anything in the dark. We had a good hour to sunrise, and in that time, a lot of shit could go down. "Anything?"

"Not a fucking thing," Dash responded. "What do you want to do?"

Our options weren't great. Staying here, we were sitting ducks. But going out there in the dark, where we couldn't see, didn't know who was after us or why, and not being able to check our vehicles thoroughly…that was a shitty position to be in.

"This was supposed to be a simple fucking vacation," I muttered. "Alright, sunrise is in an hour. We stay put until then. At dawn, we haul ass and get the fuck out of here."

"What about the girl?"

What about the fucking girl? I was the one that was shot at, but she'd been with us practically from the first day. Whoever was after me had to have seen her with us. That put a target on her back. If we left her behind, she was as good as dead.

"We have to take her with us."

He snorted a laugh. "I'll let you tell her that."

"I'm going to check in with FNG. Damn, I wish we had comms."

"I have them in my truck—not that they're helpful there."

"As soon as we get to the trucks, you contact Cash and tell him what's going on."

"Do you want me to tell him you were shot?"

I glanced down at my arm, having completely forgotten about the wound. "It's superficial."

He laughed slightly at that. "Sure it is. Put some pressure on it."

I nodded and receded further into the tent to slip out the back. As I passed Bree, I held my finger to my lips, telling her to be quiet. She nodded, but I could already see the tears rolling down her cheeks. Christ, she would be hysterical when I told her she was in danger.

I slipped through the back of the tent, carefully sticking to the shadows in case there were more of them in the back. FNG was carefully positioned behind a rock, giving him just enough cover to watch from three angles. He was still vulnerable to an attack with his back to the yurt.

I slipped in beside him, kneeling as I took one side. "Anything?"

"Not a thing. Maybe it was a hunter."

"A hunter shooting at the yurts?"

"There are some stupid people out there. Remember that one politician who shot his friend while hunting? Tell me that was really an accident."

"So, your theory is a hunter is trying to get rid of a friend and shot at the yurts instead of killing his friend."

"It's a working theory."

"It's a terrible theory," I muttered. "What did you bring with you?"

"Socks, underwear, a few changes of clothes—"

"Not socks, you idiot," I snapped. "Weapons."

I heard the implied eye roll in his tone. "Two guns. Christ, you're no fun in a shoot-out."

"That's because I was the one that was shot."

"If anything, that should make you more fun."

"I'm not IRIS or Fox. Or you, for that matter."

"What we really need is a good theme song. When I was running with Cash, some good music really got things going."

I shook my head at him. He was fitting in more and more every day. "If you start eating Funyuns, you're definitely off the team."

"I already am off the team, remember? You can't trust me."

"With secrets, definitely not. Help me keep this woman alive and I'll reconsider."

"How magnanimous of you. So, what's the plan?"

"We're leaving at dawn."

"That's a terrible idea," he disagreed.

"Have any better ideas?"

"Yeah, watch my back."

He took off without another word. "I hate it when he does that."

I watched the ridgeline for any movement, but it was silent. For ten minutes, I sat there, watching for any sign that the shooter was still out there or moving closer. I didn't hear a damn thing as FNG was off doing whatever the hell he did.

Then a flame lit up the sky to the east of us. That flame quickly transformed into a raging fire. "That's the signal," I said, shoving up from my position and running to the back of the yurt. "Let's move!" I shouted as I ran through and grabbed Bree by the arm. I snatched my bag and tossed it over my shoulder as I ran for the front of the tent. Dash was already outside, clearing the area as I shoved Bree through.

"On his six!" I shouted.

"What?" She stood there with a dumbfounded look on her face. I surged forward and grabbed her hand, placing it on his back. "Grab his shirt and stay at his six."

"What the hell is his six?"

"Twelve o'clock," I motioned forward with my hand. "One o'clock, two o'clock..." I said, moving my hand clockwise. "You're at six o'clock."

"Then just say to stay behind him!"

"Stop jackin' your jaws and move!"

Dash started moving toward the truck as I turned and covered his back. Moving quickly, we made our way to the parking lot. I knew FNG was out there somewhere covering our asses, but I couldn't see anything but that fucking fire right now.

"Get in!" Dash called to Bree, hauling her into the truck by her shirt.

I hopped in the front and slammed the door, turning around to face her. "Stay down unless you want to be the bullet magnet."

"I don't know what you're saying!" she cried.

Dash jumped in the front and put the truck in reverse, spinning the tires as he got us out. "This vacation is FUBAR."

New Guy spread the back windows wide and grinned at us. "This isn't a vacation. This is a fucking party!"

"I don't want to be at this party!" Bree cried from the floorboards.

"Oh, yeah," I said, leaning over the seat to see her. "We're under attack, and you're coming with us. Welcome to the team."

"Anything?" Dash shouted as we tore out of the parking lot.

I scanned the surrounding area with my scope, but it was impossible to see anything in the early morning light. The fire was still blazing as we drove away, giving us just enough cover.

"I think we're clear—" I started to say just as bullets pinged off the side of the truck.

Dash jerked the wheel, taking us away from Moab and back toward Arches. "Fuck!"

A bullet pierced the glass, lodging in the backseat just inches above Bree's head. She was screaming like crazy as New Guy tried to console her, but nothing was working.

"Lady, you gotta stop screaming in my ear!" he shouted as she crawled into his lap and wrapped herself around him.

"We're gonna die! I'm too young to die!"

"You'd be young if you were a child. Technically, you've already lived a full life," he said, trying to soothe her. "In the Middle Ages, most people didn't live past thirty-one, so you're already over the hill!"

"That's not comforting!" she shouted.

"FNG, stop fucking around!" I shouted, just as we took on another round of bullets. "The target is too far away. We need to find cover!"

"I'll take us into the park. We can set a trap from there," Dash said, turning on the road back to the park.

From this distance, the shooter could no longer reach us, but I could see dust kicking up around him as he got in his vehicle and came after us.

"We've got ten minutes," I said, calculating his speed with our own. Once we got into the park with the winding roads, we wouldn't be able to keep up this speed for long. With nobody in the tollbooth yet, we shot past the entrance and started winding our way through the park. Thankfully, there weren't many people out here at this hour, so casualties wouldn't be an issue. At least, I hoped they wouldn't.

Bree popped up from the back seat, looking out the front window. "Why are we back in the park?" she sniffled. "I've already seen the park. I didn't like it."

"We need to lose the shooter," I said, checking my weapon and preparing for battle.

Her eyes dropped to my weapon and went wide. "It's illegal to carry a gun in a national park."

"I'm aware."

"We need to go back. You need to leave it behind!" she said urgently. "We could get a ticket, or worse…arrested! If they find you on that, my clean record is out the window!"

"If I get rid of this, your life is out the window. Make a choice," I snapped.

In her hysteria, she grabbed me by the shirt and jerked me to her. "You don't understand. I'm a law-abiding citizen. I've never gotten a speeding ticket or even a parking ticket! One day with you and I've ruined a yurt, been shot at, and now we're breaking the law!"

"Well, if you didn't like that, you're definitely not going to like this part," Dash said as he pointed to the sign that said *No Off-roading*. He looked at me, then jerked the wheel, taking us off the main road and through the desert.

"No, no, no," Bree shook her head. "I'm not here. I'm not doing this. I did not just partake in breaking the law. I'm back home in my warm bed, and this is all a bad dream about missing a deadline. You represent my bosses that are upset with me and that cliff up ahead is the deadline!"

"Lady, you need to snap out of it," I growled.

"No! I won't snap out of it. I won't pull myself together. We are breaking the law! And when the police come and drag you off to jail, I'm going to tell them that you pulled me into this! I will not get a ticket and ruin my reputation!"

I didn't even think as I slapped her across the face, stunning her into silence. Yeah, it was a little harsh, but I couldn't concentrate on my job while she was freaking out. To my satisfaction, she sat there in stunned silence, her hand on her red face with tears in her eyes. Alright, I felt slightly bad about the tears, but it was necessary to get her to shut up.

We bounced over the rough terrain, getting closer and closer to the cliff edge. We were playing a dangerous game, one we couldn't afford to lose with a civilian by our side. The fallout if she died would be enormous.

I spun around and checked our six, my eyes widening when I saw how close the shooter was. Driving off-road had slowed us substantially. "Dash, get us the fuck out of here!"

"I'm working on it," he snapped just as bullets pinged off the vehicle again. The shooter had pulled over and was using a rifle to fire upon us. There was no way we could outrun him in this position.

Glass exploded as he shot out the back window. FNG shoved Bree to the ground, protecting her with his own body. I turned and fired out the back window, trying to buy us some time, but after only a few shots, I knew it was pointless. I was wasting precious ammo that we'd need later.

I spun around in my seat and reloaded my weapon. "We need a fucking plan."

"If we can get to the top of that rock formation, we'll have the high ground," he said, pointing ahead of us.

"How the hell are we going to get her to scale that?"

"I don't know, but—fuck!" he shouted as he lost control of the vehicle. The truck spun out of control for a few seconds before coming to a halting stop. I flung my door open and got out, swearing when I saw the flat tire.

"We're not going anywhere in this truck," I shouted at Dash. "I'll lay down cover fire. You get Bree to safety."

"Are you fucking kidding?" he shouted, climbing over the seat to get out my side. "You take her. I'll lay down cover."

"Not a chance in hell," I snapped, getting in position behind the bed of the truck. I needed a rifle to take out this fucker, but that wasn't going to happen any time soon. "Just do as I say!"

"You would rather risk your life than go with her?" he questioned.

Was I really? That was a simple answer. The woman was a hysterical pain in the ass. "You're goddamn right I'd rather stay here and risk my life."

He shook his head, but grabbed the handle to the back door and pulled Bree out. FNG quickly followed, ducking down as more gunfire hit the truck.

"Go!" I shouted. "Get her out of here. I'll cover you!"

"I'll stay with you," FNG said, shoving Bree in Dash's direction.

"This is insane!" Bree yelled hysterically. "I've never been shot at in my life. This is all your fault!" she said, stabbing a finger at me. "When I get out of here, I'm suing you for…a bad experience!"

"That's not a thing."

"Then for endangering my life!" She sobbed, covering her mouth with her hand. "I hate this vacation, and I hate you!"

I gave a curt nod. "The feeling's mutual. Get her out of here."

Dash glared at me as he grabbed her arm. "Don't think this is the end of this."

As he turned and ran with Bree, I muttered, "If only it was."

FNG tossed me another magazine that I stuffed into my pocket, then ran to the front of the truck, ducking behind the hood. We had limited ammunition, and no way of drawing this guy out. I fired off several shots, giving Dash enough time to get Bree out of range from the rifle.

"We'll run out of bullets before we take this guy out!" I shouted to him.

"I have an idea, but it's fucking crazy as hell."

I rolled my eyes. When were any of his ideas not insane? "I'll take whatever you've got."

He looked behind us to where Dash was whisking Bree to safety. "I'm gonna let him shoot me!"

"You're gonna do what?" I asked incredulously.

He nodded, laughing slightly at me. "Yeah, I told you it was fucking crazy. I'm going to let him shoot me. And then I'll lay on the ground and draw him out."

"He knows I'm here!"

FNG looked at me apologetically before raising his gun and firing at me. I was so stunned that I didn't immediately react. My eyes slowly drifted down to the spot where he shot me in the thigh. "What the fuck did you shoot me for?"

"You were supposed to fall over!" he shouted.

"Well, I didn't! You didn't have to shoot me. You could have just said, *Hey, Thumper. Pretend you were shot and fall over.* And then I would have fallen to the ground and pretended I had been shot!" I yelled, tossing my hands up in the air.

"What are you bitching about? It's a flesh wound!"

"In my bad leg, you moron!"

"Would you just fucking fall over already—ah!" he shouted, falling to the ground as a bullet pierced his body. "Fuck, that really hurt!"

"Yeah, it hurts to take a bullet, doesn't it?"

He rolled his head to the side so he could see me. "It was part of the plan. I'll be okay."

"I fucking won't," I snapped. "I swear to God, if you ever shoot me again, you'd better hope I'm out of bullets. You're definitely not on the team now!"

"Seriously? I thought you'd like my ingenuity."

I pointed to where my leg was oozing blood. "You thought I'd like that you shot me? Again, what the fuck is wrong with you?"

Another shot rang out, pinging off the truck. I ducked down, rolling my eyes when I saw FNG motioning with his eyes for me to lay down. Sighing, I dropped to the ground and pretended I had been shot. And although technically I had been shot, it wasn't life-altering. Laying on the ground made me feel like a pussy.

"What now?" I asked, glaring at him from where I laid in the dust.

"Now we wait. He'll be looking for any sign of movement."

"I know what a fucking sniper does," I gritted out between clenched teeth. "I meant what was the rest of your plan?"

"To draw him out."

I was two fucking seconds away from getting up and snapping this guy's neck. Fuck, I was turning into Fox, eager to kill just to let off some steam. "I know you wanted to draw him out. So, let's say we lay on the ground for the next half hour and he finally comes over here. What's your fucking plan?"

"We attack. Wasn't that obvious?"

I sighed, rolling my head to stare at the rising sun. "Good plan."

10

BREE

I WAS PULLED to my feet and shoved away from the truck. Gunfire pierced the air around me, making me fear this would be the last time I ever saw another person again.

"Hurry!" Dash shouted, grabbing me by the elbow as more gunfire sounded.

I covered my head, screaming as the sharp noises echoed around the canyons. I already hated the desert, but now being shot at while running through it made me despise ever coming out here.

I hobbled across the rocky landscape as sharp edges cut into my feet. With our rush out of the yurt this morning, I hadn't had time to put on shoes, let alone any clothes. I was running for my life in nothing but a t-shirt and Thumper's boxer briefs. My boobs were flapping all over the place, and if it weren't for the fact that we were being shot at, I might care a little bit more about that.

"Bree, you need to pick up the pace!" Dash shouted at me.

"I'm trying! In case you haven't noticed, I don't have any shoes on!"

He glanced at my feet just long enough to confirm what I was saying was true. Then he spun around and hauled me up over his shoulder with an oomph. "Why the hell aren't you wearing any shoes?"

"Because I was shoved out of the yurt!" I shot back. I screamed and covered my head as more gunfire sounded. Terrified that I was about to be shot, I started wriggling in Dash's arms. "Oh, God! I don't want to die!"

"You're more likely to die if you keep moving! I'm trying to save your ass!"

I pushed off his back to stare at him. "This is what you call saving me? People are shooting at us!"

"Probably because they can hear you talking!"

"Are you implying that people find me annoying?"

"No, I'm literally saying it," he huffed, picking up speed as we climbed up some rocks. I braced myself against his back as we climbed higher. The sight of the sharp rocks below us had me squirming even more in his grasp.

"Dash, I don't think this is such a good idea."

"Why? Are you afraid we'll fall to our deaths?"

"That's just one thought."

"If you want, you can go back to the truck. I'm sure it's much less dangerous around the gunfire."

"Has anyone ever told you you're not the nicest person?"

"Most people love me."

"Most people don't have your shoulder digging into their stomachs," I grimaced, pushing off him again. "Can you please put me down? I feel like I'm going to throw up!"

He took a few more steps, then slowly lowered me to the ground, shoving me back behind a rock. "We can't stay here. We have to keep moving."

He peered around the rocks, assessing the situation down below.

"What do you see?"

"Not much."

"What do you mean? You have to see something!"

Without thinking twice, my head popped up over the rock, only to have Dash shove me back down.

"Are you trying to get killed? You really have no sense of danger."

Scoffing, I put my hands on my hips and gave him my best bitch face that I used at work. "I actually have a great sense of danger, which is why I know you and your...cowboy friends have put me in a really shitty position."

"My cowboy friends?" He burst out laughing, throwing his head back. "Lady, we're people just like you, except we have more sense."

"I have plenty of sense."

"Right, that's why you decided to come out to the fucking desert by yourself."

"Hey, Thumper came out here by himself."

"Yeah, but he's a guy."

"Are you implying that because I'm a woman I can't make it in the desert on my own?"

"Yes."

My jaw dropped open at his blatant insult. "I can't believe—"

"I'm not saying all women can't make it out here. In fact, there's one woman I know that would probably last longer than all of us. Not that I would tell her that. But you came out here with all the wrong stuff. Your backpack alone would kill you because of its sheer size."

"I really wish everyone would stop talking about my backpack. Like that's the indicator of whether or not I could survive on my own."

"It gave us a pretty good idea. Can we continue on?"

"But...we're hidden," I said, peering over the rock. "There's not even any gunfire anymore."

"You're right," he sighed, sitting down on a rock. "There's no gunfire, so we should take that to mean we're out of danger. We'll just wait here and see what happens."

He grabbed a rag out of his back pocket and started wiping the sweat from his face. He looked so relaxed, but I didn't believe for a second that he actually felt we were out of danger. I peered over the rock again, but couldn't see anything at this distance.

"What do you think is going on down there?"

"I think my guys are down."

"What?" I spun around and squinted into the light to see what he

96

was talking about. Now that he said it, it did look like there were two bodies laying on the ground. "Oh my God! What are we going to do?"

"Well, you said the danger was over, so I figured I'd just wait it out up here with you. Eventually, someone will come along and find the bodies."

"The—don't you care at all that they could be dead?" I shouted.

He shrugged. "Yeah, it's a heartbreaker. They were good men, but I'm sure it'll be fine."

I was seething at his callous tone. Even though these men got me into trouble I had no desire to be part of, I still didn't want them to end up dead. "I don't understand you at all. I thought you came out here to make sure he was safe, and now you've abandoned him when he needs you most? How selfish of you."

He stood with a grin. "Relax. They're fine."

I pointed at the ground where they were lying. "They're not moving!"

"They're drawing out the shooter," he said in a bored tone. "No doubt FNG's idea."

"But...how can you be sure?"

"Because I know my guys. However, they didn't send me up here with you so they could risk their lives for nothing. We have to keep moving."

"Fine," I huffed out. "But how exactly do you expect us to get up there? We don't exactly have any climbing gear."

He looked up at the rock face, grinning when he turned back to me. "I'm sure we'll figure something out."

"Why does that not make me feel better?"

"Because you're a pessimist. Leave it to me. We'll be fine."

Twenty minutes later, the sun was beating down on my face and sweat was dripping from me in the most uncomfortable places. My muscles were straining from the climb, and though we'd taken a less direct route up the rock face, it felt like harder work than if we'd just climbed straight up.

"Wait," I cried, collapsing against a rock. "Crap, I can't go on." I breathed harshly, gasping for the tiniest bit of air. "I can't breathe up here."

97

"The air is cleaner than in New York," Dash said, shooting me an incredulous look.

I nodded, still trying to suck in air. "That must be the problem. My lungs need the car exhaust and factory smoke to function."

"That's ridiculous."

"Is it? I feel like I'll collapse at any moment." I started fanning myself as dark spots filled my vision. This was it, the end of the line for me. My whole body was giving out. "I can't make it any further. My legs are like jelly and I have this weird tingling feeling in my body."

"It's called a workout. Your muscles are fine, but I can't do anything about your head."

I ignored his jab. "My feet are killing me." I moaned, just thinking about a nice footbath. "What I wouldn't give to go to the spa right now. They'd probably look at me like I was crazy."

He sighed heavily, sitting down beside me. "If that assassin is still out there, he'll come for us next. I can't protect you if you don't get up off your ass and move."

"Just let him take me. I'm too tired to go on."

"Stop being dramatic."

I huffed out a laugh. "If you think I'm joking, think again. I've never been so disgusting in my life. Even when I moved, I didn't sweat this much. Do you know how much work it was to direct all those movers where to go? There were boxes everywhere, and I had to tell them where to go...It was hard work."

He snorted at that. "Lady, I'm not sure if you know the true meaning of hard work."

"I resent that," I snapped. "Just because I'm not good with physical labor doesn't mean I don't work my ass off."

"If you'd stop bitching about how hard this is, maybe I wouldn't harass you so much."

I turned to him, ready to give him a piece of my mind. "And where do you get off calling me lady? I have a name."

He shrugged, pushing off his knees as he stood. "It suits you."

"Jackass suits you," I snapped.

"I won't deny that's true. Now get your ass up and let's keep moving."

I grimaced as I pulled the sweaty shirt from my chest. "I feel so disgusting. I have sweat in places where sweat should not linger."

"And where does sweat not linger?" he said, laughing at me.

"For your information, I have boob sweat. *Boob. Sweat.* Do you have any idea what that's like?"

His brows furrowed as he stared at me. "Is it anything like ass crack sweat?"

"You're disgusting," I sneered. "But yes, it's very similar, and equally uncomfortable."

"I gotcha. Here," he said, pulling out his rag. "This'll clean you up."

He tossed the rag at me, hitting me in the face. I held up the disgusting rag with two fingers, not willing to touch any more of it. "That's disgusting. It's filthy!"

"So are you. What's the difference? Do you want boob sweat or not?"

As disgusting as I felt, there was no way I could wipe myself down with this rag. I'd probably catch a disease. "Not. I'd rather be sweaty and gross than let that thing come within an inch of my skin."

He snatched it out of his hand and wiped down his face. "Your loss. Now, can we continue, princess?"

"Oh, so now I'm a princess?"

"If the shoe fits," he grinned.

"I'm not wearing shoes!" I yelled, pointing at my feet.

"Shh," he hurried over, covering my mouth. He glanced at our surroundings as my heart beat out of control. I felt nauseous and light-headed, but that was nothing compared to the terror racing through my veins. I'd take it all back. I didn't want an assassin to kill me. I wasn't ready to die. I still had a good life to live.

Just as I thought I was going to pass out, Dash removed his hand and turned away from me, climbing upward, as if he hadn't just scared the shit out of me.

"What was it?" I asked, racing after him. I nearly tripped on a rock and fell, but caught myself at the last second. "What did you hear?"

He stopped and glanced over his shoulder, shooting me a confused look. "What are you talking about?"

"You covered my mouth and told me to be quiet."

He grinned at me. "Yeah, and it worked. Let's go. We're burning daylight."

11

THUMPER

"I DON'T SUPPOSE you had a timeframe for how long it would take for this guy to come assassinate us." I was bored out of my skull. We'd been lying here for a good hour, just waiting for this asshole to come shoot us. Still, he hid out behind his vehicle.

"It can't be too much longer. People are coming into the park."

I moved my head just enough to see underneath the truck. The guy's car was still parked there. "I doubt he cares about that too much. Fuck, my ass is starting to hurt."

"Would you quit whining? Enjoy the fact that you're over here laying on the ground, waiting for this guy to make his move. You could be where Dash is with Bree."

I snorted in amusement at what he was going through. Poor guy, he didn't seem to catch any breaks. Just like the time he had to fetch Fox with Rae. After being thrown up on, any man would have distanced himself from the show tune singing psycho.

"Poor bastard. Do you think he's contemplated suicide yet?"

"She's not that bad. I mean, I wouldn't want to be him, but when you think about it, she's just scared."

"She's a whiny brat," I said scathingly. "When this is over, we'll send her ass on a plane back to New York and never have to deal with her again."

"Do you really think it's going to be that simple?"

"Why wouldn't it be?"

"Because you like her."

I almost burst out laughing, but remembered at the last second that we were supposed to be dead. "What the fuck are you talking about?"

"I've seen the way you look at her. You can't tell me there's not some level of attraction between the two of you."

"I'm a guy. Of course there's a level of attraction. That doesn't mean she doesn't annoy the hell out of me."

"Yeah." I could hear the grin in his voice. "But opposites attract, and I've never met anyone so opposite of you. Hey, he's coming. Play dead."

"Play dead and then what?"

"Just follow my lead."

Excellent fucking plan. I waited with my eyelids half-closed. I could see the man approaching carefully. I held my gun loosely in my hand, as if I fell to my death with it still in my clutches. His footsteps were light as he made his way around the truck. Just a few more steps and—

"Arg!" FNG shouted, sitting upright as he fired his weapon. With the element of surprise gone, I rolled and fired just as the assassin slipped around the corner of the truck.

"Nice fucking plan, asshole!"

"I thought I had the jump on him!" he said, jumping to his feet.

I backed up against the truck, ready to swing around the corner. I motioned for FNG to go around the other way to ambush this fucker. With his nod, I gave the forward motion and we both sprung from our spots, ready to fire. But when I stepped around the truck, the only one there was FNG, who I nearly shot.

"Jesus, I nearly shot you—" I caught the movement out of the corner of my eye and immediately shifted to the attack coming at me from above the truck. But it was too late. A foot came flying at me, kicking the gun from my grip as a ninja slammed into me, knocking me to the ground.

I hit the ground hard, the air whooshing out of me in a swift gust as I heard grunts coming from nearby. I rolled to my side, sucking in a breath as I watched a woman with her hair up in a bun wearing tight leather kicking FNG's ass. I shoved to my feet and ran at her hard, having no gun to fight back with.

I slammed into the woman from behind, knocking her into the truck with all my might, only to have her slam her elbow back into my face. I didn't even see her shift her body weight. One second, she was facing the truck, and the next, she was slamming her foot into my chest and knocking me back a good five yards.

"Holy shit," I muttered, pressing my hand to my chest as I struggled to breathe. Who the hell was this woman? My eyes drifted to FNG, who was pulling his punches. "Take her down!"

He ducked just as her foot swung at his head, then he shook his head at me. "I can't hit her! She's a woman!"

Her fist hit him hard across the face, sending him sailing through the air. I jumped to my feet, feeling slightly off balance. "She's a woman who's kicking our asses. No mercy!"

I got back in the fight, not willing to admit defeat just yet. I tackled her from behind, only to be flung over her shoulder like a sack of onions. I landed hard, wincing at the pain in my spine. This woman fought harder than any man I knew, and that was saying something.

FNG charged her, swinging his fist at her face and following it with a hard strike to her ribs. She barely even flinched at the pain. I jumped to my feet and tackled her again from behind, this time not being so careless. I quickly got her in a headlock, grinning as I brought her to the ground. FNG was breathing hard as he stepped closer to her.

"You fight like a man, but we'll still take you down like a woman."

He was still grinning when her foot connected with his balls, but his face soon slipped into a grimace as he crumbled to his knees. I could feel her energy depleting, but she still shoved back, slamming me into the tire of the truck. Then she flipped her legs over head, wrapping them around my neck. My eyes went wide as she flung me through the air. I was getting really tired of being tossed around so carelessly. It was time to get my gun and put a stop to this.

As FNG went after her again, I ran for my gun that she knocked out of my hands. But before I got there, she was on me again, kicking my ass.

"How are you doing this?" I asked as she landed a kick to my face. I spit out blood and refused to go down. I got in a few good punches, but it was clear she was going to win this if I didn't end it. I needed to get her over to the cliff's edge. It was the only way I stood a chance of ending her. Either that or I'd fall to my death.

"FNG!" I shouted, ducking her fist. "Arizona!"

He came up behind her and swung, knocking her forward. "Arizona what?"

I snatched the gun off the ground and turned to make a run for it. "The fucking job Arizona!"

He took a hard hit to the jaw and stumbled backward. The assassin was on my ass in seconds, just as I was approaching the edge of the cliff. I spun around and aimed at her, firing just as she shoved my arm out of the way. She kicked me hard, just as I thought she would, laying me out flat just by the edge. It was a toss-up if I'd make it or not. And I sure as hell hoped that FNG remembered what Arizona was.

She bent over and sent a swift strike right into my chest. I blocked the second hit, and luckily, FNG arrived, saving my ass from being beaten to hell. He shouted like a warrior as he ran toward her, body slamming her to the ground. With a crazed look on his face, he slammed his forehead into her nose, then gave two swift strikes to the face. She tossed him off as I scrambled to my feet. Together, we both attacked, but could barely fight off her kicks and punches. The woman was a powerhouse.

FNG grabbed her by the waist, a horrified look crossing his face as he held up a mini grenade, sans pin. I grabbed her from behind, hoping to hold her arms out of the way as she screamed at us. FNG took advantage and shoved the grenade in her mouth, releasing the safety. I flung us backward, kicking her with my bionic foot over the cliff, but my foot got caught in her clothing, dragging me with her.

I grappled for something to hold onto just as the clothing ripped, leaving me dangling over the edge. The explosion had me gripping hard to the rock, hoping it didn't reach me as she fell to her death.

FNG flopped down on the ground in exhaustion as I rested my

head in the dirt, still dangling over the edge. "That didn't exactly go as planned. I thought we were pulling an Arizona."

"So did I," I sighed. "We're just lucky the grenade didn't go off in your fucking hand."

"Maybe I could get a bionic hand," he laughed. "We'd be twins."

"But you wouldn't be nearly as cool as me."

"Of course," he sighed. "Who the fuck would send her after us?"

"Maybe she thought one of us was Fox."

He snorted out a laugh, then sat up and held out his hand to me. "Come on, let's get you up before you fall over."

He hefted me up and we both turned, sitting on our asses as we watched the sunrise. "Did you see my foot get caught?"

His cheeks rose in laughter. "I thought for sure you were going over."

"Me too. This wasn't exactly the way I thought I'd be watching the sunrise in Arches."

"It's a good story, though."

I nodded, glancing over at him. "But who's going to tell Cash?"

"Rock, paper, scissors?"

I held out my hand and grinned at him. I was awesome at this game. "Let's do it."

I glared at FNG as I dialed Cash's number. There's no way I should have lost that game. He had to have a trick up his sleeve. I wiped the dirt and sweat from my face as we sat by the cliff watching the smoke slowly dissipate from below. I hadn't seen Dash since we sent him off with Bree, and I was secretly hoping they had found their own way out of here.

"Calling already? Who did you kill?"

I chuckled because...well..."It's funny you should say that."

"Christ," he muttered. "That wasn't meant to be a serious question. Alright, was it Dash or FNG?"

"Neither."

"You murdered someone else? Thumper, you're supposed to be on vacation."

"I'm aware of that, but—"

"You said," he interrupted me, "and I quote… 'I need to get out of here away from all the women and relax.'"

"I know that's what I said."

"No, clearly you didn't or you wouldn't be calling me, telling me you murdered someone!"

FNG grimaced. "He said clearly."

"I know," I snapped.

"Is that FNG? Ask him what the fuck happened. He was supposed to keep you alive."

"And he did, sort of."

"Oh, so you're sort of dead?"

"No, but—"

"I know. Someone else is." I could already imagine him pacing in his office. I didn't mean to call with such horrible news, but better that we killed an assassin than she killed us.

"Look on the bright side, instead of being down three agents and a civilian, you're down one assassin."

"I'm sorry, did you just say assassin?"

"That's what I said."

He was silent for a moment. "Fox is here."

"Okay," I said slowly.

"Where the fuck is Knight? Did you kill Knight?" he shouted.

"No! Fucking hell, it was a woman!"

Again, more silence followed. I wasn't sure if this was a good thing or a bad thing. Silence could go either way when dealing with Cash.

"You killed a woman instead of capturing her and interrogating her?"

"Well…see, it wasn't that easy."

"Thumper, there are three of you. How is it possible that you couldn't capture her?"

I winced and looked at FNG, who just shrugged. "Well…see, the thing is…there was this civilian staying with me after her yurt got torn up by a Bighorn Sheep."

"Okay…"

"And…in the middle of the night, someone shot me."

"You're telling me that you were sleeping, minding your own business, and someone shot you?"

"That's about the gist of it."

"For what reason?"

"If I knew that, I wouldn't be calling you."

"Fucking hell," he muttered.

I noticed he did that a lot lately. The man was wound up tight, and I wasn't sure if it was because of us or something to do with Eva. After learning what FNG knew about the situation, I wouldn't be surprised if Eva had something to do with his constant state of anger.

"Boss, do you still have Betty?"

"Of course, I still have Betty!"

"Alright, alright. I was just checking."

"Okay, here's what we're going to do. You're going to send her picture over for facial recognition. While we're working on the identity of your assassin, get your ass out of there and on the road west. Do not bring this to our door."

"Understood. Um…what about the civilian?"

"I forgot about that," he griped. "You said it's a woman. Can you drop her somewhere?"

"I'm not entirely sure that's a good idea. She was with us for several days. This assassin might have mistaken her for part of our party."

"Then you're going to have to take her with you until we're sure she's safe."

"I was afraid you were going to say that," I grumbled.

"Just get me that facial recognition."

FNG and I both leaned over the edge of the cliff and looked down at the fire dying out below. "Um…about that…there's sort of an issue."

"Of course there is. What's the problem?"

"Well…in our attempt to…" I looked to FNG for help.

"Remove her from the situation," he added.

"Right…um…FNG got ahold of a mini grenade and sort of shoved it in her mouth."

"And then Thumper shoved her over the cliff," FNG finished. "We're pretty sure there's not much to look at down there."

"So, let me see if I've got this straight. Not only were you not able to disarm a woman with just the two of you—"

"That was no woman, boss. She was like…Rae or something."

"And you couldn't take her down. So, you decided to blow her up and shove her off a cliff where she exploded. And now you have no way to identify her."

I looked at FNG, who nodded comically. "That's an accurate assessment."

"Find me something. A thumb, a fiber of hair. I don't care what you have to do, but get me something to identify this person so we have something to go on."

"Will do, boss."

"And Thumper."

"Yeah?"

"I hope you enjoy the rest of your vacation with this woman."

FNG burst out laughing. "God, boss. If you only knew."

"I have a feeling I do."

He hung up without another word. I ran my fingers through my sweaty hair, sighing heavily as I thought of the task ahead of us. Not only did we have to get down there and retrieve some kind of information about the assassin, we also had to get out of here before anyone connected us to her.

"We need to call Duke and see if he has any connection out here. We need to ditch the truck ASAP."

"And the body?" he asked, jerking his head at the cliff.

"Yeah, that too."

"I guess we should get to work."

We both nodded, staring at the cliff. "So, do you want to retrieve the finger, or should I?"

"Rock, paper, scissors?"

I slowly turned and glared at him. "What do you think?"

He swallowed hard and got to his feet. "I'll just go retrieve the finger."

"Good idea."

A half-hour later, I was watching FNG climb back up the cliff just as Dash was approaching with Bree. Both of them looked like they'd been in a fight just as deadly as the one FNG and I had just been involved in.

"What happened to you?" I asked, staring at the smears of dirt all over his face.

"Boob sweat. I don't want to talk about it." He jerked his head at me. "You?"

"Female assassin. I don't want to talk about it."

FNG hauled himself the rest of the way up, flopping on his back as he panted heavily. "Thanks for the help."

"Did you get it?"

He pulled a Tic-Tac container out of his pocket and held up the bloody thumb. "This was all that was left."

"Hand it over. I'll scan it on my phone."

"Why does he have a bloody thumb?" Bree squealed.

"Because her face was blown off," I answered nonchalantly.

"Nice," Dash grinned. "So, pizza?"

BREE

"How can you be so nonchalant about all this?"

We were sitting in the back of a pickup truck. Someone in Arches saw us and was nice enough to offer us a ride back to our yurt. Of course, with our state of dress—or undress in my situation—he assumed we'd had a terrible accident and was more than willing to help us out.

"There's no room for panic," Thumper replied, leaning casually against the back window. "What we need is a plan. We already called our boss, so we need to find out who's behind this and move forward from there."

"But...someone tried to kill us!"

"Yes, but we killed her first," FNG stated. "So...aren't you glad you're on our side?"

"You hardly look like you fared well. Look at you! Both of you! Cuts all over your bodies, bruises forming everywhere...and you're bleeding from where you got shot earlier!"

Thumper closed his eyes, leaning his head back. "And your point?"

I scoffed at his less-than-thrilling response. "Oh, I don't know. Maybe you would have some concern for your life?"

"This wasn't even close to the most dangerous situation I've been in," he responded. "Maybe unique in that it was a female assassin, but other than that, I've seen worse."

"Well," I huffed. "That makes me feel so much better."

"It should," Dash grinned. "Think of it this way, you can't kill us!"

"Especially not me," FNG added. "Trust me, I've tested it."

"Well, that's just wonderful for all of you, but unlike you, I don't have the skills to survive a female assassin."

"We could train you."

Thumper cut a deadly look at Dash. "Don't even go there. The last thing we need is one more female knife enthusiast."

"I can assure you, that will never happen. It's not that I'm opposed to guns in general, *other than in restricted areas*," I emphasized, "but I don't happen to be that coordinated."

"*No.*" Thumper's eyes went wide as he sat up and grabbed my hand. "You mean to tell me that you aren't used to this stuff? I never would have guessed it."

"My point is...as enlightening as this little adventure has been, I think I would prefer to head home and forget this whole thing ever happened."

The three of them shared a look that made me shiver in my barely-there clothes. I had a feeling that this adventure was not only not over, but was just beginning. How it ended, I didn't know.

"That's...not possible," Thumper said. "We can't allow you to go home, not after the assassin saw you with us."

"But, she's dead. What harm could come from me returning to New York? Surely, that's far enough away."

"It could be, but if she let anyone know that you were with us, it's very likely you won't be out of danger," Dash supplied. "Our boss is working to find out who she was and who sent her after us. Once we know that, we can end this and get you back home."

"And in the meantime, we'll meet up with an old friend," Thumper added.

"I'm not sure I want to meet any more of your friends," I muttered as we pulled into the parking lot.

The guys all stood and headed for the tailgate, while I stood there, thinking someone would help me down. I wasn't a princess, but I did have huge blisters on my feet and barely any clothes on. A little help would be nice.

But as I stood there with my hand out, ready for someone to grab ahold, I realized nobody was coming to my rescue. With a huff, I got down on my butt and scooted off the tailgate just in time for the driver to swing it closed and give me a nod goodbye. The guys were already making their way to the other truck, as if I was just a thorn in their side.

"Um...not to be a pain, but I wonder if I could grab just a few things from the yurt," I called after them.

"No time," Thumper said, hauling his own bag from his shoulder into his truck. "With Dash's vehicle in the open, there's no telling how long we have. As much as it pains me, we need to get out of here, ditch my truck, and get on the road."

"Wait, why do we have to ditch your truck?" I asked in confusion.

"Because my truck is here. I'm registered here, which anyone could find out if they come looking."

"Then wouldn't taking your truck be bad luck?"

He turned to me with a laugh. "Bad luck? Lady, this whole fucking trip is bad luck, but we need to get out of here. We'll have to do some finagling, but we'll be fine."

"I'm sorry, but what exactly is finagling?"

He rolled his eyes. "We need to lose them."

"Then why can't you just say that so I understand what you're saying?"

"Maybe I don't want you to understand," he growled, taking a step closer. "Maybe I just want to get the hell out of here and figure this shit out so I can put as much distance between you and me as possible."

I crossed my arms over my chest, trying to hide my hurt. I knew I wasn't his type, and he wasn't mine either. But his absolute hatred for me was unfounded. "I would say the feeling is mutual, but I'm not that rude."

"You think *I'm* being rude? You have been a pain in my ass since day one, and I've tried to help you. You took over my yurt—over my bed—and now that we're trying to help you again, you're being a pain in the ass about it."

"Think about it from my point of view. Everything that could go wrong has gone wrong. And now you're telling me I have to go on the run because somebody's after you? Is that supposed to make me jump for joy? All I want is to get a few things out of the yurt—like my purse, so I don't lose my ID and all my credit cards. And I wouldn't mind putting on something other than a t-shirt and a pair of boxers that aren't even mine!"

I was huffing and puffing like I'd just given a long-winded speech before going off to war. I knew I was acting hysterical. I could hear it in my voice and see it in my actions, but who wouldn't be like this? I'd never been in the military. I had no training for what to do when I was brought on the run. There was nothing about my life that would prepare me for a situation like this.

"Fine," he bit out. "Hurry up. We leave in five."

I turned, rolling my eyes to the sky to beg for calm. I would not lose my shit over this. I would stay calm and figure out a way to survive this horrible trip if it was the last thing I did. I marched over to his yurt and tossed back the canvas. Just a few hours ago, I was relaxing in his nice warm bed. Now I was disgusting and my feet were killing me. I had dragged a few things over from my own yurt, but unfortunately, my clothes hadn't survived the killer sheep. At least, last night I had considered it a total loss. I should have thought about possible killer scenarios before I threw them out. Like, being shot at and going on the run in only men's underwear. Had I known that might happen, I would have taken my own torn clothes in an instant.

I looked longingly at the shower, as pathetic as it was, and wished I could take a few minutes to clean up, but that wasn't possible. I grabbed my purse and headed for the entrance when a thought crossed my mind. It would be stupid to run with these men and not let a single soul know that I was in trouble. Not that many people cared about me, but I should at least let my sister know.

Making sure the coast was clear, I dialed my sister's number and waited for her to answer. "Wow, now, this is a record. I don't think I've heard from you this much since—"

"Grace!" I cut her off. "I don't have much time. I got myself into this huge mess and now someone's after us. They tried to kill us this morning, and now I have to go on the run with these men and I don't know what's going to happen!"

"Wow, that's…it's a cool story. I didn't really take you for the type to make up something like that—"

"Grace!" I hissed. "I'm not making this up. There was this killer sheep last night and he tore up my yurt. So, I stayed with these guys, except their ex-military or something. Someone shot at them, and because I was with them, it's not safe for me." She was silent. Great, the one time I was in serious trouble, she didn't believe me. "Grace, I wouldn't lie about this. Believe me, I would much rather be anywhere else in the world right now."

"Wait, so you're serious?"

"Yes!" I practically shouted. Glancing back outside, I knew I didn't have much time. "I don't know what's going to happen, but don't call me. I'll keep my phone on me and check in when I can. But if you don't hear from me, you need to contact my boss and let him know what's going on."

"Okay, does he have someone he can call for you? Someone that can help?"

"No," I shook my head, confused by her question. "Why would he?"

"Well, why else would you need me to call him?"

"Because I just got a major promotion! I can't have him thinking that I ran off and joined the circus!"

"Ah, see, that makes more sense. Here I was, thinking you were worried about your safety, but you're really worried about this job."

"I've worked my ass off for that job. I've put up with so much shit to get there. Men that hate me because I do a better job than them. The son that's too lazy to do the work properly, and then shoots me dirty looks because his father likes my work better than his. And let's not forget about the secretaries that are pissed at me for going farther than them."

"Hey, I get it. It's a man's world, but if what you're saying is true, your safety is more important than your job."

I couldn't believe her narrow-minded way of thinking. "What's the point in being alive if I lose the one thing that I've worked for my whole life?"

"You're right. Clearly, staying alive isn't important if your job is taken by the sniveling son that doesn't do the job the same as you."

I knew she was mocking me, but there was some truth in what she said. She had no idea how hard I worked, how much I sacrificed to get to where I was today. I wouldn't let it go without a fight. Not even this female assassin would stop me from achieving my goals.

"Bree!" Thumper shouted from outside.

"I have to go, Grace. I'll call within two days."

"Right, have fun."

"This isn't a vacation," I scoffed.

"I know, but what else am I supposed to say? Don't get dead?"

"It seems more appropriate."

"Well, don't get dead then. Talk to you later."

She hung up without another word. I couldn't believe the lack of concern in her voice. Throughout the whole conversation, it was like she was taking it all with a grain of salt. My own sister! If I survived this, we were going to have serious words.

I shoved my phone in my purse and headed out to the truck. Thumper was waiting impatiently while the other two sat in the truck waiting for me. "I'm ready."

"About time. That's all you grabbed?" he jerked his head toward my purse.

"Um...yeah. I just wanted to make sure I didn't miss anything."

"Let me see."

"See what?"

"Your purse."

He snatched it from my hand before I could attempt to keep it to myself. As he dug through, I wondered what he was looking for, but when he came up with my phone, I felt like a kid that just shoplifted candy.

"Really?"

"What?"

"You can't take a phone with you. That's the easiest way for someone to find us." He tossed my phone on the ground, then stomped on it, crushing it beneath his robotic foot.

"What are you doing?" I screeched. "That was my phone!"

"And you'll have to get a new one. We can't risk anyone tracking you."

"But they're not after me. They're after you."

"Maybe, but like I said, if they know you're with me, that'll be the first thing they look for." He tossed my purse back at me, hitting me in the face with the strap. "Let's move."

"Such the gentleman," I muttered under my breath. "I can tell this is going to be a great trip."

"It's not supposed to be great."

He jerked open the back door, holding it open for me. I climbed up, all too aware of my underwear being the only thing hiding my body from him and all other prying eyes. When I sat down, I could have sworn he was staring at my ass, but he slammed the door closed before I could be sure. Within minutes, we were on the road. Not one of them spoke as we headed out of Moab, heading west to some unknown destination. At least I could take a nap.

13

THUMPER

"WE SHOULD HEAD TO OPS. Hop on 70 and head straight east," Dash insisted.

"Cash said not to lead them back to OPS" I replied. "He's right. Until we know who's after us, we can't risk going home."

FNG leaned up between the seats. "Not to mention that Rafe would be pissed if his love child were to be discovered."

"His love child?" Dash questioned.

"His secret underground facility. You know how he is about hide-outs. Not to mention that the last thing we need is for Cash and Rafe to meet up again, especially after what happened with Eva."

"I thought you weren't going to talk about that anymore?"

"I don't know what happened," Dash cut in. "Fill me in."

"You know *something* happened. Let's just leave it at that," FNG grumbled. "I'm already in enough trouble."

"You know, it's impossible to get any sleep with the three of you arguing about where we're going. I thought you already settled this," Bree snapped.

With a heavy sigh, I turned around and stared at the woman. "Look, this is what we do. We work shit out, so why don't you close your eyes and think about spreadsheets while the rest of us figure out how to keep you alive, okay?"

"They weren't aiming at me."

"Maybe not, but do you think they'd let you go if they found you with us? Do you think they'd listen to your begging and pleading as they gutted you for answers? Or maybe you think they'd make your death easy. In fact, if they caught you, they'd most likely torture you for information on us. So, why don't you keep your mouth shut and let us do what we do."

I turned around, satisfied that it was quiet in the backseat. At least, for the time being. However, it didn't last long. I should have known that antagonizing her would only send her into a meltdown. The small gasps from the back seat were the first sign. New Guy's heavy sigh was the second. And finally, the jagged crying made me realize just what an ass I really was.

I turned around, ready to eat crow. "Bree."

"This is wrong. This is so wrong," she said, shaking her head from side to side.

I motioned to FNG to do something, but he shook his head at me and motioned for me to console her. *You do it.* I mouthed, not wanting to go near the woman breaking down behind me.

He shook his head, crossing his arms over his chest like a petulant child. It looked like I was going to have to be the adult in the room. "Bree," I said again. "I'm sorry I said that. You don't have anything to worry about. We won't let anything happen to you."

"Nope, this is not happening. Why would anyone shoot at me?"

"They didn't shoot at you. I'm the one bleeding."

"I work hard," she continued, completely ignoring me. "I pay my bills. I pay my taxes! I put in eighty-hour weeks. I'm always the last one to leave the building. Who would want to kill me?"

"Again, they didn't try to kill you. I was in the chair, not you."

"It could have been me. I could have been laying there, and just… poof. My life would be over. And what have I done? I haven't even started my new position yet. I came out to fucking die in the desert!"

I turned around in my seat, refusing to listen to any more of this. "Well, I tried."

"A valiant effort," Dash nodded. "Cash would be proud."

"What more could anyone ask of me? I tried to console her. You saw it."

"I did."

"She's practically catatonic."

"Muttering to herself like a crazy person," he agreed.

"So, that settles it. She can sit her ass in that seat for the rest of the trip if she has to. I did my part. I wash my hands of it."

"As you should."

I nodded, but as much as I didn't want to help her, I couldn't ignore the niggle of guilt that crept into my mind. This wasn't how I would handle any other client. She was basically being dragged along for no reason other than she met me at the wrong place, wrong time.

"Anyway," I said, shoving the guilt aside, "once we get orders from Cash, we'll plan our next steps."

FNG leaned between the seats again. "I was thinking of where we should head. Looking at the map, I found this road. Apparently, it's called the Loneliest Road in America. From what I can tell, it's the perfect place to be in our situation. Hardly any traffic, not many towns…If anyone comes after us, it's a great place to get rid of a body."

"We have to get rid of my truck first. We can't have someone tracking our movements."

"I'm on it," FNG said, scooting back in his seat.

"Man, I love this truck," I murmured, running my hand over the dashboard lovingly. "She's been good to me."

"With any luck, Cash will find a way to keep her."

"Let's hope so. I don't want to drive a minivan."

"But they're a hell of a good chick magnet," Dash grinned.

"Hardly. What do you say, Bree?" I asked, trying to draw her out of her depressed and worried state.

"Huh?"

"We were discussing minivans. Chick magnet or not?"

The disgust on her face said it all. I nearly laughed at how absurd she thought the idea of a minivan was. "In what world would a woman look at a minivan and have her ovaries explode?"

"Hey, I happen to know a few ladies who love them. It's a sign that you're willing to expand your family, or some shit," Dash argued.

"Yeah, and you can fit a lot of bodies," FNG answered, still engrossed in his phone.

"That's what Dash just said," Bree reminded him in confusion.

FNG looked up, realizing his mistake, and struggled to explain. "Right…um…bodies, as in other human beings. I know that."

But Bree wasn't falling for it. "You're a horrible liar. What exactly did you mean?"

"Bree, I don't think we should—" I tried to help him out, but Bree wouldn't allow it. She held up her hand, effectively cutting me off.

"In what way did you mean bodies?"

FNG's eyes grew wide as panic set in. I shook my head at him, not wanting him to explain what he meant. That would only send her into a tailspin that would take hours to pull her out of. And in the meantime, we'd all have to listen to her bitching.

"New Guy, stop looking at him and tell me what you meant!" Bree snapped.

"Don't you do it," I yelled.

"Tell me what you meant!"

"Don't you fucking dare!"

New Guy's head swiveled back and forth as we continued to shout at him.

"FNG!"

"Not a fucking word!"

"Tell me!"

"No!"

"Tell me right now!"

"I meant stacking dead bodies!" he shouted.

Everything went silent in the van as FNG closed his eyes and took a deep breath. Bree, on the other hand, was stunned into silence, hardly breathing at all.

"Okay," she said quietly. "Okay." She started doing this nodding thing, which I could only assume was her way of processing. "Dead bodies stacked up…it's normal in this line of work. I'm sure in… protection duty…you have to get rid of a few bodies to protect your clients. It's perfectly reasonable to assume that not everyone comes out alive. And, of course, you can't just leave those bodies laying around. You have to move them somewhere—someplace they won't ever be found. And that's why you have the minivans. You use them for transporting bodies and not being found out by police and other people that might want to arrest you or do terrible things to you. Perfectly normal," she nodded.

"Bree," I said hesitantly.

"I bet you could fit three, possibly four bodies across the back. If you took out the middle row, you might even fit in a stack of bodies horizontally. Based on the height of the van, I'd say you could stack them four high. Maybe five depending on the weight of the bodies. Then again, it might be hard to get the bodies in on top. You can't exactly slide one body over another. But I would say you could get on average twelve bodies in the back."

"Fifteen," New Guy cut in, shrugging when I glared at him.

"Right," she continued to nod. "Fifteen bodies. That's a good day's work. And no one would suspect a man driving a minivan. It's a very good cover story. Everyone would think you cart around little kids for soccer games, hand out cookies on Saturdays, and go to PTO meetings. When you think about it, it's very clever. As long as you don't actually go to a school, or other places where someone might want to take a look in the back seat."

"Bree," I said again. "Look at me."

She did as I asked, but said nothing more.

"Bree, we don't actually haul bodies around in the back."

"Aside from the one time we hauled around a mummy," FNG added, making me want to smack him.

"Right, but no dead bodies from this century," I nodded encouragingly.

She nodded slightly. "No bodies from this century. I think I can handle that."

Assured that she wasn't going to lose it, I turned back around in my seat. "I think I'm getting the hang of this."

Dash snorted. "Yeah, we'll just use mummies for everything that goes wrong with this case."

14

CASH

I STORMED down the hall to the conference room and flung the doors open. Everyone sat silently awaiting orders. I nodded to Rae who pulled up Thumper's location on the screen.

"At approximately 0400 hours, Thumper was the target of a sniper at the yurt he was staying at in Moab. FNG and Dash are with him, along with a civilian woman. Luckily, the bullet only grazed Thumper, but there was an assassin after him—a woman. He sent over a fingerprint. Rae, I sent it to you. I need you to dig into this and find out who she is."

"Awesome," she grinned. "It's a shame they killed her. I might have wanted to meet her."

Great, another person in my company that would lose their mind over an assassin. That was just what I needed.

"We need to dig into all old case files and find anyone that might have it out for someone on the teams. Let's start with cases he's worked, but I want a second team researching other avenues. He could have been attacked simply because he was away from OPS headquarters and was an easy target."

"Who's the civilian woman?" Lock asked.

Rae pulled up her profile on a second screen. "Bree Wilton from

New York. She's an executive at a financial company. She's on sabbatical. I've talked with her boss and informed him that we're doing everything we can to keep her safe."

"Are we positive she's not involved?" Johnny asked.

"At this time, we have no reason to suspect her. She didn't even make her plans until a few days ago when she found out she would have to take a vacation. After running a background check on her, Rae didn't find anything suspicious."

That seemed to appease them for the moment. "Boss," Fox raised his hand. "I hate to point out the obvious, but we know someone with very good connections."

"No," I said firmly.

"You can't deny he's a great asset."

"Fox, the answer is no."

"Come on," he whined. "I've got connections to him."

"He fucking hates you," I snapped.

"No, see, that's just a front so no one sees how great we are together."

"I'm not sending you!"

A throat cleared, which only pissed me off. I turned to Jack, sending him a clear message with my eyes that he wasn't to say a word. But did he listen?

"Not that I particularly want to involve that fucker, but Fox is right. As a former assassin, he has access to information we need. If this was a hit, who better to ask?"

I hated that he was right, but I hated the toothy grin on Fox's face even more. "If we're going to do this, someone needs to go with Fox."

It was silent for a moment before the whole room burst out in laughter.

"Good one, boss," Scottie laughed.

"Yeah, sorry, but a road trip with Fox sounds about as good as a bullet to the head," Slider said.

"You work with IRIS," Fox interrupted. "How is that any different?"

"He doesn't eat weird shit like Funyuns and pickled pig's feet," Slider retorted.

"Alright, enough!" I yelled over the chaos. Christ, I hated to be put in this position, but someone needed to go with Fox, and it had to be someone that could control him to some degree. "Rae, call Eva."

Fox's face dropped. "Boss, are you entrusting me with your woman's life?"

"It wouldn't be the first time."

"I'm honored, boss. Truly. I'll do something really special for you when I get back. Like...carve a special box for Betty."

"Hey, I already got him a box," IRIS argued.

"But it doesn't have any special designs on it," Fox said. "It's a plain fucking box. A woman like Betty needs a pedestal."

"I'm really going to regret this." I rubbed my temples as I felt a headache coming on. After the last disaster with IRIS and Jane, I should be wanting to stay home, but the need to get back in the action was hitting me hard. I needed to get away from the chaos of running a business, and back out where I belonged, with Sally 2.

Fox shoved back from his chair with a big grin. "I need to get ready. Do you think I should wear a suit?"

"Do you think that will piss him off less?" I asked.

He frowned. "Right, I should pay homage to him. It's time to get out the leather jacket."

15

THUMPER

"YOUR HITTER IS one Alexandra Desario. No known associates. She worked alone and from the chatter, hasn't missed a single kill until she met the two of you," Cash said over the speakerphone.

"Lucky us," FNG grinned, slapping me on the shoulder.

"Unlucky for her," I retorted. "Just because she's an assassin doesn't mean she would have been able to take us out."

"She had moves. You gotta admit it."

"Yeah, and she would have had less moves if you hadn't been pulling your punches."

"She's a woman! I can't use my full strength on a woman!"

"Uh...didn't you stick a grenade in her mouth and shove her over a cliff?" Dash asked.

FNG cleared his throat uncomfortably. "Well...yeah, but I only did the first part. He's the one that shoved her over the cliff."

I rolled my eyes and watched as Bree emerged from the bathroom. Cash put us up in a suite since there were four of us. I also might have convinced him to do it simply so we could try and calm Bree down. She was rapidly losing her sanity, and in return, bugging the shit out of us.

"Getting back to the hit," Cash said, redirecting the line of thought, "We put Fox on trying to track down anyone that might be able to help."

"Wait, when you say you put Fox on it...what exactly does that mean?"

"Eva's with him," Cash said after a moment. "It'll be fine."

I started laughing, unable to comprehend what Cash just did.

"What? What's going on?" FNG asked.

"You sent him to see Knight? Are you crazy?"

"Oh fuck," Dash laughed. "Were you really that desperate to get rid of Fox?"

"Knight is going to kill Fox?" FNG asked. "Why?"

"Because Fox is an annoying fucker," I answered. "And he's bound to start fangirling over Knight again. He already stole his boots and shoes."

"I thought those were a present?"

"That's what Fox would have you think," Dash answered. "He tried them on, and when Knight woke up, Fox was still wearing them."

"That wreaks of a stalker," I chuckled.

"Anyway, I've worked it out for you to meet up with Jones. Since the disaster at his Montana ranch, he's relocated. You should reach him by tomorrow."

I winced at the thought of seeing Jones again. He was a good guy, but damn, he fucking hated Cash. "Are you sure that's a good idea, boss? Dragging Jones into more of our shit might not be a good idea."

"I won't be there, so it should be fine. Besides, he has a thing for damsels in distress."

As much as it shouldn't bother me, it pissed me off to think he might get attached to Bree. She wasn't anyone to me, and I'd be glad to see the back of her. Still...I shook off those thoughts and finished the call with Cap.

"And my truck is safe?"

"Yes," Cash sighed. "Duke made sure he bought your truck. You owe him big time."

"I shouldn't owe him anything. You should see what we're bringing back for him. He'll be down on his knees thanking us when he sees it."

"Yeah? Just how much work does it need?"

I thought back to the 1967 Chevy Camaro we purchased from the used car lot. It was in rough shape, but was perfect for us. It still had a good engine and wasn't too flashy in its condition.

"It's...got some repairs that need to be done."

"I'll let you tell him that. Check in when you get to Jones's place."

"Will do."

I hung up and leaned back in the chair. I was exhausted from the late night, early morning, and all the fucking driving. We were desperately hurting for supplies, and while it was nice to stay in a luxurious hotel, I knew it was only for one night. And it wouldn't be a restful night.

"I'm going to do a perimeter check," I said, pushing up from the table.

"I'll go with you," Dash said, glancing at FNG. "You've got the room."

"Hey, I'm not complaining. I'll order room service for us."

"I want steak, a big one."

"I second that," Dash said, rubbing his belly. "I'm so fucking hungry."

"I was actually thinking of getting a salad," FNG said thoughtfully. "I think I've been eating too much lately. Can't afford to get chubby."

I shook my head at the fucker. "There is so much wrong with what you just said."

I headed for the door, unable to stop myself from looking into Bree's room as we passed. She had on a silk robe, courtesy of the hotel, and was bent over putting on lotion. I groaned as I watched her run her fingers up her thigh. Before I could see any more, Dash was pulling me to the door and shoving me through it.

"No," he said, pushing me against the wall.

"What are you talking about?"

"No boinking the client."

"Get your hands off me," I snapped, tearing his hands from my shoulders. "I don't know what you're talking about."

"Yeah, like we can't see it."

"See what?" I asked as we headed down the hallway.

"You know what. Do you think I didn't hear that groan as you walked past her room?"

"I was groaning because I want to get in bed and not wake up for three days."

"Yeah, it had nothing to do with her long legs or her smooth skin. No, it was the bed you were drooling over."

"It's been known to happen. I need to rub down my leg. It's bothering me."

"I'm sure Bree would be happy to put her hands on your stub and give it a good rub."

I got an image of Bree on her knees in front of me, taking off my bionic foot and rubbing lotion into my leg. From my position, I could see down her robe to her beautiful breasts. "Yeah, I'm sure that's just what every girl wants to do."

"You know I wasn't talking about your leg, right?"

I rolled my eyes and hit the button for the elevator. "Would you shut up? No one needs to hear your opinions."

"Plenty of people happen to like my opinions."

"Like Rae?" I poked.

"Hey, that woman is a she-devil."

"That woman takes great pleasure in driving you crazy." The elevator doors opened just as the second elevator rose to the same level. I stepped on and hit the button for the first floor. As the doors were closing, I saw a dinner cart being wheeled off the other elevator. I didn't think much of it until I saw the waiter sling back his coat, showing a gun at his hip.

"Shit!" I swore, trying to stop the doors from closing, but it was too late. I hit the button to open them, but nothing happened. "Call FNG. Trouble's on the way."

"Why, what did you see?"

"That waiter had a gun."

I hit the button repeatedly, but the elevator was already moving. I hit the button for the floor below, relieved when we jerked to a stop. I raced into the hallway, looking both ways before I spotted the stairs. Racing over to them, I shoved the door open and ran up one flight.

"Did you get ahold of him?"

"He's not answering!"

I flung open the door in front of me and pulled my gun as I raced down the empty hallway. I could hear a shout from down the hall and knew it was from our room. A loud thunk hit the door as we approached. I nodded to Dash as he took up a position on the other side of the door. I tried to shove the door open, but something was blocking it, most likely the dinner cart.

Glass shattered inside and Bree screamed as the destruction continued. I shoved the door with my shoulder, but made it no further inside. Stepping back, I kicked hard at the door, but it only gave an inch.

"Bree!" I shouted, hoping she could get to the door and move the cart.

"Thumper! Help!"

"Bree, get to the door!"

She screamed again and my heart kicked into overdrive. If we didn't get in there, it was likely someone wouldn't be going home with us. Together, Dash and I both charged the door repeatedly. On the fifth try, the door finally gave way enough for me to slip through. The cart was wedged into the hallway bathroom, splintered from us pushing the door into it.

I grabbed the cart and shoved it down the hall and out of our way. The room was a mess, completely trashed from whoever FNG was fighting in the corner. Bree was crouched in the corner, shaking and scared, but unharmed from what I could tell.

I couldn't get a clean shot as FNG grappled with the intruder, so I did the only thing I could. I charged forward and tackled the man from behind. His elbow shot out, but I quickly dodged it as I pulled him off FNG and flung him across the room. He only stayed down for seconds as FNG stumbled out of the corner, looking a little worse for wear. Then I heard the rumbling of the cart. I spun around just in time to see

Dash rushing forward with the cart, straight toward the floor-to-ceiling windows.

The man looked up for a second, his eyes calculating what was about to happen. But just as it looked like it was all over for him, FNG stumbled over, not seeing what Dash was doing.

"You son of a—"

His voice cut off as the man grabbed him and pulled him toward the window. It was too late to stop the momentum of the cart. I saw the surprise on FNG's face as he realized what was about to happen. I ran forward, hoping to grab onto him, but it was too late. The cart crashed into both of them and shoved them through the window.

"Oh shit!" FNG shouted, his voice echoing as he fell backward through the shattered glass.

I leapt forward and tried to grab onto something, getting the corner of the tablecloth. I was surprised when it jerked in my grasp, pulling me to the floor. I quickly swiveled from my belly to my butt, pressing my foot to the window frame for support.

"Dash!"

"I'm on it!" he shouted.

Together, we pulled the tablecloth up, praying that it was FNG and not whoever tried to kill him. "FNG! Tell me that's you!"

"Fuck, it's me. Get me inside! You have no idea how terrifying this is!"

"I thought you liked the idea of almost dying!" I shouted, hoping to keep his mind in a positive light.

"This is a little closer than I'd like at the moment."

I heaved with all my might until finally, we could see his hands just outside the window.

"You got it?" Dash asked.

"Got it."

He let go and rushed forward, holding out his hand for FNG. When he let go of the tablecloth, I released it and laid on my belly to help pull him up. With a few heaves, we finally had him inside. The tablecloth caught in the wind, fluttering down to the screaming below.

I collapsed on the ground with the rest of them, breathing hard as I considered just how close that was. "I think we need to find a different hotel."

"How did he find us?" FNG asked.

I shook my head. I was baffled by it. "Maybe he was tracking us all along."

"A secondary hitter at Arches?" Dash wondered.

"Possibly." I shoved off the ground and dusted the glass off my clothes. There was food scattered on the ground, and when I saw the steak, I picked it up and bit into it. "God, that's good."

"Is there any salad?" FNG asked.

"Only if you like it mixed with glass."

Dash grabbed his own steak and gnawed on it. "Mm, so fucking good. How did they prepare it in time?"

"I don't think this is our order, but I don't fucking care."

I heard whimpering coming from the corner and realized that my growling stomach would have to take a back seat to the terrified woman I had sworn to protect. I walked over, kneeling in front of her.

"Hey, it's okay."

She didn't say anything, but she didn't have to. The shaking of her body was all I needed to know she was not okay, and wouldn't be any time soon.

"Bree, we have to get out of here."

"He just went out the window."

"I know."

"No," she shook her head. "I mean, he flew out the window. And he grabbed New Guy. Why would he do that?"

"Because it's the easiest way to kill someone."

"But...he could have moved, but he didn't. He..."

"Yeah, I know."

Her eyes finally locked with mine. "You know? A man just voluntarily went out the window, and you know?" Her voice was getting hysterical, and we needed to get the hell out of here.

"Bree, we can't help what he did. For now, we need to move."

"Yeah," she snorted. "We need to move, because more men will come after us. Or maybe women. Women will come after me and try to kill me because I'm with you."

"I know, but—"

"There is no reason I should be here. I need to go home. I need to get my purse and get the hell out of here. This is insane," she said, stomping away from me. *"You're* insane!" she spat as she spun back around.

It was clear there would be no calming her down anytime soon. She was too hysterical to see a way out of this. I looked at Dash, who nodded. I hated to do it, but we had to move. I walked up behind her and quickly put her in a sleeper hold. Dash winced as he watched her face, but she dropped off in my arms in no time.

"Yeah, I don't think you're getting laid after that."

"I wasn't planning on it," I snapped at Dash, swinging her up in my arms. "We're leaving," I barked, turning to the guys.

Dash looked at his steak with a sadness only a desperately hungry man could appreciate. He took one last bite and tossed it on the ground before grabbing my bag and tossing it over his shoulder.

"That's okay!" FNG shouted. "I'm good to walk. I mean, my legs are shaky as hell, and I think I have a blister on my hand from catching the tablecloth as I fell, but I'll be alright."

"Let's go!" I shouted over my shoulder.

"Yeah, yeah. I'm coming."

Bree was knocked out, her head buried against my chest as we stepped off the elevator. The looks we received were only amplified by the sirens wailing outside. I didn't bother waiting to see if the police would stop us. Cash would have to deal with them. Dash shoved open the door at the end of the hall, opposite the lobby. We took the stairs down to the garage and quickly made it to the car. Normally, I would sit up front, but with Bree passed out in my arms, I knew there was no way I was letting her go.

"Get the door," I said to Dash, who ran around me to open it. He pulled the seat forward, allowing me to slide into the back. It was cramped in the back compared to the minivan, but would have to do.

"Bree?" I checked to make sure she was still out of it. When she didn't answer, relief flooded me. "Get us on the road," I snapped at Dash as he and FNG got in the front. "We need to be at Jones's place by tonight."

"No problem there. I'll be glad to see the back of this place," Dash grumbled as he shifted into drive.

"Yeah, because it was so horrible for you as your teammate shoved a cart into you and pushed you out a window," FNG grumbled.

"Not now!" I snapped.

My protective instincts kicked into overdrive with Bree passed out in my lap. As much as she annoyed me, tonight was a glaring example of just how far removed she was from our world. When we escaped the assassin the first time, she only felt that from a distance. God only knows what exactly she went through tonight. I was positive FNG kept her safe and out of the grips of the assassin, but that didn't mean she walked away unscathed.

I pulled out my phone and dialed Cash's number. He would know the second he got my call that something was wrong. I wasn't supposed to check in until we reached Jones's place.

"What happened?"

"We were attacked no more than ten minutes after we got off the phone with you."

"How many?"

"One hitter. There's a mess to clean up."

"I expected that."

"It's very public. He went out the window with FNG. Luckily, he's still alive."

"Well, he's FNG, so he can't die."

"Thank God that's true," I muttered. "We're on the road again."

"Any idea how he spotted you?"

"He must have been at Moab. We didn't see anyone following us, but it's the only thing I can think of."

"And you're clear now?"

"As far as I can tell. We just hit the road, so I guess we'll find out soon enough."

"How are you on supplies?"

"They're dwindling. If we get hit again, we're fucked."

133

"And Bree?"

I glanced down at her, glad she wasn't awake to yell at Cash over the phone. "Surviving."

"That doesn't sound reassuring."

I didn't have anything else to offer. We were doing the best we could under the circumstances, though probably a little more lax than we should have been. I had somewhat assumed that we were in the clear when we left Moab. I knew now that wasn't true.

"Any luck on finding out who's after us?"

"Fox should be arriving in Pennsylvania soon. Hopefully, he'll be able to get some answers for us."

"And the guys?"

"Still combing through old records. So far, we're not finding anything to suggest who's after you."

That was disappointing to say the least. "Alright, let me know if that changes."

"Will do."

"I'll send IRIS and Slider to meet you. Do me a favor…"

"Don't let IRIS blow anything up," I said with a laugh. "Yeah, I got that."

I hung up and sighed, leaning my head back in the seat. The lights faded as we left the city, and the darkness filled the car. It was a dangerous position to be in, with hardly any weapons at our disposal, we were unlikely to survive if attacked. But I'd go down fighting, defending Bree with everything in me. She was innocent in all this. And despite being a royal pain in the ass, nobody deserved to get dragged into this shit.

"We have headlights coming up on us," Dash said, his eyes glued to the rearview mirror.

I looked over my shoulder, out the back window, and cursed when I saw how fast they were coming.

Bree groaned in my arms, just in time for another adventure to terrify the shit out of her.

"Um…Bree? Can you hear me?"

"What happened?" she grumbled, pushing off of me. "Why am I in your lap?"

"You passed out," I said quickly, hoping she didn't remember anything.

"But…why are we…" She caught me glancing over her shoulder and turned to look out the window. "Who's that?"

"Um…probably no one," I lied. "A fast driver."

She stared at me with a complete lack of amusement. "Are you seriously lying to me right now?"

"I was hoping you wouldn't notice."

"Is it completely impossible to go five minutes without someone else trying to kill us?"

FNG spun around in his seat. "Technically, it's been over fifteen minutes."

"That's not helpful," I spat, though I quite agreed.

"What are we going to do?"

"Don't worry," FNG grinned at her. "I'm awesome in a car chase. This one time, I totally escaped after a rocket was launched at my car. And Johnny—well, you don't know him, but he was out on top of the other guy's roof. If he had only taken my umbrella, things might have ended a little faster—"

"Would you shut the fuck up? We're not fighting with umbrellas!" I shouted.

He frowned, holding up his compact umbrella. "So, I can't use this?"

I growled at him in frustration. Was it too much to ask for a normal team? I missed IRIS's antics and Slider's witty charm.

"How much ammo do you have left?" I asked them as I checked my own weapon. Six bullets. That wasn't much, and it would have to last until we reached Jones.

"I have one magazine," Dash said.

"I have the umbrella." I glared at him, but he shrugged. "I have no ammo. What do you want me to use? I guess I could beat him to death with my gun, but the umbrella is longer."

I rolled my eyes and tried to figure out a plan. "We need to get off the main road."

"We might have better luck if we stay on the main road. A car accident won't be nearly as suspicious as a body in the middle of the desert," FNG pointed out.

"At what cost? We can't risk anyone else getting hurt."

"I'm just saying, a run-in with a semi could be very convincing, but fine, we'll do it your way."

I checked our tail again, sighing when I saw this asshole was already closing in. "Get us off this road, Dash!"

"I'm on it. Keep your foot on."

"My foot is about to be up your ass."

"How does that work exactly?" he asked as he took a hard right, causing the back end of the car to swerve wildly on the road. "If you wiggle your foot, do the pleasure sensors go off and give you a hard-on?"

"You're fucking disgusting."

"You suggested it."

The car sped up behind us until he was riding just beside our back tire. "Hang on!" I shouted as I saw him get ready to hit us. As predicted, he yanked the wheel, sending us onto the shoulder before Dash regained control. "FNG, now would be the time to get out that umbrella."

"I thought you didn't want me to use the umbrella!" he shouted.

"Do something!"

"You can't just whip it out anytime you want. There's a moment when you know."

The other car slammed into us again. I braced myself around Bree as she whimpered beneath me. We both went flying sideways, but she was held in by her belt.

Dash gripped the wheel and jerked it hard toward the other car. We were locked, racing down the road with both cars pushing against each other.

"Use the fucking umbrella!" Bree screamed when the tension of the situation reached a fever pitch.

"Fine! Dash, put down the top! I'm stepping outside!"

"You're what?" Bree screeched.

"Don't forget your umbrella," I said mockingly.

"Oh, I've got it," he grinned as the top rolled back. "You know, I was thinking I need a theme song," he shouted as the wind whipped around him. "I really like that AC/DC song from *Iron Man*!"

"You're not Iron Man!"

"I know, but—whoa!" he shouted as the car swerved and he leapt from the car. His voice echoed in the distance as we sped off into the night.

16

BREE

I sat up with a start, staring at the spot where New Guy just stood. My hair whipped around me, slapping at my face as Dash hit the gas and catapulted us forward. "What about New Guy?" I shouted to Thumper.

"He's fine. Probably."

I stared at him in shock. "But...you can't just leave him!"

"We haven't," he chuckled, staring out into the night.

The other car was further behind, but started picking up speed. I could see two outlines fighting in the dark. The other man was in a convertible also, and all I could imagine was the car flipping and both of them being crushed into the ground.

"Here we go," Dash called out. "Get ready for it."

"Ready for what?" I asked.

"Whatever New Guy has planned," Thumper retorted.

"Hey, guys!" New Guy shouted, honking the horn as he fought off the driver. He pulled up alongside us with the driver's side on our passenger side. "I don't think this one's an assassin!"

"What?" Thumper shouted, squinting into the night.

"Yeah, I don't think he's an assassin."

The driver pulled a gun, aiming it at us. I watched as New Guy's eyes went wide and he jerked the wheel to stop the guy from shooting us.

"Never mind! Maybe he is," New Guy called. "Don't you know that shooting people is wrong?" he yelled at the guy.

I watched in horror as the man shoved his thumb into New Guy's eye. It was absolutely disgusting and the most graphic thing I'd ever seen. Thumper handed his gun over to Dash and climbed into the front seat.

"Get me closer. I'll help him out."

"Wait!" I grabbed the back of his shirt, preventing him from going anywhere. "You can't just jump out of the car!"

"Why not? FNG did it."

"But he's crazy!"

He quirked his lips at me. "Sweetheart, we're all a little crazy."

Then he leapt out of the car, slamming into the outside of the car when the driver jerked the wheel away from our car. I gasped as Thumper clung to the side of the car for dear life, grappling to get inside. The man swerved closer to our car, trying to crush him between the two vehicles.

"Thumper, look out!" I shouted, terrified that I was about to witness a deadly crash.

New Guy started beating the man with his umbrella, but the driver quickly snatched it and tossed it out of the car. It landed in our front seat with a thud, leaving New Guy without a weapon.

"Aren't you going to do something?"

"I am," Dash answered. "I'm driving."

"But what about them?" I shouted.

He glanced over and shrugged. "They look like they have it under control."

"Thumper is hanging out of the back of the car!" I said as the man swerved from side to side, making Thumper fall just as he was about to climb into the back seat.

"Yeah...What's your point?"

With a huff, I turned back to the action, my heart pounding as I watched these two men battled it out as Dash drove without a care in the world. The car swerved toward us again, the front end ramming into our back end. I slammed into the back of the seat, then glared at the man trying to kill Thumper.

The driver pulled a gun and aimed it right at me. Our eyes connected for just a moment, and the glint in his eyes was pure evil. A small smile made his lips twitch, which sent me over the edge. I grabbed the umbrella from the front seat and swung as hard as I could at the man as he pulled alongside us again.

"Stop," I swung the umbrella and hit him in the arm, "trying to murder me and my friends!" I continued to shout as I hit him repeatedly in the hand. He kept trying to ram into us, and just as Thumper jumped into the back seat, he rammed us again, nearly catching Thumper's leg in the process. I sat up and reared back, stabbing the umbrella into the car at the driver. It glanced off him and hit New Guy in the face.

"My eye! She fucking stabbed me in the eye!"

"Sorry!" I called as I hit the man again.

"With my own fucking umbrella! I can't believe this shit!"

Thumper attacked him from behind as I continued to beat the driver with the umbrella. I wasn't attacking out of a need to get involved or because I was some badass. I was just tired of being shot at. When would this all end?

"You will not,"—thwack—"murder me or anyone else,"—thwack— "today! I did nothing wrong!"—thwack—"I am a good person!"— thwack—"I pay my taxes!"—thwack—"I recycle and separate my bins like you're supposed to!"—thwack—"And I give to charity!" —thwack—

I hit him a few more times before I realized that he was already passed out and New Guy was trying to get him out of the seat so he could drive the car. Thumper grabbed my umbrella on the last hit, trying to stop me from doing any more damage. Or maybe he was just annoyed with me.

I was shaking when I finally sat down in my seat. I held my umbrella tight to my chest as Dash pulled the car over to stop where New Guy was directing the other car. My breaths were coming out in harsh pants as I replayed what just happened.

But then strong arms were grabbing me, hauling me up. Warm lips crashed down on mine and everything I was so worried about fled from my mind as tingles raced down my spine. Thumper's scent filled my senses and his touch made me melt as his hand spread across my back, filling me with warmth. I whimpered as he deepened the kiss. Everything in me calmed, but then his tongue slipped inside my mouth making everything in my body kick into overdrive. Just as I was about to slide my hand around his neck, he broke the kiss, pulling back just enough to look me in the eyes.

"What...was that?" I choked out.

"A distraction," he murmured. "You were losing your shit."

The fog from the kiss lifted and embarrassment flooded me. He didn't kiss me because he wanted to, but to stop me from freaking out. I responded out of humiliation, slamming my umbrella into his arms. He flinched back, looking at me like I was crazy.

"You're an ass," I snapped.

"And you're a psycho bitch, but we'll get back to that at another time. Are you hurt?"

"Hurt? Now you ask, after you kiss me?"

"Are you hurt?" he repeated.

"I'm fine. I didn't need you to kiss me. I was just fine," I repeated.

"Sure looked like you were enjoying that kiss," Dash chuckled.

Maybe that was true, but the last thing I needed was to be coddled. When a man kissed me, it had better be without ulterior motives.

Thumper took a step back, watching me with a wary expression. "You're not going to hit me with that again, are you?"

I narrowed my eyes at him.

"Bree, hand over the umbrella."

He reached for it, but I jerked it away from him. There was something about this umbrella that brought me comfort. It wasn't a gun, but it had protected me in my hour of need. "Don't touch it."

Thumper backed off with his hands in the air. New Guy came walking around the car, holding his eye as he glared at me with the other. "Why the hell did you hit me in the eye?"

"I was trying to hit him!" I pointed at the man in the front seat of the other car.

141

He grinned at me, despite his swollen eye. "I knew you had it in you. You're a fighter."

"I am not a fighter," I snapped. "I don't want to be here. I don't want to see another gun. I just want to go home!"

"But you attacked him."

"Because he was pointing a gun at me. He tried to kill me!"

"Bree, he tried to kill all of us," Dash said plainly.

My gaze snapped to his. "He pointed that gun at me. I saw it in his eyes. He wanted to kill me."

"Yeah, well, a hitman doesn't get paid unless he does the job."

Thumper pulled out his phone as he stomped over to the car. Grabbing the man by the hair, he lifted his head and snapped a picture. Then he took his thumb and scanned it into his phone. "Give it a minute," he muttered.

I frowned, not understanding. "What are we waiting for?"

His cell phone rang and he answered, putting it on speakerphone. "Jesus, how many men are you going to kill tonight?"

"As many as they send. I don't see any other headlights in the distance, so I'm hoping we lost them finally. If the next one is a sniper, we're goat fucked. All that stands between them and us is an umbrella."

"New Guy?"

"Bree," he responded, sounding almost proud.

"I don't want to know. How long until you get to Jones's place?"

"At least a few more hours. If we make it to then, we'll give you a call."

"Watch your six."

"It's not my six I'm worried about," Thumper grumbled as he hung up his phone.

"So...what happens now?" I asked after a few minutes of silence.

"Now we get the hell out of here."

Thumper hopped in the back seat with me as New Guy sat up front. I crossed my arms over my chest with my umbrella wedged between me and the side of the car. Dash turned around to say something, but Thumper cut him off with just a look.

"Alright, never mind. We'll drive on," he said, turning back around.

New Guy turned and glared at me. "You know, it's not right, beating a man with his own umbrella."

I wasn't sure how it happened, but I fell asleep during the drive. With all that had happened, I never thought I would drift off like I had, but maybe it was the adrenaline crash that took me down. When I woke up, there was no one chasing us, and I was entirely too comfortable.

I shifted slightly, realizing too late that I wasn't sitting upright, but laying down on Thumper's lap. His fingers were combing aimlessly through my hair, and he had to know I was awake, but he didn't bother to stop. I laid there for a few minutes, trying to figure out what to do about this situation. Thumper had kissed me. I could still feel the zinging sensation on my lips from when his warmth encapsulated me.

I knew it was wrong to feel anything for him. He'd only shown hatred toward me since we met, but somehow, I was developing some-thing close to feelings for him. Maybe it was the kiss, or maybe it was the deadly encounters we kept having. Either way, it was no good for either of us. We led two very different lives, and it was clear I would never fit into his.

The way all of them so callously took life, as if they didn't care about the consequences, really put me on edge. Then again, they didn't go out looking for people to kill. They sort of just fell in our path. But that was another reason I couldn't handle this life. That man tried to kill me, and I had no idea why. Wrong place, wrong time was what Thumper said, but this felt different. He had looked at me like he wanted to kill me. That kind of evil was something I'd never experienced before.

"What are you thinking?" Thumper asked quietly as we sped down the road.

I shrugged, not willing to get up and face the facts of what was happening. I was comfortable laying on his lap, and if I stayed here, I could pretend for a few more minutes that I was in bed and everything was fine. The way his fingers played with my hair soothed me, and maybe that's why he was doing it.

"Not too much longer and we'll be at our next stop."

"Does it have a bed?"

"Yes."

"And a shower?"

"I would hope so," he chuckled.

"And nobody will be shooting at us?"

He didn't answer immediately on that one, telling me all I really needed to know. The danger was far from over, and he couldn't promise me that we would be safe.

I finally sat up with a sigh. There was no point in pretending that I wasn't in this world. Whatever happened, I had to face it head-on. "So, what's going to happen to that guy?"

"Someone will find him," Thumper said after a moment.

"Was he dead?"

His gaze shifted to mine, but his eyes were unreadable. "Yes."

I felt like he was waiting for my response, to see if I would lose it again. And while I was sure under normal circumstances I would get hysterical, I just didn't have it in me right at this minute. So, I nodded.

We remained quiet as the sun rose in the distance. All around us, there was nothing but desert and tumbleweeds. I wasn't sure what state we were in or where we were headed. I know we started out heading west yesterday, but we turned north and headed to Salt Lake City. That was where New Guy almost fell to his death at the hotel. But now? I didn't care where we were as long as no one was immediately trying to kill us.

"Did you sleep?"

"No time to sleep," he muttered, staring out the window.

"But no one followed us."

"We're safe."

I didn't miss the *for now* that he said without saying. I sighed, wondering how my life had come to this. A week ago, I was perfectly happy in my normal financial world. Now, I was camping in a yurt, fighting off Bighorn Sheep, and running from psychos. Oh yeah, and I was beating people with umbrellas.

Speaking of which...I grabbed my umbrella and held it tight, feeling relieved now that it was in my hands again.

"Are you planning on taking that everywhere with you?" Thumper asked.

"It's a useful weapon," I answered, hating that I was speaking about weapons in such a blasé way.

He chuckled slightly, shaking his head. "I never thought I would hear you talking about weapons."

"I never thought I would have a gun pointed in my face so many times in one day."

"Touché."

FNG turned around in his seat, looking at me inquisitively. "So, does this mean there's a stalemate between you two?"

"What do you mean?"

"You know, because you're having a civil conversation."

"I'm normally a pretty civil person."

His face scrunched up comically. "Really?" He shook his head with a laugh. "You seemed like a bitch to me."

"Hey!" Thumper snapped, jumping to my defense, much to my surprise. "Don't be a dick."

But that didn't stop FNG from grinning and continuing. "See, I knew you'd come around to her. You tried to pretend you didn't like her, but then you kissed her."

"Because she was hysterical."

I really hated being called hysterical, even if that's what had happened. And I liked even less that Thumper willingly admitted that he only kissed me because of it. I knew we weren't a good match. We were so different, but that didn't mean that elements of attraction didn't count for anything. I was good-looking, and I knew it. I just didn't use it to my advantage. I didn't want people to assume that because I was pretty I didn't have a brain. Maybe that gave me a bit of a rough exterior, but how else was I supposed to get ahead in a man's world?

"You can't fool us," Dash laughed. "It was bound to happen. The moment you made that big declaration, we all knew you were fucked."

"What is he talking about?"

145

"Nothing," Thumper bit out.

"He was at work, telling us all that he was tired of all the women we brought home."

"Dash!" Thumper snapped.

"What? You don't want her to know?"

"Know what?" I asked curiously.

"It's alright, man. We all knew it would happen. FNG and I could see it a mile away."

"See what?" I was getting frustrated with all this secretive talk, especially when I thought it concerned me.

"We should call your sister," Thumper said suddenly, pulling out his phone.

"My...what's going on?"

"Nothing," he answered gruffly.

"How do you know about my sister?"

He shot me an irritated look. "Just call her."

"I...um..."

"What?"

"I don't know her number."

"How do you not know her number?"

"It's saved in the phone so I don't have to."

The look on his face made me wince. If ever I felt like an imbecile, it was now. "So, if you lose your phone and need to call someone, you don't have anyone's number memorized."

"I know the office number," I answered sheepishly.

"Well, that's fucking great. While you're off getting shot at, I'm sure your boss will send for help."

"Like my sister would?" I shot back.

"She's your family. I thought you would want her to know you're okay."

"And that you have a boyfriend," FNG said from the front.

"Shut up!" we both shouted at him.

"Believe it or not, my sister and I aren't exactly close."

"Bullshit, you've called her three times in the last week."

I was baffled by how much he knew about me. "How...are you spying on me?"

"Do you need to be spied on? Is she not really your sister?"

"Who else would she be?"

"I don't know. Why are you so concerned about me knowing about her?"

"Because they were private phone calls!" I yelled, ready to smack him upside the head. "Last I checked, those are not public record. And I'm not even sure how you would have time to check a public record when we've been shot at every five minutes over the past day!"

"I know about them because I'm supposed to know about them!" he yelled at me, snatching the phone out of my hands.

I stared at him in disbelief as he dialed a number and then put it on speakerphone. When my sister picked up, I almost smacked him with my umbrella.

"You knew her number! Were you testing me?"

"Bree?" my sister said.

"It's part of—"

"My job," I finished for him. "Wow, you just wanted to know if I knew her number."

"Um...Bree? Are you trying to talk to me?"

"No, I just thought you would find it creepy if I called her without asking for her number. I was trying to give you privacy."

"You were trying to conceal that you snooped through my records!" I said, stabbing my finger at him.

"This is going to end well," Dash muttered.

"Bree, who is that? Are these the guys you were telling me about?"

FNG spun around in his seat. "You told your sister about us? Did you tell her about me? I'm very likable."

"She married!" I snapped.

"Not that you would know," Grace snorted.

"Is everyone ganging up on me today?" I cried.

"I just wanted you to call her and let her know you're safe," Thumper answered.

"Safe," I scoffed. I held up my umbrella, shaking it at him. "You call this safe? I beat an assassin with an umbrella!"

"I told you it's an excellent weapon," New Guy answered.

"Whoa, an assassin? I thought you ran from him?"

"Her," Thumper clarified. "We blew her up."

"Yes, but she had a very nice resting place at the bottom of a cliff," New Guy added.

"And you didn't get boob sweat on you," Dash grumbled.

"Boob sweat?" Grace asked. "I'm sorry, what's going on here?"

I glared at Thumper, pissed that I let him seep his way under my skin. "I can't believe I let you kiss me."

"What?" Grace shouted.

"It wasn't enjoyable for me either, sweetheart."

"I'm a great kisser!" I shot back.

"Who did you kiss? I need names!" Grace shouted.

"I wish someone would kiss me," New Guy grumbled. "Everywhere I turn, someone's kissing or having sex."

"Maybe it's the way you say *sure*," Dash muttered. "At least if you talk to Fox, it is."

"I doubt it's that. Why don't women like me? I'm a lovable guy."

"You know, the next time someone is trying to kill you, I'm going to tuck my umbrella away and watch with glee."

"If you're not hiding in a corner," Thumper snapped.

"Excuse me for not going around killing people!"

"Alright, I just want to point out that I'm really confused!" Grace shouted.

"You can thank your sister for that!" Thumper shouted. "She doesn't know what she wants! She goes on vacation, but doesn't know how to hike. She gets a yurt, but doesn't know how to camp. She packs fucking silk underwear in the desert! And when a guy kisses her, she has to dissect every second of why he kissed her!"

"So, you kissed her," Grace guessed.

"These lips aren't coming anywhere near you ever again!" Thumper shouted, turning away from me.

"Good, I didn't want them by me to begin with!" I turned with a huff and stared out the window.

Dash laughed under his breath. "You could cut the sexual tension in this car with a saw."

I rolled my eyes and ignored all of them. They could shove their protection up their asses. And Thumper could save his kisses for someone that actually wanted them. He wasn't that good of a kisser anyway.

I sighed, knowing I was lying to myself. I just had to survive until this assassin was found, and then I could leave these men behind.

"Um...hello?" Grace called out. "I'm really confused as to what's happening...hello?"

17

FOX

"Now, I don't want you to be intimidated when you meet the Kamau. He's a very prolific figure in my life."

I hit the blinker to take the exit to the small town where Reed Security was located. Man, just being this close to him again was a dream come true.

"Why would I be intimidated?" Eva asked.

"Well…he's the Kamau. You heard me say that, right?"

"I heard, but I don't see what that has to do with anything."

"It literally means silent warrior." I glanced at her, wondering if she had a brain injury and didn't understand what I was saying. "He's like…me, but with a lot more darkness."

"I find that hard to believe," she snorted.

"Hey, I've got lots of light in me. I like show tunes…I'm a chipper guy…ooh, I like Funyuns. Tell me one thing about Funyuns that would say I'm dark."

"Well, it does give you bad breath."

I cupped my hand over my mouth and blew. "Really? Anna's never said anything."

"Fox, it's a snack that tastes like onions. Of course it's going to give you bad breath."

"Well, I doubt the Kamau cares. He likes me for my skills."

"And what is your plan for talking to him?"

"Well, clearly, he's going to play it all hardass because he can't appear to like anyone. That's why he keeps returning my postcards."

"Of course," she nodded, but I got the feeling she didn't believe me.

"Normally, I would suggest we have some kind of bonding moment. Maybe we could kill someone together, but he's trying to turn over a new leaf for his girl."

"And I'm pretty sure Anna wouldn't like you killing someone just to bond with your idol."

"Probably not. Then I thought, maybe we could watch a musical together, but I don't know that there's one dark enough for him."

"I doubt you'll get his attention with *Oklahoma*," she smirked at me.

"People just don't understand the beauty in it. But I still have a trick or two up my sleeve."

"Care to fill me in?"

I rolled my eyes at her. "I already know Cash is listening in on this conversation." I stared at the button on her coat and waved. "Hello! I know you can hear me!"

"He's not there. That's literally a button."

"Right, like I'm going to fall for that. There's no way Cash would let you out of his sight with me unless he was monitoring both of us."

"And you think he settled on a button?"

"Of course not. He's got a camera in my mirror, a tracking device on both of us, the vehicle is rigged by Dash, no doubt. And I would guess there are at least a half dozen listening devices on your person and in the truck."

"And yet you still say all of this without a care in the world."

"If he didn't trust you with me, he wouldn't have let you come," I said as I hit my blinker and turned toward the gated property. A guard stepped out and asked me for my ID. When he saw the throwing knives attached to my thigh and the gun at my hip, he immediately pulled his weapon.

"Sir, I'm going to have to ask you to step out of the vehicle."

I sighed heavily. "Yeah, I figured. Can you do me a favor and let the Kamau know I'm here?"

"Sir, just step out." Another guard walked around the truck and opened Eva's door, pulling her out with just a tad too much glee. I quickly spun and pulled my knife, holding it against the man's neck as I walked him around the back of the truck. "Take your fucking hands off her," I demanded.

The man was nearly as fast, pulling his own weapon and pointing it at Eva's head. I smirked at him with glee. "That was a bad decision."

For just a split second, I made eye contact with Eva. Then I whipped my knife at the baddie holding her, lodging my knife right in his throat. At precisely the same time, a knife sliced through the man I was holding, courtesy of Eva. He dropped to the ground, still alive but bleeding out.

"Nice work."

She shrugged. "I learned from the best. But I'm not sure how this is going to get us an audience with Knight."

"Oh, ye of little faith."

The loudspeaker squeaked before Sebastian's voice rang out around us. "Fox, there was no need to kill my guards."

"Only one is dead," I answered. "And he shouldn't have touched Cash's woman."

"And I suppose you think I should let you inside now."

"I need to talk to Knight."

"Of course you do."

"And this guy out here could probably use some medical attention. The other one just needs a body bag."

"He was new," Sebastian said in defense of the poorly trained guard.

"I would vet them further before you allow them to defend your property."

"I knew you were coming. That was me vetting them."

I grinned and swirled my hand in the air, letting him know he needed to open the gate. When a buzzer sounded and the gate clicked open, Eva and I hopped back inside the truck and drove through. The building was impressive, but needed a few upgrades, in my opinion. It would be too easy to attack.

I pulled into the parking garage and we headed to the elevators. Sebastian was already waiting for us with a wry smile on his face.

"So, you need to see Knight." He studied my outfit and frowned. "That jacket looks familiar."

"It's his. He gave it to me because I'm such a big fan."

"That doesn't sound like him."

"Oh, no. It's completely true. When I was guarding him, I tried on his coat and boots, and he just gave them to me. I was so stoked."

He stared at me with one eyebrow quirked, then turned to Eva. "It's good to see you again."

"You too."

"I see your skills have grown since you were out here last time."

"Fox has been training me," she said proudly, and I couldn't help the grin that was plastered on my face.

"She's sort of my protegé."

"And how does Cash feel about that?"

"How does he feel about what? The fact that his fiancé is safe? I'd say he's pretty fucking happy."

"I have one of my own. She's...grenade happy."

"Ooh," I snapped my fingers. "We should introduce her to IRIS. They'd have a blast." Then I burst out laughing. "Get it, because they like to blow stuff up?"

"Yeah, I got it," he said, not finding what I said humorous at all. "Anyway, Knight's in the training center."

"Cool."

We followed him into the elevators and I took in all his security measures. It wasn't bad at all, though an underground bunker seemed wiser. But I wasn't here to hand out trade secrets. When the doors opened, we headed down the hall to the training center, which was filled with new recruits, by the look of things. I felt bad for the man. Such a skilled killer reduced to training the incoming newbies.

"Knight!" Sebastian shouted.

The man—the legend—turned and sighed when he saw me. Of course, he had to act like that. He could never let on just how alike we were, or the fact that he liked me. It would be bad for his reputation. So, when he stalked over to me, glaring at the coat I was wearing, I took it as a sign of affection.

"Kamau! It's great to see you. This is Eva, Cash's lady love."

Knight stared at me, not bothering to look at Eva.

I cleared my throat and leaned in closer. "Cash is watching, so I wouldn't recommend insulting the man."

His eyes flicked to Eva ever so slightly, and he nodded before glaring at me again. "What the fuck do you want?"

"Get down to business. I gotcha. We have an issue. Do you have any Funyuns, by chance?"

"Your issue is you need Funyuns?"

"No, but I could do with some. You know, build up the effect of it all."

Knight's shoulder's bunched and his fists clenched as he bit back his anger. Man, I loved this guy.

"We don't have Funyuns," Sebastian answered.

"No, that's cool. I mean, they're a delicious treat, but not everyone has excellent taste. Not you," I rushed on. "You're the Kamau. It was thanks to you that I got my lady back. Yeah," I nodded. "When you tried to give us the slip, I followed you back here and watched you watching Kate that night. Well, I'm sure there were many nights, but that night really struck me right here," I said, pounding my fist over my heart. "That's the night I left and went back to Anna to win her back. I owe you big time, man."

He stared at me with a bored expression. "Great."

"Anyway, so the reason I'm here is that we have an issue."

"*You* have an issue. The only issue I have is that you're standing in front of me."

I winked at him. "And the recruits you have to sort through. They're definitely more of a pain in the ass."

"That's debatable."

"Knight," Sebastian warned. "Play nice."

"Oh, it's cool. He and I are like this," I said, holding up my crossed fingers. "It's a thing."

"It's not a thing," Knight retorted.

"It's sort of a thing," I nodded.

"The only way it's a thing is if I'm shoving a knife in your gut. Then, we're like this," he said, holding up his crossed fingers. "And I'm on top."

I snorted out a laugh. "You make it sound so dirty. God, I love you, man."

"The feeling isn't mutual."

"See what I mean?" I asked Sebastian. "The man is just...magical."

"If you say so."

"Anyway, one of our guys, Thumper, is on vacation and someone tried to take him out. We're thinking it's a hit."

"Wow, you're a genius," he deadpanned.

"You really don't have to flatter me."

"And you think I can help."

"Oh, I know you can. I mean, you're the Kamau. If anyone can help, it's you."

"If I wanted to help, but I don't."

"Then do it for me," Eva jumped in. "Thumper is a good guy."

"Wow, my heart is breaking for you right now."

By the tone in his voice, I was getting the feeling that he really didn't want to help us. Which was so unlike the Kamau. "This is a good cause. And you're all about the good cause."

"Right now, I'm all about the promises I made to my wife. That doesn't include helping out strangers and men that think we're besties."

The frown on my face was growing by the moment. Something happened between the last time I saw this man and now. He was jaded or something. "What the fuck happened to you? Kamau is the silent warrior that fights the good fight. You help the downtrodden and take risks for the greater good. Kamau is not selfish. This," I waved at his body, "is not the man I know."

Knight rolled his eyes at me with a heavy sigh. "Fine, I'll see what I can find."

A grin split my face as I grabbed him and pulled him in for a hug. "Man, I knew it was all an act. There's no way the Kamau wouldn't get involved when it's one of your own."

"He's not one of my own."

"He sort of is," I countered.

"He's not at all."

"But if you think about it, he is. You were shot. He had his foot blown off. You're dark and dangerous, and he's got dark hair and he's muscular. He likes robotic feet. You're good with robotics," I listed off.

He quirked an eyebrow at Eva. "Have you thought of having him seen by someone?"

"We did. It's you," Eva grinned. "Congratulations on the new appointment. Oh, and he loves the boots."

"I do, man. And the same size. I told you it was meant to be."

"Yes," Knight narrowed his eyes at me. "It was the shoe size that brought us together."

I pointed at him as Eva started pulling me away. "That and the shawarma. Tell me you loved it." He stared at me, not giving in. Man, I loved this guy. "It's you and me, Kamau! Until the end of time!"

I turned and walked away with Eva, laughing at how perfect that all was. Eva didn't find it nearly as funny.

"You need to learn to read the room."

"What, that? Kamau is like that because he has to be. He can't ever show weakness. It's not in his nature."

"I'll give you this, you certainly have a way of getting people to do what you want."

"With the Kamau, you just have to speak his language."

"Yeah, that's what you were doing," Eva said as we headed to the elevator. Cash joined us and pressed his hand to the sensor.

"You're lucky he didn't kill you."

"Me?" I pointed at my chest. "It'll never happen. The Kamau only works for the greater good."

"Keep telling yourself that," he said as he stepped onto the elevator.

THUMPER

"THANK GOD," I groaned when we pulled down Jones's driveway. I laughed when I saw IRIS step out from behind a bush and Slider walk out the front door. God, I missed them.

When Dash stopped, I practically shoved FNG out of his seat so I could climb out. I ran out to meet IRIS and Slider, pulling them in for a huge hug.

"You guys have no idea how happy I am to see you."

"I guess so. We don't normally get such a warm reception," IRIS said.

"You have no idea what I've been through."

Slider watched over my shoulder with interest as Bree got out. I turned and watched as Dash held her hand as she practically fell to the ground. "So, that's the woman."

I snorted. "Just wait until you meet her."

She rushed forward, pushing past us on her way to the house. "I have to pee!"

"I wouldn't just run inside!" FNG shouted. "Jones doesn't like guests!"

I heard the door slam open and Bree's squeal, but when no gunshots were fired, I assumed everything was okay.

"Not that I don't want to stand around and catch up, but I'm beat," Dash said with a yawn.

I slapped him on the shoulder in thanks. "Go to sleep. We'll wake you up if we hear anything. You too, New Guy."

"Do you think Jones has anything for this gunshot wound? I think it's getting infected."

"You don't say," I snapped as I remembered my own wound that I got courtesy of him.

Upon the reminder, he winced and walked away, heading to the house.

"It sounds like you've had a fun vacation," Slider grinned.

"You have no fucking clue. I can't believe Cash sent them after me."

"And the woman?"

I rolled my eyes, pressing the heels of my hands into them. "She's...a complete fucking pain in the ass. I don't even know why she came out here. You should have seen the pack she was carrying to hike. It was ridiculous. I fucking told her to go home the first time I saw her. And then she was bitching about her yurt and the lack of a bathroom inside. And when the sheep attacked us, she thought she would just stroll into my yurt and take over, like I didn't need my own fucking place to sleep! And don't get me started on how much she flipped out when we had to go on the run. I mean, I expected her to be scared, but she was fucking hysterical, crying and yelling about everything. None of us wanted to be with her! At one point, I kissed her just so she wouldn't flip out!" I laughed.

IRIS and Slider stared at me with knowing smirks on their faces.

"What?"

"Yeah, it sounds like you really hate her," IRIS laughed.

"Are you fucking kidding me? I'll be happy when this is over and we can drop her in New York."

"Will you?" Slider asked.

"Of course! She's not made for this shit. She's most definitely not Eva or Zoe."

"Which is what you wanted."

I shook my head at IRIS, not understanding. "What are you talking about?"

"I clearly remember you saying, and I quote 'Why couldn't you find someone that didn't care about your job?'"

"And here she is," Slider grinned.

"There's nothing about your job that she likes," IRIS added.

"And from what you said, she's not likely to join you in the desert hiking."

"Or bother you when you have to go on a job."

"She'll want you home to take out the trash," Slider grinned.

"And help with the kids."

"It's the ideal situation when you consider the women we have now."

"And you found her while out roaming the desert," IRIS laughed, slapping me on the shoulder. "What are the fucking odds?"

"Pretty fucking slim," I muttered.

"But this is good. She's exactly the woman you wanted!" IRIS exclaimed.

"No, she is the exact opposite."

"No, she's not."

"Yes, she is," I insisted.

Slider shook his head. "She's really not."

"Yes, she is," I gritted out. "I think I know my own mind."

"Then why did you kiss her?" IRIS asked.

"I already told you, to shut her up."

"Uh-huh," he laughed. "Because there was no other way to stop the panic. That's what I usually do when I'm with a woman." He huffed in annoyance. "This woman is so irritating, and she's about to freak out. What's the best way to calm her down?" He tapped his chin annoyingly. "Ah, yes! I'll kiss her, not because I want to, but because it will help me keep her calm."

"You're such a fucking dickhead."

"He's right, though," Slider laughed. "You like this woman, and the sooner you admit it, the sooner we can all stop pretending that she's going back to New York."

"She *is* going back to New York," I bit out. Why the fuck wouldn't they believe me?

159

"Well, if you're really serious about that, you're not going to like what we have to tell you," IRIS said.

"And what's that?"

"There's a lack of space here and—"

"Because you already know her so well," Slider cut in.

"You're sharing a room with her," IRIS grinned. "But don't worry, we gave you the room with the double bed."

I stared at them, trying my best not to fume. I would not lose my shit right now. I would not let them see how much they were getting to me. My nostrils flared in anger and my fists clenched tight, but I did not fucking yell.

"You know what? It doesn't matter. I'm a fucking professional, and I can handle anything."

"That's why we figured you would be completely fine with this—because you're a professional," Slider smirked.

I was pretty damn proud of myself for not punching him in the face and walking away. I held my temper, and I didn't even pull his gun and shoot him, or IRIS. When I turned and headed for the house, my anger was on a tight leash.

And then I walked through the door.

I watched as she tossed her head back and laughed at something Jones said, placing her hand on his arm. "You have no idea," she grinned. "Thank you so much for taking us in. I really appreciate it so much."

"I'm a sucker for a damsel in distress."

"Well, while I don't like the name, I have to admit, I am far outside my depth on this one."

"That's what we're here for," he smiled. "We'll take care of you, trust me."

Then she fucking leaned in and gave him a hug. He winked at me over her shoulder as he wrapped his arms around her and held her tight.

"Yeah, you don't like her at all," IRIS laughed as he whispered in my ear.

"Where's my room?" I bit out.

"Down the hall, last room at the end."

I stomped down the hallway, refusing to look at anyone as I passed. I knew Bree was watching me, but I didn't care. I did not like her. She could hug whoever she wanted. She could flirt with whomever she wanted. It didn't make a difference to me.

I flung the door open and headed for the bathroom. Once inside, I sat down on the toilet and kicked off my shoes. With a sigh, I leaned forward, resting my elbows on my knees as I scrubbed my hands over my face. I was losing my fucking mind. She was just another job. Hell, she wasn't even a job. She was a random job, if anything.

"This is ridiculous," I said as I stood, kicking off my pants. Sitting down again, I eased off my foot and rubbed the sore skin around my leg. Thankfully, Jones had a stool in his shower, most likely because of his own amputation. It sucked to try and balance on one foot in the shower. That's why I hadn't taken my foot off in Arches.

After stripping the rest of my clothes, I got in the hot shower and sat on the bench, closing my eyes as the hot water rushed over my skin. I was fucking exhausted, with hardly any sleep over the past two nights. My days had been filled with killing assassins and running for our lives. Not that I didn't live for this shit, but sometimes it reminded me of how much older I was than when I first enlisted in the military.

I heard the bedroom door open, but still I sat there. I wasn't ready to go out there and sleep in the same bed as that woman, especially after she was flirting with Jones. She didn't act grateful to any of us when we rescued her ass and kept her alive, but one look at Jones and she was fawning all over him.

After what seemed like an hour, I finally cleaned up and decided to get out. Shutting off the water, I pulled a towel from the bar and dried off as best I could, wrapping the towel around my waist. I used the support bars in the bathroom to hold my weight as I hopped across the bathroom. I grabbed my foot, leaving everything else behind to grab later. A billow of steam followed me out of the bathroom as I hopped over to the bed where Bree was sitting.

"Can I take a shower?"

"It's all yours," I answered gruffly. She disappeared into the bathroom while I sat on the bed for a moment. I needed to get dressed and fill Jones in on everything that happened, but that meant putting my foot back on, and I really didn't want to do that right now. I flopped back on the bed, staring up at the ceiling. I could already feel my eyes drifting closed as the shower turned on.

19

BREE

THUMPER WAS PISSED AT ME. I didn't know why, but I wasn't about to argue with him right now. As I dried off from my luxurious shower, the only thing I could think about was that bed and how desperately I needed sleep. I hurried out at the sound of a knock at the door. With only my towel wrapped around me, I wasn't exactly presentable, but the pretenses of what was publicly acceptable flew out the window the moment I went on the run with these guys.

I hurried over to the door, noting Thumper asleep on the bed, laying half off it. I opened it before anyone could knock again, smiling at Jones. "Hi."

"I have some things for you. Cash said you lost all your stuff."

I gratefully took the items from him, smiling at his generosity. "Thank you so much."

"Not a problem." He was about to turn away when he saw Thumper laying on the bed. "Do you mind if I..." He motioned behind me and I quickly opened the door.

"Oh, not at all."

He strolled in and grabbed Thumper under the arms, dragging him up the bed to a more comfortable position, then tossed the covers over him. "It's the leg."

GIULIA LAGOMARSINO

"Sorry?"

He motioned to Thumper's leg. "It's a lot more work to walk with a prosthetic foot. He makes it look easy with that bionic foot, but even with the technology, it still wears on you."

"Oh, I had no idea."

"He's lucky to have only the lower leg. I didn't get to keep as much."

I looked at him in surprise. "Oh, I had no idea—"

"We make it look easy," he grinned. "Get some rest. I'll see you later."

I nodded as he walked out and closed the door. Looking back at Thumper, I had a new appreciation for just how much he did for me. Not that missing a foot suddenly elevated him to hero status, but it definitely made me rethink how he fought for me without a single complaint, ran harder and faster, all with a bionic foot. It was impressive. And it left me feeling a little like a whiny brat, just as he called me.

Pushing that to the back of my mind, I sorted through the clothes that Jones brought me, taking just a nightshirt and underwear. Normally, I had a whole bedtime routine, but I was too exhausted right now to even consider washing my face or applying lotion. All of that could wait for another time.

I dressed quickly and laid down beside Thumper. There wasn't a lot of space, but I didn't care right now. I'd gladly take my side and be happy. Just as I got comfortable, Thumper rolled over, draping his arm across my stomach. I froze, unsure of what to do. I thought for sure he would wake up and realize what he was doing, but his even breaths made that highly unlikely.

I didn't normally share a bed with anyone else, so I wasn't sure if I should wake him up or not. But as I laid there with his arm around me, I found it to be quite comforting. The weight of his body around mine lulled me to sleep in a matter of minutes.

A rough, calloused hand on my breast woke me from a dead sleep. It wasn't an unpleasant feeling. In fact, it was far from it. His thumb brushed across my taut nipple over and over again until my back arched off the bed to chase his touch. I thought for sure when he was

164

fully awake that he would yank his hand out from under my shirt and scramble off the bed, but as I turned and looked at him, I realized he was fully awake, and the desire in his eyes made me shiver in response.

The way he stared at me awakened my body in a way I'd never felt before. His tousled hair and gruff beard gave him a sexy, sleepy look that only endeared him to me more. Without thinking, I ran my hand along his jaw, inviting him in closer. In an instant, his lips closed over mine and his tongue slipped inside my mouth. I gasped as he kissed me like he needed me to breathe. I quickly got lost in him, spearing my fingers through his hair and pulling him closer to me.

His hand drifted down my body, teasing the top of my underwear just for a moment before slipping underneath. I tore my lips from his, gasping as his fingers slid through my slick folds. It had been too long since a man had touched me, and even longer since one had done it with half the expertise that Thumper had.

My eyes drifted closed as he toyed with me, building up the pleasure to a peak as his tongue slid over my neck, nibbling at me and teasing me. I wasn't sure this was a good idea, but it felt so good that I didn't have it in me to stop it. And when his fingers started circling my clit, I lost it, crying out as his mouth suddenly covered mine and he kissed me hard.

It didn't take long for him to push me over the edge. Relief came crashing down on me like a tidal wave as he continued to toy with me. And when he started stripping my panties off me, I could only open my legs shamelessly and invite him in. He stared at me for a moment, almost looking unsure that he was really welcome.

I slid my hand over his jaw, then over his chest. My eyes drifted down his body to his enormous cock jutting out. He was bigger than anyone I'd ever had before, and if anything, that made it all the more enticing. I grabbed his hip and pulled him toward me, letting him know I wanted this just as much. The moment his cock nudged at my opening, I closed my eyes and just felt every sensation of him sliding inside me.

Tears of relief flooded my eyes as he slowly filled me. I pulled him to me, allowing his body to crush me as he started thrusting inside me.

I didn't know why I was crying, or why I needed him so much. But he was here for me, and that's all I cared about at the moment. His lips found mine again, kissing me hard as he made love to me.

When a tear slipped down my cheek, I was surprised when his lips covered it, kissing away my tears. It only fueled them on, making me feel silly for crying while he made love to me.

"I've got you," he murmured in my ear.

I wrapped both arms around his neck and buried my face against his chest as he practically laid on top of me. His hips ground against mine as he chased his release. The fire inside me built until my whole body felt like it was lit in flames. I silently cried out as I found my release just moments before him.

Together, we laid there panting, his forehead resting against mine. I closed my eyes, waiting for my heart to calm down. It occurred to me that since we'd been fighting so much, there would be an awkwardness any moment now, but the longer time passed, the more content I felt. And for his part, he seemed perfectly content to lay there with me, smothering me into the bed.

After what felt like forever, he shifted off me and pulled my body closer to his. Now would be the time to question everything, but my mind was blissfully silent. Despite knowing the man only a few days, I felt closer to him than anyone I'd dated in the past. I wouldn't exactly call us friends, but there was something undeniable between us that I would no longer be able to ignore. And that had me wondering, what would I do when this was all over?

20

KNIGHT

I SHOVED the doors open to the conference room and tossed a folder down on the table. Fox looked up at me, that silly grin on his face that made me want to pull out my gun and shoot him.

"You didn't tell me that Cash has a brother."

"Cash has a brother?" Cap said in surprise.

"And you didn't tell us he's a fed either."

"Christ," Cap muttered under his breath.

"Or that he's trying to bring down a crime syndicate."

Fox narrowed his eyes at me slightly, spinning from side to side in his chair. "Technically, Rafe isn't a fed anymore. He gave that up and went rogue with his killer girlfriend."

"And the criminal syndicate?" Cap asked.

Fox shrugged. "We don't exactly exchange postcards." He turned back to me with a wink. "Not like us."

"We don't exchange postcards."

"I send them to you. You mail them back. It's sort of an exchange."

"It's nothing like an exchange."

"It sort of is. When you send them back, you're technically sending me mail," he grinned. "See how that works?"

It took everything in me not to pull out my gun and shoot this fucker. Despite being one of the good guys, he didn't have a fucking clue, no matter how hard I sent the signals. The moment I caught him trying on my boots and jacket, I knew I had a problem on my hands. And it wouldn't be one I could get rid of easily, especially when all of OPS had a special place in their charred hearts for this fucker.

"Ebarardo Zavala. The man behind the drug cartels."

Fox sat up in his seat, as did Cap, giving me their full attention. Eva, Cash's fiancé, also seemed equally interested.

"Rafe has been investigating a trafficking ring and he's pissing off all the wrong people. Nobody knows Ebarardo Zavala by name. What makes him so powerful is that nobody truly knows who they're answering to. But when Rafe went after the trafficking ring, he pissed off Zavala. He provides the drugs that keep the merchandise in compliance."

"Merchandise?" Eva snapped, her voiced laced in anger.

"That's what the women are to him. They're merchandise. They aren't human, and they aren't worth anything more than what they bring in from the highest bidder."

"What does this have to do with our guy getting shot in the desert?" Fox asked.

"Rafe is getting too close to taking out the trafficking ring. Zavala knows about Cash, but what he doesn't know is where he is."

Fox grinned at me. "He's in California, obviously."

"If he was in fucking California, Zavala would have already pulled the trigger. I've been to your compound. We ate shawarma together, remember?"

Fox smiled at me. "A very fond memory, indeed. In fact, I was just saying to Anna the other day that we should invite you and your lady out for a barbecue. We could make a weekend of it and compare knife-throwing skills. Not that you wouldn't be amazing, but I am pretty spectacular."

"Or we could figure out how Zavala is going to get to Cash," I bit out, getting us back on track.

"Maybe Cash isn't the target."

"Maybe not, but all of you have a target on your backs because of

Rafe's inability to keep his nose clean. And by coming here, you've involved us in your shit," I said angrily.

I finally had my life with Kate and everything was going right. I had a family to protect, and I couldn't do that if that shit stain Rafe got us all involved in his crusade. I couldn't risk my family, not now. I was settling down and finally learning to work with my team. Rafe just threw a monkey wrench in and blew my plans to hell.

"And the hit?"

"If I'm right, Zavala is behind the hit. He has a reach longer than you can imagine. There's no fucking way you outrun this. Your only option is to hit back hard. Cut off the head of the snake, or end up in a body bag...if you're lucky. Zavala isn't exactly the type to allow a family a respectable funeral."

Fox grinned and pushed back from his seat. "Well, this has been truly enlightening, and as much as I would love to stay and chat—seriously, we should exchange info sometime. You still haven't answered my question about your favorite show tune. Don't think I've forgotten," he grinned. "No? Still not going to tell me?"

I turned and glared at Cap. "Can I shoot him now?"

He rolled his eyes at me. "No, you can't shoot him. That would defeat the purpose of you staying on the right path for Kate."

I hated that I made those promises. "Fine."

I turned and walked away, only to find myself being hounded by Fox.

"So, I was thinking we should strategize."

"Zavala isn't my problem."

He burst out laughing. "No, not about Zavala. I meant, for our show."

"What the fuck are you talking about?" I snapped, walking faster away from him.

"You know, the show I talked about in my last letter. It'll be a massive production, but I already know what song I'm going to sing. It'll be epic."

I turned and shoved him up against the wall. "I'm not going to be in a show, or discuss show tunes with you. I don't want to talk about anything with you. What I want is for you to leave me the fuck alone," I growled.

Pappy passed behind me, shaking his head as he continued down the hall.

Fox winked at me, shoving me away from him. "I got it, man. No need to mess up my jacket," he said, running his hands down my former coat that I loved so much before he tried it on. "No need to tell me twice. I get it. I'll go ahead with the planning without you." Then he leaned in closer. "We have them so fooled. You're my hero."

He turned and walked away, wrapping his arm around Eva's neck as they followed Cash to the elevators. I heard Pappy walk up behind me, stopping beside me. "Looks like you have an admirer you can't shake."

"The problem is, as annoying as he is, he's too good to kill."

"Meaning, you can't do it?"

"Meaning, he's a psychotic mess, but he's one of the good guys. The world needs a few crazy men to keep people in line."

"So...you're not going to kill him."

"That depends on how many more postcards he sends."

"So, I'm guessing you don't want me to give you this." He held out a card to me that was clearly from Fox.

"What the fuck is that?"

He pressed down on the letter, laughing when a song started playing.

"Fuck, Kate's going to leave me."

"Why?"

"Because I might break my promise and kill him."

He slapped me on the shoulder, squeezing me hard. "Patience, my man. He can't be any worse than some of the guys we work with now."

The elevator doors opened and Fox turned back to me one last time, sliding my sunglasses on his face. I hadn't even seen him take them.

"Maybe I spoke too soon."

21

THUMPER

BREE DRIFTED off to sleep in my arms, but I was wide awake. I probably shouldn't have done that. Hell, Cash would yell down the house when he found out—and there was no doubt in my mind that Dash was already on the line with him, telling him everything he knew. Dash was good like that, sticking his nose in everyone's business.

I laid my head back and sighed as I stared up at the ceiling. I wasn't sure what happened. I was lying in bed, sleeping with my arms wrapped around her unknowingly. When I woke up and my hand was on her stomach, it just naturally gravitated toward her breast. Yes, she was a pain in the ass, but the attraction to her was hard to deny. And then fucking Jones had to get her to smile and laugh. She fucking hugged him!

And that was the crux of my situation. I didn't want her to smile for him. I didn't like that she laughed at his jokes or that she got along with him so easily. That made me a total ass, and even more so that I wanted to stake some kind of claim on her. If she ever found out that my intentions with her were not purely innocent, she would be pissed as hell at me. I should have controlled myself. I should have ignored that jealous part of my head that thought like a man in his twenties and behaved like the logical man I knew was hiding somewhere inside my head right now.

The guilt over what I'd done was eating away at me. I couldn't lie here with her any longer, knowing what a prick I'd been. I eased myself away from her and scooted to the end of the bed to pull on the sleeve for my foot. After getting dressed, I stared at Bree for a moment as she slept peacefully. She didn't deserve what I had done to her, and no doubt she would hate me when she found out.

I walked out of the room, closing the door softly behind me. FNG stood outside the door, leaning against the other wall with his arms crossed over his chest. It was clear by the scowl on his face that he wasn't happy with me.

"Don't start," I grumbled as I walked past him.

"That was fucking shitty," he hissed as he followed me down the hall. "What the fuck did you do that for?"

I spun around and got in his face. "Did it ever occur to you that I wanted to?"

"No, because all I've heard out of your mouth since the moment you met her was what a pain in the ass she is."

"And I couldn't decide that I didn't feel that way anymore?"

He shook his head at me, the disappointment evident in his eyes. "You know, I never took you to be a liar."

He shoved past me without another word and stomped out the front door. Sighing, I ran my hand over my face and headed for the kitchen. He was fucking right. I wasn't a liar, but I couldn't deny that I had feelings for her. The question was, were my feelings stronger than my jealousy?

"Quite the show you put on this morning," IRIS grinned as he poured himself a coffee. Turning, he took a sip as he leaned against the counter. "And you said you didn't like her."

"Fuck off," I muttered, grabbing my own cup.

"I thought you'd be happy," he said in confusion. "She's fucking perfect for you."

"In what way?" I snapped. "She hated everything about me. All that was," I pointed to the bedroom, "was a release. I doubt she'll think twice about me when she gets home."

His face turned serious as he set down his mug on the counter. "I thought this was a mutual thing."

"I'm not saying it wasn't mutual, but let's not kid ourselves into thinking that she'd ever want to be with me."

"She just was," he pointed out. "We all heard it. I think Jones is a little jealous."

I ducked my head, unwilling to look him in the eye. If he saw the guilt on my face, he'd fucking know. It was bad enough to get a guilt trip from FNG, but IRIS was my teammate.

"Thumper," he snapped, forcing me to look up at him. "What the hell is going on?"

"I don't know what you're talking about," I said, trying to ignore him as I sat at the table.

"I'm talking about how you suddenly went silent when I mentioned Jones." He watched me carefully, putting the pieces together in his head. This was not going to end well. "Jesus, Thumper. She's a fucking client!"

"Would you keep your voice down?" I hissed.

"What the fuck were you thinking?" he said angrily. "It would be different if you felt something for her, but you slept with her because you were jealous? Or was it just to get to Jones?"

"It had nothing to do with getting to Jones."

"No, just pissing on your territory."

When I didn't say anything, he scoffed at me, turning away and running his hands over his head in frustration. I felt the same fucking way. I knew I was an asshole, and that she deserved better than what I'd done. No matter my personal feelings about her, nobody deserved what I just did.

He spun around and stabbed his finger in my face. "You leave her the fuck alone from now on. I don't care what the fuck you have to say to her, but you will not lay a finger on her, or I swear to God, I will tell Cash and let him deal with you."

"Do you think I wanted it to happen this way?" I snapped. "It's not like I wasn't attracted to her."

"That doesn't make it better. You know, I never took you for a piece of shit."

"Neither did I," Bree said from behind me.

My eyes slipped closed as I heard her walk further into the room. I stood, turning to face her. What I did was terrible, but the fact that Bree now knew just what an asshole I was, she would never forgive me.

"Bree—"

"Don't get me wrong, Thumper. I'm a big girl and I make my own decisions. I'm perfectly capable of recognizing that what happened in there was a mutual decision, but your reasons are really fucked up."

I swallowed hard as I stared at her with tears in her eyes. "Bree, I..." I stood there, trying to come up with something to say to make this better, but my mind was blank. Nothing I said could make this right for her, and I had to live with that.

"That's what I thought."

She turned on her heel and marched back to the room. I raced after her, only to have IRIS grab my arm.

"You're not going anywhere."

"Get the fuck off me," I said, turning and slamming my fist into his face. He backed off instantly, glaring as he held his cut lip. I raced down the hall after her, catching up just as she was about to slam the door in my face. I stuck my hand between the door and the frame, gritting my teeth in pain when she closed the door on my arm. "Bree, just listen!"

"You just listen," she yelled. "You're an ass!"

"I know, but—"

"There are no buts in this situation," she argued. "You're disgusting!" She let go of the door suddenly and I shoved it open, only to flinch back when she came at me with the umbrella. I blocked her hit, not daring to take it away from her as she continued to assault me with it. I deserved every ounce of her anger.

"Bree, would you just listen!"

"To what?" she yelled, smacking me over and over again. "To more excuses?" The umbrella smacked me upside the head and I yelped. "Should I listen to all the reasons you slept with me despite only being attracted to me?"

"I'm sorry!"

"You're,"—thwack—"so,"—thwack—"disgusting!"

"I know!" I shouted, finally grabbing the umbrella and holding it above my head as she tried to take it back from me. "I know," I said, lowering my voice. "And I'm sorry."

Her shoulders sagged as she stared at me in disappointment. It was worse for everyone to look at me that way than if they just hated me. Disappointment meant that I had let someone down in a big way, and I never allowed that.

"I—"

"We've got incoming!" Jones shouted as his feet pounded on the stairs.

"Get dressed," I said to Bree. "Grab what you need. We need to move!"

I ran down the hall, leaving Bree to get ready. Jones opened his laptop as we all huddled around the screen to see what he was seeing. "There," he pointed. "At the entrance."

"How the fuck are they finding us?" I said, unable to believe that we were once again found.

"We'll figure that out later. Right now, we need to move!"

I ran back down the hall and into the room just as Bree was pulling on her jeans. She quickly slipped on her shoes and grabbed her purse and umbrella before running to me. "You know, just once I'd like to get a full night of sleep!"

I grabbed her hand and pulled her down the hall. Gunfire erupted outside, shattering the windows and piercing the walls. Bree screamed and I pulled her lower as we ran, praying we didn't get hit by anything. We made it to the garage just as everyone else was climbing inside.

"Let's move!" Slider shouted, motioning for me to get Bree into the back. I shoved her inside and climbed in after her. Jones hit a button and the opposite end of the garage opened into a back entrance, giving us an escape. Hopefully, they didn't figure it out anytime soon. Dash hit the gas and followed Jones out the back. We rode out into the darkness through the trees on a dirt road.

I looked out the back window, watching for any sign that whoever was after us was catching up. Within minutes, headlights were on our tail. "We've got company!" I climbed into the trunk of the SUV and pulled up the cargo box, finding a shit ton of weapons inside. "Thank you, Jones," I muttered under my breath.

"Thumper!" Bree shouted. I looked up into her frightened face. "What's going on? How did they find us?"

"I don't know." I pulled out the rocket launcher and spun around, getting the equipment ready. "Hold it steady," I shouted to Dash.

He lowered the back window as I lined up the shot. With three SUVs on our tail, this would only slow them down a little. With the target painted, I took the shot, watching as the vehicle exploded in a burst of flames. In the distance, a much larger explosion wrenched through the air, sending a violent burst of air at us. I could feel the heat from the flames in the back seat.

"What the fuck just happened?" Slider shouted.

"I believe that was Jones blowing up his house," Dash chuckled. "The man has a flair for the dramatic."

"He blew up his house?" Bree said, her voice laced with panic. "Why would he blow up his own house?"

"Don't worry about it. He did the same thing when they found him in Montana," Dash said over his shoulder.

The vehicle behind us burned, blocking the path of everyone else. I climbed back over the seat and sat down just as Slider got into the front seat, yanking open the glove box. "I knew Jones would hook us up."

He pulled out earpieces and got them connected, handing one back to me. "Dash, did you get Jones's number?"

"Yeah, I got it," he said, handing his phone back to me. "It's under 'gimp'."

I rolled my eyes at him. "Wow, that's so nice of you."

"Hey, he would do the same fucking thing if the situation was reversed. Hell, he'd probably do it to you," Slider chuckled.

I ignored them as I scrolled through Dash's phone for gimp. Finding it, I hit send and glanced out the window. "Shit!" I shouted, leaping across the seat to Bree and pulling her seat belt across her, clicking it into place just as we were hit from the side.

"Thumper!" she shouted as metal crunched.

My body flew into the door and my head smashed into the window, then everything went black.

22

BREE

My body jerked from the crash, but the seat belt held me in place. Thumper's body collapsed into my lap, but he didn't move. The SUV spun to a stop and Dash pulled out his gun and started firing at whoever hit us.

Panic washed over me at the sound of the gunfire. I started shaking Thumper, hoping he would wake up. Then Slider was slamming his shoulder into the door, trying to open it.

"Goddamnit!" he shouted, sending my heart into overdrive. We were going to die here, with Thumper lying in my lap. I was safe because he protected me with his life—just as he said he would.

Tears sprang to my eyes as I shook him, trying to wake him up. He didn't move, and the next time I shook him, his head slid slightly in my lap, leaving a streak of blood on my legs.

"Oh, God," I murmured, terrified of what I would see if I flipped him over. My vision blurred the longer I stared at him. I swiped my dripping nose and tried to pull it together as chaos unfolded around us.

Slider got into the back seat, shouting in my face, but I didn't hear a word he said. Finally, he unbuckled my belt and shoved me down in

178

the seat. His face reappeared in front of my own. "You stay down! Understand?"

I nodded, finally hearing all the gunfire and shouting around us. Bullets pinged off the vehicle, and more people than just Dash were firing their weapons. Slider jerked at the handle of my door, and when it popped open, he turned back to me.

"I'm going out there. Stay low and cover your head, got it?"

I nodded, trying to pull Thumper's body closer to me. Slider crawled over him and slipped out, shutting the door behind him. When I looked up, Dash was no longer in the vehicle. They both left me. Terrified and not knowing what else to do, I slowly lowered Thumper onto the floor, then scooted around until my body covered his. My face was just inches from his, and I closed my eyes, terrified by every bullet that was shot.

It felt like it lasted for hours until finally, it went quiet. I lifted my head and waited for someone to yank open the door and shoot me. I had no idea if anyone was still alive. What was I supposed to do if they all shot each other? And what about Thumper? I slid my fingers over his neck, searching for a pulse. When I felt his steady heartbeat under my fingers, I breathed a sigh of relief. But with that relief came a wave of uncertainty and fear. He was alive, but I had no idea how to take care of him. If everyone was dead, what was I supposed to do for him? Should I try and go find help? Would leaving him here be the death of him?

The sound of crunching outside had me snapping my gaze to the opposite side of the vehicle. I held my breath as the steps stopped just outside the back door on the driver's side. The handle jiggled, but the door didn't open. I slid my hand around the floor, trying to find something to protect myself with. My fingers brushed over the fabric of the umbrella and I clutched it tight.

The steps moved slowly around the back of the SUV, approaching the other side of the vehicle. If someone attacked, I wouldn't be able to defend myself from this position. Making as little noise as possible, I got into the seat and sat on my knees, staring at the cracked window. Thumper groaned from the floor, his head shifting slightly, but I ignored it and focused on the footsteps outside. My heart beat in rhythm with each step, until whoever it was stopped right outside.

It couldn't be Dash or Slider. They wouldn't move so slowly, knowing I was inside. No, this had to be someone that was after us. I licked my dry lips and adjusted my grip on the umbrella. If I was going to do this, I had to attack first.

The door clicked open slowly, making my heart skip a beat. It opened centimeter by centimeter, then was flung open. I didn't wait for an attack. With a scream, I shoved my umbrella forward and slammed it into the man outside the SUV. He gasped, stumbling backward and falling to the ground, as the door swung back toward me. I shoved the door open and jumped out. The man lying on the ground was someone I didn't recognize. He was holding his neck and gasping for air, his eyes wide as he stared at me. Then I heard shouting in the distance and knew there was someone else coming for me.

Footsteps pounded on the ground, so I made a split-second decision and wrestled the gun out of the man's hand, then took off into the trees. Branches scratched at my face as I raced away from the vehicles. Terror gripped me with every step I took. I didn't know if anyone else was alive, and Thumper was in no position to rescue me. I was all alone, and with my luck, I wouldn't be alive for very much longer.

Panting and barely able to fill my lungs, I searched for a place to hide. My only reprieve was a huge tree that might cover my body, so I rushed over there and shoved my back up against it. Sitting on my haunches, I closed my eyes and tried to control my breathing. I'd seen enough horror movies in my younger days to know that the easiest way to get caught was to not be quiet.

Despite my best efforts to be strong, my hands shook and tears streamed down my face. I wasn't ready to die. And while I was scared before, I always had the guys around me, doing their best to keep me safe. I was on my own now, and whether I lived or died rested solely on my shoulders.

"Pull it together," I whispered quietly to myself. I swiped the snot from my nose and forced myself to take deep breaths. I wouldn't last more than five minutes if I kept panicking.

The snap of a twig behind me had me stiffening against the tree. I wasn't sure if I should turn around to get a better look, or if I should stay where I was so I didn't make any noise. It was impossible to tell where this guy was, or if it was only one man. I wished now more than ever that I had at least the most basic knowledge of survival.

I looked down at the gun in my hands and wondered if it was even ready to fire. I knew exactly nothing about guns other than you pulled the trigger. A noise to my right made me jerk my head in that direction. There was a man just feet from me, walking slowly as he looked around for me. Any second now, he would turn and find me.

I wasn't ready for this moment, but that didn't matter. Whether I was ready or not, he turned and the second he saw me, I knew I was in trouble. I could see the grin on his face by the sunlight filtering through the trees. He wasn't here to talk things through. He was going to kill me, and he would enjoy it.

With the first step he took, I raised my gun and pulled the trigger, but it wouldn't go back all the way. I squeezed hard, but still nothing happened. Panic filtered through me, and the man laughed when nothing happened. A second later, he was running full speed toward me, slamming me into the ground with his full weight. The air was knocked from my lungs, and the gun flew from my grip.

"Not so easy to kill that bitch," he laughed. "We'll see."

Large hands wrapped around my neck and squeezed the very life from me. I choked, grasping at the man's hands, trying everything in my power to get him off me, but he was too strong. Tears slipped down my cheeks as I realized I was going to die out here. Spots danced in front of my eyes as my lungs burned with the need for oxygen.

And then suddenly, the man was flung off me and air rushed into my lungs with the first full breath I drew. Rolling to the side, I gasped, sucking in breath after breath. Two men were fighting in the distance, but my head was still fuzzy and I couldn't make out who was there.

I breathed deeply, calming down the panic of my near-death experience. With every second that passed, my vision cleared. Thumper knelt like a warrior over the man that had tried to kill me. He glanced back at me once, then turned to the man and quickly shifted behind him. I didn't know what he was doing, but one minute he was struggling on the ground, and the next, Thumper violently twisted his neck. His body hung limply from Thumper's hold.

He tossed the man on the ground, then got up and ran over to me. I scrambled to my knees, grateful that he was alive and that he had rescued me.

"Bree—"

I didn't give him a second to say anything else as I flung myself into his arms and cried into his neck. He held me close, his hands running soothingly up and down my spine. With every choked gasp and cry, he held me close and whispered that it was going to be okay.

I wanted desperately to believe him, but the last ten minutes had left me feeling drained of all hope. Minutes passed with him rocking me and doing his best to calm me down. I knew I was probably annoying the hell out of him, but after almost losing my life, I thought I deserved five minutes of crying.

"Hey," he said, pulling back from me. I grabbed for him, but then his lips covered mine and his hands cupped my cheeks. He kissed me just as passionately as he had while he made love to me. Like a warm blanket, he wrapped himself around me and calmed my fraying nerves.

A throat cleared somewhere behind us, but he didn't stop kissing me. It was as if nothing else mattered at this moment, and the deeper he kissed me, the more I got lost in his touch, ignoring everything around us. When he finally pulled back, he stared into my eyes with gratitude that I didn't understand.

"Okay?" he asked.

I nodded slightly, my lips quirking up at the side. "Did you kiss me to shut me up?"

His lips turned up in a smile. "No, that was all for me."

I didn't know what brought on this change, and frankly, I didn't care. He was here and I was alive. That was all that mattered right now. He stood and pulled me to my feet. His hands slid over my neck as he checked the damage, though I wasn't sure what he could see in this light, but I could feel the shift of anger in his body.

"Let's get back to the SUV."

I took one step, but my legs gave out, wobbling like jello. "I think I need a minute."

He didn't give me the minute I needed. He scooped me up into his arms and started carrying me back to the SUV. I wrapped my arms around his neck and buried my face against his warm body. I ignored the smirk on Dash's face as he watched us walk past. My fingers slid up his chest, over the massive amount of blood on his shirt.

"Are you okay?" I asked.

"A little bit of a headache. I'll be fine."

I blocked out everything else as he carried me back to the SUV. I didn't want to know anything other than who was alive, if anyone. I could only assume the danger had passed if we were walking slowly back to the road.

"Head count?" Thumper asked.

"Thirteen down. Jones and IRIS are interrogating the last two."

"Any casualties?"

"A few minor scrapes and bruises. FNG is patching up."

I felt Thumper nod, and then we were back at the SUV, the one Jones was driving. Thumper set me down and I leaned against the vehicle. Looking back at ours, I was surprised we survived the crash. If Thumper hadn't been so fast, I probably would be dead.

"I need you to wait inside."

I looked up at him, my entire body stiffening in fear. "No," I said immediately. "Please, don't leave me." Tears filled my eyes at the mere thought of being alone inside. My mind flashed back to those moments of waiting for the man to open the door and kill me. I knew if I went back into the SUV alone, I would lose my mind. I wanted to believe I was strong, but I knew that mentally I couldn't handle the strain right now.

"Hey, it's okay. I'll stay with you," he said, running his hands up and down my arms. "Let's go check on everyone else."

I nodded and turned with him, my panic receding, knowing I wouldn't be alone.

"Dash, let me see that," Thumper said, turning to his friend.

I finally took a good look at Dash and nearly fainted at the amount of blood gushing from his shoulder.

"It's nothing," Dash said, holding back a wince.

"Yeah, and you don't look like you're about to pass out, either," Thumper muttered. "Sit your ass down before you fall down."

"I could say the same to you," Dash shot back.

I took a good look at Thumper and gasped at the large cut just below his hairline. "Both of you sit down. Just tell me what to do and I'll take care of it."

They looked at each other with uncertainty, which only fueled my anger. And I needed something right now besides fear to get me out of my head.

"Sit down now," I said more forcefully. Finally, they complied and sat down, both of them holding back a groan in the process. "Right, now where can I find something to clean you up with?"

"Trunk," Thumper muttered, leaning back against a tree.

With a nod, I headed to the back of the SUV, careful to step over the dead man just outside the door I had fled from. A wave of dizziness washed over me as I popped the trunk. I wasn't injured really, but seeing a dead man and knowing how close I'd come to dying was nearly my undoing. I leaned inside where Thumper couldn't see me and took a fortifying breath. I could handle this. I wouldn't freak out right now.

After another minute, I grabbed the medical kit and spun around, nearly having a heart attack when I saw Thumper standing directly behind me. "Jesus, you scared the shit out of me."

A beautiful frown marred his face. "Are you okay?"

"I told you I am."

"Bree, you don't have to be strong. You nearly died. That would shake anyone."

I wanted to cry at the understanding in his voice, but there was no time for tears right now. I wouldn't stay alive two minutes if they both passed out and died. "I'm okay. I promise. I just had to take a minute."

He studied my face for any sign I was lying, then nodded and grabbed the medical kit from my hands. "Take care of Dash first. I think he's about to pass out."

"Okay."

He walked with me back to where Dash sat on the ground. Thumper was right, Dash's eyes were barely open, and the blood was still seeping from his wound. Thumper sat gingerly on the ground beside me, nodding at Dash's shoulder.

"Strip the fabric on both sides."

I reached forward with shaky hands and tore the fabric where the bullet entered. Blood oozed between my fingers, making it slippery and hard to hold. But I would not let Thumper down. He needed me right now. After several seconds of struggling, I was able to tear the fabric, making it wide enough to treat the bloody mess. I wasn't normally squeamish, but seeing the insides of a person's body changed that. I took a deep breath and waited for instructions.

"Here." Thumper held out a packet to me, nodding at his shoulder. "Pour it on both sides. It'll cauterize the wound."

"Won't that hurt?"

He shook his head slightly. "We don't have a choice. He can take it."

I tore the packet open and sat up, making eye contact with Dash for just a second. With a slight nod letting me know it was okay, I leaned forward and poured it over the wound on the front side.

He clenched his jaw as sweat poured down his face, but he didn't make a sound. I moved him forward and repeated the process on the back side of his shoulder. This time, his hand came up and gripped my hip as the powder covered the back side of his shoulder.

When I finished and a few minutes passed, his grip eased and he sank back against the tree. I looked to Thumper, who nodded and handed me a gauze pad. "Cover it. FNG can clean him up when we stop."

I quickly covered the wound, noting that Dash seemed to have passed out. Then I shifted my attention to Thumper. "Okay, what about you?"

He grabbed a small bottle out of the kit and handed it to me. "Just clean the wound. There's some antibiotic ointment in the kit. We'll cover it for now and FNG will handle it later."

"It sounds like he's going to be busy," I muttered, getting to work on cleaning Thumper up. After putting on the ointment and covering his cut with gauze, I sat back on my heels. "What now?"

"Now we go check on the others."

I nodded and gathered up everything from the kit, closing it to take with me. When we rounded the SUVs, I wasn't prepared for what I saw.

23

THUMPER

MY POUNDING head and the nausea swirling in my stomach was a clear sign of a concussion. But we were all down for the count, and I couldn't afford to leave Bree all alone to deal with the chaos around us. We still had to get the hell out of here and find someplace safe to hide. The longer we stayed in the open, the more likely we were to get caught again. But there were too many of us injured to move without patching up first.

"Why don't you go help New Guy," I said, motioning in the distance to where FNG was working on Slider, who was sprawled out on the ground, barely moving. I pressed a kiss to her temple just before she stepped away from me.

I watched her walk away, my breath catching in my chest as I thought about how close I came to losing her. Waking up in that SUV, hearing her scream, but being unable to move to help her, scared the shit out of me. I'd never felt so helpless in my life. When I finally shook off the dizziness enough to get up and climb out of the SUV, she was nowhere to be found. It was pure luck that I saw that asshole running after her.

The anger I felt when I saw her on the ground, being choked to death sent me into a rage unlike anything before. I wanted to make that asshole pay for laying his hands on her. I could have ended him a lot faster than I had, but I wanted the pleasure of snapping his neck. I wanted him to know he'd lost and fucked with the wrong man. That wouldn't redeem me in Bree's eyes, but it gave me the satisfaction I needed to live with myself.

I pulled out my phone, dialing Cash to distract myself for just a few minutes. "I was just about to call you. I heard from Fox."

"Too late," I muttered. "We got hit again."

"I'm gonna kill him."

"Who?"

"Rafe," he muttered. "This is all due to him. He went after a trafficking ring and pissed off the wrong man."

I looked over at Bree, feeling dread seep into my bones. "Cash, we need a solution. We're bleeding out here."

"How bad is it?"

"Dash took a bullet to the shoulder. He's passed out by a tree. FNG is working on Slider. IRIS and Jones walked away mostly unscathed."

"And you?"

"Concussion. A fucking nasty one," I said as my stomach churned. I closed my eyes and breathed through the need to vomit. At this rate, none of us were going to survive that much longer.

"You have to leave it all behind. Go dark and lay low. I'll send another team out to you. Send me a location when you have it."

"Will do."

"How are you on supplies?"

"We're good. Transporting them is a problem."

"Take what you need. Lock will bring whatever you need."

I glanced around me, checking out the damage we'd already sustained. I wasn't sure we'd make it to a second location, but we didn't have much choice at this point.

"When the going gets tough—"

"The tough get going," I finished, hanging up the phone. We didn't have a choice. Stay here and die, or get the fuck out of here with whatever we could and pray our luck held out a little longer. Then again, I was never a big believer in luck. We made our own luck, and if it wasn't in the cards, it didn't happen.

I walked over to where Slider lay on the ground and took in his wounds. One round to the head, one in the leg. "How is he?"

"Head wound is superficial," FNG filled me in. "He's fucking lucky. The bullet just grazed his head. He's unconscious, but he should be fine. He's not going to be walking around anytime soon."

"And you?"

He shot me a self-deprecating smile. "You know I can't die."

I slapped him on the shoulder and headed into the woods where IRIS and Jones were. A scream tore through the air, leading me to where they were holding their hostages. As I approached, I saw one man had already been discarded like trash. Only the final man remained, bleeding from his fingers and crying his eyes out. I would hate to be on the receiving end of IRIS's torture. When he was pissed, he was just as crazed as Fox.

"Fuck you!" the man spat.

IRIS drew his knife and slammed it into the man's throat. A few gurgles later, any light remaining in the man's eyes died, along with the rest of him. IRIS shoved him to the side and let him fall to the ground, wrenching the knife from his body.

"Anything?" I asked.

"True professionals. We didn't get jack shit."

I nodded, expecting as much. "I talked to Cash. Basically, we're fucked. This has to do with Rafe."

Jones huffed out a laugh. "Fucking Rafe. It always comes back to him."

"We have to leave it all behind and go dark. Cash is sending Lock's team to meet up with us. It's on foot from here."

"And Slider?" IRIS asked, concern lacing his voice.

"Unconscious, but he should survive. We'll have to haul him out of here. You can strap him to my back and—"

"Are you fucking kidding me?" Jones spat. "You can barely stand. You have a concussion. The last thing we need is to carry your ass out of here too."

"I'm seeing double," I confessed. There was no need to go into greater detail. They all knew I had a concussion, but the severity of it was the real sticking point. I'd pushed through the pain and side effects of the concussion because Bree's life was on the line, but I was going downhill fast. I wouldn't be able to shoot straight, let alone fight off the pounding in my head for too much longer.

"We need to get the hell out of here. I'm no use with a weapon right now, but I still have a little in the reserve tank. Use it while you can."

Jones nodded, but IRIS looked less than thrilled to allow me to take on this responsibility.

"Just don't push it so hard that you can't make it out."

I smirked at him. "I have something to fight for right now, and it sure as hell isn't your ass."

"Oh, so now you've decided you want her?"

"He always wanted her," Dash said from behind me. I turned and studied his pale face. A little worse for wear, but he'd make it. "He was just too chicken shit to admit it. It's easier to lie to yourself about your motives."

I wasn't going to dig too deeply into what he meant. Right now, we had to get the hell out of here. "We need to leave in five. IRIS, I need you to help me strap Slider on."

He nodded and followed me back to the vehicles. Bree stood up and walked over to me.

"What's going on?"

"We have to continue on foot. Are you good?"

She bit her lip for a moment, but nodded as determination took over. "I'll be okay."

IRIS came walking over with straps from the back of Jones's SUV. It wouldn't be the most comfortable for either of us, but it was better than using vines. "Alright, let's get him on my back."

Ten minutes later, Slider was strapped to my back and Jones had gathered everything he could from the SUVs. We were going to have to move fast and use the cover of dark for as long as possible, which meant few stops.

"And for you," Dash said, handing Bree her umbrella. "We can't let you continue without your trusty weapon."

She grinned at him as she clutched it. "What's wrong? You don't trust me with a gun?"

"Do you know how to use one?"

"No."

"Do you want a gun?"

"Not at all."

"Then I made the right call," he said, motioning us forward.

"FNG and I will take the rear," IRIS announced. "Jones and Dash will lead us out. Bree, stay close to Thumper."

She nodded as we took off through the trees. I stumbled more than I'd care to admit, but kept pushing on. There was only one way out of here for us, and I was determined not to slow us down.

IRIS caught up to me, huffing alongside me. "You holding up?"

I grinned. "Embrace the suck."

"Alright," he smiled, falling back into position. And that was all that was said on the subject until we arrived at the motel three hours later.

"We won't be able to hide out long," Dash said as he spoke to Cash. "They've been attacking nonstop since yesterday."

I couldn't hear what Cash was saying, but at this point, I didn't care. My head was pounding, and that bed was calling my name. I waited with as much patience as possible while FNG and IRIS unstrapped Slider from my back. I didn't know how he was doing. I was in too bad of shape to give a fuck at the moment.

When the weight was gone from my back, I stumbled over to the bed and collapsed. The light streaming in from the windows was killing me, and I shoved a pillow over my head to block it out. I needed pain meds, but we didn't have anything left after patching everyone up. Slider was decidedly in most need of meds at the moment. A bullet to the head, even a graze, would cause a massive concussion.

"Roll over, asshole." FNG sat down beside me, shoving at my body.

I rolled over as asked, but did nothing more to help. He pulled the pillow off my head and damn near made me throw up when he shined the bright light in my eyes. I took a deep breath, swallowing down the pain as he continued his exam.

"How's Slider?"

"He woke up. Said you give a shitty ride."

"He's lucky I took him at all. I should have left his ass behind."

"He agreed," FNG chuckled. "How's the pain?"

"Two."

"So, pretty fucking bad."

"I said two."

"And you lied," he continued, not bothering to hash it out with me. "Your girl is worried as hell about you, so why don't you just help me out so I can tell her you're going to be okay."

"I am okay."

He flicked me on the forehead, immediately sending shocks of pain down my spine. I gritted my teeth, biting back the groan forcing its way to my lips. "Yeah, you're fine. You need food and plenty of water, but I don't have any more pain meds."

"What about Lock? When is his team arriving?"

"A few more hours. We'll lay low until then. You should get some sleep."

"They'll be back before then," I mumbled, already feeling myself slipping into unconsciousness.

"Then we'll fight them off and drag your ass out of here."

I nodded but was quickly losing the battle of staying awake. My whole body was giving in to the aches and pains streaming through my body. And the harder I fought the need for sleep, the more my head pounded.

"Jones is getting some food. You need to eat something before I give you anything for the headache. Until then, get some sleep."

I nodded and allowed myself to drift off into a restless slumber for the next twenty minutes.

"Thumper!"

I could hear her calling me, her painful screams echoing in my head, but I couldn't find her. I stumbled out of the SUV, searching all around. My vision spun as I searched for her. In the distance, I thought I saw someone running. I couldn't waste another minute, or she would be dead. I took off at a dead sprint, praying that I got there in time. I stumbled over roots and shoved at branches that scraped my face. Her desperate pleas sent my heart into overdrive.

She cried out to me again, but it was coming from a different direction. I stopped and listened for her again, closing my eyes to focus on only what I could hear. "Thumper!" I spun around and took off in the opposite direction. Minutes passed as I ran flat out toward her. I broke through the trees to a clearing only to find her on the ground with a man standing over her with a smirk on his face.

He turned and ran, leaving me with the choice of chasing him down or getting to Bree. With her body lying limp on the ground, there was only one thing to do. I rushed to her and knelt down, hoping she was just unconscious.

"Bree!" I shook her, trying to wake her up, but as I stared at her tear-streaked face, it was clear she was already gone.

I jerked upright, searching for her, only to find her lying beside me, sleeping peacefully. I rolled over and pressed my fingers to her throat, reassuring myself that she was still alive. Breathing a sigh of relief, I rested my head against her chest as I calmed myself down.

"You okay, man?" FNG asked.

I rolled back over, laying my arm across my face. "Yeah." My voice was gruff, but that could be chalked up to how shitty I felt.

"Here, eat something," FNG said, shoving food in my face. It smelled terrible, and the nausea swirling in my stomach said eating was a bad idea. But I needed meds. I shoved bread in my mouth, sure that was the only thing I could stomach at the moment.

"Is she okay?" I asked around a mouthful of food.

"She pretty much passed out next to you not long after you fell asleep. Didn't say much."

"But she…"

"She's doing okay," he reassured me. "I'm surprised she's held it together based on our previous experience with her."

I wanted to say she was toughening up, but in my heart, I knew it was more likely that her silence was a defense mechanism against all the trauma.

He nodded at her. "What's going on with you two? When we were at Jones's place, you were at each other's throats."

I couldn't answer him. I wasn't sure if anything changed other than how I looked at her. I couldn't deny I made a shit ton of excuses for all the reasons we couldn't be together.

I thought she was annoying.

She freaked out way too much.

We lived different lives.

I would never be good enough for her…

I wasn't sure if any of those excuses were valid or not, but the one thing that had changed was the fact that I could no longer deny that not only did I care about this woman, I was terrified that I would lose her.

FNG grabbed a bottle and shook out a few pills. "Here, take this. Lock should be here within the hour, and then we're moving."

"Slider?"

"About as good as you."

He stood and walked away, leaving me alone with Bree. Everyone else was keeping watch, probably outside the building. I had expected to get hit again, but things were quiet. Unless they were waiting for us to get to an unpopulated location.

"How are you?"

I turned at the sound of Bree's voice, surprised when she smiled at me. I rolled to my side and slid my hand along her cheek, needing to touch her. Her eyes fluttered closed at my touch, and that wrenched at my heart, knowing how I had treated her just the day before. I didn't deserve for her to smile at me, let alone take comfort from me. She should hate me for what I did.

"How are you?"

"That's my line," she grinned.

"But I ask it so much better." Her smile lit up the room, surprising the hell out of me. "I bet you wish you went on a different vacation."

"Preferably one without a Bighorn Sheep," she added.

"And rabbits that take over your yurt."

"I could do without the sand also. I didn't realize how much I would hate it."

It relieved me to see her cracking jokes, but it wasn't good for her to hide behind what she was really feeling. If she was falling apart, I needed to know it. "So, how are you really?"

Her smile faded the longer she stared into my eyes. "I've been better."

"Scared?"

"For you," she said quietly. "And me, but seeing you...in the crash...I don't think I've ever been that scared in my life. You protected me and you could have died."

Her eyes were glossy with unshed tears, but no matter how hard she tried to fight it, they fell and coated her cheeks.

"I'm sorry I wasn't there to protect you sooner."

"Well, you were sort of unconscious."

I drew in a shaky breath when I remembered the sight of that man sitting on her, choking the life from her body. "I thought for sure I was going to lose you."

"You killed him. For me."

"And for me. I needed to kill him." I watched for any sign of disgust, but she just continued to stare at me. "I can't tell what you're thinking. You're usually so vocal."

"I think I've lost my ability to freak out. It's buried somewhere deep inside."

"It's a defense mechanism. Your brain is protecting you."

"And you? Are you still protecting me?"

"With my dying breath," I whispered, leaning in and brushing my lips against hers. I thought for sure she would pull back or smack me, but instead, she pulled me closer to her, wrapping her arms around my neck. Despite the pounding in my head, with her in my arms, my whole body calmed down and finally felt at ease.

"Please don't have sex," Slider muttered. "I'm not unconscious."

LOCK

WE ROLLED INTO TOWN, expecting someone to be waiting for us. Either that or to find Thumper's team already dead. So, when we pulled up to the motel and found everyone alive and mostly well, it was an odd feeling. Something was off.

I got out and looked around, shaking my head when I didn't get the feeling of being watched. "Scottie, do a perimeter check with Brock."

"On it," he said, taking off at a jog toward the back of the motel. Brock went in the opposite direction.

I approached Jones, who was posted outside the door. "Everything good?" I asked, holding out my hand to shake his.

"Oh, yeah. We're all great," he said sarcastically.

I nodded, looking around some more. "It's been quiet?"

"I can't figure it out either. It doesn't make any sense."

"They sure as fuck didn't realize they were dealing with OPS and just decide to walk away," I said. "So, what are we missing?"

"I don't have a fucking clue."

"And the guys?"

"Dash took one to the shoulder. He's holding up, but he could do with a few stitches."

"And Slider?"

"Grazed with a bullet to the head. Rung his bell pretty good, but with some rest, he should be fine. FNG removed the bullet in his leg, but had to do with the supplies we had. Thumper decided to take out a window with his head, so he's not exactly in top form."

"Well, these guys like to pretend they're shatterproof," I grinned. "You don't look too bad. No uglier than before, at least," I said, eyeing the cuts on his face.

"That was my intention. I figured as long as I was still better looking than Cash, I had it in the bag."

I chuckled at his ability to find humor even in the shitty situation they were stuck with. "So, lay it out for me."

He shrugged slightly. "From what I understand, they were hit three times before they reached me. They weren't there even one day before we were hit again. I lost another fucking house to Cash, and you'd better believe I'm getting paid for it."

"So, what's changed? You left the vehicles behind."

"Yeah, but they didn't arrive in the same vehicle they left with in Arches. So, it's not the vehicle. The guys all checked. They haven't been tagged in any way. Bree's phone was smashed the minute they left Arches, but she's not the target anyway."

"It doesn't make any fucking sense," I said again, still baffled by it.

"Honestly, I'm not gonna quibble over the fact that they haven't chased us down yet. We've got three out of six men down. Let's get to a safe house, and then we can figure this shit out." He jerked his head at me. "You have some place in mind?"

I laughed under my breath. "You're never gonna believe it."

"Try me."

"If I told you, I wouldn't be able to laugh when I see the look of shock on your face," I said, slapping him on the arm.

I turned and opened the door, finding Slider sitting up in bed, holding his head. He looked like shit—pale and in some serious pain. The tension in his body magnified the true extent of his injuries.

Keeping my voice quiet, I sat beside him. "Sitting down on the job, huh?"

He huffed out a laugh. "Fucking Thumper, dragging us all over the fucking country. All because of a woman."

I glanced over my shoulder to the other bed where Thumper was passed out with a woman curled up in his arms. "That's new."

"That's a fucking disaster waiting to happen."

"Why do you say that?"

"Have you ever seen Thumper obsessed over a woman before?" I shook my head. "It's fucking terrifying."

"So, it's the real deal?"

He shrugged. That seemed to be the only movement he was capable of at the moment. "I guess we'll find out when this is over."

"How are you holding up?"

"Peachy. You ever been shot in the head?"

"Can't say I have."

"Well, I wouldn't recommend it. It fucking sucks."

"You should be sleeping."

"I had to piss," he grumbled. "FNG wanted to stick a fucking catheter in me. Can you imagine letting that asshole near your dick?"

"A scary thought, indeed," I nodded. "Let me wake up sleeping beauty and we can be on our way."

I went to stand when he grabbed me by the arm. "Lock, whoever the fuck this is, they're good."

"Then it's a good thing I'm here. You need a team that actually knows what the fuck they're doing," I smirked.

He flipped me off and laid back down. The sooner we got on the road, the faster we'd get to the safe house. Thank God we were headed to Colorado. With any luck, we'd figure out how the fuck to get this hit off us and keep everyone safe. We couldn't hide out forever, but we couldn't fight when three guys were seriously injured. Our luck had to change fast.

25

THUMPER

WE'D BEEN DRIVING down this road for a half hour without another fucking car in sight. If I didn't already know this was private property, I would have alarm bells going off like crazy. We pulled up to a gated private property and Lock hit the buzzer, announcing our arrival. A scanner popped up, taking Lock through various scans. I was surprised when we didn't all have to go through the same thing.

The gates opened, allowing us entry to the property. I stared out the window in utter shock at what I was seeing. This wasn't a house. It was a fucking mansion.

"Who the hell do we know that owns a property like this?"

"I don't think you're going to like the answer," Lock answered, pulling into the circle drive at the front of the house.

I opened the door and stepped out, grateful to be at the safe house where I could finally relax and get some fucking sleep. Up until now, every minute I was asleep was filled with nightmares of Bree being strangled. With so few of us uninjured when we arrived at the motel, it was hard to let my guard down. But with a head injury, I couldn't stay awake, no matter how hard I tried.

I turned and held my hand out for Bree. She looked just as rough as I felt. She'd hardly said a word since we left the motel, and I could only contribute that to the past horror-filled twenty-four hours. I wrapped my arm around her shoulders and led her inside. It wasn't at all what I expected, but if we were truly safe here, I'd take it.

And then he walked around the corner.

I rolled my eyes and groaned.

"Told you you wouldn't like it," Lock muttered.

Knight eyed us all warily. Whether we were on his side or not, he didn't trust us, and I could hardly blame him for that. He was still adjusting to this life even after a few years of being with Reed Security.

"I have a room set up down the hall for Slider. I also have a doctor here to get you guys cleaned up. But before we go even one step further, you need to know something. My wife is that doctor, and if you so much as look at her the wrong way, I will gut you alive, then throw you out on your asses. Am I clear?"

A loud clapping sound came from behind us, and we all turned to see who it was. Everyone shifted, finally giving me a peek at who was bold enough to give Knight shit at a moment like this.

"The Kamau, ladies and gentlemen!" Fox grinned from ear to ear as he stepped inside. "I don't have to tell you, but I'm going to. That was a remarkable speech. I love the whole murder and veiled threats thing you have going on. You've still got it," he laughed. "Fucking amazing."

"Fox, what the hell are you doing here?" Lock spat.

"He slipped in behind you," Knight announced. "Did you really think I wouldn't see you arriving? I nearly shot you the moment you crossed my property line."

"But you didn't," Fox laughed. "Because you have something special. I told you, you can't get enough of me. I'm like mold. I grow on you until I take over."

"Or until I kill you off," Knight threatened. "Just stay the hell out of my way."

"No problem. You've got shit to do. But since we're here, I thought I'd bring my lady love along. I thought since we're so close that our respective wives should meet."

"You're not married," Lock pointed out.

"Not yet. But I thought since I'm here with my bestie, this would be the perfect opportunity to solve that problem. Anna?" he called out.

She slipped in the door behind him with a smile on her face. Strolling right past all of us, she walked right up to Knight and wrapped her arms around him in a hug, whispering something in his ear.

"Uh…Anna, you're making me jealous. I love him too, but not enough for you to leave me for him," Fox said nervously.

Knight nodded to her, then actually did something that resembled an almost smile. I couldn't be sure. It was there and gone so fast. "Kate!"

He turned back to us all, glaring as his wife entered the room. It was a clear threat to be on our best behavior while we were there, and I'd gladly abide. Hell, I was just happy to have a roof over my head.

"There are a few rules while you're here," Knight said, pointedly looking at each of us before he continued. "One, you do not look at my wife. Two, you do not touch my wife. Three, you will never be in the room alone with my wife."

"I'm getting the feeling you don't trust her with us," Fox grinned. "And that's just silly because we're all so awesome."

He stared at Fox, not giving an inch. "If you break any of these rules, I'll have you shot on the spot, and Kate will not be allowed to help you in any way. Do I make myself clear?"

"Hudson," Kate admonished. "It'll be a little hard to take care of them if I'm not allowed to touch them or look at them."

"You're allowed to take care of them. They aren't allowed to touch you in any way. That's what we agreed to," he snapped.

She pressed her hand to his arm and instantly, he eased just a smidge. Then she turned to all of us with a smile on her face. I didn't quite get the attraction, but who was I to say what man she chose to fall in love with?

"Hey, guys. I have rooms set up for all of you. Slider, Thumper, and Dash are all in rooms on the first floor. The rest of you can choose rooms on the second floor. Let me know if there's anything you need."

"We'll take first watch," Lock announced.

"Just a minute," Knight stopped him. "This is my house. If you'll follow me, I'll show you the layout and the security systems. I don't need any of you getting electrocuted because you didn't fucking pay attention." He turned to walk away, then looked back at us. "And watch out for Eugene."

"Who's Eugene?" Lock asked.

Knight turned back to us with a grin. "A robot prototype I'm working on. You'll know him when you see him. Just don't pull a gun and you should be fine. For the most part."

He walked off without another word. Lock's team followed while the rest of us stood there in shock. Or awe.

"Can I help you with something?" Anna asked Kate.

"Do you know anything about medicine?"

"No, but I can be an assistant. I don't have complete use of my right hand, but I can manage."

"Alright, we'll look at Slider first." Kate turned to Jones. "Can you help him down the hall? First door on the right," she pointed off to the left under a large staircase.

Jones and IRIS both propped Slider up under his arms and helped him down the hall. Dash followed, looking even worse than right after he was shot. I wasn't sure if Kate had a blood supply around here, but without it, Dash would take a lot longer to recover.

"Are you ready?" Bree asked, looking up at me tiredly.

"Yeah, let's go lay down."

"I want a shower," she grumbled as I wrapped an arm around her and we followed the rest of them.

"Want some company?"

She smiled up at me. "I'm not going to freak out, if that's what you're thinking. That time has come and gone."

"I was actually thinking you could support me," I said with a self-deprecating smile.

She stopped and studied me. "Are you okay? Should I get Kate?"

"No," I said tiredly. "Just a little dizzy, nauseous, tired as fuck...the usual."

"How is that the usual?"

"It comes with the territory of a head injury. My second in a few months. Can't say I would recommend it to anyone."

We continued down the hall to a lavish bedroom that could easily fit three rooms in one. I thanked God that it had a private bathroom where I could take off my foot and shower in peace. I was too fucking tired to deal with anyone else's bullshit right now.

I eased down on the bed and bent over, untying my shoes. Fuck, even bending over sent me into a tailspin.

"Here, let me help," Bree said, kneeling down in front of me.

"I've got it."

"You're about to pass out, and it's all because of me. Because you put me ahead of yourself."

"It's who I am," I said, trying to downplay just what I would do for her. I wasn't ready to admit to her or myself just how bad I had it for her. It snuck up on me so quickly and bit like a snake.

She smiled to herself as she helped me take off my shoes. "And this?" she asked, running her hand over my bionic foot.

I wasn't sure she had it in her to handle this part. It wasn't for everyone. And while I didn't give a shit about my metal appendage, some couldn't help but look at me with pity. And that just pissed me off.

"I've got it."

"Just tell me what to do." She shot me a look that brooked no arguments. So, I took her through the steps of removing it and the sock. Her fingers ran over the scar and up my leg. Before I knew it, her fingers were at my hips, running along the waist of my pants. "We have to take these off if we're going to shower."

I really fucking hoped I could contain myself. Despite feeling like crap, my body was still drawn to her, and I knew I wasn't in any condition to be doing the things I really fucking wanted to do. Luckily, she kept things clinical as she helped me out of my clothes, and when she went to start the shower, I took a few minutes to calm down my raging hard on.

Pushing off the bed, I hopped over to the bathroom and grabbed the mat to lay down on the floor. A slippery surface was a sure-fire way to end up on my ass.

She opened the door and held out her hand to me. "I lied about freaking out."

"I lied about being okay," I admitted.

I got into the shower with her and sat down on the ceramic ledge, letting the water wash over me. To my surprise, she straddled my hips and wrapped her arms around my neck. "Tell me we're going to be okay," she whispered.

"I won't let anything happen to you."

She ran her fingers through my wet hair, her eyes staying on my forehead. "And us?"

I knew this question would come eventually, but I still didn't have an answer. Maybe that's why I shoved away the idea of actually liking her. How could we ever work? We were complete opposites.

"I have no fucking clue," I answered honestly.

"Do you want to be with me?"

"If you asked me that two days ago, I would have said hell no."

"And now?" Her voice held a note of confidence, but I could see the vulnerability in her eyes.

"And now I think I've been lying to myself. But where does that leave us? You live in New York, and I live in the ass end of nowhere."

"Does your job ever bring you to New York?"

"Occasionally, but less often than you'd think."

She contemplated all that, then slipped from my lap, standing under the water. I watched as she washed her hair, wishing I could stand behind her, running my hands over her body. But I was unsteady on one foot in the shower, and falling on my ass and risking cracking my skull open would hardly be sexy. It was funny because I hadn't really hated having one missing foot until this very moment. It was a battle wound, one that I was proud of. I knew what I signed up for when I joined the military. I'd seen vets missing limbs and go through some rough shit. I had no illusions about what might happen to me.

But at this moment, as the woman I was falling for stood in my shower, I cursed the foot I was missing and wished like hell I could be any other two-legged man that could take his woman in his arms and fuck her up against the shower wall.

"What are you staring at?" Bree asked, rinsing the shampoo from her hair.

"You."

"And?" she quirked an eyebrow.

"And I'm wishing I could stand up and take you against the wall."

She watched me for a moment, then her hips swayed as she walked over to me and climbed back into my lap. "Then I guess we'll just have to get creative in how we have sex in the shower."

A grin split my lips as she grabbed my throbbing cock in her hands. Then she sank down on me, and I forgot why I was so fucking pissed about not being able to fuck her against the shower wall.

"What are you doing?" she asked as she towel-dried her hair.

I grabbed the lotion from the counter and hopped out to the bed, sinking down with a sigh. "Just taking care of ol' stumpy."

She crawled onto the bed and watched as I squirt some lotion into my hands. "How often do you have to do that?"

"Every night when I take it off. If the skin cracks, it can lead to infection."

"Here, let me," she said, pushing me back on the bed.

"I can do it."

She refused to look at me as she squirted some lotion into her own hands and started to massage it onto my leg. "I know you can do it. But you've taken care of me through my hysterics and people shooting at us. I can do this one thing for you."

I was so used to doing it myself that I hadn't really thought about how nice it would be to have someone else taking care of me. And the longer she massaged my leg, the more I realized how relaxing it was to have her hands on me.

A knock at the door barely drew my attention. When Kate popped her head inside, she smiled at my woman taking care of me. Christ, I had a woman. When did that happen? I was so fucked in the best way.

"I see you already have someone to take care of you. How's your head?"

"About as well as can be expected."

"Let's check it out."

I didn't need her to check me out to know that I needed some fucking rest. That was about all I could do right now. But if she had some meds, I wouldn't say no to them. Anything to kill the pounding in my head for five minutes.

After examining me, she gave me some pills, which I was eternally grateful for. There wasn't much more she could do without access to the proper hospital equipment. I laid back in bed as Bree snuggled up to me.

"It's weird. Now that we're safe, I can't fall asleep," she murmured.

"You're waiting for the other shoe to drop."

"I can't stop thinking about it," she whispered. "His hands around my neck...I was so scared. I thought for sure that was it."

"I'm sorry I wasn't there." I pressed a kiss to her temple, wishing I could get the same thoughts out of my head.

"I don't blame you. I didn't mean to make it sound like that. It's just...he said something I can't get out of my head."

I frowned. "What did he say?"

"Something about it not being easy to kill me."

I shifted so I could face her. "He said exactly that?"

"I don't know. I mean... it was something like that."

"Bree, this is important. I need you to think. What exactly did he say?"

She closed her eyes, her lips moving as she thought back. "Not so easy to kill that bitch." She took a deep breath. "Yeah, I'm pretty sure that's what he said."

I sat back and ran it over in my head. Why would he be concerned about killing Bree? Every time someone was after us, they attacked all of us first, which was in line with us being the targets. Why would anyone worry about killing Bree, unless it was for the sole purpose of getting to me? But if someone was after us because of Rafe, Bree wouldn't even be on their radar. None of this made any sense.

But then I remembered what Bree said after we were attacked on the road. She said the man pointed the gun at her, and looked like he wanted to kill her. I dismissed it because he was a hired gun. Of course he would want to kill her. I sat upright in bed, tossing off the covers. I looked at the pills on the bedside table and knew they would have to wait. They would knock me out, and no matter how bad my headache was, I couldn't afford to go to sleep right now.

"Thumper, where are you going?"

"I have to talk to the guys. Stay here."

"Thumper! Wait!"

I slipped my sock on, then my foot. I shouldn't have it on so soon after putting on the lotion, but I didn't have a choice right now. I had to talk this through with the guys. If I was right, we were looking in the wrong direction.

"Just stay here for a little bit. I won't be gone long."

"Hey!" she snapped, getting my attention. "I have done whatever you've asked for days now. If something's going on, I need to know."

"I don't know for sure. That's what I intend to find out."

"Then I'm coming with you."

That was the last thing I needed. If Bree knew what I suspected, she would really freak out. "Bree, please, just do this for me."

She pursed her lips at me, which was never a good sign coming from a woman. "If this has to do with me, then I'm coming. But if you can tell me that you're not running out of here because of something that concerns me, then I'll stay here. But you'd better be honest with me, because if you lie, I'll know, and I'll be pissed."

I didn't want her to find out like this. It would most definitely send her into a tailspin, but if I lied to her now, she might never forgive me. "Alright, let's go."

We quickly got dressed, and then I dragged her down the hall after me. Knight was walking toward the stairs with Fox hot on his tail.

"I know we didn't plan on this little get together, but when I heard they were meeting up at the Kamau's house, I just couldn't resist. This is fucking amazing."

"Knight!" I shouted, stopping him on the first stair. "Where is everyone?"

"The study. Why?"

"I need to talk to them now."

He nodded and led the way. Sensing my urgency, he moved quickly down the various halls until we reached the back of the house.

He swung the door open, leading inside to where Lock's team was with IRIS, FNG, and Jones.

"You should be sleeping," Jones chastised.

"We're wrong on the target," I said, getting directly to the point.

"What? What are you talking about?" FNG asked. "We were there when you were shot the first time, and every time after that they tried to kill us."

"Right, they were trying to kill us, but only to get us out of the way."

"What are you talking about?" IRIS asked. "Who else would they be after?"

I felt Bree's hand tighten around mine as silence weighed heavy throughout the room. "They were after Bree," I said after a minute. "It was never us."

"How sure are you on this?" Knight asked.

"Pretty fucking sure."

He exchanged glances with Lock. "Then we need to find out if any of these hits have to do with Zavala, or if that's just one massive coincidence."

"Thumper, you're going to have to fill us in," FNG said. "I was there. I don't remember anyone going directly for Bree."

"That first night," I explained. "Bree was in the chair. I got up to use the bathroom, and she slipped into bed. So, I took the chair. It was a matter of minutes. The distance that sniper was at, he probably didn't even know she moved. He saw a body and took the shot."

"That's assuming he took his eyes off the target for several minutes," Lock pointed out.

"It wouldn't be the first time it's happened," Knight muttered.

"And then Bree said the hitter in the car looked like he wanted to kill her."

"That's his job," FNG said. "We've already been over this."

"Yeah, but you and I were both in the car with him. If he wanted to take us out, why was he pointing a gun at Bree when he had two of us in the same fucking car? It doesn't make any sense. And last night in the woods, he said to her *Not so easy to kill that bitch.*"

Everyone looked around at each other as I said that last part. It was a clear threat to her, and only her. Nobody would be worried about taking her out alone if we were the target.

"This changes everything," FNG said, his brows crinkling. "But one thing doesn't make sense. Why were there so many people after her? What's so special about her that someone wants her dead? And how the fuck did they keep finding us?"

I turned to Bree, hoping she had some clue about that. She looked shell-shocked, shaking her head. "I don't know," she whispered. "I go to work. I go home. I…"

"It's okay," I said, squeezing her hand. "We'll figure this out."

Her eyes flicked to mine and anger surged. "But how did they keep finding me? You crushed my cell phone at Arches."

I did. We switched cars, we didn't use her name or ours…We even bought that car under Cash's fake name. No one should have been able to track us.

"Her purse," I finally said, running my hands through my hair. "She had her purse with her until last night. We didn't check it because I thought they were after me."

"That was a fucking stupid assumption," Knight muttered.

"And there hasn't been anyone around since you escaped Jones's place," Lock said, nodding in agreement. "That's why this felt off. If they were after you, they would have kept sending someone. But since they're after Bree, they can't find her now that the tracker isn't on her."

"What do we do then? How do we find out who's after me?" Bree asked, her voice quibbling in fear. I pulled her in close to me, wrapping my arms around her. "We'll take it from here. This is what we do."

She grasped my shirt in her hands as she buried her face against me. Whoever was after her had better run. Now that we knew who the real target was, we wouldn't stop until that asshole was buried six feet under.

BREE

"WHAT ABOUT OLD BOYFRIENDS?" IRIS asked. "Anyone that might have dated you that didn't care for your tone or—"

"I'm sorry, are you trying to suggest that someone wants to kill me —would go to all this trouble—over the tone of my voice?"

"Shouldn't you know better by now?" FNG whispered to him.

I rolled my eyes, irritated with this line of questioning. The thought that someone wanted me dead was hard enough to swallow, but knowing that it might be because of something as stupid as my tone of voice was really cutting.

"It doesn't necessarily have anything to do with your tone of voice. That's not what I'm trying to get at. Psychopaths don't need a logical explanation to go after someone. But knowing anyone that might have a beef with you gives us a pool of suspects to look into."

I sighed, knowing I was overreacting. They were just trying to help, and I was making this more difficult. I sat down, ready to get to work. "I can't think of anyone that I might have pissed off. I literally go to work every day for at least ten hours. I work weekends and rarely see a single friend. I can't even tell you the last time I was home to visit my family."

He nodded, looking down at his notes. "Well, Dash is running backgrounds from people you work with. Maybe that'll give us some insight into who would go to such great lengths to kill you."

"IRIS," Thumper snapped, walking into the room. "Maybe a tad more delicacy."

"Right, I forgot you're in love with her."

I ignored the jab, knowing he was just egging Thumper on. He didn't love me. How could he? We barely knew each other.

"Don't you have a woman to call?" Thumper asked him.

"She probably followed me out here."

"Let's hope not. The last thing we need is them trying to sneak into Knight's house. He'd probably shoot them on sight," Thumper muttered.

"Why would they follow you on a job?" I asked. "Isn't that dangerous?"

IRIS tossed his head back and laughed. "You know, you'll be a refreshing change to the bunch. Maybe you can talk them out of being so crazy."

"Me?" I asked with wide eyes. "What could I do?"

"That panic stuff you do…maybe teach them that."

"Too late," FNG sighed, shaking his head. "I heard Eva just got a new set of knives from Fox."

"For cooking?" I asked hopefully.

"Throwing," Thumper grimaced. "He…" He swore under his breath. "I shouldn't even tell you this. You'll probably want to join them."

"Join them with what? I'm not following."

Thumper and IRIS exchanged some kind of look that I just didn't understand.

"There's only one way to know, man," IRIS said. "Might as well show her now."

"I'm going to fucking kill him if he changes her," Thumper snapped.

I was so confused right now. They were speaking some kind of language that I didn't understand. And I really hated it when people talked about me as if I wasn't there. It wasn't fair to me.

"Look, if you have something to say, just say it."

"It's not something you'd understand. We have to show you," IRIS smirked. "Are you ready to see the kind of crazy that comes with being part of OPS?"

I wasn't sure about anything at this point. I went on vacation, thought I was wrapped up in some kind of mad hit on the men, but it turned out, I was the actual target. There was exactly nothing in my life that I was prepared for right now.

"Show me the way."

Despite Thumper looking like he was about to pass out, he led me out of the room and down the hall. Then we headed for the back of the house and outside. The guys had some kind of target practice set up, but only some of them were there.

"Alright, alright! Who wants first dibs?" Fox shouted, standing next to a tree. I only knew about him from when he walked into the house when we first arrived. I wasn't entirely sure what his position was at OPS. Frankly, he seemed like a bit of a wild card, but then all these men had a twisted sort of humor to them.

"I'll go first." Knight stepped forward, tossing his beer into a trash can.

"The Kamau!" Fox shouted. "Now, this is going to be awesome! I can't believe the Kamau is going to throw knives at me!"

"He's going to do what?" I asked, leaning over to whisper to Thumper.

"It's a thing. You have to see it to believe it."

"But what exactly am I seeing?" I questioned. He couldn't really be throwing knives at Fox. That was insane—something you'd see in the circus.

"Just watch."

Irritated as I was by his answer, I waited as Fox backed up against a tree, spreading his arms wide. Knight stepped up to a table I hadn't seen before. Spread out on it were various knives, but they didn't look like normal knives.

"What are those?"

"Throwing knives," Thumper answered. "You use them in throwing competitions. Fox, however, uses them to—"

At his abrupt stop, I had to know what he was about to say. "To what?"

He glanced over at me, his eyes wary as he watched. "For killing people."

I swallowed hard, doing my best not to panic. This was me turning over a new leaf. I had to learn to control my anxiety over situations and not let it control me. "Oh, that's..."

"Insane. Yeah, that's Fox. But he's a good guy. As long as you stay on his good side, you're golden. Make friends with him, and he'll have your back for life."

That seemed simple enough, but then again, most of these guys seemed to have that same air to them. I wasn't about to question the crazy man standing by the tree, about to have knives thrown at him.

"You ready?" Knight asked.

"Give it to me, Kamau."

"You'll regret saying that."

"Hey, and if you don't get me, there's a bag of Funyuns in it for you. Maybe I'll even throw in some shawarma."

"Great," Knight said, though he sounded less than enthusiastic.

"Is he really going through with this?" I whispered. "What if he misses?"

"I have the feeling that Knight doesn't miss. And if he does, it's probably because he meant to. In Fox's case, that's very likely."

"That doesn't make me feel better about the man we're staying with."

I watched with bated breath as Knight picked up several of the knives and stared at Fox for what felt like minutes. The metal slipped back and forth between his fingers as he shuffled them around in his grip. I needed to remind myself to breathe as I waited for the inevitable. At least Kate was here and could hopefully patch up any injuries.

The first knife left his grip so fast that I almost missed it. The four after that were flung through the air in rapid succession, leaving me gasping for breath and clutching Thumper's arm as I squeezed my eyes shut. I couldn't handle this. No matter what I had already seen, watching men deliberately throw knives at each other for entertainment was taking things too far.

"Man!" Fox shouted. "Did you see how close he got to my dick? Not that I approve of you shredding my favorite jeans."

"Care to up the ante?"

"You know it, buddy. Let's give it up for my bff!" Fox shouted.

I stared at him, shaking my head at how idiotic this was. "He's actually proud that another man almost cut off his penis?"

"You have to know Fox to really understand."

I turned to Thumper in shock. "And this is the man you want me to befriend."

He winced slightly, but I couldn't tell if it was because his head was pounding or if he understood my objection to the friendship. "He's really not that bad."

I huffed in irritation as I turned back to the scene that was about to unfold. No amount of cool tricks could make me applaud this ludicrous behavior.

"Not impressed?" Anna asked as she stepped up beside me. She was beautiful, with the most perfect skin I'd ever seen. She didn't even wear makeup. I was jealous of her just because of that. She looked vaguely familiar, like one of those faces you've seen before, but you knew you'd never place. I didn't get why she was here.

"Of a man that eagerly awaits being shot by his best friend?"

"They're not really friends," she grinned. "Fox thinks so, but Knight just tolerates him."

"Why?"

"Because...he's Fox. He's a good guy."

I turned to her slightly. "You arrived with him. You're his fiancé."

"The one and only," she grinned.

"Can I ask a personal question?"

"Of course."

"Why...how..."

She smirked as if she already knew what I was thinking. "Fox has known me since we were kids. I only met him when he kidnapped me from my life and took me away from it all."

Wow, talk about a pile of emotional luggage that needed to be unpacked. "Um...You're not still his hostage, are you?"

"No, but I would gladly be. See this?" She held up her right hand which was mangled in the most hideous way. The whole palm of her hand looked like it had been severely damaged. I couldn't imagine what had happened to cause such damage.

"What happened?"

"A bad person came after me. It's because of Fox that I lived. And I got to watch as the man suffered a very terrible death."

"And you're okay with that?" I asked incredulously.

She turned to me, her face completely serious. "It's how I sleep at night. Some day, you'll meet a man who calms the fear inside you. He'll take every worry and care out of your world, and put them on his shoulders to bear the burden. When you find that man, never let him go. He'll protect you with his life, and make sure you never have to suffer another day in your life."

With that, she walked forward, clapping her hands and cheering for the man currently waiting for the madman in front of us to fire his gun at her fiancé. I didn't really understand it. But then I looked over at Thumper and remembered how he saved me in the forest—how he held me in his arms and quieted the world around me.

I may not understand this part of his world, but she was right. He made me feel safe in a way I never thought I needed. He made me wish I could always be in his arms, to have that security of knowing he would always be there for me.

I linked my fingers through his and squeezed his hand. "Are you ready to go to bed?"

"I thought you'd never ask."

27

THUMPER

WAKING up with Bree's body tangled around mine was something I wouldn't have relished just five days ago. But since then, I'd come to grips with the fact that despite how different we were, something about her gripped me by the heart and pulled me into her radius.

I didn't quite understand it myself. How did I go from wanting to strangle her to insane jealousy, to needing to hold her and remind myself that she was safe as long as I was with her? I didn't even really know her. She was a workaholic. That's it. That was the extent of my knowledge about her. Yet, I couldn't deny my attraction to her.

And then there was the way she looked at me with all the trust in the world, knowing I would do anything to keep her safe...My heart-beat doubled every time she looked at me with that fierce loyalty. But my greatest fear was that when all this was over, she would go her way and I'd go mine. The intense attraction we both felt would fall away as we got back into the routine of our lives. She would forget about me, and the time we shared together this week. And what would I do? Go back to living my life the way I wanted without a care for any woman? I couldn't do that. I didn't have it in me.

I was never a love 'em and leave 'em kind of guy to begin with, but this job made it impossible to form any sort of relationship—especially when we moved states, and then left for work every few weeks. Bree wasn't the type to sit around waiting for a man. She was too driven, too focused on her own life to let any man rule her world.

And yet, that might be the key to our happiness.

Her breath slid over my bare chest as she wiggled in my arms and finally woke up. Watching her over the past hour was a little creepy, but I needed it to reassure me that I hadn't lost her yet. Her eyes fluttered open and an insanely beautiful smile lit up her face. My breath caught as I watched her watching me. I'd never get tired of seeing her look at me like that. I wished I could capture it on camera, so if and when this fell apart, I would have more than memories to help me remember.

"Good morning," her voice lilted as she snuggled in closer.

"How did you sleep?"

"Amazingly well, considering all that's happened. What about you? How's your head?"

"A dull ache," I lied. The headache still persisted, but I shoved it to the back of my mind, refusing to let a little thing like a head injury get in the way of enjoying my time with her. It would come to an end soon enough.

"So, what's on the agenda for today?"

"I need to check in with the guys, see if Dash found out anything while I was snoozing on the job."

"You weren't snoozing on the job. I think you've more than earned an entire night of sleep."

I sighed, sinking deeper into the bed. This thing was luxurious as hell, and for the first time in a long time, I didn't really want to get up and face the day. If I could, I'd lay here all day with Bree. But the fact was, we needed to figure out who was behind the attack on her, and even though I knew delaying would keep her with me, I couldn't allow her to live in fear even a minute longer than necessary. Her safety outweighed everything else, even my desire for her to stay.

I sat up in bed and swung my legs over the edge. My body ached with the aftereffects of the crash, but it wasn't enough to make me stay in bed. I massaged my stump, getting ready to put my bionic foot in place. At least nothing had fucked that up. There was nothing worse than being laid up because my stump was hurting. It didn't happen often, but when it did, it was because I wasn't taking care of myself.

"Do you have to go?" Bree asked, sitting up and wrapping her body around my back. Wet kisses pressed against my skin, making it damn impossible to turn her down.

"I just need to check in. If there are no updates, I'll come back to bed. You should go back to sleep."

She yawned wide and laid back down. "That sounds good."

I drew the covers up over her and pressed my lips to hers. Seeing her all warm and cozy did silly things to me, made me think of a life where we were normal with 9-5 jobs. But that wasn't in either of us, and I doubted we would be happy that way.

I finished pulling on my foot and locking it in place. When I glanced at Bree a second time, she was already fast asleep. After dressing quickly, I headed down the hall to the kitchen and grabbed some meds from the kit. I would have to forgo anything stronger if I wanted to stay awake. But if I could shove this headache aside, I would be golden for at least a little while.

"Is this wise?" IRIS asked from behind me.

"What's that?"

"You haven't really gotten any rest."

I shrugged, knowing I would say the same thing if the situation was reversed. "I got a full eight hours last night. That's more than I usually get."

"Still, I think—"

"Where the fuck is the coffee?" Slider asked as he hobbled into the kitchen.

"You too? Fucking hell, go back to sleep, Slider," IRIS snapped.

"I've slept too much as it is. Now I need coffee."

"You need to take a fucking break. What is it with you two? What part of *concussion* made you think that you should get up instead of taking it easy? And slider, you have a fucking leg wound. We're in the safest place we could be at the moment, and you're up wandering around to find fucking coffee! I'll bring a damn cup to your room!"

Slider shot me a sideways glance as he poured himself a cup. "You want some?"

"Fuck yeah," I grumbled. "How's your headache?"

"Same fucking hell as yesterday. You?"

"Same."

"Then go to bed!" IRIS shouted.

"FNG filled me in on the case. You really think your girl is the target?"

I nodded, hating that it was the most logical reason shit when down the way it did. "It's the only thing that explains this new turn of events."

"You mean, nobody's trying to kill us."

"Which is why you should both take advantage of the break and go back to fucking bed."

Slider shook his head. "I can't imagine anyone wanting her dead. For what reason?"

"I'm hoping Dash has something to tell us."

"It won't be good news. Nobody says *Good news, I know who wants to kill you.*"

"But it is good news if we can go kill the fucker."

He snorted, taking a sip of his coffee, grimacing as he drank it. "This tastes like piss. Who made this?"

Anna walked into the room, grinning at us. "I did. Don't let Fox hear you say you don't like my coffee. He'll lose his mind."

Slider instantly schooled his features. "It's...tasty piss. Like...something I'd drink if I was stranded in the wilderness with no water to drink."

I chuckled at his terrible attempt to make it better. Anna just smirked at him, getting her own cup down. "I never said I made good coffee."

She started to pour her cup, but the pot wobbled in her right hand, spilling coffee all over the counter. "Shit!" I rushed over to help her. She flexed her right hand, grimacing when it cramped up. I snatched a towel off the counter and cleaned her hand off, then started to massage her palm.

"You need to have Fox massage lotion on your hand every night at bedtime. See these cracks? That's not helping the healing process. And massages will help encourage blood flow."

219

"Why the fuck are your hands on my girl?" Fox snapped as he walked into the room. Then he noticed the spilled coffee on the counter and me massaging her hand. "Baby, what's wrong?"

"Nothing, I just—"

"She needs daily massages. It wouldn't hurt to do some strength training too. And you need to apply lotion every night. These cracks could lead to infection."

"Fox—" she started, but he interrupted her.

"Why didn't you tell me your hand was bothering you? I'm going to kill that doctor the next time I see him." His face turned dark as he stared at his fiancé in pain.

"I'm fine. It was a cramp."

"It starts as a cramp," I told her. "That's a warning sign that you need to step it up. Use it or lose it," I shrugged.

"Baby, you should have let me get your coffee."

"Actually—" I was about to tell him that the more she used it, the better it would be for her, but the death glare from Fox had me backing off.

Anna was no wilting flower. I might have thought so when I first started protecting her, but after seeing the strength she drew from Fox, I knew she could handle a lot of shit.

"Don't drink this piss," Fox said, pouring the coffee down the drain. "I'll get you real coffee, the good shit."

"I made that coffee," Anna smirked.

Fox stood there in shock for a moment, then stumbled over his words, trying to make it better. "Uh…it's…fantastic shit. I mean, not shit, but good…"

"You guys are too easy," Anna smiled as she walked away.

Fox looked at me in confusion. "Does that mean she didn't make the coffee or that she's fucking with me?"

"Maybe a little of both."

He nodded, then chased after her, calling her name. Slider smirked at me as he continued to drink it.

"I thought you didn't like it?" I asked.

He shrugged. "The way my head is pounding, I'll take just about anything right now."

"Yeah, don't listen to me and actually go take care of yourself," IRIS muttered, now sitting at the kitchen table, flipping through a magazine. "What would I know? I only had to drag both your asses out of a firefight."

"Actually, I walked out and carried Slider, so…"

He lowered his magazine and glowered at me. "So, what?"

"So…" I narrowed my eyes at him, not sure how he wasn't seeing where I was going with this.

"I'm going to check in with Jones. Hopefully, he has some idea what the fuck is going on."

"What do you mean?"

"Where the hell are we?" he scoffed. "I know we don't have any safe houses like this."

I laughed, only to hold my head when it started to throb. I forgot that he'd been out of it most of the time. "FNG didn't tell you?" He shook his head. "We're at Knight's house."

"Knight? You mean, Fox's obsession, Knight?"

"The one and only," I grinned. Man, this headache was more than worth it to see the shocked expression on Slider's face.

"Fuck, no wonder he came. I was wondering what would make him drag his woman out here."

"I actually told you last night, asshat," IRIS muttered. "Not that you would pay attention to me anyway. What would I know?"

"His wife Kate patched you up."

He grinned, nodding as he remembered. "Yeah, hot chick."

"I wouldn't let him hear you say that. You'll end up buried in the back yard."

I slapped him on the shoulder and set my coffee down. "I'm going to check in with Dash."

"I'll come with you. I need the distraction from the pain."

"Yeah, don't listen to me," IRIS snapped. "I'm only trying to keep you guys alive, but what the hell do I know?"

I stopped behind IRIS and pressed my hands into his shoulders. "Are you alright, IRIS? You seem a little stressed."

"Because you won't fucking listen to me."

"Are you still going on about that? Christ, it's a concussion. We've all had them before. Feel the pain, am I right?"

Slider nodded in agreement. "Death before dishonor."

"That's taking it a tad far," IRIS argued.

Slider's gaze narrowed in dangerously on IRIS. "Not in my eyes."

I laughed as he turned on his heel and stormed out of the room. Well, he limped, but he made it look badass.

"Look on the bright side, he's not unconscious anymore."

"But for how long?" IRIS asked.

I pulled out a chair and sat down beside him. "What's going on with you? Where's badass IRIS that's not afraid of anything? Now you're babying the fuck out of all of us."

He sighed, hanging his head. "Ever since the accident...you and Slider nearly died in that accident."

That was taking things a little far. Neither of us was ready to meet our maker.

"And I couldn't do anything for you. Jane was gone and my only thought was keeping her safe. But when it was all done, I felt... horrible because I left you guys behind. I mean, I stayed until the ambulance arrived, but you were in the hospital. What kind of teammate leaves one behind, let alone two? That was me, chasing after a woman instead of taking care of the men who had my back? That guilt is eating me up inside. And I know you guys don't blame me. If we had been even a minute later, Jane might be dead. But then you guys were injured again, and all those feelings came rushing back. You're my brothers. I need you to be there. I need to take care of you and know I'm not letting you down again."

I stared at him for a moment, nodding my head as he let out a deep breath. Then I stood and slapped him on the shoulder as I passed. "Well...good luck with that."

"Dash, you've been digging into her life all night. You're telling me you still don't have anything yet?"

He stopped typing and turned to glare at me. "Yes, I'm working a little slower, seeing as how one of my arms isn't fucking working."

I winced, my eyes drifting to his bandaged shoulder. "Sorry."

"It's okay," he sighed. "I want to find out who tried to kill us just as much as you. It's just taking a little longer than expected."

"You could call Rae for help."

He snorted, shaking his head at me. "Are you fucking crazy? And admit that she might be able to do my job better than me at the moment?"

"You're not admitting she's better. You're saying you need help."

"Which she would take as a sign that she's better. You don't get how she works."

I was pretty sure I completely understood the relationship between Rae and Dash. It was based purely on sibling rivalry, except they weren't siblings. "What can I do to help?"

"Nothing," he muttered. "I'm just running through this list of names." He slammed his hand down on the keyboard in anger. "It's just taking me twice as damn long!"

I snatched the list and looked it over. I didn't actually think I could help in any way, but when I was looking at the names, one in particular caught my attention. "Hey, what was her boss's name again?"

"Preston Hobbs. I already looked at him. He's clean."

"What about his son?"

"I haven't gotten to him yet. He's not exactly high ranking in the company."

"Exactly," I said, tossing down the papers. "Bree said the son didn't like her, that she was promoted before him."

"And that's a reason to take out a hit on her?" he said skeptically.

"I don't know, but it's worth checking out."

"Alright," Dash said, running the background on him. He let out a low whistle after several minutes of digging. "He's not hurting for money. Daddy must pay him well. At least, he had money until he paid one million dollars to an unknown account."

"A million dollars? That sounds an awful lot like money for a hit."

"But a hit usually gets paid half up front, half when the job is completed."

"Except, we didn't have a single hitter coming at us," I said, thinking it through. "We had multiple attempts on her life within hours of each attempt. That suggests he put out a major hit, and he thought he'd get his money back fast if he put out a million dollars."

"Yeah, but how do you get back a million that fast?" he asked. "Uh-oh…"

"Uh-oh, what?"

"It looks like Liam likes to gamble."

"Christ," I rubbed a hand over my jaw. "How much is he in for?"

"Give me a minute."

His fingers on one hand flew over the keyboard as he did some searches. I didn't know where the hell he got his information from. The man had contacts all over the place, and despite the rivalry between him and Rae, he was just as qualified for his job as her. That's why Rae got such a kick out of their rivalry. He was a challenge for her.

I sat by, my heel bouncing on the ground as I waited impatiently for any information he would find. This was why I never stuck around while the research was being done. I felt like I would crawl out of my skin waiting on the information.

Finally, he leaned back in his seat and sighed. "You're not going to like it."

"Just tell me."

"Two million to some pretty big players. Interest is beyond what this job would cover."

I sat back in my seat, trying to see where Bree figured into this. "She couldn't have gotten a raise that would cover that, not in the timeframe he would need it to pay off the debt."

"We need to talk to Bree and find out what this raise of hers entailed."

"I'm not sure I want her to know what's going on yet."

"You don't have much of a choice. If we're going to find out if this guy had anything to do with the attempts on her life, we need as much information as possible."

I knew he was right, but I wanted to protect her from reality for as long as possible. "Alright, let's go talk to her."

I pushed up from my seat and headed back through the enormous house toward our bedroom. When we were just outside the door, I turned and pressed my hand to his chest. "You wait out here."

He held up his hand, stepping back with a smirk on his face. "No problem, man."

"And get that smirk off your face. I don't like that you've seen her naked."

"I do, and I know it bugs the shit out of you, which makes this so much better."

"Do you want me to shoot you in the other arm?"

"Then how would you get the information you need?"

"I'll call Rae. I'm sure she'd love to hold this over your head for the next year."

He narrowed his eyes at me. "That's just mean."

I turned and opened the door. Thankfully, Bree was fully clothed, so at least I didn't have to worry about anyone else seeing her naked.

"Hey," she smiled. "Are you coming back to bed? I just got dressed to come find you."

"Actually, I need to talk to you about something."

The smile on her face vanished and she nodded. "Just let me put on my shoes."

"I'll wait outside."

I turned and opened the door, stepping out into the hall. "She's coming out."

"Damn, so I don't get to see her in the bedroom again."

"Keep pushing," I snarled.

Bree stepped out behind me with a strained smile on her face. "Wow, a party waiting in the hall for me. This must be good."

"Let's head back to the study," Dash said, leading the way.

Bree slipped her hand into mine and squeezed. I knew she was nervous. Hell, this was no picnic for me either. I wanted to take this off her shoulders and know she wouldn't have to worry about a thing.

Dash shoved open the door and took a seat in front of his computer. "Bree, what exactly do you know about Liam Hobbs?"

She stood there in shock. "Um…he's Preston's son. I know he wants my job, but he's never shown that he's up to the task. Well, that's not entirely true. He works hard, but his ideas don't run along the same lines as the company. He wants to take things in a different direction. And every time he fails, his work gets worse." She looked between the two of us nervously. "Why? Do you think he's the one after me?"

"It's too early to say," Dash said, brushing off her worries. Right now, it looks like he owes quite a bit of money to some pretty bad people."

"That doesn't really surprise me," she muttered.

"The thing is, he has money, but not enough to cover the debts. What were the terms of the contract when you were offered the raise?" I asked.

"About two hundred thousand more a year with stock options. Most of the benefits the company could offer me, I was already taking advantage of. Preston knew how hard I worked and increased my benefits before he should have."

"So, there was no bonus at the beginning of your new job?"

"No, not that I'm aware of. I guess it might have been different for his son."

I looked to Dash. "That makes sense. If he was expected to take over one day, it stands to reason that he had a lot more to gain."

"But I stepped into that position," Bree said nervously. "I was going to take over one of the executive positions in the company."

"I think it's time we paid Liam a visit," Dash grinned.

2 8

THUMPER

"You want to do what?" Cash shouted into the phone.

I pulled it away from my ear, wincing at how loud he was being.

"Cash, listen to me—"

"No, you listen. A day ago, Knight was certain this had to do with Rafe. Now you want to go off and chase down a businessman's son based on a hunch and torture him."

"We don't intend to torture him," I lied.

"I do, boss!" Fox shouted. "I can't wait to get my hands on this fucker."

I glared at him in the backseat, rethinking my decision to bring him along.

"You brought Fox?" he shouted.

Again, I pulled the phone away from my ear. "Boss—"

"You're supposed to be the sane one."

"I thought that was Lock."

"Him too, but now he's got longer hair and he looks like a fucking hippie. What the hell is going on with you guys? Falling in love and growing out your hair? Where are the guys I hired?"

"Right here, boss!" Fox shouted. "Just as eager as ever to kick some ass and eat some pig's feet. Hey, did you know there's something called Turtle Soup? I can't wait to get my hands on that."

"You're not going. I won't allow it."

The engines roared to life and Scottie turned around, giving me a thumbs up.

"What is that sound?" Cash asked.

"Uh…"

"Is Scottie flying my plane?"

"Do you want the truth or a version of the truth?"

"Thumper—"

"Don't worry, boss. We've got the plastic in place. And since this isn't a dangerous mission, it's highly unlikely he'll even vomit."

"Tell him to shut down the plane."

I stalled as long as I could while Scottie turned us down the runway. "Uh…we're being waved on."

"Stop the plane."

"They're saying to go," I insisted.

"Shut it down!"

"Oh shoot, we're taking off. I guess I was too late." I snickered as I exchanged looks with Fox.

"Turn around right the fuck now!"

"What's that, boss? I can't hear you. You're breaking up."

I hung up, hoping that was the last I heard from him. Walking up to the front of the plane, I pulled the plastic aside and sat down in the copilot's seat. "How's it looking?"

"Should be a steady ride," he said, pulling back on the yoke as we reached full speed.

"I lied to Cash and told him we already took off. He might be pissed at you."

"Hey, I was listening to Lock. He ordered me to fly you out to New York. As far as I'm concerned, I was just doing my job."

"Do you need me to stay up here?"

He slowly turned and looked at me. "Do I look like I need help?"

"No, but—"

"Do you know how to fly a plane?"

"No, but—"

"Then get the fuck out of the cockpit and leave me alone."

"Geez, somebody's grouchy."

"Because I haven't seen Quinn in a fucking month," he grumbled. "I'm working on getting her a job in Kansas."

"What does she say about that?"

He winced slightly. "She doesn't exactly know. But I didn't spend all that time building the fire only for the flames to go out."

I nodded, not quite understanding what he was saying. "Sorry, what?"

"You didn't hear about the fire?"

"Do I want to know about the fire?"

"Man, I can't believe no one told you. When I met Quinn, I knew she wasn't just some random hookup. We had this chemistry I couldn't explain. So, I built a fire."

When I didn't immediately say *ah,* he shot me a dirty look.

"I laid out the groundwork to build a fire with her. I didn't want to explode into flames with her and burn out fast. I wanted to build the heat between us so she wouldn't want to leave. I fanned the flames until we were so hot we were ready to burn up in the atmosphere."

I frowned, thinking back to what I knew. "Didn't she run away to Alaska to escape you?"

He huffed in irritation. "That was before I fully ignited the flames. She didn't exactly know what I was doing."

"It sounds like you didn't either," I muttered.

"So," he grinned. "Are you going to build a fire with Bree?"

I stood up and clapped him on the shoulder. "Your metaphors are as bad as you're flying."

I headed to the back and sat down with IRIS. Slider was still at the house with everyone else. He wasn't in any condition to travel yet. In fact, Lock argued that I wasn't either, but I wasn't about to miss out on something so important. Besides, I needed time to think about my situation with Bree.

"You ready for this?" IRIS asked, cracking his knuckles in anticipation.

"Seriously? I think I'm in the most control out of any of us. You'll want to strap a bomb to his car. Fox will want to dunk him in acid, and

Scottie will be lucky if he makes it off the plane not covered in vomit. I think I've got this."

"Yeah, but are you ready for what happens when it's over?"

"Not even fucking close," I sighed, resting my head back against the headrest.

"What is it about this woman? You seem like complete opposites."

"We are. That's the problem. Or maybe it's a good thing. She's got her own life and her own ambitions. I could never be with someone that sat around waiting for me."

"I hear ya. Jane's the same. She's buried in her books more times than not. And when she gets wrapped up in writing, not even sex will distract her. I have to practically force food down her throat."

"See? That's what I'm talking about. It could be good. But would she be happy in the middle of nowhere? She just got this big promotion."

"Yeah, I have a feeling that if Fox gets his hands on the son, her boss won't be so interested in keeping her at the company."

"So, I've fucked it up for her."

"Better out of a job than dead," he said reassuringly. Or, that's how it was supposed to sound.

"I guess, but I don't want her to end up resenting me."

He leaned forward, shooting me an odd look. "You guess? Like you have to question whether or not it's better if she's out of a job than dead?"

"That's not what I meant, and you know it."

"Look, when I was courting Jane—"

I snorted in amusement. "Is that what you call that?"

"It was dating," he snapped.

"It was *not* dating. You kissed her while she was dating another man. You made her question her relationship. You got fucking pissed that she slept with him."

"She didn't," he grumbled. "Thank God for that. I might not have recovered. It's bad enough I have to compete with IKE."

"He's a good guy. I like him," I nodded. "I was actually thinking he might make a good fourth for us."

"Excuse me, I couldn't have heard you right. Are you seriously suggesting that I work with the man she wrote about in her books?"

"Is there a problem with that?" I egged him on.

"Have you seen him? He looks like something out of a James Bond movie. Hell, even the way he smokes a cigarette is endearing, and I hate smokers!"

"So, get a pack and try it out."

"And look like I'm trying to be him? Not a chance in hell."

"Is that what you're really worried about? That you'll look like him?"

"No, I'm fucking worried that Jane's going to continue working around him and fawn all over him."

I rolled my eyes at him. "Is that likely? I mean, you've seen how obsessed with you she is."

"She was obsessed with Alexander fucking Pierce, and look how that turned out."

"Yeah, he tried to kill her. Don't do that and you should be fine."

He sat back, scrubbing his hand down his face. "There are too many fucking new people. The Young Squad, IKE, this fucker Officer Tate."

"Fox's friend? Yeah, that should be interesting," I grinned. "I can't wait for him to get out here."

"What is it with you and being so fucking gleeful about new recruits? I don't like it."

"That's because you're not seeing the bigger picture. The more recruits, the less we have to go out on job after job. The more time we have to spend with our women."

"If we can hang onto them," he sighed. "Fucking IKE and Liam Hobbs."

I nodded. I couldn't agree more.

Dressed in full tactical gear, I approached Liam Hobb's house from the back. Fox was somewhere being Fox, and IRIS had the front. Scottie was waiting in the SUV, having made it all the way here without vomiting once.

Peering through the back door, I slowly turned the handle, feeling it give in my grip. "Back entrance is clear."

"We're good at the front," IRIS said over comms.

"You guys are not gonna believe this," Fox snickered. "I wish you could see things from my point of view."

"What?"

"He's got a lady in the room with him."

I rolled my eyes. "And what's so hilarious about that?"

"I guess you'd have to see it upside down."

That gave me pause. "Fox, where the fuck are you?"

"Hanging off the roof, looking in his window. Should I freak him out and tap on the window?"

"The idea is to go in silent," I said tersely. "No witnesses."

"Welp, that's going to be a problem while he's entertaining a lady."

I thought through our situation, coming up with a solution. "I'll go in first and make some noise. We just need enough to distract him and get him downstairs. We'll snatch him while she's still upstairs."

"And then she'll call the police when she realizes he's gone."

Again, Fox snickered. "She's not likely to call the police in the position she's in. I've never seen a woman so tied up before. Seriously, let me have some fun with them."

"Fox, stay out of sight," I snapped. "I'm going in."

I carefully pushed open the door, then crept through the house, careful to keep my steps light until I was in the right position. "IRIS, meet me in the front hall."

"Roger that."

After a moment, I saw his shadow moving through the house, and when he was in position, he gave me a thumb's up. Glancing around, I found a glass on a table and knocked it to the floor. Slipping back into the shadows, I waited for the footsteps on the stairs. Within seconds, the asshole was running down the stairs, flipping on lights as he went. I remained hidden until he passed me, then slipped out behind him, quickly covering his mouth with my hand as I dragged him to the back of the house.

IRIS hurried over, syringe in hand as I got him out the back door. After IRIS stuck him, it was only seconds before he passed out. "Scottie Dog, we're ready to go."

"On my way. Street's clear."

"Fox, get your ass down."

"Just a minute," he said, his breaths coming out in huffs.

I got a bad feeling, my gaze snapping up to meet IRIS's. "Fox, what are you doing?"

"Nothing, I swear."

I rolled my eyes, knowing whatever he was doing was bound to come back on us. I heaved Liam up in my arms as IRIS grabbed his feet. "Fucking prick," I muttered. I was pissed just to have to haul his ass around knowing what he did to Bree.

"You'll get your turn," IRIS said, trying to calm me down.

"Not if Fox gets his way."

"Fox," IRIS hissed over comms. "Are you here to help or to be a pain in the ass?"

"Coming," he said in a sing-song voice. "I checked out his movie collection, and let me tell you, I'm not impressed. He doesn't have a single musical in his entire collection. And don't get me started on all the girly movies he has."

"Fox, that doesn't matter right now," I argued.

"I'd say it does. It gives us a good idea of who we're working with. He should be easy to break."

"I already have that covered. There's no need to get out the vat of acid."

"What? What are you talking about? Why wouldn't I need the acid?"

"Because I have something scarier."

"Then why the hell did I come out here?"

"Good question," I muttered. I was beginning to wonder why I thought it was a good idea to bring him.

"You know, I'm starting to feel very used," he said, now running toward us.

IRIS and I were nearly to the SUV where Scottie was waiting. He popped the trunk and we shoved Liam inside, then slammed the door and got in. Fox got in the front, turning around with a scowl on his face.

"I had plans," he muttered. "Good fucking plans. I got quite a few ideas from those pickled pigs' feet. I was looking forward to testing them out."

"Sorry to disappoint you," I said sarcastically.

Scottie pulled away and headed through the gated community toward the shitty end of the city. Thankfully, we didn't have to find a location to interrogate this asshole. My contact had that covered for us.

"So, are you going to fill the rest of us in on who you brought in?" Fox asked.

"Trust me, it'll be worth the suspense when I reveal him."

Fox shook his head, clearly agitated that he wasn't my go-to scary guy on this job. "You know, it's not right. This is my thing, and you're cutting me off at the knees."

I pulled out my secret weapon and handed it up to him. "I know, and I'm really sorry."

He stared at the bag of Funyuns for a second, then a grin split his lips. "I'm not saying all is forgiven, but I'm not quite as angry as I was."

Fifteen minutes later, we arrived at an abandoned warehouse. I slammed the door as I got out and IRIS walked around, shaking his head at me. "Do you ever wonder why interrogations always take place in abandoned warehouses?"

I slowly looked at him. "Because they're abandoned."

"Right, and then someone comes around and turns this into an apartment complex, having no idea what shady shit happened here. I'm never living in a warehouse."

"I'll keep that in mind when we head back to Kansas."

IRIS and I grabbed Liam out of the back and headed to the entrance. Scottie pulled up the rear, while Fox sat munching on his Funyuns without a care in the world.

"Not joining us anymore?" I asked Fox over comms.

"What's the point? It's not like I get to have any fun."

"But then you'll miss my surprise," I said, knowing I had him.

After a minute, I heard the SUV door slam and his heavy footsteps jog up behind us. "Alright, you got me, but only because I need to know if this is really better than me doling out some punishment."

"I promise, it'll be worth it."

Scottie flung the door open, shaking his head at me. "I'm really fucking glad I'm not on his team."

"I was really hoping for a reenactment of the famous tango. It's the perfect opportunity."

We headed down a dark hallway that opened up into a large space.

"I can leave your ass behind," he threatened. "I'm sure Cash would love to pay for commercial flights for all of you after his own plane was used to haul you out here."

"I would not."

Cash stepped out of the shadows, his arms hanging at his side, but he was anything but relaxed.

"Boss," IRIS said. "Funny meeting you here."

"Is it?"

Cash narrowed his gaze on the fucker in my arms. I shifted him slightly, getting ready to drop him if Cash came after me. He was pissed as hell, but I could see the excitement twinkling in his eyes. He needed this.

"How'd you beat us out here?"

"Easy, I have connections too." He left it at that, not saying anything else as he turned on his heel and headed to the chair strategically placed in the middle of the room. We arrived early and I staged the room how I wanted it, but he'd clearly been here after us and made a few changes of his own. The tools I had laid out were all gone, and the chair was now facing some chains that were hanging from the ceiling.

"I see you redecorated."

"I thought we'd go for a more rugged approach this time. Acid is so overrated."

Fox scoffed behind me. "Boss, you're attacking my work. I'm not sure I appreciate that."

"Well, that's the brilliant thing about me employing you. I don't have to care what you think."

Fox walked over to the wall and slid down, pulling out some more

Funyuns. "Clearly, I'm not wanted. I'll just sit over here and munch on these fantastic treats."

IRIS and I dropped Liam into the chair, not bothering to strap him down. The little weasel wouldn't get far from us, no matter how much he tried. Besides, half the torture was knowing he could run, but it wouldn't make an ounce of difference.

I nodded to IRIS. "Let's get this show on the road."

Cash stepped in and held up his hand. "No more drugs. You took it this far. Let's do this right."

He cracked his knuckles, then slammed his fist into Liam's face. He groaned, rolling his head to the side, nearly falling out of his chair. I had to admit, I liked Cash taking things old school. There was a simplicity to it that made me yearn for days before Fox got into his crazy torture.

"What...what's going on?" Liam muttered, his head still in a haze from the drugs.

"Somebody hasn't been playing nicely with others," Cash said, shaking out his shoulders. "We're going to get to the bottom of this, and how that ends for you depends on what you're willing to tell us."

The man looked utterly terrified, but he didn't say a word. His lips pursed together as he watched Cash walk slowly around him. His nostrils flared when Cash walked behind him, out of sight. Then he saw Fox sitting against the wall eating Funyuns, and the panic really set in.

"I...I don't know anything. Why am I here?"

"Bree Wilton," I said, studying the way his eyes got wide when I said her name. "I see you recognize the name."

"Of course I do. She works with me. What does that have to do with anything?"

I walked forward, resting my hands on the arms of the chair. "I think you know," I whispered. "The question is, how long until you break? I give it five minutes."

In a panic, he swung his gaze from me to IRIS to Scottie. "You gotta believe me. I have no clue what's going on here. I...I didn't do anything."

"No?" I questioned, nodding to Cash.

He immediately grabbed him from behind, wrapping his arm around the fucker's neck. He choked and squirmed, pulling at Cash's arm, which had the opposite effect of what he intended. Cash only squeezed harder until the man turned bright red and a wet spot appeared at the front of his pants.

When Cash released him, the man choked and coughed, crying as he sat before us like the sniveling weasel he was. "I swear, I don't know what you're talking about!"

"The hit," I snapped. "Tell me who you hired."

"What are you talking about? What hit?"

"The one you put on Bree's head!" I yelled, slamming my fist into his face. His nose crunched with the blow and blood spewed down his face. Tears mixed with the blood, making it run in tiny rivulets down his neck. "Tell me who you hired!"

"I didn't," he cried. "I didn't hire anyone." His sobs did nothing to make me feel sympathy for him. I could break him with my fists in a matter of minutes, but I had more than one motive here tonight. I had to consider what happened when the hit was gone, and how Bree would move on with her life. And that required evidence that would keep his father in check and off Bree's back.

I nodded to IRIS, who whistled over his shoulder. Fox perked up, immediately standing with his bag, shoving more Funyuns into his face faster than before. "Man, the suspense is killing me," he grinned.

Out of the shadows stepped the one man that could really lay the fear of God into Liam. The mobster that Liam owed money to was as slick as they came, dressed in a pricey suit with two goons at his side. Normally, I wouldn't get them involved, but I needed Liam to pay out the money. If they thought his plan to take out Bree would work, they'd let Liam carry out his plan.

"Mr. Hobbs. It's so good to see you again. I hear you've failed to deliver what you promised."

"Man!" Fox said excitedly. "You're right. This is so much better!"

Liam's entire body shook as he stared at the man. His eyes flashed to mine pleadingly, but fell on deaf ears. "Mr. Santini," he stumbled over his words. "I can still get you the money. I just need a few more days."

Benny Santini was ruthless. He didn't give second chances or allow extra time to pay a debt. If you didn't pay, your life was over. And then he went after your family, friends, and anyone else that meant anything to you. Then he killed your dog.

Santini clucked his tongue as he took a few steps closer to the man sitting in the chair. "You had your chance and you failed. Either I get my money tonight, or I'll have to allow my friends to teach you a lesson." He got in Liam's face and grinned. "Remember, we discussed this when you first came to me, telling me of your plans to get rid of the girl."

Liam swallowed hard, his eyes shifting to mine. "I...I swear, I didn't want to do it. You have to believe me," he cried.

"You lied to Santini," I said, hoping he would spill his guts for the camera I had rolling right this very minute. "Bree's position wouldn't have allowed for a two million dollar payout. Not in the timeframe you had."

He looked to Santini nervously. "It would." He ducked his head, his whole body shaking wildly. When he finally looked up, he had tears streaming down his face. "The company had an insurance policy on her."

"What? That doesn't make sense. Why would they buy insurance on an employee in finance?"

"Because of the training that goes into the employees," he argued.

"She would have known about it," I countered.

"Not when she started. Back then, you didn't need employee consent," he whimpered. "And when she got this new job, the policy went up. It would have been enough to cover all my debts. It's called Dead Peasant Insurance. You can look it up. It's completely legal."

"Killing the employee for profit is not," I snapped.

"It's not like I wanted to do it," he cried. "I had no choice!"

"You always have a choice!" I shouted. "And you thought you could get away with stealing the insurance money from your father's company?"

"I would have paid it back. Every dime."

I looked up and nodded to IRIS, who walked over to the hidden camera and turned it off.

"Send it over."

"Send…" Liam looked at me nervously. "What are you doing?"

"I think your father deserves to know that you planned to embezzle money from his company. Because you're his son, I'm sure he'll pay your debts. If not, you can try to persuade Mr. Santini for an extension, but I wouldn't bank on that, so you'd better work on your begging. Now, about this hit…"

Liam was quickly losing it. His eyes were glassed over as he stared into space, knowing he was well and truly fucked. Even if his father paid his debt, there was no way he'd have a job any longer. He could kiss any kind of inheritance goodbye after the shit he pulled.

I slapped him across the face, getting his attention again. "Who has the contract?"

He shook his head, closing his eyes as tears slipped down his face. "I…I went through a broker. There wasn't just one guy. He assured me this was for the best, to ensure the job was completed," he pleaded.

"So, call it off!" I yelled.

"I can't! The money's been paid. It's in an escrow account until the job is completed."

I sucked in a breath, running my hands through my hair as the reality of the situation came crashing down on me. Bree would never be safe. As long as that money was out there, it wouldn't stop until she was dead.

I turned around and kicked him hard in the chest. Cash moved out of the way just in time, allowing the chair to tip backward and crash to the floor. I turned and yelled as rage swarmed through me. I wanted to kill this fucker, but he would have to stay alive until I figured out how to protect Bree.

"Want me to dunk him in acid now?" Fox asked, wiggling his eyebrows at me.

29

BREE

I WAS COMPLETELY restless as I waited for any word from Thumper. He'd only been gone for a few hours, not nearly long enough to have solved my problem. Yet, I found myself wishing he would just call and check in with me. I hated that I needed to talk to him, that I had become this woman that was clingy and needed her boyfriend's reassurance that everything would be okay.

Boyfriend?

Shit, when had that happened? I'd gone from a woman that rarely dated to a woman that considered herself attached after only a week. And for half of that time, Thumper and I couldn't stand each other.

"Bree?"

I spun around, panic building inside me as I stared at Anna. "This is it, isn't it?"

"This is...what?"

She stared at me in confusion. Of course, I had to actually open my mouth and tell her what was going on if I wanted her help. But instead, I stood there like a fool with my mouth gaping. I was never this incoherent. I was the master of conversation back at the office. The appropriate conversation, that is. I could draw in a crowd and make them listen to the most boring financial speak. How? I made it interesting with fancy phrases and exciting facial expressions. But talking about romance?

"I don't know what's wrong with me." I started flapping my hands, not knowing what else to do. I was nervous, felt like I would throw up, and my heart was racing in my chest.

"Okay," Anna said, rushing over to me. "I think we need to get away."

"Yeah? Like to a spa?"

"I'm afraid we won't be able to leave, but Kate was telling me about this great place. Why don't you get a swimsuit on and we'll head out there?" she said gently.

God, I was back to the Bree that Thumper despised, freaking out over small things and annoying everyone with my whiny attitude. "I don't have a swimsuit. I don't even have a change of clothes!"

"Bree, take a deep breath and calm down. There are spare swimsuits upstairs. I'll grab the towels and everything we need. You just go get changed. You can do this, alright?"

I nodded, even though I felt anything but okay. I was a wreck. I knew it, Anna knew it, and soon everyone else in the house would know it. Hell, it was already too late to hide the mess I was. I scurried upstairs to my room, flinging open drawers in an attempt to find what I was looking for. Not even the knock on the bedroom door could distract me from my task. It was like this one step would help me set my head straight. At least I hoped it would.

"Bree? What's going on?" Dash asked.

"Nothing. I just need..."

"You need what?"

I shut another drawer, then rushed over to the closet, flinging the doors open.

"Bree, what's going on? You're panicking."

I laughed at that. "Panicking? No, that's not me. I don't panic. If anything, I'm cool and calm. I'm the opposite of panic."

"Then what do you call this? Because it sure as hell isn't calm."

"I just need a swimsuit," I muttered. "Get the swimsuit. That's what she said."

"You know, I love this whole muttering to yourself thing. It's new…different."

I spun around and faced Dash for the first time. "Look, I need a swimsuit. It will help me…calm down or something. But I can't find the swimsuit, and until I do, I'm going to be a little chaotic because the swimsuit isn't here and I'm supposed to be in it."

"Um…" He looked at me funnily, clearly not understanding what I just said. Hell, I wasn't even sure what I just said, but it made sense in my head.

I turned around and got back to work, flipping through the hangers for any sign of these elusive swimsuits. A throat cleared behind me and I spun around, only to find Dash holding up a swimsuit.

"Is this what you're looking for?"

It was skimpy, something I would never wear. But Anna told me to get a swimsuit, and Dash was holding one. One step was complete. Now I just had to get dressed. I hurried over, snatched it out of his hands, then started stripping.

"Okay," Dash cleared his throat, quickly turning around. "Give a guy some warning. Thumper would kick my ass if he knew I saw you stripping."

I huffed out a laugh. "*Thumper* would. I don't even know the man's name. What the hell is wrong with me? Who goes and falls for a man without knowing his name? First name. Last name. I have none of those details. And he's out there fighting for me. And I don't know his name!"

"Tate," he answered uncomfortably.

"Tate. Ha! It suits him. Perfect for him, actually. But did I ask? No, and you know why not?"

"Do I really want to know?"

I pulled the bottoms of the swimsuit up, not even aware that I had just totally stripped in front of Thumper's teammate without a care in the world.

"Because I'm selfish. I care about me. That's the definition of selfish. If you looked me up in a dictionary, the word selfish would be written next to me."

"I think you have that backward."

"And it's true! I should have at least asked him his name before I allowed him to do the most indecent, amazing, dirty things to me."

"Yeah, I really don't need to know this," he said awkwardly.

I pulled on the top and spun around. "He deserves better than me. I'm just some...horrible person from a different world, and he's this amazing man that almost died saving my life!" I cried. "What kind of person am I?"

He stared at me with wide eyes, not answering at all. Anna rushed into the room, wrapping her arms around my shoulders. "Okay, I think it's time for that girl's day. What do you say?"

I wiped the tears from my face as I nodded. "Yeah."

"Okay, let's go."

She led me out of the room, past Dash who still stood there with a dumbstruck look on his face. I was a crying mess. I knew it, and soon the rest of the house would too.

"Are we going to the pool?"

"Something like that."

"Yeah?"

She nodded, rubbing my arm as she guided me to the back door. "We're just going for a little walk."

That stopped me in my tracks. "Walk? No, I don't do walks. That's the way this whole thing started. I went for a walk and ended up being shot at. I don't do walks."

"Yeah, but we're at Knight's house. Nothing will happen to us here."

"Are you sure? Because nothing should have happened at the national park, yet Thumper brought a gun in there! I went from a law-abiding citizen to this!"

"Mmhmm. I know, but it's just a short walk. Ah, Kate's here!"

She looked relieved at seeing the other woman walk over. Kate was just like Anna, beautiful without even trying. It was no wonder they were so put together. They oozed confidence. I used to ooze confidence too. Then I was shot at and slept with an insanely hot man. Now I just oozed doubt. There was entirely too much oozing.

They ushered me out the door, past the tree line. "This doesn't look right. This is the opposite of relaxing. You're taking me into the woods, where people hike and get eaten by bears. Did I tell you about my run-in with the sheep?" I rambled. "This massive thing got stuck in my yurt and tried on my underwear. And then everyone was standing around commenting on the color and texture of my underwear, all the while a sheep was trying to eat me alive. And that was after the rabbit attacked me!"

"It's okay," Kate said reassuringly. "It's a two minute hike."

"There's that word again. Hike. I'm pretty sure I already said I didn't hike. God, what does Thumper—Tate—I really have to remember that. What was I saying?"

"Bree, you have to calm down," Anna said. "I know this is a lot to take in, but you're losing it."

"I know!" I shrieked. "This is me!" I waved at my body. "Crazy me that somehow got Tate to fall for me. At least, I think he fell for me. But that was after we nearly died. I was calmer then. Mostly because I had nearly been killed and was internalizing my panic. But now it's back, this irrational side to me that I can't seem to put a lid on. And when Tate sees this, he's going to run all over again. He'll drop me on my doorstep and never see me again."

"I think you're jumping to a lot of conclusions," Kate said soothingly. "If ever there were opposites, that would be Knight and myself. I'm a doctor and he—well, he wasn't the most upstanding person. But we made it work."

"But how?"

She shrugged slightly. "You have to find the right balance. That's what we did. And in the end, the love I felt for him outweighed my worries."

"Yeah, but that was your decision. Tate will look at me and his love will not outweigh his worries because we're not in love!"

"Are you sure about that?" Anna laughed.

"How can you love a person after a week? It's not possible! God, my feet hurt already. We've gone too far. And it's so hot out here. I can hardly breathe through the humidity."

"It's not humid out," Anna pointed out unhelpfully.

"Then the air's too clean or something. It's clogging my arteries."

"We're here," Kate said, stepping ahead of me to pull back a branch. A hot spring sat hidden on the property, completely surrounded by trees for the utmost privacy. And all around the hot spring were large boulders, perfect for laying on.

"Wow," I whispered.

"Close enough to a spa?" Anna asked.

I nodded, unable to speak. She set the towels down and kicked off her flip-flops, dipping her toes in the water.

"It's perfect."

Kate was already getting in as I stood there uncertainly. I wasn't even sure what I was worried about. It was like a hot tub, but even those could be deadly if not cleaned properly. And we were in the wilderness. Could you clean a hot spring?

"Bree, stop thinking and just get in," Anna smiled.

How could she be so calm at a time like this? My boyfriend was out there, risking his life for me, and I was going to relax in a hot spring? It didn't seem right. But since we were already here, and I was wearing the swimsuit, I dipped my toe in and instantly felt calm at the refreshing warmth.

Slowly, I sank into the spring, the warmth wrapping around me like a blanket. I couldn't remember ever feeling this relaxed. The tension seemed to seep out of my body the longer I sat here, and it had only been seconds.

"Better?" Kate asked.

Nodding, I finally started to relax.

"So, why don't you tell us what's really going on?" Anna asked, swishing her hands through the water as she rested back against a rock.

I swallowed down my fears, refusing to let them silence me. These were women that worked with dangerous men. If anyone understood, it would be them. "Thumper is this great guy. I mean...perfect in every way. He's a protector and the way he looks at me..." I shook my head, unable to even do him justice when speaking about him. "I'm just me. I'm not a country girl that likes to go hiking. I get wrapped up in financial information and find it thrilling. And when this is all over, and the excitement wears off, where does that leave us?"

"Don't you think we all wonder that?" Anna asked. "Remember I told you that Fox has known me since I was a kid?" I nodded. "He knew everything about me and what I needed before I did. You'd think something like that would get old, but it hasn't. I feel like he knows me better than anyone. He knows what I can handle, when I need space, and when he needs to pull me out of my head," she said, raising her hand. "Courtesy of a psycho…And even though Fox makes me stronger and teaches me how to deal with that fear, there are still moments when I'm too afraid to move. And that's when Fox swoops in and takes away all that fear. He shoulders the burden so I don't have to."

"That's what Thumper does for me, but…"

"But what?" Kate asked.

"What if I'm not enough?" I admitted.

They were both silent for a moment, until Kate finally spoke. "You know, I used to wonder the same thing. Hudson has this exciting life, but when he was with me, it was different. You'd be insane not to wonder how your lives will fit together. But you have to remember, you can't decide what he wants or needs. That has to be a decision he makes."

I sighed, leaning my head back against a rock as I let the sun bathe me in warm rays. This was what I should have done. A spa day would have been perfect, but instead I went hiking. But if I hadn't, I never would have met Thumper. And thinking back on my life, I realized how lonely it was before he came around. My life was devoted to work with no real friendships or relationships. Even my sister was shocked to hear from me. Maybe my perfect life wasn't so perfect after all. Maybe it was time to consider a change.

"Just what in the fuck do you think you're doing?"

I jerked at the sound of the angry male voice behind us. Kate, however, didn't even flinch. "Relaxing. What does it look like?"

"How many times have I told you I didn't want you to come out here by yourself?" Knight grumbled.

She opened her eyes and looked around. "I see two other people with me. What do you see?"

He narrowed his eyes at her. "What are their swimming qualifications? What would happen if one of you started to drown?"

"Highly unlikely," she muttered, closing her eyes.

"Yeah, I can't say Thumper would be happy with this either," Dash said as he broke through the trees with FNG.

"He wouldn't like you staring at her," FNG corrected.

"She's underwater. How exactly am I staring at her? Then again, she did strip in front of me."

FNG snorted. "Wow, he's really going to kill you."

"Hey, I turned around," Dash snapped.

"Would you two shut the fuck up?" Knight snarled. "Kate! It's time to get out."

"Mmhmm," she hummed, resting her head back and relaxing.

"Don't make me come drag you out of there."

"Sure, Hudson. Whatever you say."

Splashing to my left had me squealing as he stomped down into the spring and then swam over to her, clothes and all. She grinned as she wrapped her arms around his neck, and then a moan slipped from her lips.

My head jerked to Anna, who was laughing behind her hand. I quickly scrambled out of the spring, not needing to catch the show. Anna was on my heels as we rushed back to the house, not even bothering to gather up our things first. I could hear Dash and FNG tromping after us, making all kinds of racket. When we reached the tree line, we turned to each other and burst out laughing.

"I'm pretty sure Thumper would not have been okay with that either," Dash grumbled, storming past us.

30

THUMPER

I SAT IN THE WAREHOUSE, still running through all the possibilities in my head. I couldn't see a way out of this for Bree. Any way I sliced it, she would be in danger for the rest of her life. The only solution I could come up with was to bring her back to OPS with me. And then what? She'd live her life in hiding? She'd resent me for the rest of her life—whatever life that might be. Yeah, she'd be alive, but that didn't make up for her inability to function as a normal person.

"It's a conundrum," Fox said, flipping his knife in his hand.

I looked up and glared at him. "Thanks, I hadn't realized that."

"I mean, you can keep her safe, but what then? She doesn't exactly strike me as the type to be satisfied living in a bunker. And what happens then? Do you get married? Change her name and hope no one realizes who she is?"

"Yeah, I got the point," I snapped at him. "I'm fucked, and so is she."

"Not necessarily," IRIS spoke up. "There's one way out of this that you haven't considered yet."

I highly doubted that. I'd considered all my options, and couldn't find a single one that would give us all what we wanted. "Please, regale me with your wisdom."

"It's simple. You need to kill her," he shrugged.

"Yeah, that solves all my problems," I snapped. "Kill off the woman I love. Why didn't I think of that?"

A huge grin split his lips. "Dude, you love her? I knew this was intense, but I didn't realize…I'm so happy for you, man!"

"Yeah, it's fucking great. And you just suggested I kill her."

"Well, not seriously kill her. What you need is proof that she's dead to take to the broker so he'll release the funds. Once the funds are gone, no one will come after her."

"Except the broker when he realizes he's been duped," Cash pointed out. "His business will tank when people find out he released a hit and the funds, but the subject wasn't actually dead. And then he'll be coming for us."

"A minor problem," IRIS admitted. "These things have to be taken one problem at a time."

"The problem is, we don't have a fucking solution," I snapped.

"Technically, it's only a problem if anyone finds out he released funds without the subject being killed," Fox spoke up.

"And it would be pretty fucking obvious she wasn't dead when she walked into work completely alive," I pointed out.

"Hear me out on this," Fox continued. "We already have the black-mail on Liam and his father. Liam won't want it getting out that he hired someone to kill Bree, and his father won't want it getting out that his own son planned to swindle the company. Neither of them are going to mention that Bree is in fact alive."

"That's fucking thin," I grumbled. "You're basically placing Bree's life in the hands of men that fucking hate her. There's no way her boss is going to want her around after this blows over. No matter how good she is at her job, she's a liability now. She knows too much, and no matter how much her silence protects her, her boss can't afford to keep a woman alive with that much intel on him. And he'd do it the right way, taking her out in an apparent accident. I can't be there with her twenty-four, seven. There's no way I could keep her safe."

"So, tell her to come home with us," Cash answered. "It's the easiest way to keep her safe."

"And a sure-fire way to get her to hate me."

Fox jumped to his feet, his smile stretching wide across his face. "Alright, hear me out again. I've got the perfect solution!"

"I would love to hear this," Cash muttered.

"The problem is the broker. He's the only loose wheel in this cog. We've got enough blackmail on the boss and his son to keep them quiet if they don't want to end up in jail or have the company fall into ruin. So, put them aside. We fake Bree's death, making it as convincing as possible. We send the broker the evidence and get the money. Easy peasy. Then, we send Bree back to New York, with a team for protection, and make sure the broker finds out he was duped. Now, the pressure's on him. He's going to want retaliation, but we'll be ready for him. And when he strikes, we take him out. The broker is out of the picture, Bree's in the clear, and since the hit has paid out, no one is coming for her."

I thought it over in my head, running through all possible outcomes. It could work, and because the broker fucked up, he would be expecting retaliation in some way. We could even make it look like Liam went after the broker for fucking up the hit.

"Am I brilliant, or what?" Fox grinned. "Man, I did all that thinking without my Funyuns on me."

"You ate a whole bag just a half hour ago," IRIS pointed out.

"Right, but a half hour is a long time. Ooh, and I volunteer to take out the broker. I can make it exceptionally painful. Come on, boss," he pleaded. "You know you want me to do this!"

Cash looked to me for guidance. "What do you think? It's your girl."

"I think...we don't have much of a choice. She's going to be pissed to have to deal with more shit, but it's the only way out that I can tell."

"Yeah, but we have to get in and tap the broker's phone. We need to be sure he doesn't send someone out to finish the job to make up for his failure."

"I'll get Rae on it. She can get us ears on the inside."

"How the hell do we even find him?" I asked. "I doubt he left a forwarding address."

"Liam had to get ahold of him somehow," Cash grinned. "I think it's time we put him to use."

I got out of the minivan and let out a deep breath. Staring up at the mansion, I tried to reason with myself that this was for the best. I was pretty sure Bree would freak out when she learned of our plan. Not only did it potentially place her in danger, but it effectively ended her career. And I had to be the one to tell her.

IRIS clapped me on the shoulder as he stood beside me. "It'll be okay. We'll work shit out."

"You're not the one that has to work it out. She's going to hate me," I grumbled.

"You don't know that."

But I did. Even if we could find a way to work past this, I still took her life away from her.

"You can't blame yourself, man. You didn't put the hit on her. You're just trying to keep her alive. She needs to be rational about this."

I shot him a sardonic smile. "Since when have the words rational and woman been used in the same sentence?"

"I wouldn't say that," he pointed out. "That won't help your case any."

"Neither will telling her I have to pretend murder her."

"Well, not you. Fox is more than willing to play that part."

"Yeah, and terrify the ever-loving shit out of her."

"Well, better him than you. Besides, he'd find some way to make it fun for her."

"You say that like it's comforting."

The front door opened and Bree stepped out, watching me hesitantly before running toward me. I hauled her against me as she jumped into my arms, hoping she wouldn't freak out too much when we explained what had to happen. I had a feeling these last few moments with her were the last I'd have any time soon.

Fox strolled over grinning from ear to ear. "Ready to get dead?" he asked her.

She pulled back, still resting her hands on my shoulders as she frowned.

"Fox—"

"Don't worry. I'm the best in the business. Well, aside from the Kamau, but he doesn't do wet work anymore."

"Wet work?"

"Killing people," he nodded. "Yeah, he's gone straight for his lady. I suppose this isn't technically breaking the rules since you won't actually be dead, but it must cross a line somewhere."

"I'm sorry," she shook her head, turning to face me. "What's going on? You want to kill me?"

"Fake kill you," I clarified.

"Don't worry," Fox laughed. "Anna will help you with the acting. She's a natural, and she can teach anyone."

"Tate, what's going on?"

I was taken aback by her use of my name. I wasn't even sure I had told her. "Let's go inside and talk about this."

"No, I'm fine out here. Tell me now."

I looked to Cash, who was hovering nearby, listening in. "Well, the thing is, Liam put a hit on you, but he put the money in an escrow account."

"Okay, I know what an escrow account is, but what does that mean for me?"

I swallowed hard, hoping she didn't hate me. "It means they'll keep trying until the job is done. Liam can't call off the hit."

She paled considerably upon hearing the news, taking a step back as her hand cupped her throat. "They're going to keep coming for me."

"There's no way for us to stop it," I answered gravely. "But we have a plan. The only way to stop the hit is to kill you ourselves. Once the broker that set it in motion receives confirmation of your death, he'll release the funds."

"To me," Fox interrupted. "But don't worry. You'll get the money. You've earned it," he winked.

"From there, we need you to be seen so the broker finds out you're still alive. We'll take him out, and that should be the end of it. All loose ends will be tied off."

"But what about Liam? That doesn't solve his problem of wanting me dead!"

"We've got enough blackmail on him to keep him and your boss quiet."

"My—" She stepped away from me, tears filling her eyes as she realized what was happening. This was the point I knew I'd lose her. There was no way to make any of this right for her, and it didn't matter that I didn't cause any of it. I was tainted by association.

She swiped the tears from her face, steeling her spine as she turned around. "I think I need a minute to myself."

"Bree—" I started, wanting to go after her, but Cash grabbed me by the arm and held me back.

"Just give her some time to process this. Her whole life is going up in flames."

"She's going to hate me," I grumbled.

"You don't know that. It's a lot to take in. Just give her what she asked for."

But the thought of her thinking about it at all drove me insane. I couldn't allow her to run off on her own and process this shit without me. I needed to know what she was thinking, and figure out a way to help her.

I shook off Cash's grip and rushed after her. Fuck giving her space. She was mine, and I wouldn't allow her to push me out of her life. I stormed into the house and followed her out the back door. She was practically running through the back yard to get away from me.

"Bree!" She didn't bother turning around, so I ran faster until I caught up with her, grabbed her by the arm, and spun her around. "Don't fucking walk away from me."

"I just need some space," she cried. Her tears covered her cheeks and her eyes were sad and lonely.

"No, what you need is me. You're already on your way out."

"I'm not—"

"You're running!" I argued. "I know this is bad. I know it fucking sucks for you, and I know you probably blame me for everything going sideways, but I'm trying to make this right for you."

"Right for me?" she laughed. "How can any of this be right? My boss will hate me. I won't be able to get a job anywhere, and some random guy wants to kill me simply because he screwed up a job that you tricked him into screwing up! How is any of this fair?"

"It's not," I snapped. "I know this all sucks, but what else am I supposed to do? You can't go into hiding for the rest of your life. You need to be able to go do whatever it is you want when this is over!"

She huffed out a laugh, stepping away from me. "When this is over. So, I'm disposable now?"

I frowned, not understanding what she was saying. "You're not disposable."

"But it's so easy for you to send me away when all this is over. I've become too much of a burden to hang onto."

I shook my head, wondering where she got that idea. "Just the opposite. I want to keep you with me for as long as you'll have me, but I won't do it by trapping you with me. If you stay, it's because you want to. And if we don't go through with this, that's exactly what will happen to you. You'll start to resent me because everything you've worked so hard for will be stripped away with the snap of my fingers. Your sister will have to mourn you. Your job will be gone. Hell, you won't even be able to go back to your apartment."

"So, you're saying you do want me," she asked in confusion.

I tossed my head back, laughing up at the sky. "Bree, you are beyond a doubt the most infuriating woman I've ever met, but there's no way I could ever want anyone more than I want you. Can't you see that by now?"

"I just assumed...I've made such a mess of your life already."

"You didn't do anything. You didn't do anything to ask for someone to kill you. That's all on the selfish prick that doesn't know how to handle money. And it was a stupid fucking plan."

"He would have succeeded if you weren't there."

"But I was there. I will always be there, for as long as you let me."

"But why?"

I could hear the uncertainty in her voice. I knew as well as she did that nothing about us made sense. And maybe that's why it worked. "Because despite everything we've been through, how different we are, you're still the one I want to come home to. And maybe it won't last. Maybe this is something amazing that happened, but will fizzle out over time. But I'm willing to risk everything to see where it'll go. The question is, will you risk it with me?"

Her eyes flicked to the ground. I was so sure she was going to say no. I could feel it in my bones. Bree was a rational person, and nothing about this was rational. So, when she looked up into my eyes with a smile on her face, my heart fucking melted right there on the spot.

"You've kept me alive this far. I think I'd be stupid not to give you one more chance."

A huge weight was lifted from my shoulders at her words. I shifted closer to her and pulled her into my arms. "You won't regret it."

"No, but you'll regret crossing me," Fox shouted, an evil laugh escaping his lips. "It is time to kill you, my sweetness. Are you ready to meet your fate?"

I glared at him as he stood in a fucking cape with his knives strapped to his sides.

"Way to ruin a moment," Dash said as he walked out, slapping him on the back.

"They were having a moment? Shit, I didn't realize. Go back to it. I'll come out and do my bit in three minutes. Is that long enough?"

Bree laughed and snuggled into my neck, just as I liked it. Maybe we would be okay. I really fucking hoped I had worried for nothing.

"I'm just saying, I was ready," Fox argued. "You totally killed the mood for me."

"And you'll play *Phantom Of The Opera* and be back in the mood in no time," I retorted. "Can you give her at least half a day to adjust to this?"

"Fine," he grumbled under his breath. "It's not like we're on a timeline or anything."

"Not a timeline that fits into a half day," I snapped, getting irritated with his pouting.

"The problem is going to be drawing out the broker," Cash said, continuing with our previous conversation. "If we send in Liam, he'll smell a trap."

"Not if we send Liam in with photos of Bree still alive," I pointed out.

"But what are the chances he'll get a face-to-face with this guy?" Slider asked. "The broker's not stupid. He's not going to leave himself vulnerable, even for someone like Liam."

"Except this is a botched job," IRIS pointed out. "His entire business is riding on his credibility. We have to hope that Liam can do his job and draw him out."

"And if he doesn't?" I asked. "We can't bet Bree's life on this. The moment the broker finds out the job was botched, he'll have to start the hit again. Not to mention, I don't trust Liam as far as I can throw him. If he gives us up, then the whole fucking company is in trouble."

Knight walked into the kitchen, pretending to ignore us, but the tension in his body said he was listening in.

"We'll have to make sure Liam asks for a specific meetup. We have the blackmail on him," Cash insisted. "If he values his life at all, he won't pull any shit."

Knight snorted. "Liam won't keep his mouth shut. I've seen this before. Trust me, that guy is out for his own skin, and if he thinks he can get the broker to take you out, he won't hesitate to flip on you. With his dad's money, he can flee the country within hours of the meeting."

"Then what do you suggest we do?" Cash snapped. "This is your world. Tell us how to get around the problem."

Knight studied us for a second, then walked over and pulled out a chair. "There are only three men in New York that have the ability to pull off a job like the hit on Bree. Most would hire a single gun. It's cheaper, but you aren't paying for the best. Jobs that have a big payday are the ones that go to the best hitters. That's why it's basically a free for all. Whoever gets the job done first gets the money. And they're the best not just because of their proficiency, but because they take jobs where the hit needs to appear as an accident."

"But Bree's didn't look at all like an accident," I pointed out.

"No, but it was an out-of-town job," he added. "It adds to the mystery of why she was killed, taking the heat off whoever paid for the hit. Now, of those three men, only one of them has the number of hitters on his payroll that went after Bree. He happens to be a man I worked with a few times."

Cash's eyebrows went up at that. "And I'm assuming you can tell us where to find him."

Something that resembled a smirk crossed Knight's lips, but it was hard to tell through his rough demeanor. "I can tell you where to find him."

Fox's face lit up as he jumped up from his seat. "Alright, here's the plan. Thumper, you can hang back with your team while the Kamau and I go in. We'll have a little fun, do our thing, boil his ass in acid, and then walk away as if nothing happened."

"Why would I go if you're just going to boil him in acid?" I asked.

"Well…I just thought you'd want to be there," he said, rolling his eyes at me. "But hey, that's fine if you don't want to join in the festivities."

Slider leaned forward on the table. "Just a thought, but have you ever considered getting rid of someone in a way other than boiling them in acid?"

Fox's brows wrinkled in confusion. "You mean, like just burying the body?"

Slider shrugged. "Something like that."

"Well, first of all, it's best not to leave any evidence behind. Acid is great for that. Second, I find the screams soothing as the body slowly disintegrates into the barrel. And finally, why mess with the classics?"

"Don't you ever get tired of it?"

Fox scoffed. "It's not like this is a weekly occurrence. Although to be fair, it has happened a lot more since I joined the company. You could even say that I was relatively docile before I met all of you. So, if you think about it, you really have yourselves to blame."

"Not that this isn't a thrilling debate," Knight bit out, "but taking him out at this location is impossible. It's a dead zone."

"What does that mean?" Cash asked.

"Nobody can move against anyone else at this location. It would trigger a string of deaths, essentially taking out anyone involved. It's a way to keep the meetings neutral and everyone in check. Your best bet is to stake out the location and follow this guy."

Cash nodded in agreement. "We send Liam in with evidence that Bree's alive, then wait at the dead zone. From there, we follow him home and take him out."

Fox held up his hand. "So, does that mean no acid?"

31

BREE

"So," Fox clapped his hands together. "How should we do this? Pick your poison!"

I watched his cheerful demeanor with a guarded sense of safety. Sure, he looked like he wanted to help, but he was way too cheerful about killing me off. I leaned over to Thumper and whispered, "And you're sure the whole killing thing is just an act."

"I'm not going to lie, he'll make it look real, but he won't actually kill you."

"Will it hurt?"

"No, I swear to you."

I looked at him, knowing I could trust him, but that didn't erase the fear. Whatever happened today would set the wheels in motion for my future. And while I was happy to be making forward progress, I was terrified of what that meant for me along the way.

"We could do the whole hanging thing," Fox continued, cocking his head from side to side. "Not nearly gruesome enough, if you ask me. I was thinking something along the lines of a brutal slaying. Now, normally, I love a good acid dip, but since we're not actually going to show this live, it sort of takes the fun out of it. Plus, then we'd have to have fake skin and blood floating around in the water with you. Totally doable, but maybe a little too dramatic for our current plans."

"Fox," Thumper snapped. "How about we just go for something simple. A good throat slashing would work just fine."

He nodded slightly. "I know, but where's the fun in that? Come on, man. This is our chance to be inventive! And think about this," he said to me. "You get to choose your death, like you're in a horror film! Isn't that exciting?"

I tried to summon up the excitement he felt, but found myself lacking in the ability. Somehow, plotting my own death had never been on my to-do list. "I think a basic gunshot wound would do just fine. That's simple enough, isn't it?" I asked, looking to Thumper for guidance.

"Of course," he reassured me.

"Yeah, if you want to be boring," Fox muttered. He held up both hands as Thumper glared at him. "But hey, it's your death. We'll do it how you want. Now, it would be best to stage it tonight. Best to get this show on the road. I'll require some roadkill, my cape, some sheep brains, and…" He frowned, tapping his finger on his chin. "I know I'm missing something."

"Funyuns?" I asked, noting that he really seemed to love them.

"Yes!" he snapped. "See, you already know me so well."

"I'm beginning to wish I didn't."

"Everyone says that, but they hardly ever mean it," he chuckled. "Now, I'll get the Kamua—not that I can't do this on my own—but I really feel this will be a good bonding experience for us. You know, something to help us bond even more."

"Maybe you should put on his boots," Thumper suggested.

Fox winked at him. "That's what I was thinking. He'll be so stoked."

Fox sauntered off, leaving me alone with Thumper. I was doing my best not to freak out. After all, they were only fake killing me. Still, everyone would assume I was dead. There would have to be an obituary and everything.

"What happens with my sister?"

"Well, she should be safe. This shouldn't blow back on her in any way."

"No, I mean…with my death. Can't I warn her what's about to happen? I can't put her through that."

"That's not a good idea, Bree. If she doesn't act the right way, it could give away the game too soon. We need you to have a funeral and appear dead, then reappear afterward."

"But she's my sister," I said, my lips quivering. "I can't do that to her. Not after all the crap I've put her through over the years."

"She'll understand," he tried to reassure me. "We'll make sure she's okay until it's time for you to reappear again. And when she finds out what happened, she will forgive you."

I blinked back tears, knowing it was easy to say these things. "I've already let her down so much."

He stepped into my space, wrapping his hands around my biceps and giving them a firm squeeze. "And when this is over, you'll have a chance to make things right with her. But we can't risk blowing this in any way. We need time to make sure everything falls into place as it should. If we blow it early, we might not be prepared for any actions the broker takes."

I knew what he was saying was true, but that didn't make it any easier to deal with. Being on the run had given me a new perspective of just how bad of a sister I'd been. Hearing the dismissive tone in her voice when I informed her I was in trouble was unsettling. Had I been a better sister, maybe she would have been more concerned, but being out of her life for so long must have felt like I was already dead. The reality that the only person that cared if I lived or died was Thumper crashed into me hard, sucking all the breath from my lungs.

I vowed that when this was all over, I would be a better sister and aunt. I would be there for my family the way I should have been all along. Whatever happened, my life was going to change.

"Alrighty-o!" Fox grinned as he reappeared in black with a cape wrapped around his neck. "Who's ready to get dead?"

"You're sure about this?" I asked as I stood in disguise at my own funeral. The veil over my face did a good job of concealing who I was, but Thumper took extra precautions to ensure that nobody would recognize me if my veil came off for any reason. The mask felt foreign and gross on my face, but Fox considered it a work of art, so I went with it.

"It'll be fine." Thumper squeezed my hand, still not understanding why I needed to be here. If it were up to him, I would have stayed back at Knight's mansion as we waited for the fallout. But something inside me told me I needed to be here today.

Nerves bubbled up inside me. I felt hot and cold as I stared at my closed casket. The bullet to my face was enough to ensure that no one would question why it wasn't open for viewing. Not that I would want that anyway. I found the whole ordeal morbid. I already decided that I wanted to be cremated when my time was up.

My sister stood by my casket looking a little somber, but not nearly what I expected. I thought there might be a few tears at least, but she actually looked like she had better places to be. And there were fewer people than I expected. Most of the people that came were coworkers.

"It's a good turnout," Thumper said, trying to make me feel better.

"Are you kidding? More people showed up at my grandpa's funeral, and most of his friends were dead at that point."

"Well...maybe they were put off by the circumstances of your death."

I rolled my eyes, knowing that wasn't the case. "Then why is it whenever someone tragically dies, there's an outpouring of mourners who barely knew the victim?"

He didn't have an answer for that, and I wasn't really expecting one anyway.

"Come on, let's take a seat."

He guided me to the chairs, behind a few men I knew from work. They were talking about office stuff, something I would have done at one point. Now, I realized how tacky it was.

"Did you hear how she died?" one of them said.

"Bullet to the face," another scoffed. "Brutal way to go. Can't say I would wish that on my worst enemy."

"She is your worst enemy," another laughed.

"Was," the man corrected. "Now, she's out of my life for good. Thank fuck. What a bitch."

Thumper squeezed my hand as they continued to bash me. I tuned them out and did my best not to cry. I knew I wasn't a favorite around the office, but I always assumed that people generally liked me. Now, at my very own funeral, people bashed me and called me a bitch. It was a massive reality check, one that I didn't brush off.

My sister stepped up to the podium and cleared her throat. I prayed that she had something good to say about me. She looked up at the sparse crowd, then looked over at her family.

"Bree was...different."

Okay, that wasn't the send off I was hoping for.

"Since we were kids, she was always focused on achieving her goals, whatever those were at the time. But she always knew she was going places. I wish I could say that we were close, but the reality is, we hardly talked or saw each other."

"Who would want to hear from the ice queen?" one of the men laughed under his breath.

"But deep down, she was a good person, just hard to relate to. I wish I had gotten to know her better before she passed, but now all I can hope for is that she's at peace."

She took her paper and stepped down. That was it. My final farewell was a humbling experience, indeed.

"Let's go," I whispered to Thumper.

He didn't bother to argue as we stood and exited the funeral home. I didn't need to see anything else. Everything I needed to know was laid out in front of me in a wooden box of loneliness and regret.

"Bree—"

I smiled at Thumper, trying my best not to start crying. "It's fine. I received a gift today."

He shot me a strange look. "And that would be?"

"I got to see how others really view me. Even my own sister couldn't muster up more than a short paragraph to honor me. That says a lot about the kind of person I am."

"No," he insisted. "That says neither of you took the time to

263

develop a relationship. Maybe you were distant, but when was the last time she reached out to you?"

He had a point, but I knew deep down that it was my fault. Grace gave up on me because of my own decisions, and I had to live with that.

I squeezed Thumper's hand, trying to reassure him. "It's okay. I get a chance to make it better. We just have to get through the next few weeks. Then I'll take some time to visit her, maybe figure out what I really need out of life."

"And does that include me?" he asked hopefully.

I wanted to jump and say yes, but after seeing how badly I'd screwed everything up, I knew I needed to take some time to fix the relationships I'd already ruined.

"I really hope so. But I know now I can't go back to how things were with my sister. I have to fix this."

I knew that wasn't the answer he was looking for. "That doesn't mean I don't want to be with you. But I can't move forward without fixing what's already broken."

He nodded in understanding. "It'll be fine. We should get going. We have to plan out the next phase."

He took my hand and led me to the vehicle, his eyes on our surroundings the whole time. He was making excuses because of what I said. He'd already planned out the next phase and was ready to go, but if it made him feel like he had an out, I'd give it to him.

"To our last night in Colorado," Thumper said, raising his glass in the air, his speech slurring as he swayed with the motion.

Everyone was lively tonight as we prepared to head home for the big reveal. I was especially excited to put all this behind us, but Thumper was acting strangely. He was drinking more than he had the entire time here, and IRIS knew it too based on the way he was watching him.

"And to our host, Knight, for providing us with a safe house until we could get a plan together. Even if you are a crazy fucker, we're still grateful."

Knight quirked an eyebrow at him, clearly unimpressed with the way he was acting.

"Yes!" Fox shouted. "To the Kamau! And many more sleepovers!"

The guys all laughed, but Knight pushed back from the table and walked out. Kate shook her head with laughter as her grumpy husband left. Despite only spending a small amount of time with her, I already felt I understood the dynamic of her relationship with her husband. Though not the same as my relationship with Thumper, there were parallels I was beginning to understand.

"And to Bree," Thumper announced, drawing my attention. I blushed from the eyes on me, and prayed he didn't say anything too embarrassing. "When I first met you, I was sure I was going to find you dead in the desert. Or at the very least, you would leave after that first day. And then you surprised the hell out of me when you stayed," he grinned. "I would say it would have been better if you'd just gone home, given the rabbit and the bighorn sheep, but then we never would have been on this…ridiculous adventure together."

"And don't forget the guys that saved your ass!" FNG shouted.

Thumper nodded, then turned to IRIS. "And to my teammates. Thank you for not using my foot to beat someone, use it as a torch, or shoot at it. I really appreciate going home with it in one piece."

"It was one time!" IRIS shouted, laughing along.

"It's fifty thousand dollars to replace," Thumper pointed out. "And I'm still waiting for your money, Cash!"

"Good luck with that. I saved your ass."

"You were fucked up and shot me in the foot," he laughed.

"Sorry, I was busy being held hostage."

"Just don't allow it again, or Rafe will slip in and steal your girl again," he laughed.

It went silent around the table as Cash's eyes turned glacial. He turned to FNG, who was doing his best to hide from his boss. I had no idea what was happening, but Thumper dropped some kind of bomb unintentionally.

I shoved my chair back and rushed around the table. "I'm exhausted. I think we should head to bed."

"And how exactly did Rafe take my girl?" Cash bit out.

"It wasn't her fault, boss. She thought he was you," Thumper snorted. "Blow jobs aren't really considered sex, right?"

He stumbled backward, his chair screeching across the floor as I reached out for him. I sent a pleading look to IRIS, who immediately got up and stormed over, grabbing his other arm.

"You knew and didn't say anything?" Cash bit out.

"Hey, it was FNG that walked in on it," Thumper chuckled. "Man, he just can't catch a break."

FNG stared around the table with wide eyes. "Uh…"

"You knew all along?" Cash snapped.

He swallowed hard. "You know, knowledge is a tricky thing."

"We should really go to bed," I insisted, trying to push Thumper out of the room, but he just wouldn't go.

"It could have been worse. Just thank God that Rafe has a conscience. Or maybe that FNG walked in. Who knows how far it might have gone. Am I right?" he laughed.

But no one else was laughing right now. In fact, everyone was doing their best not to look at Cash, and rightfully so. When Thumper woke up in the morning, he was going to feel like shit, and not just because of the amount of alcohol he'd consumed.

I dragged Thumper from the room with IRIS's help. "Man, you really know how to stick your foot in it," IRIS muttered.

"And how to take it off. Because it detaches," he laughed. He turned solemn and faced me with an abrupt stop. "Tell me the truth… if we get in an argument, are you going to take my foot off and beat me with it?"

I stared at him, unable to think of a response to such a ridiculous question. But before I could answer, he burst out laughing, wrapping his arms around my shoulders as he leaned heavily on me. IRIS had to grip him under the arms to keep him from crushing me to the floor with his weight.

"Alright, I think you've done enough damage for one night. Maybe it's time to get you in bed."

"Bed," Thumper mumbled. "With my lady love, as Fox says. Except, she might not be my lady love for long."

I looked at IRIS in confusion. Clearly, he thought I was no longer there.

"What are you talking about?"

"She's going back to her sister," he slurred. "After everything…" He sighed heavily as IRIS lowered him to the bed. "Maybe it's the foot. It can be a turnoff."

"It's not the foot. Although, you're depressing as fuck right now. That could have something to do with it."

I lowered myself in front of him to help him with his foot, but it was like he didn't even see me.

"You should have seen those fuckers at her funeral. Pissants," he slurred. "Like they'd know a good woman if they saw one."

"Well, it's a good thing you have her. Maybe you should tell her."

IRIS looked at me, quirking an eyebrow. What was I supposed to do? The man didn't even know I was here. Hell, I wasn't sure he knew where he was or the fact that he'd just blown a secret sky-high. IRIS sighed as he pushed Thumper down in bed.

"You got this?" he asked me.

"Yeah, I know what to do."

He clasped me on the shoulder. "Try not to be too hard on him. I've never seen him like this before."

I nodded as he left the room. Thumper was already passed out on the bed, hopefully dreaming of better things than what was going to happen when all this was over. I had no idea he was taking it quite so hard, and seeing him like this made me question if we'd rushed into things too fast. Because no matter the connection between us, it felt like we were drifting further apart.

32

THUMPER

THE POUNDING in my skull was the first sign that I had way too much to drink last night. The second was the fact that I was laying on the bathroom floor with Bree passed out beside me. I groaned, rolling over as I tried to remember something about last night. I had to have been drunk, but I didn't recall drinking that much. Then again, my head was in a fucked up place with every minute that drew closer. I knew Bree would leave me soon. She hadn't said it specifically, but her lack of enthusiasm for staying with me told me all I needed to know.

I couldn't blame her. After that funeral, anyone would question their life and those in it. Even her own family was less than upset about her recent demise. It only proved how much the distance between them had hurt their relationship.

I shifted on the floor, my eyebrows shooting up in surprise when I saw my foot no longer attached. Even in my drunken state, Bree had looked after me. I slid my hand over her cheek, wishing I could beg her to stay, but that wouldn't be fair. Whatever happened from here, she had to make choices best for her going forward.

She yawned, stretching as she came awake. She blinked up at me, her eyes not nearly as bright this morning. "Morning," she mumbled sleepily.

"Morning. Please tell me I didn't throw up."

A happy smile graced her face. "No, you just insisted on sleeping in here."

I frowned. "In the bathroom?"

She nodded. "You said it was cooler and more comfortable. Something about it reminding you of the military."

"So...you slept in here...with me."

"You were very insistent."

"But you could have taken the bed."

"I wanted to be with you. Besides, now I can say I know what it's like to sleep in the military."

I snorted at that. "This isn't like that at all. But I appreciate you putting in the effort."

"And on that note, I'd like to get up off the floor and feel like a human again."

She groaned as she sat up, and I rubbed my hand over her back, working out the kinks. I wasn't exactly feeling great myself, but Bree wasn't used to roughing it on cold, hard floors.

"Do you want some help getting up?" she asked.

After what I put her through last night, I wouldn't allow her to help me in any way. "I've got this. I'm going to take a shower. Why don't you go lay down for a little bit?"

"Mmm, that sounds good."

I kissed her, waiting for her to leave before I got up and hauled my ass into the shower. I was desperately regretting whatever the hell I drank last night, but no more than when I got out of the shower and ran into IRIS.

"Hey," I jerked my head at him. "What the fuck happened last night?"

"You don't remember?" he snorted.

I frowned, thinking back again. If he was stating it like that, it must have been a night to remember. "My head is fucked up. I don't remember a thing."

He clapped me on the arm, grinning at me like a fool. "Well...today should be interesting."

269

He walked away without another word. I shook my head and continued down the hall, running into FNG next.

"Asshole," he muttered, shoving past me.

I turned with the hit, shaking my head at him. "What the fuck did I do to you?"

But he didn't turn around. He just kept walking. I shook my head and continued into the kitchen. If I was going to tackle this day, I needed a fucking coffee. When I walked in, Fox was already leaning against the counter in the kitchen. With a knife in one hand, he sharpened it against a block, studying the blade with great intensity.

"You ready for today?" he asked.

"Just grabbing some coffee."

I walked over to the cabinet and pulled down a mug, pouring myself a cup.

"I'm surprised you're alive and well this morning." His tone was just a little too gleeful, but I didn't read anything into it. Fox was always a little odd.

"Bree took care of me last night—took off my foot and everything."

He pointed his knife at me. "Now, that's a good woman. Yeah, I'm surprised how well she handled the whole thing last night," he laughed.

"Handled what? Me getting drunk?"

He shook his head, chuckling as he flipped his knife. "Man, it was classic Thumper." He walked out of the room without another word while I tried to figure out what was so "classic" about what happened last night. I couldn't remember a time I had ever done anything where someone referred to me behaving in a classic way.

Cash popped his head into the kitchen, barely acknowledging me. "We leave in ten. Make sure your shit is packed."

He turned and stormed out, leaving me shaking my head. Either I drank more than I realized last night, or I woke up in an alternate universe where I had done something really fucking stupid. And that couldn't be right, because I never fucked up anything.

Bree and I quickly packed up and headed for the entry. She was unusually quiet this morning, which I chalked up to the impending mission. It would have rattled anyone.

"Hey, FNG, can you take Bree's bag out?"

"Fuck off," he snapped, walking right past me.

Slider stepped up beside me, grinning like a fool. "Man, you sure know how to have a good time."

"Is that what this is about? Did I do something last night?"

He eyed me with a grin. "You really don't remember?"

"Remember what? Last night is a blank."

"Well, this should be interesting," he grinned.

"What should be interesting?" I shouted as he walked away.

Fuck, I couldn't get a straight answer out of anyone, but I had somehow managed to piss off several people. Bree walked past me in a hurry, and I grabbed her by the arm.

"Hey, what exactly happened last night?"

She glanced at the guys, then back to me with a nervous smile. "You know, I don't really know the story."

"But what did I do?"

"Hey, Bree!" IRIS shouted. "You've got the middle seat!"

"Oh, hey, look at that. It's time to go."

She hurried off, leaving me shaking my head. Not even Bree would say what happened. And the longer this went on, the more a gnawing feeling in my stomach grew. Somehow, I had fucked up. Just what happened was still to be determined. And until then, I was fucked.

"Package has been delivered," Cash said over comms. "We're headed to you."

I breathed a sigh of relief that part one of our plan was underway. We still couldn't trust Liam, no matter how threatened he felt by the blackmail. He was stuck between a rock and a hard place, and that made him a major liability.

"Copy that," I answered.

"So, now we sit and wait," FNG snorted from the back seat.

I was getting really tired of his attitude. Ever since we left Knight's house, he'd been a pain in the ass. "You didn't have to come."

"Right, because that would have been a good option for me."

"We have enough guys. You could have stayed home. Or were you afraid someone might risk their lives and you wouldn't be there to do the same?" I shot back.

"I was afraid Cash would have me taken out back and shot," he muttered under his breath.

I rolled my eyes at him. He was so fucking dramatic. "You would have to give Cash a really good fucking reason to kill you."

"You mean, like witnessing his brother getting a blow job from his fiancé?"

"Well…yeah, that would do it," I huffed out a laugh. "If you tell him, it's your funeral."

"It's about to be yours. I should just hand you over to the broker and call it a day."

I spun in my seat, tired of his shit. "What the fuck is your problem with me? Is it because I said you couldn't be on the team? It was a fucking joke!"

He burst out laughing, but he didn't look happy. Slider sat uncomfortably next to me. "You really don't fucking remember."

My brows furrowed in confusion. He was talking in riddles. "What are you talking about?"

"I'm talking about you betraying your friends. I had your back in the desert. I took a fucking bullet for you!"

"You shot me!" I shouted, lowering my voice when I realized I would draw attention. "You shot me, you asshole," I hissed.

"Is that why you did it? To pay me back for shooting you?"

"I didn't do anything. And unlike you, I don't go around shooting my friends!"

"That's not entirely true," Slider said, shrugging when I shot him a death glare. "I'm just saying, if the circumstances were right…"

"Whose side are you on, anyway?"

"I'm on the side of not getting murdered. IRIS?" he asked, looking to the back seat.

I had completely forgotten he was back there. It was unusual for IRIS to be so quiet about anything. And here we were, having a huge fucking argument, and he was silent.

"I know nothing. I am a lone wolf."

"You're an asshole," I retorted.

"Hey, you dug your grave. You have to lie in it."

"What is with all the cryptic bullshit?" I snapped. "Whatever the fuck the—"

"He's here," Slider interrupted, looking through his binoculars. "That didn't take him long."

"Cash," I spoke into comms. "He's on scene."

"We're moving into position now. We've got things covered to the south. When he comes out, we'll push him to the east and take it from there."

"Copy that," I answered.

"Be advised, we've got a snitch on the scene," Slider added, still looking through his binoculars.

"Who?"

He looked at me with a grin on his face. "Liam."

I shook my head in disgust. "He had one fucking job, and he couldn't even stick to it."

"More fun for us," he laughed.

In just a few hours or less, this asshole would be a blip on the radar and Bree would finally be safe. I didn't condone taking out random people, but this guy wouldn't stop until she was dead. There was no way around it.

I waited impatiently, wishing I had eyes and ears on the inside. I pulled out my phone and dialed Rae's number.

"Yes, Thumper?" she asked in a bored tone.

"How's Bree?"

A huge sigh filled the silence. "She's sitting right beside me. Is that good enough, or do you need to hear her voice?"

I rolled my eyes at her tone. "I just wanted to check in."

"Right, because I would really let anything happen to her. In an underground bunker. Where nobody knows we are."

"There's no need for sarcasm. I'm allowed to worry."

"You're halfway around the country. What exactly do you think is going to happen?"

That was a good question, one I hadn't figured out, but something was nagging at me. I just couldn't put my finger on it. "Fine, you're right. I'll let you go."

"How magnanimous of you."

She hung up without another word, which should have pissed me off, but instead made me smile. If Rae was worried, she wouldn't be nearly as sarcastic. I tapped my fingers on the steering wheel, trying to shake the odd feeling bubbling up inside. We had this guy covered from all angles. We all knew our jobs, yet something was just off.

"Would you relax?" Slider grumbled. "We've got this. After tonight, this will all be over. We just have to wait for him to leave the meeting."

I nodded, knowing he was right, but then it hit me, the one thing that was wrong with this scenario. "Shit," I hissed, flinging my door open. I took off at a sprint for the dead zone. If I didn't get there in time, we were fucked.

"Thumper!" Slider shouted into comms. "What the fuck are you doing?"

"We covered the broker, but we didn't consider that he would already put the hit out again on Bree!"

"Oh fuck!"

I heard commands being shouted through comms and feet pounding behind me as the teams moved in. Neutral zone or not, we didn't have a choice but to take out anyone in that building. If a single hitter left, Bree would be in danger all over again.

I pulled my gun and sidled up alongside the building, peering around the corner. Cash was at the back of the building, signaling he was in position to move in. We had no schematics of the inside of the building because we hadn't assumed we'd need them. Now, I wished we had grilled Knight for the information.

Slider tapped me on the shoulder, letting me know he was behind me. I signaled to Cash that I was moving in, then stepped out of the shadows and booted in the door with one swift kick. Gunfire exploded around me as Cash moved in with Fox and Dash.

The few men left standing quickly took cover, returning fire without hesitation. But we had the drop on them, taking them all out within minutes of entering the building. When the gunfire stopped, I moved around the room, kicking bodies to ensure no one was left alive. It was a bloodbath, and the repercussions would be great if we were caught.

"Well, that didn't exactly go as planned," Cash muttered.

"What do we do about the bodies?" I asked.

"Burn 'em," Fox grinned. "Burn the whole fucking building down."

"Yeah, that won't draw attention," Slider said.

"What other choice do we have? Any evidence left behind could cause blowback. We need this mess cleaned up, and the sooner the better," I said, actually agreeing with Fox. I checked out the bodies, noting Liam wasn't among them.

"This wasn't exactly what I thought we'd be doing when I started this business," Cash sighed. "But...I never thought we'd befriend an assassin either, so I guess we go with the flow or sink."

"That was beautiful," Fox said, pretending to wipe a tear from his eyes. "Can I set the place on fire now?"

"Hold on," IRIS cut in. "If anyone is going to blow this place up, it's going to be me. We need this controlled, to appear as if it was an accident."

"With seven bodies inside?" I questioned.

"Hey, there are ways to make it happen. Now, I'm going to need to find the gas line, a few..."

I didn't hear what else he said as he rushed off through the building, muttering to himself as he planned his massive explosion.

"Slider, go with him and make sure he doesn't blow himself up," Cash sighed.

"Oh, sure. Send me, because I don't care if I live or die." He rolled his eyes and took off after IRIS.

"There's no way this will look like an accident, not with all the bullet holes in these men," I said, staring at the bodies. I started moving around the building, opening doors to find our snitch. If he had kept his mouth shut, he would have lived another day. Now, he was going to die, and there was nothing I could do, or even wanted to.

"I'll put a call into Rafe," Cash nodded. "He still has contacts at the FBI. I'm sure he can get this cleared up."

"Are you sure you want to do that, boss? I mean, knowing what Rafe did?" Fox laughed. "You're a better man than me."

I frowned, not understanding his line of thinking. "What did Rafe do?"

Fox snorted. "You know, the thing he did with Eva?"

My eyes bugged out of my head as I spun to face him. "You fucking told him?"

"I didn't tell him," Fox laughed. "Man, that whole drunken schpeel was so fucking awesome!"

"Not from where I was standing," Cash bit out.

"But you had to admit, you didn't see that coming," Fox continued to laugh.

"Yeah, and he tossed me right in it," FNG snapped.

"And I'm still eager to know why you didn't fucking tell me what my own fucking brother did!" Cash roared.

FNG held up his hands, backing up as Cash advanced on him. "What was I supposed to do? Eva begged me!"

"And you should have fucking told me! This has been eating her up inside, and you could have prevented it!"

"Better *that* eating her up than the alternative," Fox snorted.

I turned to FNG, shaking my head. "Wait, so this is why you've been so pissy with me?"

His eyes bugged out. "*I've* been pissy with *you*? I've been getting death glares from Cash for three fucking days!"

"Then why didn't you fucking tell me?"

"Because—" FNG started, but stopped when I flung open the last door and saw Liam crouched down inside.

I shook my head in disappointment at the little fucker. "So, not only are you a shitty liar, but you can't hide for shit either."

The little weasel sat in front of me shaking like a leaf, and the gun in his hand was hardly a threat when he wasn't holding it properly. I grabbed him by the collar and dragged him out of the closet, tossing him into the center of the room.

"You just couldn't stay out of it," Cash said, stalking toward him. "So, you decided to team up with the broker. How'd that turn out for you?"

"What do you want?" he asked, his voice shaking. "I'll get you money. I can pay you!"

"I don't need money, and we wouldn't take it from someone that tried to get us killed."

"But..."

"But, but..." Fox mimicked, laughing hysterically at him. "Man, there is nothing better than a puny shithead pleading for his life. Can I boil him now?"

"Boil?" Liam screeched like a girl.

"Fox," Cash sighed. "We talked about this. Not everyone needs to be boiled. He doesn't even have anything to tell us!"

"Yeah, but that doesn't mean it wouldn't be fun," Fox said, his brows pinched in confusion. "After all, that's the whole point of it."

"I thought it was to get information," I said.

"Well...sure, but as Cash said, this guy doesn't have any information."

"So, why waste the time?" Dash asked. "Wouldn't you rather be home with Anna?"

"She's actually working on a screenplay with Zoe right now. It's kind of killing my jam. See, the storyline is that this handsome man woos a woman with flowers and shit. It sounds kind of boring to me. I mean, where are the explosions? Where's the killing?"

"Maybe she just didn't get to that part yet," I said.

"Or maybe she doesn't think every movie needs to involve someone dying," FNG snorted.

"And what's wrong with that?" Fox cut in.

"Um...I would be really happy if I didn't die," Liam held up his hand.

"No one asked for your opinion," Fox snapped. "Who wants to watch a movie where there's no explosions, no killing, no fun?"

"Some people like that stuff," I shrugged.

"Like women," Dash pointed at him. "I guarantee, if you take a chick to a movie, nine times out of ten, she wants to see a chick flick."

"Not Eva," Cash smirked. "Thank God for that."

"Yeah, but she also nearly slept with your brother," Dash said. "Her judgment can't be trusted."

"Maybe don't bring that up," I muttered under my breath.

"Yeah, let's not bring up the gigantic secret you've all been hiding from me," Cash snapped. "I thought I could trust all of you."

"In our defense, we only found out recently," I said, hoping that would get us off the chopping block.

"How does that make me feel better?" Cash snapped. "So, you've only been hiding it from me for a few weeks instead of months? How the fuck is that better?"

A shot rang through the building and we all turned to face the pipsqueak on the floor. His eyes were wide as he stared at all of us in horror. "I…"

Fox stepped forward, holding his shirt away from his shoulder. "You shot me, you little prick."

"I didn't mean to," he stumbled over his words. "I…there was yelling and…you have to believe me!"

Fox stared at him for a moment, pointed at him as he laughed hysterically. "He wants us to believe him! Man, I love this guy!"

Liam looked between all of us as we joined in the laughter. After a few seconds, Liam joined in, clearly not understanding the joke was on him. Then Fox went silent as he stalked toward him and grabbed him by the shirt. His whole demeanor shifted from playful to deadly.

"I'm going to have fun with this."

"Nervous?" Cash asked as we got off the plane in Kansas.

I shrugged, pretending I was totally okay with this. "Nah, it'll be fine."

"You're not worried she's going to run off to find another job?"

I stopped walking and turned to him. "Are you trying to fuck with my head?"

"No." Then he grinned. "Well, maybe a little. After all, you guys have been keeping secrets from me."

"Yeah, but…you have to understand, Eva didn't want you to know. She knew you would freak out."

He nodded, then continued walking. "I'm not freaking out. She thought it was me. I can't be upset with her for trying everything possible to keep me by her side. It's really fucking sweet if you think about it."

"So, you're not going to do anything about it?"

"I didn't say that." His jaw grew tense the further we walked. "I'm definitely going to put Rafe in the hospital. He should have found a different way to handle the situation. He should have fucking trusted my teams."

I almost found myself defending the guy. He was trying to get his brother back. For that alone, it was hard to judge him so harshly. Then again, it wasn't my fiancé he nearly slept with. "So, what are you going to do about Eva? Are you going to tell her?"

"Of course. I can't have her blaming herself. Besides, it makes sense now why she's been so hesitant to get married."

A grin split my lips as I clapped him on the shoulder. "Boss, you're gonna get married?"

"Of course. I've been trying to get her to marry me since I bugged her car when she tried to leave me."

"You're a role model for all of us," I said sarcastically.

"And what about you? Are you going to ask Bree to stay?"

"I'm not sure what to do yet. She wants to go make things right with her sister, but…"

"But what?"

"I'm…afraid she'll take that time away to reevaluate our relationship."

"Then don't give her the chance. Go with her."

"Seriously? You don't think that reeks of desperation?"

"Of course," he snorted. "But either you're desperately in love with her or you're not." He clapped me on the shoulder and walked away.

Desperately in love…Was I desperately in love with her? I wasn't sure we'd known each other long enough to put that kind of label on what we had. I knew I didn't want her to go. When she was in danger, I was terrified that I wouldn't get to her in time. But desperately in love? That was something only time would tell. But Cash was right, if I gave her the opportunity to walk away, things would most likely fizzle out instead of growing stronger.

Despite the fact that we were so different, I didn't want to let her get away. I liked that she wasn't like all the other women, desperate to throw knives with Fox or learn how to blow something up with IRIS. I liked that she was softer than everyone else. There was a delicate femininity to her that made my protective instincts surge. I could take care of her and protect her. She needed me, and that was something only a true man could appreciate.

So, was I going to let her go to her sister's all alone? Not a chance in hell.

33

BREE

MY HEART RACED as I waited for Thumper to come back to me. I knew
he landed. Everyone was talking about how successful the trip was.
But none of that mattered to me. It probably should since it had to do
with my life, but all I cared about was seeing Thumper again. I had
been a nervous wreck since he left, waiting for him to check in like a
needy wife. I wasn't like these other women. I couldn't just go play
with knives and watch movies while my man was out risking his life
for me. I knew he could take care of himself, but this wasn't my life. I
didn't live or die by the gun. It terrified me to even think of him
getting a scratch. Which was sort of ridiculous considering that he was
missing a foot and didn't let that stop him.

Still, I had every right to worry. He was my...well, he was mine.
Plain and simple. He took a massive risk going after this broker guy,
and so did the rest of his team. They all had my back, and for the first
time in my life, I realized what it was like to have people surrounding
me that cared what happened.

Three minivans pulled down the long driveway just minutes later. I
shoved the door open and rushed down the drive, not even waiting for
them to stop. The passenger door on the second vehicle was flung open
and Thumper jumped out. I ran hard at him, leaping into his arms as he

easily caught me. I wrapped my arms around his neck, squeezing him tight to me. The relief that filled me was enormous. The weight that was lifted off my shoulders the moment he was home was indescribable.

"You came back," I whispered, feeling tears well in my eyes.

"Did you doubt me?"

I couldn't speak, so I shook my head as a sob rose in my chest.

"Hey," he said, concern filling his voice as he tried to pull back from me. But I wouldn't let him. I just needed him to hold me. He got the message and ran his hand up and down my back as everyone else filed out of the vans and walked around us toward the building. "Bree, what's going on?"

"I just..." I sniffled, unsure how to express what was going on in my head. "You...did this amazing thing for me. All of you. It was dangerous!" I snapped, feeling anger bubble up inside me. I stepped away from him and smacked him on the chest. "Don't ever scare me like that again!"

He cocked his head at me, the look on his face was one of confusion. "Did you want me to stop them or not?"

"Yes, but I don't ever want you to risk your life like that again!"

Uncontrollable tears fell down my face the longer I stood there. I knew I was acting ridiculous, but what I felt for Thumper was unlike anything I'd ever known. I couldn't lose him now that I had him.

"Baby, you know this is my job."

I sniffed, swiping my hand over my nose in a very unladylike manner. "I know," I cried. "And I'm trying to be okay with it, but..."

"But what?"

I took a stuttering breath, trying to reel in my tears. "But the thought of you not coming home..." My face crumbled the more I thought of it. "I've never had anyone...I never cared about anyone the way I do you."

"You have your sister."

I shook my head. "I didn't understand when I was younger. I was so driven that nothing else mattered. And now you're here," I cried. "You irritate me with your...amazing skills and the way everyone loves you. And I hate that you like hiking when I suck at it." He smirked at me. "And I will never go camping with you unless you get me one of those luxury campers. I don't do bugs or dirt or bighorn sheep! And if you laugh at me again because a rabbit is trying to attack me, I'll leave you. I won't even look back."

He nodded at me solemnly. "Rabbits are dangerous creatures."

"I know," I cried, swiping at the tears that continued to fall. "I know I can be ridiculous, but if you love me, or even like me a lot, you have to like or love all of me, ridiculousness and everything."

I stood there, breathing heavily as I waited for his reply. I had just laid a crap ton of information on him, and I wasn't entirely sure how he would respond. But I had to take this chance for once in my life. If he didn't want the same things as me, it was better to know now.

He watched me carefully as I worried myself into a tizzy. "Are you saying you love me?"

Taken aback by his question, I didn't know how to respond. "I—do you love me?"

He shook his head at me. "That's not how this works, Bree. You have to answer me."

I stomped my foot, irritated that he was putting me in this position. "I don't mind you."

"Because it sounded like you're in love with me. And I'd be willing to take you camping in a luxury camper if I thought you loved me. And I would chase off all the rabbits that threatened you with their cute noses if love was on the table. But I'm afraid I'll drag you along on every hike I go on if you only sort of like me. That's where I draw the line."

The stupid, stubborn man was backing me into a corner. "Of course I love you," I snapped. "Would I be standing here in the middle of Kansas, willing to stay with you for the rest of my life if I wasn't in love with you?"

He chuckled as he wrapped his arm around my waist. "Alright, calm down. Nobody said you had to answer right now."

"Ugh!" I screamed, irritated with him. "You know, I don't want to go on your stupid—" But I never got to finish my thoughts as he pressed his lips to mine and slipped his hand over the nape of my neck, pulling me in closer to him. I melted into his touch, my anger quickly dissipating the longer he kissed me.

"I love you too, Bree," he murmured against my lips. "Especially when you're scared of rabbits."

"It was a big rabbit," I murmured, pulling him into another kiss.

"Don't be nervous," Thumper said, squeezing my hand. "She's your sister. She's going to be happy you're not dead."

I took a deep breath and stared at the house skeptically. "You say that, but you heard her at the funeral. Honestly, I'm not sure that she cared I was dead."

"Of course, she did. She was in shock."

"Shock." I turned to face him. "My own sister heard of my untimely demise, having been killed in a cruel way, and her eulogy to me was less than three minutes long. Correction, less than a minute!"

He winced at the reminder. "Well...maybe she's a nervous speaker."

That had me snorting in amusement. "My sister is great at many things. And I'm sure she's perfect with her own family. But with me? It's always been different."

Thumper handed his phone over, staring at me pointedly. "Call her."

"She'll hang up!"

"Call her," he insisted.

Sighing, I snatched the phone out of his hands and dialed the number. I chewed my lip in anticipation, knowing she would probably yell at me the moment she heard my voice. It rang several times before she answered.

"Hello?" she huffed out.

"Grace?"

"Yes, who is this? Hey! Stop chasing your sister!" she shouted to the kids in the background.

"Grace, it's...it's Bree."

"I'm sorry, what?" she said over the noise.

"It's Bree."

"You know what? That's really funny, asshole."

Then the line went dead. I stared down at the phone, not sure what to do now.

"That was quick," Thumper said.

"She called me an asshole and hung up."

"Did she know she was actually speaking to you?"

"I don't think so. She must have thought it was a prank."

Thumper shoved the phone at me again when I tried to hand it back. "Try her again."

But that was the last thing I wanted to do. "You know, I think we should just leave. The timing is bad. It's almost dinner time and the... light is not as bright."

He narrowed his eyes at me, not buying my excuses at all. "Do it."

I had a stare-down with him, determined not to follow his orders, but it turned out, Thumper was really good at making me fold. "Fine, but don't say I didn't warn you."

I dialed again, this time refusing to be nervous as the phone rang.

"Yes?"

"Grace, it's Bree. Don't hang up!"

"Whoever this is, you'd better pray that I don't find you. Because if I do, I'm going to rip off your nuts, soak them in vinegar, then shove them down your throat!"

The line went dead and I jerked at the threat. Holy shit, my sister had moxy. "Um...she's less than thrilled that I called again."

"Alright, time to take it to the next level," Thumper grinned. "Let's go knock on her door."

"No!" I shouted as he reached for the handle. "We can't do that."

"Bree, we're already here. What do you want to do? Wait until she comes out of the house and jump out at her?"

"No, but...maybe we could contact the police and have them break it to her gently."

He rolled his eyes at me. "We're here. We're doing this, okay? You wanted this."

I wasn't thrilled with the idea of knocking on her door, but he clearly wasn't going to let me get away without at least trying. "Fine, but when she punches me in the face, you have to take me to the hospital. You know she threatened to chop off my nuts."

He grinned at me. "You don't have any nuts. Thank God."

"Yeah, but that doesn't mean she won't chop off a boob or something. Are you telling me you'd be happy with a one boob girlfriend?"

He frowned slightly at me. "Do I get to keep the boob?" I rolled my eyes at him. "What? I'm being serious," he shouted as I got out of the car. "We could put it on display like a fish!"

I slammed the car door and started marching up to the house. Thumper was beside me seconds later, snatching my hand to hold in his.

"She's going to hate me."

"Not when we explain what happened."

"Right, she's going to look at me and wonder why the hell I bothered to come visit. This is going to be a disaster."

"Positive thoughts."

"Yeah, that'll help me right now," I grumbled.

I could hear the kids yelling inside as I stood on the porch. My sister had her hands full, and I was here to interrupt her night and make everything worse. This was going to be awful. Taking a steadying breath, I knocked on her door and waited for the impending shock.

After minutes, the door swung open and Grace stared at me with wary eyes.

"Surprise!" I said, waving my fingers in the air like an idiot.

"I'm sorry, would you hold on a minute?" She slammed the door shut and walked away.

I stood there, unsure of what to do from here. "That...was sort of how I thought it would go."

"Really? I assumed you were just freaking out."

"No, that seems like a logical response."

He nodded, but I could tell he wasn't seeing it the same way as me. "So...she seemed really nice."

I nodded. "She's always been super family oriented."

"Right, she has kids."

"And her husband is super busy."

I watched out of the corner of my eye as he frowned. "He wasn't at the funeral, was he?"

"Nope," I shook my head. "Not that I blame him. I was late for their wedding."

"Well…maybe he was late for your funeral and we just didn't see him."

"Yeah," I agreed, mostly to make myself feel better.

We continued to stand there in awkward silence for several more minutes. I was about to just turn around and leave when the door finally swung open again. My sister didn't look like she had done anything, other than make me wait just because she was pissed at me.

"So, you're alive."

"I am."

Her eyes flicked to Thumper. "And this is?"

"Tate Parsons, ma'am."

Her eyebrow quirked up at the greeting. "Tate, I'm guessing you're somehow involved in this mess?"

"If we could come in, we'll explain," I answered for him.

She looked me over then sighed, stepping aside for me. "I'm sure this will be good. Can I get you anything? A water? A beer? I could use a drink."

"No thank you," I answered, standing in the foyer, not sure where to go.

"Wow, so formal, even in death," she muttered as she walked past me. She plopped down in a seat, leaving the couch open for us. I sat down, nervous as hell as she watched me intently.

"So, what is this miraculous story?"

"Well…it's actually…not funny at all," I laughed. "Um…I went on vacation like we talked about. That's where I met Thumper."

"I thought you said your name was Tate?" she questioned.

"It's a nickname."

"And while we were in Arches, someone tried to kill me," I laughed, hoping she would laugh along to break the tension.

She narrowed her eyes at me. "Is this a joke? Were you trying to get money for work?"

"No!" I snapped, shocked she would think that. "I really was shot at. Well, Thumper was shot at. And at first, we assumed it had to do with his company. He's in private security. But then we kept getting attacked by hitmen, and one thing led to another..." I rambled, snapping my mouth shut for a moment. "Um...and Thumper figured out I was the target."

"Wow, big surprise," she said, less than surprised by the news.

"It's not like someone wanted to kill me because of my personality," I argued. "It was over gambling debts, and I was an easy target, I guess."

Her eyes skimmed over me just like my mother's always had. I hated that look, like she was dissecting every inch of me. I wished she would just believe me and get this torture over with, but she was determined to drag it out. "So, you weren't really dead."

I looked at Thumper out of the corner of my eye. "Obviously."

"And that moving speech I gave at your funeral—"

"It really wasn't that moving," I muttered.

Her face lit up. "So, you *were* there."

"You knew?" I said in shock.

She waved her hand, brushing me off. "I knew from the moment you walked in."

"But...I wore a disguise. How did you know?"

"You have a nervous tick," she grinned. "Always have."

"I do not," I insisted.

"Yes, you do. You flick your ring finger nail with your thumbnail."

I frowned, looking down at my hands. I'd never noticed that before. "Really?"

She nodded, a huge grin stretching across her lips. "Since you were a kid. When I saw it at the funeral home, I knew you weren't really dead."

My jaw dropped in shock. "Is that what the horrible eulogy was about?"

"Well, I couldn't make it too nice. After all, you did fake your death and forget to tell me about it."

Two kids ran into the room that I assumed were my niece and nephew. They stopped when they saw me, staring at me like an alien. "Who's she?"

"That's your aunt," Grace answered.

The girl frowned. "The dead one?"

"Yep."

"She doesn't look dead."

"Because I'm not," I cut in, not wanting my niece to remember me this way.

"If you aren't dead, why was there a funeral?"

"Because…" I looked to my sister for help, but she offered none. "Because…people thought I was dead."

"Were you in the hospital?"

"No."

"Did you hit your head?"

"No."

"Were you really pale?"

I didn't understand where this line of questioning was going. "No."

"Were you bleeding a lot?"

"No."

"Then you should have told my mom you were alive," she said matter-of-factly. "Mommy says if there isn't blood, you're fine."

The kid had a point, but if I hadn't faked my death, there would have been blood. A lot.

"Hello!" her husband shouted from the back door. "I'm home. God, I'm so hungry. I had this meeting at lunch, and I didn't get to—" He stopped talking when he saw me sitting in the living room. "So, the witch lives."

I puffed out my cheeks, blowing out a harsh breath. "Good to see you too, Mike."

"So, what's for dinner?"

"Pizza," Grace answered. "But I guess I'll have to order two since we have a woman that returned from the dead standing before us."

I stood quickly, not wanting to be an inconvenience. "Oh, that's okay. We'll go and let you eat."

"No, it's fine. Isn't it, Mike?"

"Sure. I mean, she didn't make it to our wedding on time, but yeah, we can feed her after she resurrects herself from the dead."

I nodded, knowing I deserved that. "Great."

"Great," Thumper nodded. "You know, this is actually going much better than I thought."

"Agreed. You haven't chopped off my nuts yet, so that's a bonus."

Grace gave a strained smile. "Great. I'll order the pizza."

She turned and walked out of the room, leaving us with the kids and Mike. Thumper grabbed my hand and gave it a squeeze.

"So…what's it like going to your own funeral?"

34

THUMPER

"So, the visit with the family went okay?" IRIS asked as we stood at the bar waiting for our drinks. The bartender slid them in front of us with a nod. I took my beer and watched Bree from across the room. She didn't look particularly comfortable with the other women, but she was trying.

"It was okay. They weren't exactly thrilled to see her, but I guess that's to be expected when you disappear from someone's life for so long."

He shook his head with laughter. "Man, I would have loved to be there to see the look on the sister's face."

"She already knew Bree was alive. Apparently, Bree has some tick she recognized. And the brother-in-law wasn't exactly welcoming."

"Well, not everyone gets along with their family."

Duke strolled up, plopping some money on the counter. "Can I get two beers?" he asked the bartender. Then he turned to us, leaning on the bar. "So, you want to tell me why the fuck Rae is so pissed at me?"

I shook my head, not knowing the answer. "I would assume you did something to piss her off."

"All I did was look at her car. Apparently, I didn't do it right," he snorted, grabbing the bar the bartender placed in front of him.

291

"Well, she is finicky about her cars."

"And her men," he huffed.

I grinned as I watched him watching Rae. She was shooting him evil looks that could almost be misconstrued as a form of love. Or hate. It was hard to tell when they were both glaring at each other.

"You could always try talking to her," I suggested.

"Yeah, if I wanted to get kicked in the nuts," he muttered, taking a sip of his beer. "It's the mechanic thing, isn't it? She doesn't like the grease or something."

I laughed in amusement. "I really doubt it's that. You've got all the women going crazy any time they see you. It's not exactly a thrilling thing for the rest of us."

"Everyone except her," he grunted, swiping his beer and the second one off the bar and stalking over to Rae. She seemed even more irritated by him handing her a beer, which I found hilarious.

"Fuck," FNG grumbled as he stumbled over to the bar. "Bartender! A round on me for everyone in the bar!"

I placed a steadying hand on his shoulder as he nearly slid off the bar when he tried to lean on it. "You okay?"

"You mean besides the fact that Cash hates me, Eva hates me, and tonight is my last night on Earth?"

I burst out laughing at his dramatics. "Cash won't kill you because you caught Eva giving Rafe a blow job."

"Really? Because I got this feeling," he slurred. "Tonight's the night."

"But you can't die," IRIS pointed out.

"Yeah, I used to think the same thing. But…"

"But what?" I asked, not sure where he was going with this.

"Everyone has to die at some point. You know, it's like they say… Everyone dies, and when you're…in battle, you owe a death to God. That's me. I owe him a death. And it's tonight."

I didn't know what to say to that, so I gripped him on the shoulder. "Well, it's been an honor working with you. Like you said, everyone's got to go at some time."

"Right? It's only right it should be me. I mean, I don't have a team or a woman, so I'll take the hit for you guys."

"That's very nice of you," I laughed. "Maybe you should go home and sleep this off."

"Hell no!" he grinned. "If tonight is my last night on Earth, I'm going to drink until I'm drinking no more."

He snatched another drink and stumbled over to one of the tables. I grabbed my own beer and the drink for Bree, sitting down beside her. "Here, baby."

"Thanks."

"How's it going?"

"Um…well, they're all talking about guns and bombs, so…I'm a little out of my depth here."

"You'll get used to it."

"That's if I decide to stay."

"Hey, you already told me you were staying. You can't walk away now."

"I could if I wanted. There's nothing holding me here."

"You mean aside from me," I grinned, pressing my lips to hers.

"Well, there is that. I do kind of like you."

"Love me. You love me. You told me, and you can't take it back now."

"I might be able to help with that," Cash said as he approached.

"Help with what?"

"Keeping her here." He sat down and eyed Bree. "So, Thumper tells me you're a financial wizard."

She blushed furiously under his penetrating stare. "I can hold my own."

"Because I think I have a very good deal for you. I need someone that can handle the finances of the company. Not only the books, but the investments and expanding our portfolio. Even with paying clients, the cost of running an operation like ours isn't getting any cheaper."

"I could definitely help with that," Bree said excitedly.

I rolled my eyes. "I've lost her now. Thanks a lot, asshole."

He chuckled as he drank his beer. "I'm keeping her here, aren't I?"

"You said finance. That's practically porn to her."

She slapped me on the arm, but her attention was already back on

GIULIA LAGOMARSINO

Cash. "I would need to review all the books and look at all your current investments. Plus, I'd need access to all upcoming jobs so I can accurately map out and plan for future operations and advise just how much you're able to invest without risking overextending yourself or the company. And then from there, we could work on employee investments. The best offer you could make your employees is a secure future."

He shrugged at that. "I would think a guarantee of coming home from a job is more urgent."

"I'm not following."

I laughed and wrapped my arm around Bree's neck, pulling her closer. "He's kidding, baby."

"Financial planning is no joke. I'm going to need to get started on this right away. We should really get back to the office."

"Tomorrow is good enough," Cash grinned. "Tonight is about drinking and hanging out with my beautiful fiancé." He stood and walked over to Eva, pulling her into his arms. I could understand the appeal now.

"Alright," Lock sighed as he stared down at us. "I hate to point this out, but the table is all out of whack. We need to shift. The girl-to-guy ratio is all off, and this is not safe for any of us."

"The table situation is fine," I said, not wanting to get into the whole table rotation thing with him right now.

"Are you kidding? You sat down, and now we've shifted every-one...Do you see how many of us have our backs to the door? It's unacceptable."

"You're unacceptable!" FNG shouted as he stood.

Lock rolled his eyes. "Good one. I'm so glad you set me straight. Now, about the seating—"

"Yeah, you work it out, Lock. I'm going to save FNG. He's about to make a huge mistake."

I stood and practically ran as he headed for Cash and Eva. What-ever he was about to do, it wouldn't end well.

"Eva, I'm so sorry. I had to tell him. I was forced!"

"You didn't tell me at all, fucker."

"I would have," he slurred, "if the rabbit man didn't beat me to the punch."

"Okay," I grinned, slapping my hands on FNG's shoulders, turning him away from the crowd. "How about I take you home?"

"Are you going to kill me?" he asked with wide eyes.

"FNG, nobody is going to kill you."

He grabbed me by the shirt and pulled me close. "The time is nigh."

"The time is time for you to go sleep this off." I spun him around, catching him as he nearly fell on his ass. "Come on. I'll drive you home."

I marched him to the door just as Slider walked in. "You're leaving already?"

"I'm taking FNG home."

"The time is nigh!" he shouted.

"The time is nigh for what?" Slider asked.

"His imminent death."

"But he can't die. He says so all the time."

I shrugged. "Maybe he finally realized he's not immortal."

FNG shoved open the door and stumbled out into the night.

"Hey, do you want me to take him home?" Slider asked.

"You don't mind?"

"Nah, I'm not really in the mood for company. My head's still killing me."

I didn't like the sound of that. He hadn't said anything about his head hurting in the weeks since we'd come home. "Let me grab Bree and I'll go with you."

"It's okay, man. I'm just gonna chill."

"No, give me a minute," I said, turning for the door. "Bree!" I shouted across the crowd. She looked relieved to hear me call her, and immediately got up to hurry over.

"Are we leaving already?"

"FNG's drunk and Slider's not feeling good. I want to keep an eye on him."

"Okay."

"You don't mind?"

She shot me a look. "Really? Does this look like the place I want to hang out?"

I looked around at all the guys and shrugged. "It's not bad once you get used to it."

She ran her hands up my chest and grinned. "I'd much rather be in bed with you than at a bar with a bunch of guys."

"Well, alrighty then," I laughed. "Peace out, bitches!" I shouted, wrapping my arm around Bree as we headed out the door. I'd take her in bed over the guys any night of the week. And it looked like this was my lucky day.

35

SHADOW

"Shadow, check in."

I looked through the scope at the crowded bar. Until he stepped outside, I didn't have a clear shot. "Negative, no shot."

The mission was clear. Take out the target and get the fuck out without being caught. With a whole fucking company of ex-military hot on my trail, that would be difficult for anyone else. But I wasn't anyone else. My exit was mapped out perfectly. They'd be so distracted by the disaster playing out in front of them that they'd be slow to respond.

The music filtered into the night as the front door opened. The target stepped outside with several others, but I was only supposed to take him. That was the mission, and making a critical error of removing more than one of them would cost me more than a paycheck.

He moved away from the group of men, laughing as he raised his hand in the air as he tossed a few jokes their way. He was almost to his truck.

"Target acquired."

I activated the signal and waited for him to open the door. With one look back at his friends, he opened the door. Just a few seconds more...

With the slam of the door, I pulled the trigger. The explosion ripped through the night sending flames shooting into the sky. They wouldn't be able to reach him until I was long gone. I quickly took apart my rifle and stashed it in the case. Brushing away all evidence of my location, I hopped off the roof and disappeared into the night.

ALSO BY GIULIA LAGOMARSINO

Thank you for reading Embrace The Suck. Don't miss out on my next book in Owens Protective Services. Click here for *Assume The Position!*

Join my newsletter to get the most up-to-date information, along with new content in the Reed Security series.

https://giulialagomarsinoauthor.com/connect/

Join my Facebook reader group to find out more about my obsession with Dwayne Johnson!

https://www.facebook.com/groups/GiuliaLagomarsinobooks

Reading Order:

https://giulialagomarsinoauthor.com/reading-order/

To find the individual series, follow the links below:

For The Love Of A Good Woman series

Reed Security series

The Cortell Brothers

A Good Run Of Bad Luck

The Shifting Sands Beneath Us- Standalone

Owens Protective Services

Made in the USA
Middletown, DE
04 April 2023

28249604R00184